RULES FOR ENGAGING THE EARL

"A moving tale of hope and redemption."
—*Kirkus Reviews*

"MacGregor strikes the perfect balance between brilliantly rendered characters and deft plotting, both of which provide the solid foundation for a gracefully written, immensely satisfying historical romance readers will treasure." —*Booklist*

"Jonathan's lovable, matchmaking butler steals every scene he's in and Constance's fellow widows remain a delight." —*Publishers Weekly*

"*Rules for Engaging the Earl* is one of my favorite reads of the year." —NovelsAlive.com

The Cavensham Heiresses

WILD, WILD RAKE

"Passionate, tumultuous." —*Publishers Weekly*

"Incandescent." —*Booklist*

"Will delight those looking to warm their hearts with a tender read." —*Library Journal*

ROGUE MOST WANTED

THE GOOD, THE BAD, AND THE DUKE

Also by
Janna MacGregor

WILD, WILD RAKE
ROGUE MOST WANTED
THE GOOD, THE BAD, AND THE DUKE
THE LUCK OF THE BRIDE
THE BRIDE WHO GOT LUCKY
THE BAD LUCK BRIDE
A DUKE IN TIME
RULES FOR ENGAGING THE EARL

How to Best a Marquess

Janna MacGregor

St. Martin's Paperbacks

For those who are like Beth and have fought the good fight and persevered.

This is a work of fiction. All of the characters, organizations, and events portrayed in this novel are either products of the author's imagination or are used fictitiously.

First published in the United States by St. Martin's Paperbacks, an imprint of St. Martin's Publishing Group.

HOW TO BEST A MARQUESS

For information, address St. Martin's Publishing Group, 120 Broadway, New York, NY 10271.

www.stmartins.com

ISBN: 978-1-250-76163-7

Our books may be purchased in bulk for promotional, educational, or business use. Please contact your local bookseller or the Macmillan Corporate and Premium Sales Department at 1-800-221-7945, ext. 5442, or by email at MacmillanSpecialMarkets@macmillan.com.

Printed in the United States of America

St. Martin's Paperbacks edition / May 2023

10 9 8 7 6 5 4 3 2 1

Acknowledgments

When you write historical novels, you rely on your people. I mean the friends who write in the same genre. A huge shoutout to my dear friend Dr. Vanessa Riley. When you have a friend with a Ph.D. in mechanical engineering who writes brilliant stories set in the Regency period, you can ask anything about compound engines and receive excellent advice. I couldn't have done it without her. I'd be remiss in not thanking Elizabeth Essex, who helped me with the maritime and naval ship terms used in the second book of the Widow Rules series, *Rules for Engaging the Earl*.

A special shoutout to my plotting partners, Lenora Bell and Charlotte Russell. You both are brilliant!

Thank you to my agents, Kimberly Witherspoon and Jessica Mileo, who were charmed by these three widows. You both are the absolute best. Thank you to Kim Rozzell for her friendship and all her creativity in helping me share my books and ideas with you. I appreciate the team at St. Martin's Press, who helped me bring the stories of Kat, Constance, and Beth to life. I know Meri appreciates everyone as well!

Thank YOU for spending time with the three wives. My readers are the best in the world.

Finally, my heartfelt gratitude goes to my husband, the author of my romantic life.

Prologue

The last notes of the supper waltz hung suspended in the air much like Miss Beth Howell's heart. In that moment, everything stopped. No one moved.

Yet the ballroom vibrated with energy.

Her life was about to change forever. She could feel it in every pulse, heartbeat, and breath.

Julian Raleah, the Earl of Weyhill and heir to the Marquess of Grayson, would undoubtedly propose tonight. He'd expertly swept her across the dance floor this evening. All the while, his gaze had never left hers. Every one of his smiles had turned the night into something extraordinary.

"Will you accompany me outside?" He kept his voice low so no one could overhear.

"Of course." Though it was quite scandalous for an unmarried lady to leave the ballroom with a gentleman, this was no ordinary man. Nor was this an ordinary night.

Finally, he let go of her waist, then extended his arm. Together, they exited the ballroom through the double French doors that led outside to the grand terrace.

Beth's breath caught at the sight of the formal garden. Lanterns glowed on the pathways that framed two long rectangular wading pools blazing with floating candles.

"It looks like stars have fallen from the sky," she said in awe. The light reflecting off the water made it appear as if they'd stepped into another world.

"Do you like it?" Julian's voice deepened with a hint of uncertainty.

She took his hand and squeezed. "It's enchanting."

A playful smile tugged at both corners of his mouth. "I did this for you. I asked Lady Chelsfield if I could decorate the pools this evening."

Her heartbeat joyfully tripped in her chest. "What do you mean?"

"I wanted this evening to be stunning . . . like you." His smile grew even bigger, promising her that tonight would be memorable in so many ways. "I placed small candles on wooden squares and lit them right before our waltz."

With her free hand, she playfully tapped him on the arm. "So, this is where you ran off to. No wonder I couldn't find you for the last hour." She stepped a little closer. "It's beautiful, Julian. I'll never forget tonight for as long as I live."

He cleared his throat, then turned toward the pool as he squeezed her hand gently. "I'm a little unsettled. I've never done this before." His thumb gently brushed over her knuckles.

"I'm a little nervous too," she confided. "I don't think I've done this before either."

"Believe it or not, that makes me feel better." He took a deep breath. "If we do *this* together, I think I can manage."

When he returned his gaze to hers, there was an intensity there that she had never seen before. This was a man who was determined to succeed. She'd always found such a trait attractive, but Julian wore it like a superbly tailored suit. It fit him like a glove, making him even more handsome than ever.

He angled his tall body until he faced her. He reached for her other hand and entwined their fingers together. "Beth, I have something to ask you."

"Ask away," she said breathlessly. The thundering in her heart pounded so loud he had to hear it.

He brought their interlaced hands to the middle of his chest. His heart was pounding as hard as hers. "I've been calling on you for over three months now. It's enough time to know what our next step is. I hope you want the same thing as me." His gray eyes smoldered with longing and desire, almost as if lit from within. "I want us to be together. Forever."

Good heavens, this was it. She'd known their night together would be special. When she'd received a small bundle of violets and a note from him asking for the supper waltz, she'd suspected he'd propose this evening.

But being in the moment with him was completely different from her expectations. Her heart swelled with emotions that were difficult to explain. Should she immediately answer or wait until tomorrow?

She'd answer immediately. She wanted this more than anything and so did Julian.

Her nervousness grew faint as a newfound sense of contentment filled the air. Even though her father had passed away several years before, his pledge was coming true. He'd promised her that she would have the man of her dreams. And that man stood before her. Starting tonight, they would share a future, create a life together, and raise a family. It was all she'd ever dreamed of.

"I'd very much like to call on your brother tomorrow and ask for your hand in marriage." Julian's stalwart gaze never wavered as his voice deepened. "If you're amenable?"

She shook her head and smiled. She felt like a princess who'd found her charming prince.

"You don't want to marry me?" His whisky-dark voice lowered. There was a tightness around his eyes that indicated she'd shocked him.

"No. I mean yes." The words tumbled from her mouth. "I shook my head because I want to remember you standing in front of me and asking me to share your life. I don't want to forget anything about tonight." Tears welled in her eyes as her heart pounded to reach him. She squeezed his hand hoping he could see how much this all meant to her. "This is the happiest day of my life."

He sighed in relief, then chuckled. "I thought you were saying no." He grew serious again as he pressed her hand against the middle of his chest a bit harder. "This heart is yours. Do with it what you want."

Her breath caught at his tender and heartfelt words. In return, she pulled their hands to her heart. "And this is yours to do what you want."

Now they were tied to each other creating a bond, an intimacy, that would never be broken. She was certain of it. Then he brought her wrist to his lips, kissing her throbbing pulse. The softness of his lips contrasted with the evening stubble of his face. With such a sweet gesture, he'd stolen her heart forever.

It didn't make any difference that she'd just given it to him.

"I adore you," she said softly. "But I have a request when you see my brother tomorrow to ask for my hand."

"Anything, my dear Beth." He smiled against her skin, then his tongue caressed her pulse as if promising her untold delights that they'd share together in the future.

"Ask for my other hand also." She smiled when he laughed softly, the movement of his lips tickling her.

"This is one of the countless reasons why I want to marry. You always find a way to make me laugh even when I'm nervous." He released her hands, then took her into his embrace. "Let me share a secret." He lowered his voice, then pressed his lips against the tender skin below her ear. "I'm greedy when it comes to you, Blythe Elizabeth Howell. When I see your brother, I'll ask for all of you."

Finally, Julian relaxed . . . just a tad. His beautiful Beth had said yes. That simple word meant that his life would be tied to the woman he held in his arms. He vowed, then and there, that he'd do everything in his power to give her what she deserved. But he had to make certain she understood what their life would be like in the beginning.

"Beth, I've been honest about my financial state. I can't afford a special license. We'll have to wait three weeks while the banns are called." He forced his gaze to hers.

"I think special licenses are highly overrated." She pressed her cheek against his chest and wrapped her arms around his waist. "I prefer waiting. It'll give me time to tell everyone that you're the man I'm marrying."

Only Beth could turn his lack of fortune into something that she preferred. He was the luckiest man in the world to have her as his bride.

Her lips twitched as she tilted her head to regard him. "Plus, that will give us time to visit our rabbits, Beatrice, Bonnie, and Bertram."

"Of course." He laughed softly. The first time he'd called upon Beth, they'd walked to Hyde Park with her maid trailing closely behind them. He didn't have an open carriage to drive her properly through the park, so he had to find other ways of entertaining her. When they'd discovered a warren of nesting rabbits, he'd made up a story about their lives, trying to charm her. Since that day, she always asked about the rabbits. In return, he'd make up some tale about their imaginary lives. He'd woven those stories with his ideas and dreams of their future together.

A beautiful blush darkened her cheeks. "I want to tell them about our marriage."

"Our marriage." He spoke the words like a benediction. His fingers brushed the soft skin of her cheek. "I promise I'll do everything in my power to make you happy. I want you proud to claim me as your husband."

"If you can't tell, I'm already proud of you," she said tenderly with a smile.

Throughout the last several years, he'd always felt as if he was an outsider when he attended these social events. He didn't wear the latest fashions. He didn't have a fortune to waste in the card rooms. He didn't belong to any gentlemen's clubs. Nor did he have a carriage that proclaimed he was the heir to the impoverished Marquess of Grayson.

That was why it was so hard to believe that the most beautiful and eligible heiress in all of society had agreed to marry him. That simple fact meant she had faith in him.

"Beth, I'll find a way to make money, so you'll be able to buy anything you want. I've been designing steam engines. One of my ideas, if I can make it work, will revolutionize the mill industry." The admiration in her eyes made him feel ten feet tall.

Her eyes widened. "How did you learn to do that?"

"I studied physics when I was at university. I'm good at it, Beth. I'll not stop until I succeed. I'll be able to pay

off all my father's debts and give you everything you desire." He held out his arms as if offering her the world.
"Gowns, jewels, a fashionable home, and carriages in
every color. Anything you want, I'll provide for you."

"You can use my dowry to fund your work," she said
softly as she cupped his cheek with her gloved hand. "But
money doesn't buy happiness, Julian. I learned that when I
lost my parents. I don't need or want any of those things.
I only want you."

His heart swelled at the affection in her eyes and
the softness of her touch. She believed in him. That
was the greatest gift a man like him could ever receive
from his partner in life.

"Come. I need to get you back inside before anyone notices how long we've been gone."

"I don't care," she declared. "I think we should an-
nounce our betrothal tonight."

He brought one of her hands to his lips. "Not tonight,
dearest. I must see your brother first."

Her radiant smile was brighter than a midsummer's
sun. "St. John will welcome you with open arms. He only
wants me to be happy."

He leaned toward her, and she matched his movement,
closing her eyes. Gently, he pressed his lips to hers as he
took her into his arms. She fit against him perfectly.

Like his darling Beth, Julian would remember everything about this perfect night.

It was the start of their life together.

Chapter One

London, 1816
The Mayfair home of the Marquess of Grayson

Blythe Elizabeth Howell had enough life experience to know when a situation was hopeless and when to take matters into her own hands.

Determined, Beth marched up the steps of the lovely Palladian manse that belonged to the Marquess of Grayson. Tonight proved that she must create her own future and define her own ideals of a perfect life. No longer would she abide by her brother's edicts. Nor would she cower behind society's machinations of her ruined reputation.

The only way to accomplish all of this was to convince the marquess to lend assistance and travel to Hampshire with her.

As soon as possible.

She'd laugh if it weren't so ironic that she was turning to Grayson for help. Especially since he'd been the one to run from her all those years ago after he'd asked her to marry him.

With her brother insisting she marry again, drastic situations required drastic actions. Beth had vowed tonight that she would no longer delay. She would find the lost dowry that her late husband, Lord Meriwether

Vareck, had taken with him when he'd left her after two weeks of marriage.

That dowry represented her freedom.

Her traitorous gaze ventured skyward as she studied the gray brick home that was as intimidating as its owner, Julian Raleah, the Marquess of Grayson.

He'd been the first man to ask her to marry him. She'd fancied herself quite in love with the marquess. Beth had found him honest, polite, with a hint of devilment in his eyes.

When her brother had refused the marriage, Grayson hadn't tried to convince him. He'd simply left without saying goodbye.

She'd been devastated by his actions. Obviously, the blasted man hadn't cared for her the way she'd cared for him.

But none of it mattered now. This was business and a chance for her to reclaim her dowry.

He was the one she'd ask for assistance since he was in the same position as she. He needed a fortune and so did Beth.

Yet the heartache still lingered. After Grayson had walked away without even fighting for her, she'd never given any other man the same regard. It was as if she'd become an empty shell of who she once was.

But once she found whatever remained of her dowry, at least her reticule would be full.

Standing in front of the imposing black entrance doors, Beth straightened her shoulders, then knocked. Grayson helping her attain her goal was not a certain outcome. But he was the only person she could turn to.

He didn't have a wife or a family. Nor did he have any commitments that would require him to remain in London. More importantly, they were not friends. Beth would classify their acquaintance as merely that—confrères who had a past with each other. He would be the perfect partner in her bid to recover her lost dowry.

With a creak, one of the massive oak doors swung open.

"Good evening," a man said. He must be the butler. In his early thirties with black hair and green eyes, he was dressed in the Grayson livery.

"Is the marquess at home?" Beth nodded as she stepped across the threshold.

"Your name?"

"Beth Howell."

He nodded, then smoothed his formal livery. "This way, my lady."

"I'm a miss, not a lady," Beth corrected him.

One black brow rose a fraction. "Come with me." After a few steps, he stopped in the hallway. "I apologize for my manners. Lord Grayson rarely has visitors. I should have introduced myself earlier. I'm Cillian Patrick, his lordship's butler."

A hint of an Irish lilt colored his voice. But it was the twinkle in his eyes that gave Beth pause. He seemed delighted to have her here.

"Shall we?" Without waiting for her answer, he continued his path down the main hallway.

She followed. Though it was rather dark, there was enough light to see the contrast of faded wallpaper that once had surrounded large paintings or perhaps family portraits. "Is the marquess redecorating?"

An exaggerated sigh of unerring patience escaped Cillian. "In a manner of speaking, Miss Howell." He stopped outside an open door and waved her in. "Lord Grayson?" His earlier lilt had been replaced with a perfect formal accent. "Miss Howell to see you."

The Marquess of Grayson glanced up from a journal,

methodically replaced a quill pen in its stand, then rose slowly from his desk.

With his great height and massive shoulders, Grayson intimidated most people. His perfectly angular cheekbones appeared sharp enough to cut a diamond. An appropriate comparison as his gray eyes glimmered in recognition. A hint of a smile pulled at his lips. His relaxed manner was in sharp contrast to his black formal wear. All the times she'd ever seen him, it was the only color he wore.

Odd. He must like to appear imposing, wearing all black except his shirt. It certainly lent him an air of formality.

"Miss Howell." The low rumble of her name on his lips sent goose bumps across her flesh. He bowed slightly. "What are you doing here?"

"I was wondering if I might have a moment of your time?" A plate with a single meat pie sat next to his journal. "If I've interrupted your meal, I apologize."

Her timing may not be perfect, but she wouldn't leave until she said her piece.

An untied cravat dangled from his neck, revealing a glimpse of his bare chest. She forced herself to look away. It was unseemly that she noticed such a sight. Instantly, her body became overheated. The temperature in the room had risen by twenty degrees.

Hadn't it?

Such an inconvenient thought didn't even deserve consideration. Yet there was no denying how handsome he was. The candlelight enhanced the silver in his gray eyes, while his black hair gleamed. There was even a hint of danger about him in his state of undress.

This was simply ridiculous. Grayson was a beau from long, long ago. He was merely a man from her past.

Yet she would admit there had been a time when she'd

have counted the hours until she would see him at a *ton* event and dance in his arms.

But not now.

He turned his back to her and faced a mirror behind his desk. Several times his reflected gaze latched with hers as if trying to divine her thoughts. He'd needn't worry. Soon, he'd know what she wanted from him.

He quickly tied the neckcloth into a simple mathematical knot. When he turned to face her, a slight scowl appeared. The earlier fire in his gray eyes had now transformed into smoldering embers.

"Won't you sit down?" He lowered his voice. "Your lady's maid is free to join us."

"No need. She's with my brother," Beth said.

His eyes widened at the pronouncement. "Your brother requires your maid's assistance?"

She cleared her throat, determined not to let him or this evening upset her even more. "No, of course not. She's still at the house. I didn't ask her to accompany me."

"If anyone saw you come to an unmarried man's house, they'll reach to the wrong conclusion."

"And what conclusion would that be?" She baited the bear when he pursed his lips into a thin line. For the most part, she didn't care a whit for what he or anyone else thought.

At least, that was the attitude she exhibited to most people. The truth was her self-worth felt like a piece of metal. Every time she read about herself in the gossip rags, there was a new dent. It was exhausting being pummeled by rumors and judgments that she had no control over.

That's why she needed to recover her dowry and get on with the rest of her life. If society thought her a woman of loose morals, that was their misjudgment and not hers.

"Thank you for your concern, but there's no need." She

blinked, an outward appearance of calm as a storm of nervousness raged within her. "I'll only take a moment of your time. I have a proposal for you." She straightened her shoulders in a show of emboldened self-confidence.

Grayson's bergamot-orange scent followed her. She inhaled the fragrance and held her breath.

"You're the only one I can turn to." She closed the distance between them. "I wouldn't ask if the situation wasn't dire."

He nodded.

"Will you accompany me to Kingsclere? My former husband . . . I mean Lord Meriwether . . . left each of his wives including me a packet of receipts. It's a trail of where he spent his money. I believe those receipts hold the key to my dowry. I'll make it worth your while." The room turned deadly silent, but she refused to look away from him. She tightened her stomach in preparation. If he said no, she was determined not to collapse into a heap.

"I can't do that." Her gaze pierced his.

Her lungs burned from the breath she'd been holding. Slowly, she released it.

Bloody hell. Why couldn't anything be easy?

"I'll split whatever I find with you. Equal shares. My dowry was worth twenty thousand pounds." In seconds, she was in front of him. "Ten thousand pounds for each of us." She hesitated for a moment. "I know you need the money as much as me."

He shook his head once, then walked to the fireplace. He picked up a poker as if to tend the unlit fire, then discarded it. "I always need money," he murmured.

It wasn't for her ears, but she heard it anyway. That's why he was perfect to accompany her. The truth was that a woman traveling alone was an easy target to be taken advantage of even if she minded her own business. As a viscount's sister, she'd always had outriders and grooms-men to protect her. But this trip would not include any of those protections. Anyone who accompanied her she had to trust that they'd not tell her brother the true reason for travel. If she found her dowry, she had little doubt that St. John Howell would try to weasel her money into his own pocket.

She'd rather share her dowry with the devil before she'd give another shilling to her brother.

Even sharing with the man who had asked her to marry him, then had forsaken her the very next day, was better than sharing with her brother.

How much better?

Time would tell. She only hoped Grayson was worth the risk.

Chapter Two

I don't know what to say." Julian Raleah, the Marquess of Grayson, stared into Beth Howell's face. It was inconceivable. She was standing in his study. He never thought he'd see the day.

She *actually wanted* him to travel with her, in hopes of recovering a dowry that in all probability didn't exist anymore.

In all his thirty years, he couldn't recall a single woman visiting him alone. What made her appearance even more confounding was that they weren't friends. Whenever they attended the same parties and events, they were cordial to each other. But any fondness they shared had been extinguished eight years ago when her brother had pointedly told Grayson that he wasn't good *ton* and refused his request to marry Beth.

Hard to believe that it had been eight years since he'd courted her. Yet she was still beautiful. Her heart-shaped face and high cheekbones made him want to cup them in his hands and feel her warmth. The shade of her lips would put a perfect summer rose to shame, and her brown hair glistened as if the sun had painted streaks of copper in her locks. But her eyes, those magnificent blue orbs, reminded him of the deepest sea depths. You could drown in them and never want to be rescued.

What completely inappropriate thoughts.

She was a woman who barely acknowledged him. Yet he'd seen her play with babies and pet stray dogs that others ignored. He'd even heard that she comforted her brother's detested racehorses when they were foaling.

Thus, it was easy to comprehend where she placed him in the order of the universe.

Dead last.

But tonight, Beth Howell stood in his study asking him to travel with her.

Alone.

He crossed his arms against his chest and regarded her. "I'm a man of honor. I can't travel with an unmarried woman. People would think I'm taking advantage of you. I'm trying to convince investors that my steam engines are sound." After her brother had smashed his dream of marrying Beth, Grayson had gone on with his life. From then on, he'd worked on steam engine designs while struggling with the upkeep of his marquessate.

"Hear me out. If we could sit down and discuss it, I'll tell you my thoughts." Beth waved toward a small sitting area in front of the fireplace.

"I'm going out this evening." He cleared his throat. "I'm attending the Duke and Duchess of Langham's ball."

Beth stood silent for a moment. "I didn't know they were giving one."

Ever since her name had been tangled with that of her supposed husband, Lord Meriwether Vareck, society had shunned her, and in like Beth fashion she'd shunned it. She only mingled with her closest friends and family.

"It's their annual fundraiser for their Haley's Hope charity." He swallowed his discomfort. "I have some business to attend to. Several members of the Six Corners Consortium are attending. I plan to discuss my inventions."

Why was he telling her this? It was akin to proclaiming that he was tired of needing to budget every halfpenny he possessed. All because his father had foolishly invested in gold mines across the ocean without any proof they were viable. Then when it became obvious that he'd lost almost everything, he'd gambled recklessly in more foreign investments trying to recoup his losses. Grayson had learned quickly that only investments a person created on their own were worthwhile.

"Good luck with the consortium." She smiled slightly, wearing her indifference like a suit of armor, but he caught the glimpse of hurt in her eyes.

Beth bit her bottom lip, and he tightened his stomach to keep from groaning aloud. She always did that when she was worried or anxious. At least, that's what he remembered from their time together in the past. As soon as she stopped nibbling that tender flesh, her lips would swell as if she'd been recently stung by a bee. That would be all he'd think about tonight when he discussed his engines.

He had to cast such nonsense aside. If he didn't succeed with the consortium, then he'd have to restart his hunt for an heiress to marry. He'd avoided it for as long as possible. It's not that he wanted to avoid marriage. On the contrary, but it was quite humbling to have his proposal refused without consideration.

Failure was not an acquired taste. No matter how many times he experienced the phenomenon, it never grew easier to accept.

"Pardon me, my lord. Your coach is ready." His butler,

valet, coachman, and sometimes footman, Cillian, sailed into the room like a clipper ship ready for battle. Abruptly, he stopped and stared at Beth. "Miss Howell, may I say that your gown is exquisite? I didn't notice when you arrived because there were no candles lit in the entry."

Grayson flexed the fingers of his right hand. Cillian didn't mean it as an insult, but it still burned Grayson's pride. He was now cutting back on candles as a means of saving his coins. Once he found investors interested in his inventions, things would change.

"Thank you," Beth answered politely. "It's an old gown, but I embroidered a new pattern I'm currently designing on the matching shawl." She handed the delicate silk garment to the servant. "Take a closer look."

Cillian approached and reverently took the material. Immediately, he lowered his gaze to the glimmering silk. "That's exquisite needlework. None finer in all of London, I wager." He lifted his gaze to Grayson and winked. "My lord, you should have such a pattern embroidered on a waistcoat." The butler turned to Beth. "He only wears black, but with such a design, perhaps he could be persuaded to wear a more colorful garment."

Beth bent her head close to Cillian's as her fingers traced the exquisite pattern of Greek keys that she'd carefully woven into the cloth. "What kind of pattern were you thinking?"

Cillian glanced back at Grayson and wagged his eyebrows. The wily valet knew that Grayson could care less about fashion. "I was thinking something simple such as a white waistcoat with black embroidery."

"Why only black, Lord Grayson?" Beth slid a curious gaze his way.

"Well . . ." How to answer such an innocent question? He donned black as it was easier to wear such fashion repeatedly without anyone the wiser. He only owned two formal suits of clothing.

"He wears the color well, Miss Howell," Cillian offered with a nod. "Wouldn't you agree?"

"Cillian," Grayson said curtly.

"Interesting." Beth's eyes seemed to be shooting daggers his way. "During my debut, I don't recall you being so . . . somber."

He held her gaze, never flinching.

Cillian continued as if he weren't even in the room, "Back to his waistcoat. I was thinking something meaningful to the marquess."

"Cillian," Grayson growled in warning. "Perhaps you should see about the carriage."

His valet's eyes widened. "*I have it.*" A grin stretched across his entire face, making his freckles even more apparent. "Puffs of steam. Perfect and unique. Just like Lord Grayson."

Grayson rolled his eyes at the exuberance of his valet. "Miss Howell didn't come here to have you freeload her exquisite craftmanship."

Beth shook her head. "Such embroidery would look like clouds. I'm afraid people would think him fanciful." Her defiant gaze darted to his. "I don't mind your butler's high spirits. I enjoy the work. Besides, it allows me to create new designs. Perhaps it'll be the latest fashion craze in our linen shop."

During that infinitesimal pause, it was just the two of them in the room as the outside world was forgotten. It took the strength of Hercules for him not to tilt her face to his so he could see all the varied and wonderful emotion reflected in her eyes. No one else had intrigued him like she did. A grin pulled at his lips and all he wanted that evening was to spend the time with her.

"Pardon me, Miss Howell." Cillian bowed, then turned to Grayson before he left the room. "I should see to the horses."

The silence in the room grew to an uncomfortable roar.

Beth turned to face him. "Now that your butler is gone, I'll tell you why I need you." By the mulish look on her face, she was determined. "My brother."

Those two words explained everything. Grayson walked to the side table and poured two glasses of port.

"What did he do this time?" Grayson strolled toward her. It had to be bad if Beth walked to his house without an escort to ask him to travel with her.

"He . . ." Her voice caught, betraying the extent of her distress.

"Beth?" By then, Grayson was by her side. She didn't even object to his use of her Christian name. He handed her a glass. "I take it that he's behaved badly."

She nodded. "It's unbelievable." She held up her glass in a salute. "Here's to a way out of this mess in my life."

"Let's sit down, and you can tell me how I can help you." He waved a hand toward the small seating area in front of his desk. He'd never really cared how worn the upholstery on the matching Queen Anne chairs in front of his desk appeared until now. With Beth here, they appeared absolutely dismal.

Beth moved with a grace that queens would envy. She settled herself in one of the chairs, and Grayson took the other.

"Thank you for the fortification." She took another sip of port, then smiled gently. "Where to begin?"

"From the start," he answered.

"You'd never make it to the Langham ball tonight. I'd have to first share how St. John stole the fruitcake my governess had baked for my fifth birthday." She set her glass on a small table to her side, then angled her body to face his.

It was such a simple but sensual move. His mind went to places that it didn't belong, including imagining her as his. He cleared his throat, hoping to sweep such musings from his thoughts. He was a gentleman. As such, it was his duty to help her if he could.

"Grayson." She sat silently for a second, twisting her fingers together. Finally, she lifted her gaze to his. "I can't do this anymore."

"What are you referring to?" He sat perfectly still and watched as pain flashed across her face.

"St. John. I can't live with him." She stood abruptly and pointed in the direction of her home. "At this very moment, the Marquess of Siddleton is sitting in our formal dining room." She hmphed slightly. "He's waiting for me to return from the retiring room so he can ask for my hand in marriage."

"Siddleton?" His shock couldn't have been any greater than if she'd told him that she'd sprouted wings last night during her sleep. "He's ancient."

"He's seventy-eight years old and needs an heir."

"Isn't Lord Stanton his heir?" Grayson asked.

Beth shook her head. "Lord Stanton is related to the marquess through his mother's side of the family. The title must go through the male line per the laws of primogeniture. My brother needs funds, and St. John plans to use me as the means to replenish his coffers."

Grayson was caught off guard by the sudden vibrancy in her tone. "So, you left the house in the middle of dinner?"

The defiant tilt of her chin warned she wouldn't accept any criticism. "I came here." She took another sip of port, finishing the glass. "My . . . I don't know what to call him. Husband? The man who duped me?" Her hand fluttered in the air, revealing her unease.

"Lord Meriwether?" he asked.

She nodded. "Yes. The man I married . . . who also happened to have two other wives at the same time. So, I really wasn't married, was I?" She tilted her stalwart gaze to his. "Forgive my sarcasm. I simply want to find out what happened to my dowry once and for all. It may be gone, but I want proof. Call it intuition, but I think it's hiding in plain sight."

"Don't you think it would have been found by now? Your husband has been buried for quite some time."

"You mean my *supposed husband*," Beth corrected.

Grayson leaned forward and rested his elbows on his knees as he regarded her. "In all likelihood, your *supposed husband* spent it. Even his own brother, who's one of my best friends, said he probably wasted it on horses and gambling."

She flinched slightly, then gazed out the window to the overgrown courtyard outside his study.

When Beth turned in his direction, nothing indicated that she'd noticed how unkept the formal gardens were. "How could someone waste twenty thousand pounds on horses and gambling?" Before he could reply, she continued, "He left his first wife, Katherine, a prized Hampshire pig. He left his second wife, Constance, an income from a lease on an iron ore mine."

"There's quite a difference between a pig and a mine lease." He lowered his voice, trying to ease the truth from creating a new wound. "Constance, the Countess of Sykeston, was Meriwether's legal wife. That lease is worth ten thousand pounds a year. He was taking care of his wife and daughter."

"He didn't know she was carrying when he passed

away," Beth argued. "How do you explain Katherine's bequest?"

"How does anyone explain a pig?" He laughed gently. "Perhaps Meri had a fondness for pork roast?"

She grinned slightly.

"Don't you make enough as a partner at Greer, James, and Howell to live comfortably?" Most considered it rude to discuss money, but it was always at the forefront of his mind. What would he have to sell next to keep the marquessate from tipping into insolvency?

"It's enough. But this is about me having choices in my life. If you're worried about expenses, I have enough coin for the trip," she murmured.

He tried to keep his expression impassive. "Whatever money I can spare, it's yours."

Slowly, she raised her gaze to his, then lifted her chin an inch. "Thank you, but there's something more important that I need besides money. Your escort."

"Your reputation will be ruined if you're discovered gallivanting across the country with me." He fought not to cringe at the words. He sounded like an elderly aunt giving her unsolicited opinion.

"When word had spread throughout London what Meri had done, I became a pariah. No one of good *standing* wants anything to do with me." She grew quiet. After a moment, she turned her gaze to his. Pain dulled the sparkle in her blue eyes. "I don't have a reputation to ruin. Some might say it was destroyed when Meriwether's three wives, Katherine, Constance, and I, lived together."

"You might care if you want to marry again," he said.

"I have no marriage prospects. Unless you consider Lord Siddleton one." She tangled her fingers together. "The truth is I don't want to marry. I want to be free from all the machinations that people like me are subjected to.

The evaluations of my worth based upon the size of my dowry. The finagling of my brother to find another to marry me so he can reclaim the wealth that he willingly gave to Meri. The innuendos and averted looks that greet me when I walk down Bond Street shopping for a new bonnet." She chuckled slightly. "Of course, that's not an issue anymore. I have no extra coin for such frivolity."

Grayson clenched his hand into a fist. It sickened him how her circumstances had changed because of her so-called marriage. He stole a glance her way. No matter how she dressed, he'd always thought her beautiful.

Beth Howell had once been the most sought-after heiress in the *ton* during her introduction to society. When Julian had asked Beth's brother for her hand, he'd been rebuffed by her good-for-nothing brother. Beth's brother had threatened to sully Grayson's reputation by calling him a fortune hunter if he continued to woo Beth. Since Grayson's reputation was the only real asset he possessed, he'd been forced to walk away.

Sadly, if Howell had let him marry Beth, Grayson's estate would be solvent, and as importantly if not more, Beth would have wanted for nothing. He'd have given her the life she deserved. Now she worked in trade. Just like he did.

"Please say you'll come with me?"

The pleading in her voice was something he'd never heard before. Another aspect of Beth Howell he'd never thought he'd see. The proud beauty before him had never in her life begged or cajoled anyone for anything.

"There might not be any money left." He walked away to escape her and her scent. The soft wafts of honeysuckle seemed to tangle his thoughts into knots.

"We won't know for certain unless we try." She joined him by the study door that led to the overgrown courtyard.

"It's a bad idea."

Her shoulders slumped slightly as if the wind had gone out of her proverbial sails. She creased her brow for a moment, before her enticing blue eyes flashed with light. "I just need three weeks of your time. I'll wear a disguise, and so can you."

She started to pace. The speed of her movement indicated her growing conviction that she could convince him.

"Three weeks? Absolutely not." He leaned against the closed door and regarded her. "Disguises? Those only work in gothic novels."

A sly smile tugged at her lips as she lifted her gaze to the ceiling. "I swear you've become ancient in your thinking."

"I beg your pardon," he protested. "Ancient? I'm only four years older than you."

"I'm twenty-six and you're in your third decade. That's pretty ancient."

"You make me sound like a dinosaur."

"As the cobbler says, if the shoe fits." Before he could volley a response, she dropped her voice. The sultry sound reached deep within him and flooded every part of his body. "You're simply scared."

He couldn't argue with that reasoning. Traveling with her would be the ultimate test of his restraint, his sanity, not to mention his dignity. "I'm sorry, but I must decline."

She stopped her pacing and stood before him with a mulish look in her eyes. With little effort, he could sweep her into his arms and kiss away her arguments as he explored her luscious lips and mouth with his own.

Perhaps that was the reasoning she needed to dissuade her from her recklessness.

Without considering the ramifications, he closed the

distance between them but stopped before he pressed his lips against hers.

Her breath teased his lips as his gaze slowly catalogued each delicate feature of her face. "Do you know what can happen when two people attracted to each other travel together?"

"No, but I can imagine all sorts of things."

The sparkle in her eyes taunted him, demanding he move closer. But he kept his distance. "So can I."

Her tongue lightly swept across her lower lip, making it glisten.

He almost groaned at the sight. To even think of kissing her would be catastrophic on so many levels.

"Then it's a good thing I'm not attracted to you." She took a step back, smoothing her hands down her dress. Her demeanor was once again that of a woman on a mission. It was no wonder she was a successful businesswoman. She knew what she wanted and went after it with gusto.

"You'll be at Willa Ferguson and Jacob Morgan's wedding the day after tomorrow at the Duke and Duchess of Randford's home?" she asked with a sweet smile.

He nodded.

"Please think about what I'm offering. You can give me your final answer then." She turned on the ball of her foot and strolled toward the exit, picking up her shawl on the way. She glanced over one shoulder and smiled at him. "Just remember, ten thousand pounds."

How long he stood there staring he didn't want to calculate.

Now he understood the plight of Achilles and his vulnerable heel.

Chapter Three

Beth decided on her way down the stairs that she'd not engage her brother on the disastrous dinner with Lord Siddleton last night. When Grayson had escorted her home, she'd slipped through the back hallway of the servants' entrance, then taken the exact route she'd used last night to escape her brother.

Thankfully, St. John had kept to his normal routine. After dinner, he'd visited his club.

She let out a deep sigh and hoped he had better sense than to gamble last night. It was one thing to be a wealthy aristocrat and place money on idiotic wagers. It was entirely another when he had no money to spare. Besides his racehorses, stables, and the general upkeep on the family estate, her brother didn't have two pence to rub together.

He was her only family. Her mother had conceived late in life and had died from giving birth. The babe was stillborn. Her father had succumbed to a heart ailment before her first Season in London. She'd been on the verge of turning seventeen, and St. John had just reached his majority, leaving him in charge of their futures.

She'd always assumed that her brother loved her. Yet he demonstrated time and time again that he loved himself more. That was the problem with men. She audibly blew out a breath. Of course, she was exaggerating. Her friends' husbands proved that not all men were self-centered.

Just thinking of exceptional men brought to mind Julian Raleah, the Marquess of Grayson. His unique name fit him perfectly. She hadn't made up her mind whether he was self-centered or not. He'd hurt her deeply when he walked away. Yet she still found it amazing that he created steam engines. What peer had the knowledge or aptitude to do that?

Her brother should strive to follow Grayson's example and find some ingenious way to deal with his lack of fortune.

She paused slightly on the fifth step when she saw him. With his ruddy cheeks, red hair, watery eyes, and barrel chest, St. John resembled a boiled lobster freshly pulled from the pot. He'd be difficult to ignore this morning.

"Blythe, where were you? We waited for a half hour before we ate." He narrowed his eyes for effect, but instead, his cheeks expanded like those of a puffer fish ready to defend its territory.

"Upstairs," she answered. She'd learned early on in life that it was easier to stick with the truth than to lie. You didn't have to remember as much.

"I sent one of the footmen to see if you were ill." He sniffed for good measure. "You were gone."

There was no need to answer, as he'd lecture her no matter what she said.

"Where did you go?"

"Lord Grayson's house," she answered politely.

He stuck out his arm for her to take. "Grayson?" The word lolled on his tongue as if he'd taken a bitter medicine.

With as much poise as she could summon, she slipped

her hand around his forearm and allowed him to escort her to breakfast in a small dining room.

Two liveried footmen stood at attention near the buffet that held an abundance of food. St. John took servings of everything while Beth preferred her toast, jam, and tea. It was her standard breakfast fare.

He waved the footmen away. "Close the doors behind you."

That sentence ensured the staff would be aware that St. John was taking her to task for leaving last night. She supposed she should feel guilty for her treatment of Lord Siddleton, but she owed nothing to St. John.

Beth exhaled her frustration. He should have told her his plans. Of course, if she'd known, then she never would have appeared for the dinner anyway. She'd have gone to the home of her friends Kat and Randford for the evening. She loved to play with their son, Arthur, Randford's heir. She could spend hours just watching the handsome little man sleep.

Of course, he was only six months old, but she had little doubt he'd grow up to be as handsome as his father and as kind as his mother. Truth be told, she loved babies and children of all ages. It had been her fondest wish to have had a family of her own, but sometimes fate had other ideas.

Such as having to deal with her brother.

He threw his serviette to the table and stared at her. "I forbid you from having anything to do with him. He's bad *ton.*"

She knew exactly whom he was referring to, but she wouldn't give St. John an inch. "Do you mean Grayson?" She took a sip of tea, then looked over the edge of the cup. "I don't see how you can forbid me anything. I'm of age, and I'm no longer in society." She gently placed her cup back on its saucer with nary a sound. This was a conversation she should have had with him months ago. Better late than never. "Besides, he's no different than we are. Only he doesn't spend money that he doesn't have."

"There's a world of difference between us and him. He's always been poor. We're just down on our luck." St. John shook his head so hard it was a wonder it didn't fly off through the open window. "Typical that you would only think of yourself," he grumbled as he gripped the edge of the table so tightly that she could see the whites of his knuckles. "You must marry again. Lord Siddleton is wealthy, kind, and, as importantly, he's old."

Her brow crinkled at the words.

"Which means that you won't have to tolerate marriage to him for decades. A couple of years at most. Give him an heir, and he'll leave this world a happy man."

"That's ridiculous." She pushed back from the table.

"He's not that bad. Just make certain all the candles are out." St. John blinked innocently.

"It's disgusting that you would reduce a marriage between me and Lord Siddleton to such a common and vulgar purpose." She inched her chin in defiance.

"You'll consider it?"

"St. John," she retorted. "Enough. I'm not marrying."

"Blythe," he cajoled. "We need money. You must see the beauty of the arrangement. His homes are breathtakingly elegant. You'll be a darling of society again and can host a multitude of events there." He rested his chin in one hand. "Think of the balls and soirees you could plan. You'll be a grand dame of London society. You'll have friends galore. Everyone loves a come-from-behind story."

She quirked a brow. "Does society, really?" As if becoming a grand dame was what she wanted. But then, her brother had never been the most astute individual. He made a rusted ax look sharp. "You've offered me up like a trussed goose ready for Christmas dinner. I decline. I *will not* marry again."

"But you weren't married. Meriwether . . ." Her brother's words trailed to nothing.

She clamped her teeth hard.

"The truth is that I only have about two months of funds before we're insolvent." His voice choked on the last word.

"If you're so inclined to replenish the viscountcy coffers, I suggest you find an heiress and marry her," she replied. "I'll not go through another marriage ceremony."

"Blythe," he said in his most persuasive voice. "I can't marry."

"Why not?" she demanded in return.

"Because . . . I'm not the marrying type. At least, not yet." The look of feigned sincerity on his face reminded her of all the times he tried to finagle an extra dessert from Cook before dinner. Of course, Cook had always given in. St. John was a staff favorite and the heir.

Beth sighed. "I'm not the marrying type either."

"But you're a woman. You must marry." His face was turning that awful shade of red again. "I need you to be biddable."

"No."

"A caring sister would do as I ask." A brief glance of irritation appeared, making his eyes shine with an unholy lightness.

"I'm afraid not." She took another sip of tea. "I have another trip planned. I'll need my carriage. I'm leaving at the end of the week."

He cleared his throat and sat upright in his chair. "You can't have the carriage."

As silence descended between them, her gaze never left her brother's.

"I . . . I . . ." Struggling for words, he swallowed. "I sold it."

"I'm done." She stood from her chair with as much grace as she could muster and discreetly clenched her fist. Pieces of her brittle heart broke apart. She stared at the teacup and plate in front of her. Ordinary items that had always been a part of her life, but now seemed unrecognizable. Much like her brother. Her only family.

She swallowed the tears that threatened. She hadn't noticed that her carriage was gone, as she always walked to the workshop. But she needed that carriage as much as she needed air. Her carriage represented more than a vehicle to go from place to place. She used it for work and travel to help her business succeed. She could visit her best friends, Katherine and Constance, Meriwether's other two wives, whenever she wanted or if she needed to get away from her brother.

But more than anything, it represented her freedom to live her life as she wanted. Her own brother hadn't even considered the impact selling it would have on her. "You had no right."

"I had to," he answered.

"That was the last gift Father ever gave me." She raised her eyes to his. "Did you sell yours?"

"I'm a viscount. I must maintain a certain status," he said with his nose tilted in the air.

"You're in this predicament because of your own actions." She swallowed the bitterness of her words.

"My horses are investments," he said sharply in defense. "Don't do anything you'll regret."

Her gaze latched onto his. "What does that mean?"

"It means that if you don't marry, then you'll be as destitute as me. I won't have the funds to keep you in a manner that you're accustomed to." He waved a hand in her direction. "No new frocks, gloves, shoes, baubles." He stood, indicating he hadn't lost all his manners as a gentleman when a lady was about to depart a room. "You understand."

"What I understand is that you need me to marry so you'll have enough money to keep your stables and racehorses. I also understand that marriage would curtail my freedom to work." She smiled slightly. "I'm sorry, but no one will tell me what I can and cannot do anymore. My frock?" She waved a hand down her dress. "I purchased this with my own earnings because of my work. Perhaps you should consider earning an honest wage?"

"What?" he sputtered. "The aristocracy doesn't work for a living."

Her stomach clenched as she realized that her brother was a stranger standing across the table. They'd lived together for years, but she wondered if she ever knew the real him. For the first time ever, she doubted if her brother loved her.

It made little difference now. She was responsible for only herself.

"If you can't stomach earning an honest wage, perhaps you should consider selling your horses and renting out your stables," she said. "That should provide some necessary funds."

"Nonsense," he retorted. His upper lip twitched, a sure sign that his anger was pulled tighter than a French knot. "If you don't want to marry Siddleton, marry Monty."

"Montague Portland?" she cried. "He's hardly better than Lord Siddleton."

St. John shook his head, sending his jowls jiggling. "He happens to be my best friend in the entire world. Said if you wouldn't marry Siddleton, he would offer for you. Of course, with the proviso that I give him half of my stables in exchange for fifteen thousand pounds. It's a sacrifice I'm willing to make."

"No, St. John." Beth bit the inside of her cheek. Truth be told, she'd rather marry Lord Siddleton than Montague Portland. He was as horse crazy and as big a wastrel as her brother. "It's a sacrifice for me more than you. You'll not issue such dictates anymore. Nor will I be a consolation prize."

Without waiting for his reply, she exited the breakfast room with her head held high.

At the entry, their butler, Mr. Fremont, nodded. "Off to work, Miss Howell?"

"Yes," she answered, taking her cloak and gloves from his outstretched hands.

"Very good, ma'am. The devil is partial to idle hands," he answered.

"Indeed, Mr. Fremont," she said, quickly pulling on her kidskin gloves. They were her last pristine pair. "Have you been reading Chaucer?"

"Yes." He bowed slightly.

"Will you inform Lord Howell that I'll be dining at the Duke and Duchess of Randford's house this evening?" She started to descend the front steps, then turned around. "Mr. Fremont? Once you're finished with your book, perhaps you would consider loaning it to my brother. We were just talking about the rewards of working to improve oneself. I'm sure he'd enjoy reading it again. Good day." Beth gracefully maneuvered the steps, then took her customary route to her workshop.

⁓

Julian should be thinking about steam engines instead of Beth Howell and her outrageous request. Any second, the consortium representative would arrive. Last night at the Duchess of Langham's ball, Julian had met with several men looking to invest with him. Yet Beth and her tender lips and saucy mouth were holding court center stage in his musings.

"My lord, Sir Jeffrey Baker from the Six Corners Consortium is here."

Grayson pushed aside his thoughts. He could tell by the formal tone Cillian used that his visitor stood nearby. Gone was the lyrical lilt in his valet's voice only to be replaced by a stuffy and typical English-butler tone.

Julian resisted the urge to chuckle at Cillian's antics. The man could have made his fortune on the stage. It was hard to keep track of which part he was performing throughout the day with all his different personas.

"Send him in, please."

Cillian nodded, then turned on his heel to escort Sir Jeffrey inside Julian's office.

Julian's gaze swept across the study. Freshly cleaned, the wood furniture practically sparkled. If he could keep the envoy from the consortium interested in his work and his ideas, then perhaps the man wouldn't notice the worn upholstery. Cillian had already placed a coffee service and a small pot of tea in the room to hide the lack of real servants.

Pillows had been strategically placed on the furniture to hide the shabbiness of the room. He'd have to thank Cillian for his quick thinking. Wherever he purchased them, they had to be returned this afternoon. Julian didn't have any extra coin for such fripperies.

Only his closest friends knew how close he tittered on the brink of financial ruin. He didn't want that information floating through London society. Julian had little doubt that the consortium wouldn't look too favorably on a peer who needed an infusion of funds quickly to keep his estate and properties habitable, no matter how ingenious his designs were.

He forced himself to take a steadying breath. Nothing good would come from such thoughts. Sir Jeffrey had called upon him specifically to discuss his designs. He wouldn't care about the furniture.

Grayson stood when his visitor entered the study. Cillian soundlessly closed the door behind him.

"Good morning, my lord," Sir Jeffrey announced. "I've been looking forward to our conversation since last night."

"As have I. Thank you for coming." Julian walked to his guest. "Would you care for anything before we start?"

"No, thank you."

A simple reprieve from having to serve refreshments eased the clenched muscles in Julian's stomach. There would be no need to explain why there weren't any servants other than Cillian.

"Shall we begin?" Julian waved toward a small library table in the study. The mechanical drawings of his various compound engines were stacked neatly into two piles. One was for a two-stage machine, while another had a three-stage design.

Wearing a finely tailored morning coat of brown wool and navy breeches, Sir Jeffrey sat at the table, then placed a pair of wire-framed spectacles on his nose. He had to be Julian's age or even younger.

"My wife says I read too much," Sir Jeffrey confessed as he tapped the side of his glasses. "Hence, I need these." He leaned his lanky frame in the chair and studied Julian. "Tell me about your design."

Julian pulled a drawing from the pile and placed it in front of his guest. "Are you familiar with steam engines?"

Sir Jeffrey nodded. "Steam is produced in a boiler. The pressure generated is pushed through a valve that moves a piston up and down that's connected to a rod and flywheel, thus producing energy."

Julian nodded. "I've taken a similar concept and changed it. It's my own design."

"Tell me more." Sir Jeffrey studied the drawing.

Julian stood closer, and with a pencil, pointed to the compound steam engine he'd created. "Instead of one chamber, I've connected two chambers or stages, as they're called. The steam in the first chamber has less energy after it's done its work, but there's still more to harness. Thus, it goes into the second chamber and produces more energy in a more consistent . . . let's say smoother fashion."

Sir Jeffrey's eyes widened. "By your drawing, an engine this size could perhaps be manufactured for helping the operation at the mills up north."

Julian nodded his head. "I believe that this design can have multiple chambers, thus making it ideal for large applications."

"If your design works, that would mean that investors like me could help build factories and other industries without having to be located next to rivers." Sir Jeffrey looked at the drawing again.

"It works," Julian said confidently. "I have an operational model at a London warehouse. If you have the time, I could show it to you."

Sir Jeffrey smiled as he studied the drawings. Finally, he looked Julian's way. "I do not claim to have the knowledge necessary to evaluate such a device. I'm more enamored of numbers." He chuckled slightly, but the gleam in his eyes betrayed his intelligence.

"You're modest." Julian sat in the chair opposite Sir

Jeffrey. "I imagine you are aware of far more than you let on."

His visitor shrugged slightly. "I'm simply a man who notices things. Times are changing for the aristocracy in power, and the middling classes are ready to step in. Most men in the peerage believe they can act in any fashion they want. But people in trade, like us"—he waved a hand between them—"must maintain high standards for work and behavior."

"I'm in complete agreement," Grayson said. "I focus on steam engines and not soirees." He meant every word. People in trade didn't look favorably on aristocrats who behaved as rakes and wastrels with no accountability. Tradespeople were trying to create new industries, and they had to be held to the highest standards for society to accept them. To bridge the two worlds he found himself straddling, Grayson had to hold himself to the same high standards.

Sir Jeffrey chuckled. "It's one of the reasons I admire and want to work with you. I do have a man of science who should see it. Afterward, he'll write a full report and present it to the consortium membership." He took off his spectacles, then placed them in a coat pocket. "If it operates the way you say, then the consortium will invest in your design."

It took every ounce of control Julian possessed not to lean forward and demand to know more. If they saw how desperate he was for funds, they might not make their best offer. "Of course."

"Excellent." Sir Jeffrey whipped out a piece of foolscap and a small pencil from the satchel by his side. "When might this be arranged?"

Julian bit his lip to keep from smiling. With the eagerness in the man's tone, Sir Jeffrey was as excited as

Julian about the project. "I'll make it a priority to meet your man of science when it's convenient for him."

"He's on his way back from Aberdeen. I expect him in London sometime late next week. He'll need a rest after the trip." Sir Jeffrey stood. "By and by, Lord Grayson, one question I should've asked." Never taking his gaze from Julian, Sir Jeffrey replaced the pencil and foolscap into his satchel. "If the consortium wanted a variation of your operational model, I assume you have the capacity to cater to their interests?"

The hair lifted off the back of Julian's neck. If the man was referring to money, things were about to become complicated. "Could you expound on what type of variations and what you mean by *capacity*? So . . . I could be thinking of applications."

Sir Jeffrey nodded. "*Capacity* meaning funds and warehouse space for the new engines. Depending on the size of your engines, we might want to see one in a larger model." He chuckled slightly. "Or a smaller one. You never know what uses the other members might be thinking of for your designs. Naturally, we'd give you time to build it before we came to a decision."

"It won't be a problem." *What a lie.*

Once again, the familiar feeling of failure raised its ugly head demanding attention. This was nothing but a disaster waiting to unfold. Why couldn't an opportunity present itself without requiring money?

His friends, the Duke of Randford and the Earl of Sykeston, immediately came to mind. They both were war heroes and had money. They would help him if he asked, but he would never take advantage of their friendships that way. If the consortium didn't buy his engines, he'd never be able to pay them back.

Beth Howell immediately charged into his thoughts.

Her offer to split any monies they found might be the answer to his prayers. Even though he had said it was a slim chance of recovering those funds, it might be his only way to succeed with the consortium.

"Perhaps in three weeks?" Sir Jeffrey furrowed his brow.

"I'll await word." Julian extended his hand to the man for a shake. Immediately, Cillian entered and escorted Sir Jeffrey to the door.

Julian clenched his teeth and paced the length of the room. What was he thinking? Traveling with Beth represented a hazard on so many fronts. They'd be traveling together in close quarters. She might not feel the attraction between them, but he certainly did. Probably, there wasn't any money left. Throughout his life, Lord Meriwether had been known for being an excessive gambler with expensive tastes.

He stopped in front of the overgrown courtyard of his London home. A grim reminder of what his future might look like if he didn't find a way to successfully sell his engines.

For the love of science, why was he even contemplating accompanying Beth on such a fool's errand?

He blew out a breath. There was only one decision to make. For once in his life, he had to take a risk.

Chapter Four

That evening, Beth waited her turn to present her wedding gift to Willa Ferguson, who was Katherine, the Duchess of Randford's companion. Like a fairy tale, Willa had fallen in love with Katherine's husband's valet, Jacob Morgan. The Duke and Duchess of Randford were delighted with the match between the two. To celebrate, Katherine, who liked to be called Kat, was hosting a small party for Willa ahead of the nuptials set for tomorrow morning in the grand salon at Randford House.

It was the very room where they were now celebrating.

Beth loved Willa and was certain Jacob was a fine man. But frankly, the idea of marriage soured her stomach. She closed her eyes for a brief second, then glanced around the room. Why was it that these women seemed immensely happy with their marital state while Beth thought it akin to dancing with the devil?

All day, she couldn't stop thinking about Grayson and what his decision would be. Based upon the way luck had thwarted her at every turn, Grayson would refuse to accompany her.

Even at night, he wouldn't leave her be. Images would pop into her mind, namely Grayson's lips against hers.

She would wonder if they were as soft as they appeared. She'd love to see him sprawled on a bed with her linens underneath. She bit her bottom lip to keep from grinning at such a wicked thought.

Her gaze drifted to Constance, who was Meriwether's legitimate widow. When Beth had first met Constance, the poor woman had been carrying and close to delivering Meriwether's child.

Kat's marriage had never been consummated, as Meri had left the same day they exchanged vows. With Constance, he'd stayed a month. With Beth, he'd lasted two weeks and had only come to her bed once, their wedding night. All the other evenings, Meri had preferred St. John's company. How humiliating that your supposed husband preferred your brother and the discussion of racehorses over a new wife who sat anxiously awaiting her husband's arrival!

Thankfully, she wasn't left with a child.

Instead, her family's stables had been blessed with racehorses, while Beth had been left behind and ruined by Meriwether's actions.

"Beth?" Willa gently prodded. "Is there something special about the wool you're gathering?"

"Pardon?" Beth forced her attention to the bride-to-be.

"You've been preoccupied since the very first minute you entered." Willa sat beside Beth on the long sofa that framed a wall of windows that overlooked the Duke of Randford's famed rose garden.

Kat and Constance joined them in a set of chairs that faced the sofa.

"Lass, what ails ye?" Willa's penetrating gaze studied Beth's features.

She forced herself to smile. "Nothing and everything."

Willa laughed softly. "That's life. Everything changes

while staying the same. Like Jacob and me." A beautiful blush covered the Scotswoman's cheeks.

Kat reached over and patted Willa on the knee. "I'm so happy you and Jacob are marrying."

Willa nodded. "Thank you, lassie."

Constance scooted up to the edge of her chair. "I couldn't agree more. You'll have a wonderful life together." She turned her attention to Beth. "Would you like to say something?"

Beth shook her head vehemently. "I'll never marry."

Kat's and Constance's respective eyebrows practically floated to their hairlines, while Willa simply chuckled. She leaned toward Beth, then said in a loud whisper, "I think Constance was gently nudging you to wish me congratulations on marrying Jacob. Not necessarily your views on the state of wedded bliss for yourself. Not that I don't want to hear what you're thinking, but I can probably guess."

Beth glanced at Constance and Kat, her best friends, who were more like sisters. She shared everything with them. "I apologize. My mind is elsewhere." She leaned over and pressed a kiss to Willa's cheek.

Though the woman was in her mid-forties and a bit older than her husband-to-be, there was something youthful and exuberant about Kat's companion. Perhaps it was the glow of excitement about her that she was about to impart on a life with her true love.

Beth pushed such nonsense aside. What made many women happy wasn't what she wanted.

"Your brother?" Willa asked gently.

Beth nodded. "He invited the Marquess of Siddleton to dinner last night. Apparently, St. John wanted the man to propose at the dinner table and expected me to accept."

Constance's hand flew to her chest. "Did he even discuss it with you?"

She shook her head. "He'd mentioned it was a grand idea weeks ago, but I never thought he'd actually set the plan into motion."

"What did you say?" Kat asked.

"I explained that I needed to attend the retiring room, then I walked out the door and went to Grayson's house."

Willa tilted her head and regarded Beth from head to foot. "Aye, I knew that man was involved somehow."

"Willa," Kat scolded.

"Don't Willa me, my miss," the bride-to-be said while shaking her head. "Is it the marquess who has your head up in the clouds?" Willa was the type of person who was plainspoken, with a talent for unearthing the truth wherever it might be hidden.

"Yes and no," Beth said softly. "It's not simply Lord Siddleton. St. John told me that Montague Portland offered to marry me if I didn't accept the marquess's proposal. Seems Portland and St. John will share stables for a sum of money and my hand." She clenched her fists at the thought that she was nothing better than a broodmare. "I asked Grayson to help me find my dowry . . ."

All three women leaned close to hear the story.

"I asked him to travel with me. I planned to use Meri's receipts that he left us as a map of sorts."

"Good thinking," Constance said.

Kat's gaze never left hers. "What did Grayson say?"

"He said he'd give me his answer at the wedding. I offered to split any monies we found." Beth tangled her fingers together.

The three women looked at one another before turning back to Beth.

"Darling, what if Christian and I traveled with you?" Kat asked.

Before the words were out of Kat's mouth, Beth shook her head. "I can't and won't ask that of you." She reached over and placed her hand over Kat's. "This is a step toward my independence. I only asked Grayson because . . . well, he needs the money as much as I do."

Constance smiled slightly. "Are you hoping you can rekindle what you once shared?"

"No. That's our past." It was difficult to discuss Grayson. He'd made it clear what he thought of Beth when he'd walked away.

Which was fine with her. She'd put him in her proverbial box of disappointments, only to be viewed on occasion as a reminder of her set course in life. Independence.

Yet she was the one to reach out to him. But she needed someone, and he fit the bill.

Funny that after all these years she could walk into a room and sense whether he was there or not, much like an apparition ready to haunt her. There was always a sense of ravenousness about the marquess, a hunger that couldn't be satisfied. The way he stared at her at times, she almost felt like his prey.

When it happened, she never let on how it affected her. Deep down, she loved the feeling. His heated gazes reminded her that he'd once looked at her that way when they were courting. His eyes would darken with promises of private caresses, titillating touches, and so much more.

Late at night, much like last evening, she'd feel that same hunger. What she wouldn't give to have a man who was consumed with her and not concerned with money, lineage, or other women.

Just her.

She cleared her throat gently to disperse her thoughts about Grayson. "I've given this thought. Everything is tied together. I wanted to meet the farmer who sold Meri your Hampshire boar."

Kat tapped her chin. "I have the papers that accompanied the sale. I could give them to you."

Beth sat on the edge of her seat and turned to Constance. "Do you have the lease from the mine Meri left you?"

Constance placed her glass of lemonade on the table and rested her hand on her rounded stomach. She and Sykeston were expecting. "It's at the solicitor's office. I'll send word to Mr. Hanes that you'd like to examine it." She turned to Kat. "Does Randford still have that collection of personal items of Meri's? Perhaps Beth could look at that before she goes."

"Of course. It contains old racing sheets, notices of horse sales, and a locked box without a key. Christian wanted to throw it out, but I asked him not to. You're more than welcome to look at all of it."

"Thank you," Beth said. For the first time in a while, hope surged. Yet unease niggled its way through her thoughts. Why was it that Meri left Kat and Constance something but seemed to have forgotten her?

Did he think her unworthy of such a bequest? Perhaps she was the type of person who was forgettable. Society certainly didn't remember her. Most of her friends from finishing school had stopped calling on her when it was discovered she was one of Meri's widows. No one wanted any part of the scandal.

But everyone loved to talk about it.

What had hurt the most was that her pretend husband only spent one night in her bed. Perhaps it said more about him than it did about her. Another promise broken.

She had quite the collection of those.

Chapter Five

Beth Howell was the key to Julian finding funds for the consortium's proposal.

Plus, if he and Beth were successful, she would never have to consider Siddleton's proposal again. She could also move out of her brother's home and live on her own. It would give her the independence she sought.

Julian would do everything in his power to help her. Because by helping her, he'd help himself. God, if only they had a little luck on their side. With a painful sigh, he turned his attention to the business at hand, Willa Ferguson and Jacob Morgan's wedding.

"What are you bemoaning?" Cillian yanked the cravat tight before creating the elaborate knot that would soon be choking him.

"I didn't realize I said anything aloud. Forget—" His words lodged in his throat when Cillian tightened the *bloody* knot around his neck, making it difficult to breathe, let alone converse. Somehow, he managed to squeeze out, "Looser, if you have a care."

"I don't want my masterpiece to sag midway in the ceremony. Do you? Now buck up and take it like a marquess. Besides, you want to make a good impression with

Miss Howell." A wicked smile appeared. "I think it's marvelous to see you in such a state. You're normally"—the valet drew back and regarded his work tying the neckcloth—"much too staid. Boring even." Obviously, he wasn't satisfied, as he continued to fret with the blasted knot he'd created.

"I see that you hold me in the highest regard," Julian answered sarcastically. "Remind me again why I keep you in my employ?"

"Besides the fact I'm the only one you can afford, I think you're quite lucky to have me by your side. I have a myriad of talents that you benefit from. More importantly, you need me. I even would venture to say that you enjoy my company." Cillian lifted an eyebrow and critically evaluated Julian. "I enjoy you also, but not as much as you enjoy me."

"I never realized how pretentious you are," Julian retorted.

"I think you should help Miss Howell. She trusts you, and the idea a lady of Miss Howell's worth setting off on such an adventure without someone loyal and faithful? It would be a travesty," his valet said, then waved a hand at the mirror. That was the signal for Julian to admire Cillian's handiwork and give effusive praise.

"Loyal and faithful? You make me sound like a dog. Furthermore, I didn't ask for your opinion." Julian turned to the mirror. "Pink." He blinked to ensure that the vision in the mirror was him. Once verified, he shook his head. "You tied a pink cravat around my neck?"

"Don't make such a great fuss and clatter about a piece of fashion." Cillian pointed to a table where a bouquet of blush-colored roses lay. "The duke wants you to wear one of those on the lapel. Why he sent so many is beyond me." He waggled his eyebrows. "Perhaps you could present them as a token of your esteem to a special someone."

"Stop." Julian captured his valet's gaze in the mirror.

Julian tugged at the cravat absently, while his other hand clenched in a tight fist. Blood pounded through his veins as it always did when he thought of how he'd lost Beth years ago. Then when he told his father that Howell had refused his offer for her, his father had offered no advice or even empathy. He'd merely said, *What a disappointment.*

Perhaps his father had been referring to him.

Or perhaps he was disappointed in Grayson's sense of pride.

He'd never forget the day when Howell had called him a fortune hunter. Beth's brother had threatened to buy all the marquessate's debts and force Grayson's father into insolvency if Julian had pursued the match. Defeated and unable to find another way to win Beth's hand, Julian had no choice but to walk away. Which at the time had seemed the best course of action, since he'd never wanted to embarrass his father or Beth.

Pride was a possessive mistress.

Unfortunately, his father's financial worries hadn't lessened. If Grayson had succeeded in securing Beth's hand, their futures might have been vastly different.

Instead, he'd seen his father wither away with the remorse and anguish of seeing the coffers of the proud estate and the farms start to falter under his watch. Julian had known even before the doctor's prognosis that his father's heart problems were due to the constant anxiety of trying to find a way out of the financial burden he'd created. At his early death, that burden had become Julian's.

Perhaps he could have saved his father if he'd married

another heiress. But his heart wouldn't allow it. Those precious weeks wooing Beth were ingrained in his memories.

His saving grace might be delivered by the Six Corners Consortium. Julian had done his own research on the group. They were quite conservative in their thinking and in their investments. The fact that they were extremely interested was more than promising. He just had to find some money.

"Now that you've mentioned Miss Howell, I've decided to accompany her." Julian turned in a tight circle and faced Cillian. "I need money, or this investment opportunity will fail to come to fruition."

"I'm delighted you see this for the opportunities that it presents." Cillian frowned when he saw Julian's scowl. "What?"

"What does *opportunities* mean?" He released a breath, but it did little to loosen the knots in his chest.

"For someone who is so book smart, you can be so dense at times. You and she can start again where you left off."

"She doesn't want to marry."

"Why?"

Julian escaped Cillian's probing eyes by studying his cravat in the mirror. "She's convinced she'll be much happier if she continues through life by herself." He smiled slightly, but the bitterness of their ill-fated circumstances made him want to howl at the ceiling like a wild animal in pain. "So, it's not to be. I want a family. I want a wife by my side and children tugging on the knees of my breeches."

Cillian's look of horror almost made him laugh.

He reassured his valet. "Hopefully, by then, I'll have dozens of pairs in my wardrobe, so it won't make any difference how wrinkled and stretched out my clothes become."

All his adult life, he'd imagined it would be Beth by his side. When he'd heard she'd married Randford's half brother, he grieved. Yes, grieved for all he'd lost. Then when it was declared that Beth's marriage was void, he silently rejoiced only to be dejected once more when she'd informed him that she would never marry again. She was finished with the male species, and unfortunately, that included him.

"As an inventor, sometimes your ideas lack any imagination whatsoever." With a tad too much enthusiasm, Cillian brushed a piece of lint off his coat.

Julian kept his balance, then stared into his valet's eyes.

"You're looking at it the wrong way." Cillian took a step back and regarded Julian's formal wear. "If you help her find her missing fortune, she'll trust you." He pointed his finger at the middle of Julian's chest. "And she'll trust your dedication to her." Cillian could perfectly arch a single eyebrow better than any stuffy aristocrat Julian had ever seen. "Paving the way for you to sweep her off her feet." He straightened a nonexistent wrinkle in Julian's morning coat, then nodded his satisfaction.

Julian turned around for a final glance in the mirror. His gaze landed on his valet's. "This might be a fool's errand with no fortune at the end of the rainbow. I doubt if I'll have her good opinion then." Not to mention the fact that she acted as if she could barely tolerate him at times.

"You're blathering like a bubbly-jock," Cillian argued.

Julian lifted his own brow in answer. "If she finds her fortune, she has even more reason to stay independent. Frankly, it's her life. I'll wish her all the happiness in the world." He glanced at his signet ring on his little finger. It was the seal of the Marquess of Grayson. Once upon a time, she had wanted to marry him even when she knew the truth about his wealth.

It hadn't mattered then. But now her circumstances had changed.

"Perhaps you're right. It is her life to do what she pleases," Cillian said, but by the set of his jaw, Julian knew he didn't believe it. "Perhaps she won't accept anyone's heart. But you could leave a small piece of yours as a remembrance."

"What does that mean?" Julian shook his head. "More of your sentimental Irish wisdom?"

"It means, if you have a chance to win her again and fail, then at least you tried." His gaze bore into Julian's. "Could you actually take another woman as your wife without trying to win Miss Howell's hand?" He snorted, then brushed his own coat, an old livery uniform. "Call me a tried and true romantic, but if I were you, I couldn't." He lifted both brows in defiance. "You can't do it either." He glanced at the clock on the mantle. "Enough of the philosophy lesson. If you're not out the door this instant, we're going to be late."

"We?"

"Who do you think is going to play coachman?" Cillian said with the lift of an eyebrow.

"I'll ride over myself. You don't have to come."

"You can't. Your horse is hitched to the carriage. If you ride over to Randford House, you'll smell like horse at a wedding. Uncouth." Cillian sniffed, then slipped the tall hat on his head and tugged. It matched his uniform. With a look of satisfaction and a sly smile to match, he quickly pinned a rosebud to Julian's jacket. "Besides, you'll be like Cinderella arriving at the ball."

"Spare me," he said, chuckling. Julian appreciated Cillian as more than just a loyal servant. Many nights, Julian would work late into the early morning hours, forgetting to eat. But Cillian didn't. He'd bring a meal and keep Julian company as he ate. Many nights it kept Julian from realizing how lonely his life had turned. His friends, the Duke of Randford and the Earl of Sykeston, were married. Their futures had taken a different path while Julian was still stuck in the same position he'd been in for the last eight years.

Satisfied with his formal dress, he walked to the door, then turned to Cillian.

He should have known. His valet and coachman was straightening his own appearance again in the mirror.

"Are you trying to impress someone?" He arched an eyebrow. Cillian had never mentioned having someone in his life, but the way he took interest in the details of his own clothing made Julian pause.

Cillian nodded. "Naturally. I must keep up appearances with the other drivers. You're a marquess and need to look the part, so I must look the part."

For all his flaws, Cillian Patrick was loyal.

Without another word, Julian left his valet standing in front of the mirror rearranging his hair.

A quarter of an hour later, Julian stepped out of his carriage and straightened his coat. The Duke and Duchess of Randford's Mayfair home loomed before him. Julian had visited hundreds of times before, yet this time felt different. A couple was ready to commit their lives to each other, and he'd been invited to witness such an event. Was there ever a celebration of life more worthy than that? Perhaps the birth of a child. His parents had taught him to appreciate such occasions, whether it was a couple from high society or his own tenants who joined together in matrimony. It was all to be celebrated. He just wished he was in a celebratory mood.

Julian tugged on his beaver hat, then proceeded to the front door, where the Randford butler stood waiting for him.

"Welcome to Randford House, my lord," Wheatley called out. The white-haired butler bowed elegantly in his formal morning suit.

"Good morning, Wheatley."

The butler waved him in with a flourish. Julian stepped inside, where a footman in the red livery of the Duke of Randford stood ready to take his hat and cane. He nodded a greeting at the footman.

"Lord Grayson, you're the last to arrive," Wheatley informed him. "If you'll follow me to the family salon."

He followed the butler to the Duke of Randford's personal sitting room. Even outside the door, he could hear the joyous conversations that floated through the air. His old friend Jonathan Eaton, the Earl of Sykeston, was the first to notice his arrival.

"Grayson," he called out as he came to Julian's side.

Julian took his friend's hand for a shake. "You look remarkably well, old man."

Sykeston had been severely injured during the war, and miraculously, he'd survived. But his recovery wasn't without its own peril. He'd become a recluse. But all that changed when he married his childhood best friend, the former Constance Lysander. She just happened to be the legitimate widow of Randford's half brother, Lord Meriwether.

Julian smiled at his friend, who held Miss Aurelia Vareck, Constance's daughter by Meriwether. Sykeston loved the little girl and claimed her as his own. He proclaimed her a miracle, as she taught him to see there were bigger things in life beside dwelling on your past losses.

"My lord." Sykeston's countess joined them.

Julian bowed to his friend's lovely wife. "Lady Sykeston, you're a vision."

She blushed prettily, then smiled at her husband. The look between the two of them was intimate, as if they were having an entire conversation without saying a word. Julian marveled at such emotion and tenderness shared between the couple. It was what he wanted with his future wife.

Sykeston juggled the little one in his arms. "Grayson, when are you coming to visit us?"

"Well, I could stop by tomorrow," Julian answered.

Constance laughed. "No, he means Portsmouth. We're leaving tomorrow morning. Do say you'll come for a visit. We've asked Randford and Kat. We're inviting Beth. We could make it a party."

Randford had sidled up beside him. "You should join us. Kat and I are coming later in the week with Beth."

"I have other plans," Julian said, but he didn't add that Beth wouldn't be attending either. She'd be with him.

Randford nodded toward his duchess, who stood beside the bride and groom along with Beth.

Julian stole a glance in Beth's direction. She looked stunning today wearing a topaz-colored silk gown that accented her beautiful eyes and with her hair in an elegant and relaxed coiffure. His body tightened, such an inconvenient response.

"The vicar is ready to start." Randford nodded in the direction of his wife. "Kat and I are standing as witnesses."

"We'll take our seats." Sykeston lowered his daughter to the floor but still held her hand. With Constance by his side and his cane in the other hand, he escorted them to the front of the room.

Julian chose to sit in a chair behind the group. If he knew Beth, she'd want to sit next to Constance and Aurelia.

As the vicar welcomed everyone to the joyous occasion, the Randford servants and the remaining guests quieted. Julian purposely didn't allow his gaze to wander, but he knew the instant she slid into the seat next to his.

"Grayson, I didn't see you come in." Beth's low voice reached him, the sound deep and slightly hoarse, as if she'd just awakened.

Like a steel trap, his mind clamped down on such an image. What would she wear as she slept? Perhaps a silk nightgown that she'd embroidered by her own hands. The sound of silk sliding across her curves as she slowly woke from a deep slumber echoed around him. He could almost feel the softness against his fingers. His lower body tightened much like a compactly coiled copper wire primed to release all that pent-up energy.

He crossed his legs hoping to hide the burgeoning tautness in his breeches.

Her soft breath teased his skin just as the slight touch of her lips against his skin would. He clasped his hands together, which was the wrong thing to have done. His unruly cock jumped at the contact. Like sticking his hands in a burning fire, he jerked away and crossed his arms over his chest.

"I'll help you discover what happened to your dowry," he whispered.

Her hand shot out and squeezed his forearm. "You will?" Her smile lit up the whole room. "I thought you'd say no." The glee in her voice grew louder. "This is the best news." She glanced at Willa and Jacob standing before the assembled group of witnesses.

The look of abject joy on her face stole his breath. It

was the same smile she'd given him when he'd asked her to marry him.

Several of the Randford maids turned in their direction with scowls of disapproval on their faces. Julian simply nodded. In no circumstance would he apologize for bringing such happiness to Beth's face.

"Grayson, I can't thank you enough."

The sound of his name was like a caress. He swallowed, praying for control.

Beth snuck a peek in the maids' direction as she lowered her voice. "Just to show you that I know how to compromise, I've reconsidered my request for three weeks of your time." Her gaze was harder than a cut diamond. "If we don't dawdle, two and a half weeks should be sufficient."

He turned to face her. That was a mistake. Her eyes sparkled like a pool of water kissed by the sun. Such a vision muddled his mind from the task at hand.

"One week," he whispered brusquely. That would give him enough time to prepare for the consortium agent's visit.

She furrowed her brow and said something, but he couldn't hear over the din of applause. Just then, the family and friends cheered as the couple broke apart from their first kiss as a married couple.

"What?" Julian asked.

"I said two weeks," Beth practically shouted as she raised two fingers. By then, the noise was slowly fading. She shook her head in annoyance, then forcefully added, "I want another."

Silence descended as Beth's demand pealed through the room.

"Who am I to argue with that?" Morgan chuckled. "Another kiss for my bride!" A blinding smile appeared on the bridegroom's face, then he swept Willa into his arms for another kiss.

As the gathering of friends and family looked on, Grayson leaned close. "Two kisses. I didn't know you were so greedy for such a display. I must remember that." He lifted his brows and smiled.

"There's quite a bit about me that you don't know." She tilted her chin in challenge.

"I'm looking all the more forward to our travels then." He turned his attention back to the front but continued to address Beth. "We should offer our congratulations to the happy couple, then continue our conversation in the conservatory."

She stood but was near enough that he could smell the delicate honeysuckle scent she wore.

Slowly, he stood. "There's one thing I know about you."

"What's that?"

"You still wear the same fragrance as you did all those years ago." With an ease that was in direct conflict with the pounding of his heart, he placed his hand on the small of her back. "Come with me."

She blinked twice, but the mulish set of her mouth reminded him that the woman before him was entirely different from the girl he'd once thought he'd marry. Beth had always been confident and bright, with a novel mind, but there was a hint of cautiousness about her now. He had little doubt that her brother and supposed husband were the cause of her new wariness.

His old friend Randford stared intensely in Grayson's direction.

He answered with his own arched brow. Randford still felt responsible for the three wives his younger half brother had married. Though the duke had provided for all of them, Beth was now in need of a fortune.

And Julian had every intention to help her find it.

He turned to her, and immediately he felt as if he'd been punched in the gut. There was relief in her beautiful blue eyes. A soft glint of light captured her emotion. Any man who didn't believe she was a rare treasure was a fool.

He had never been a fool. But Beth Howell could easily turn him into one.

"You won't regret this," she said. Without another word, she walked to the front of the room with all the others.

Julian stood rooted in place, mesmerized by the gentle but tantalizing roll of her luscious hips as the realization slapped him upside the head. He'd follow her anywhere she wanted.

Which meant that he had to be completely and utterly logical about their travels together. Under no circumstance could he act upon his growing attraction to Beth.

But he had a suspicion that even if they found her fortune, this trip could be his downfall.

It was impossible for Beth not to feel breathless as she stepped into the warmth of Randford's conservatory. Humid air surrounded her, making any deep breath impossible. It had nothing at all to do with the marquess who had followed her into the room.

Beth tried to ignore Grayson as she slowed her step to marvel at the sight before her. The glass structure was the duke's pride and joy, second only to his family. The building overflowed with color and fragrance, as the duke was a connoisseur of roses.

By then, Grayson had caught up with her as they

approached a small sitting area that overlooked the formal terrace of Randford House. As expected of a gentleman, he waited until she took a seat before he sat across from her.

Without taking his gaze from hers, he slowly tugged one glove off one hand, then the other. The slow movements mesmerizing, as if she were witnessing a seduction.

Beth swallowed the lump of consternation in her throat as she watched the marquess. This was merely a mutually beneficial arrangement. She'd do well to remember that fact. She scooted to the edge of her seat prepared to discuss their trip.

He rested his elbows on his muscular thighs—not that she noticed—and regarded her.

"No matter how many times I've been in this building, I'm always amazed at the sheer beauty of it." He reached toward a pot that sat next to his chair and ran his fingers over a single rose.

Beth smiled slightly. "That crimson color is my favorite."

"Another secret I've discovered about you." He leaned back in his chair with an insouciance that made him even more attractive in her eyes.

His ease was a rare trait. At least, in her experience with men. Her father had always been a jolly sort, but he'd found a way to always keep himself busy. The only time he rested was when he was sleeping. Her brother had always been obsessed with his horses. Every free moment was spent at the stables or at Tattersall's. Though he didn't have funds to purchase horseflesh at auction, it was still part of his social schedule. Meri had been constantly on the move, as could be attested by his three wives.

But a man like Grayson wouldn't require every moment of his day be scheduled with tasks or entertainments.

The fact that he commented on the conservatory was proof of that.

Heat bludgeoned her cheeks. "We should discuss our trip."

He nodded in agreement, a teasing smile still on his lips.

Beth reached into her reticule and took out a list that she'd prepared in advance. She glanced at him, then returned her gaze to her list. There were so many things she'd written down, but it was hard to find a place to start. But she'd always been a person who didn't shy away from tough subjects. "I took a piece of my mother's jewelry to E. Cavensham Commerce. Lady Emma Somerton gave me a generous loan."

"I thought you had money saved for this trip?" A line appeared between his eyes.

The urge to reach and smooth the crease between his brows made her scoot forward a bit more.

Good lord, what was she thinking? They were acquaintances. She'd even accept *business partners*. She could not touch him as if they were intimates. "St. John sold my carriage. I'm hoping we can use yours."

"Why aren't you using the carriage money?" The gray in his eyes flashed as he leaned forward.

Her answer probably wouldn't surprise him, but it was nevertheless humiliating how little regard her brother had for her. "He didn't tell me until after he sold it, then kept the money." Desperate to keep an even keel on her emotions, she forced her gaze to his. "If we can't use your carriage, I have another piece that I can use for more funds."

"We'll use mine. Don't worry. I'm a master at economy travel." He placed one hand over hers. "We'll keep expenses to a minimum. Randford has horses at various inns for when he travels. When we head south, we can ask if we could use his horseflesh when we need a fresh team."

She shook her head. "No. Randford has already been too generous on my behalf. I need to do this myself. You understand."

"I do." He leaned back in the chair, breaking the contact between them. "Cillian will be our coachman."

She nodded, but her first instinct was to take his hand back in hers. Even though she'd always been able to handle anything that came her way, it was nice having his reassurance.

"I went to Randford's family solicitor to review the mineral lease that Meriwether left Constance. I've also read the pig's pedigree that he left Kat." She handed him another piece of foolscap she'd pulled from her reticule. "I've drawn a map of our travel to Hampshire. Obviously, we won't know where to go until we see the farmer who sold Meriwether the pig. If it's a dead end, we can investigate who had the mine lease prior to Constance."

"We can stay with Constance and Sykeston," Grayson said, then frowned when he saw the shake of her head. "Right . . . we should do this ourselves."

"We'll also save time." She chewed her lip as she calculated their travel days. "If we stay with them, they'll want to entertain us. That adds days."

He studied the map, then lifted his gaze to hers. "You've put a tremendous amount of work into planning this trip. Are you sure you need me?"

"Fair question." She let the silence envelop them along with the rich, earthy smell of soil. "You have the same hunger as I do. I'm betting you won't quit hunting until we flesh out every lead or until we find the money." He stared at her, but she wasn't intimidated. "I need a business partner, not a lady's maid, to accompany me. Anyone else might try to talk me out of it."

He nodded, then stood and closed the distance between them. He took her hands and helped her stand. "You consider me a business partner?"

The bare skin of his hands was callous, indicating that he wasn't an aristocrat of leisure. He knew work and wasn't afraid of it.

She had to tilt her gaze to his. "Yes. We're equals. How do you see us?"

He took a pair of shears that had been laid on a bench beside them. Carefully, he clipped the crimson rose they had admired. With several snips, he removed the thorns. A genuine smile tugged the corners of his mouth, and his eyes flashed with an emotion that she couldn't identify.

"We are business partners." He handed her the rose. "I hope friends too."

She opened her mouth to say that they were friends. But then she daintily closed it and presented her best smile.

How could you be friends with the man you once thought you would marry?

She had to forget her past and concentrate on her future. "Shall we depart at six o'clock tomorrow morning?"

Chapter Six

❦

The trip to Hampshire gave Beth more time to study Meri's receipts. No matter how many times she examined the papers, she couldn't figure out where Kat's pig had come from. The only transaction that could possibly involve the animal appeared to be one where Meri had parted with two of his erotic statuaries from his collection. He'd given them to a farmer on the outskirts of Kingsclere.

Tired of reading, she pulled out the ivory fabric she'd been embroidering. She'd made the decision to design a waistcoat for Grayson as a thank-you for accompanying her on the trip. If they didn't find her dowry, at least he wouldn't walk away empty-handed.

The bottom of the waistcoat would be embroidered with a Greek key pattern that would extend upward along the button closures. On the lining, where no one would notice, she'd put something special that only they would know the importance of as a remembrance of the trip. She couldn't wait to finish it and show it to him.

She glanced up from her needlework to the open journal beside her, where she'd taken notes about Kat's prize Hampshire pig and his pedigree. "Do you think Sykeston or Constance know this farmer?"

Across the forward-facing bench, Grayson was sprawled and fast asleep.

With his massive size, he took up practically the entire inside of the carriage. Gently, she set aside her embroidery and studied him. It was an oddly intimate moment. She could gaze to her heart's content and not be accused of rude behavior. Though honestly, she doubted he would even consider her study of him rude. He seemed to enjoy her attention. There were dark circles under his eyes and his face looked drawn. Still, in repose, he was a handsome man. Dark whiskers shadowed his square jaw. A frisson of something pleasant swept through her. If she'd just met him, she'd think he was someone daring and dangerous.

She was so close she could see a small cut on his neck where he'd nicked himself shaving. An image of him shirtless standing before a mirror performing his ablutions popped into her thoughts.

Heat swiftly licked her cheeks at the image of him naked from the waist up. She'd never seen a man's naked chest before. She'd never seen Meri's body. When he came to her on their wedding night, the room had been pitch-black. When he'd taken her, he'd lifted her nightgown. He had worn a nightshirt. Only his scratchy legs had touched her. Neither of them held each other as she thought lovers would do.

Her gaze slid from Grayson's neck to his chest. Inch by inch, she studied him. His wide torso tapered into a narrow waist. Her skin suddenly tingled, and her fingers yearned to touch his body to see if it was as hard as she imagined.

"Yes," he whispered.

She jerked at the deep cadence of his voice. Had she spoken aloud her musings?

A wicked smile tugged at one corner of his mouth. Her eyes met his, where a fire smoldered. He blinked slowly, then his gaze swept over her face. Instantly, his grin grew.

The scoundrel. He must have known what she'd been thinking.

"Pardon?" she asked in the most nonchalant voice she could muster.

"I said yes." The deep rumble of his baritone voice reached inside her chest and squeezed her heart. He spoke as if he were seducing her.

In response, her heartbeat raced.

Treacherous organ.

"Yes, Sykeston and Constance would most likely know all the farmers in Hampshire." He easily swung his body upright. "Are you doubting your plans?"

"No," she said. "Just curious."

He leaned toward her with his legs bracketing hers. Instantly, he surrounded her. If it were another, she might feel smothered, but not with him.

She closed her eyes briefly. To even consider wanting more with him would lead to nothing but heartache. She was wiser now. It would not happen again. When she slid her gaze to his, he was studying her lips. For a moment, she thought he'd close the distance between them and press his mouth to hers.

"My lord, we've arrived," Cillian called from the coach box. Instantly, the carriage slowed in front of the Golden Falcon, a popular Kingsclere coaching inn.

"Pity," Grayson said softly. His gaze never left hers. For that infinitesimal moment, they shared an entire conversation without breathing a word to each other. "I was hoping . . ."

"Yes?" she asked softly.

"We could finish . . . what we started," he murmured.

By then, the carriage had come to a complete stop. She forced her gaze from his, then smoothed her skirt, thankful for the distraction before she made a fool of herself. With one glance, he had the ability to make her lose all sense of reason. She could not think of him in any other way but as an associate.

Associates do not kiss associates.

When Cillian opened the carriage door, Grayson winked at her, then the handsome fiend jumped from the carriage. With a smile on his face, he extended his hand, ready to help her down. With a deep breath for fortitude, she placed her hand in his. Though they both wore gloves, she could feel the simmering heat of his hand. Gently, he squeezed hers in reassurance.

"Thank you."

"My pleasure." He bowed slightly.

Such a simple movement left her feeling unbalanced. It would only take a slight breeze to topple her into his arms.

What bloody *nonsense.*

Beth glanced around the inn and the surrounding area. It was a quaint town. The inn was a Tudor structure and appeared to be well-maintained.

A stable hand waved in greeting and came forward. "Welcome to the Falcon."

Cillian nodded in the man's direction, then pulled off their two bags. "I'll get the horses settled."

"Thank you." Grayson turned to her as he picked up their bags. "Have you been here before?"

"Yes," Beth said a little too breathlessly for her own good. "Once before with my brother. He was trying to buy an offspring of Eclipse." At Grayson's questioning gaze, she continued, "He was undefeated in his racing career. Many call him the best British Thoroughbred to ever have lived." She reached to take her bag from the marquess. "I can carry that."

Grayson stopped. "I'm well aware. You're the most self-sufficient woman I've ever met." He slid a side-eyed glance her way and delivered a smile. "You want to be responsible for your own destiny."

Beth slowed to a stop, and Grayson followed. "Are you mocking me?"

The grin teasing his lips fell away. "No. Where would you get that idea?"

"You threw my words from yesterday back at me," she challenged. "Verbatim."

"Beth, I'm trying to be courteous." He lowered the bags and stepped closer. "Are you trying to start an argument?"

"No." Perhaps she was. He kept her off-balance, and it unnerved her. So far, he'd been kind and flirtatious at times. Just like in the days when they were courting. It all made her wary. She'd once trusted him and look where that had left her.

"An act of kind respect and manners doesn't mean I'm not trustworthy." He ran a hand through his hair, then handed her the bag. "By all means."

She ignored his statement or reprimand or lecture. Whatever he thought to impart, she wanted no part of it.

"Come. Let's see about accommodations." Without waiting for her, he turned toward the inn.

Beth's feet remained fixed as he strolled toward the entrance. She took a moment to look at the bucolic scene around her. The town was in the midst of preparing for an event, a fair of some sort. People scurried about preparing tents and tables for a party. Meats were roasting on open fires, much like her cheeks from the shame of her behavior.

She *had* been attempting to start an argument with him because of their bygone courtship. It was bad form on her part. Besides, it didn't matter anymore. What happened in their past needed to stay there. They were working together, and any discord wouldn't be beneficial to either of them.

Perhaps she'd remember that if she embroidered it on a sampler.

She carried her bag into the inn to discover Grayson speaking with the innkeeper. A small public taproom located adjacent to the entry buzzed with chatter and the clanking of serving platters and jugs of ale. Delicious scents of roasting meats and baked bread greeted her in welcome. Her stomach growled in response.

Grayson smiled as if nothing was amiss.

At the first opportunity, she'd apologize to him.

"Miss Howell." A handsome young man nodded his head and smiled. "Welcome. I'm Thaddeus Jenson." Before she could greet him, the enthusiastic man continued, "As I was saying to your traveling acquaintance, you've picked a perfect time to visit Kingsclere and the Golden Falcon." His eyes grew wide with excitement. "The annual fair is in town, and we just had a cancellation." He lowered his voice to a low murmur. "I'm afraid it's only a suite. Two adjoining rooms, but there's a door between you and Lord Grayson."

"It's perfectly acceptable to me," she said confidently while peeking at Grayson. His beautiful gray eyes darkened, nailing her in place. They smoldered with a promise of something delightfully forbidden.

She had to rein in her runaway imagination.

A raucous cheer erupted in the public room.

"Are there locks on the doors?" Grayson asked Mr. Jenson.

"Yes." Mr. Jenson smiled. "It's mostly locals who attended the festivities. The best day of the year in my opinion. We're happy you're staying with us." He rang a bell on his desk.

Wiping her hands on an apron, a young woman appeared from a door directly behind Mr. Jenson.

"This is my wife, Martha." The innkeeper turned to Martha as other guests entered the Falcon. "Will you escort Lord Grayson and Miss Howell to their rooms?"

"I'd be delighted." She smiled sweetly. "If you'll follow me."

As Martha led the way, she chatted merrily about the fair. "I'd recommend eating here first before you attend."

"Why is that?" Grayson asked as he climbed the stairs next to Beth.

Martha winked at Beth before she answered Grayson. "Everyone says I'm the best cook in the county." She stopped at the landing, regarding them. "I don't mean to boast."

"We'd be delighted to dine here," Beth offered.

"Excellent," Martha said triumphantly, then opened the first door on the right. "Here we are."

Grayson waved both ladies inside before he followed. He nodded in approval.

The spotless room was decidedly different from the dark wood and decorations of downstairs. The walls were white, with matching bedding. The entire bedroom was surrounded by windows, allowing the natural light inside.

Martha escorted Grayson through a doorway that led to the other room. Beth sighed quietly in relief. She'd stayed in enough inns during her travels with St. John to know that this one was exceptional.

The innkeeper's wife returned to her side. "Miss

Howell, if you need my assistance dressing or anything at all, please don't hesitate to ask." She grinned sheepishly. "It would be my pleasure. It's not often that we receive people of quality at the Golden Falcon."

"You're too kind." Beth picked up her bag and placed it on a side table next to the bed. She opened her reticule and took out a coin to give to the woman. "For you."

Martha held up her hands as she shook her head. "There's no need. Lord Grayson generously took care of us when he arrived." She lowered her voice. "He told Thaddeus and me that you were his top priority. Whatever you wanted or needed, we're to see to it." She curtsied, then went to the door. "I'll have one of our men bring water for your bath this evening."

As soon as the door shut, Grayson knocked on the connecting door between their rooms even though it was wide open. "May I come in?"

Beth whirled around and faced him. "Tell me how much we are paying for this?"

❧

Grayson winced at Beth's irascible tone. Immediately, Dante's indelible words of wisdom came to mind: *Love is the seed in you of every virtue and of all acts deserving punishment.*

All good deeds must be punished and all that.

He exhaled. She was worried about money. How could she trust him if he didn't tell her what his plans were?

"Beth, forgive me. I acted without thinking. I wanted to provide for your comfort since we're traveling together." He didn't care if it meant that he'd be short of funds when the window tax came due. He could always sell another portrait or another family heirloom.

"You don't have to do that," she said dismissively. But he could tell by the slight flutter of her hands he'd surprised her.

"I didn't know if we'd ever have this opportunity again." The words were out before he could stop them. He cringed slightly when her gaze jerked to his.

"What do you mean?"

"Traveling together." He dipped his gaze to meet hers, then lowered his voice. "This trip will be memorable for me. I hope for you too. Are you not happy with the accommodations?"

"It's perfect." A beautiful pink stained her cheeks.

He swallowed the groan that threatened to escape at the sight of her chewing on the tender flesh of her lower lip. He wanted to soothe it himself with his own lips.

"What do you mean by *memorable*?" she asked, breaking him out of his stupor.

"I consider you my friend." He was taking a risk here by being completely honest. "Our time together will be more pleasant if you're comfortable. As such, I want you to enjoy yourself if that's possible."

"Oh." She blinked twice, then shook her head slightly. "You must think me a bear. I'm sorry if I'm abrupt. It's just . . . you've caught me unaware. I haven't really had anyone think about my enjoyment in a long time." She tangled her fingers together and looked everywhere but at him.

"You're not abrupt." In two steps, he closed the distance between them and took her hands in his. "Our first night on the road, I wanted to take care of the expense. May I?"

The supple feel of her skin beneath his hands and the softness in her eyes made the hair on the back of his neck stand at attention. It was as if they were back at the

Chelsfields' ball when he asked for her hand. She relaxed before his eyes. She trusted him at least a little bit, and it was a heady feeling.

She squeezed his hands slightly. "Of course. That's very kind."

"Beth, I . . . want you to be happy."

A slow smile spread across her pink lips. "In that case, I want to eat in the public room, then go to the fair."

"It would be my pleasure." He bowed slightly and extended his arm.

Beth twined her arm around his, but it was the smile on her face that brought one to his. No matter what happened this evening, he considered it a success. For the first time in ages, she seemed pleased with him and his company.

They made their way down to the pub. Martha quickly seated them and served a meal fit for royalty. Cillian nodded their way. He sat with the other coachmen, fitting in as if he were one of them.

By the time they finished the excellent meal, the public room was practically overflowing with people. But all sound melted away when he caught the warmth in her gaze that threatened to burst into an inferno. His heartbeat pounded in a rhythm that reminded him of the time when they'd first held hands. Such an innocent touch, but it had stirred his blood. He'd wanted her then, and as God was his witness, he wanted her now.

The din in the room required that he scoot his chair closer to her. Mere inches separated them. Though they were surrounded by a roomful of people, he only had eyes for her. "May I ask you a question?"

Beth placed her wineglass on the table, then nodded. "There's no use being formal with me." She wiped her lips with the serviette and elegantly replaced it in her lap. "We're business partners."

Bloody hell. They were back to business partners. "That's what I want to discuss with you."

This conversation was going to be difficult, but they needed to discuss the swirl of desire that seemed to surround them, or at least it surrounded him. Yet he didn't think he was imagining it. She couldn't take her eyes off him, just as he suffered the same affliction.

"Let's go outside. I think it'll be easier to converse." She stood slowly and grinned. "We can walk the fair."

He nodded and blew out a slight breath as a sudden heat threatened to consume him. Inside, every muscle seemed to tighten as an ache spread throughout his body.

Lord, he was in trouble if he didn't get his unruly thoughts under control. But once they discussed their respective expectations, this simmering desire would diminish, and they could be together without distraction.

He held out his hand and without any hesitation she took it as if she were completely comfortable taking his hand in front of a crowd. Perhaps it was the atmosphere of the fair, when anything and everything seemed possible.

"I haven't been to a fair since my youth."

She looked at him as they walked out of the public room. "When was that?"

"I was ten years old."

"You poor dear," she chided playfully. "At my father's estate in Cumberland, everyone waited with bated breath for the autumn festival. It was my favorite time of the year."

"Better than Christmastide?" he asked.

"Pfft," she said dismissively. "There's no comparison.

There were ribbons and handkerchiefs of the highest quality. Better than you find in London. Candied apples and spun sugar to feast upon."

By then they were outside, and the fair was in full swing. The smell of fires and succulent foods filled the air. Julian held out his arm. "Let's walk a bit, shall we?"

She nodded and slipped her arm around his. It was such a common act, but with the fair swirling around them, it felt anything but ordinary. Children chased one another from booth to booth. Some were enchanted with a Punch and Judy show. Men were gathered around a vendor who served ale. Women crowded around the entrance of a tent where herbs and floral sachets were sold.

"What did you want to talk about?" Beth's shoulder brushed his upper arm as a trio of boys whooped as they ran by.

With her arm tucked around his, he pulled her tighter. "You said you weren't attracted to me, but I'm attracted to you."

"Pardon me?" She stopped suddenly and her eyebrows squished together. "I don't mean that it's horrible you're attracted to me, or I don't like it." She dropped his arm and took a step back. "I'm just a little surprised at your honesty."

"Are you really?" he asked as confusion clouded her eyes. He turned away from her and looked over at the setting sun. He tried to collect his thoughts into a semblance of order. "I won't make you uncomfortable with my company, and I won't act upon my feelings."

"Neither will I," she said with a slight nod.

He tilted his gaze to hers. "So, you're attracted to me also?"

"I . . . of course I am," she said, clearly irritated. "I've always been attracted to you. But it doesn't change anything about our current situation. I won't marry. But perhaps"—she tilted her defiant chin in his direction—"perhaps we should become lovers."

Her suggestion hung in the air as if daring him to take what she offered. If the earth had hollowed out in that moment, he wouldn't have been as surprised as he was by her pronouncement.

"I think that would be a mistake." He bit his lip when he saw the hurt that appeared instantly in her eyes.

"My reputation precedes me again," she murmured.

"I hope you know me better than that," he assured her. "I wouldn't be here with *you* if that was a concern."

"What reasons then?"

"Beth, look at me," he said softly. When her gaze met his, her earlier hurt was replaced with her familiar reserve. "We share the same friends. Randford and Kat along with Sykeston and Constance. When we visited them at the same time, it would be awkward. I don't think I could ever be comfortable with you if we shared such intimacies and then tried to remain friends."

"But we're not friends," she said, shrugging. "As acquaintances, it wouldn't make any difference."

"I beg to differ. You see, I want a wife and a family one day. It wouldn't be fair to her." He closed his eyes. He was exposing his feelings more than he'd wanted to, but she had to understand. "I don't think it would be fair to me either. Every time I saw you, I'd remember the taste of your lips, the softness of your skin, and the brilliance of you."

God, he already sounded as if they'd made love. Well, they had . . . in his imagination. He had no doubt the real Beth would be even more glorious than he'd imagined.

He took her hand in his. "It might be unsophisticated, but I can't think any other way. It would be difficult when we go to see our mutual friends with our spouses. Tell me you understand?"

"I won't marry, but I wouldn't do that to your wife." Her stalwart expression didn't change.

Perhaps he shouldn't have brought it up. Now he felt lower than a toadstool. But he didn't want them to get into a tangle because neither of them could control their desires. Though he seemed to be the one feeling the brunt of that affliction. This was best for both their sakes even if it hurt like hell.

If he made a mistake with Beth, his heart couldn't stand it.

Two fiddlers commenced playing a lively jig for a country dance. Beth turned her gaze in the direction of the makeshift dance floor. Martha and Thaddeus Jenson were in front of the line. The set would probably last for forty-five minutes or more with the number of fairgoers ready to kick up their heels.

"Would you like to dance?" Julian asked, fully expecting her to say no, but he wanted her to know that he still valued her company.

And he still wanted to hold her in his arms even if it was only a simple country dance.

Before she could answer, a young boy approximately seven or eight years old tugged on Beth's skirt. "Miss? My ma asked me to fetch you. She wants to tell you your fortune."

Chapter Seven

It was as if everything had frozen in that second when Grayson asked her if she understood why they couldn't be lovers. Beth had never really considered what the long-time impact of their trip might have on Grayson. Her thoughts for the last month had been consumed with trying to craft a life for herself free and independent from her brother.

What was she thinking asking Grayson to be her lover? Heat, the kind that felt like fire, rose in her chest, making its way to her cheeks, which undoubtedly blazed in all their glory. If she had a fortune, she'd gladly give it in exchange for direct passage to her room. She wouldn't come out until the next decade arrived.

Grayson was right. They couldn't act on this attraction to each other without there being ramifications that would hurt them and their loved ones. After they parted ways, it would be awkward, to say the least. Inevitably, they would meet at either Kat's or Constance's homes for holidays and such.

If she was married to him, she wouldn't want to socialize with one of his previous lovers. She wondered how many he'd had over the years.

Again, it was none of her business.

Her friendships with Kat and Constance grounded her. She couldn't imagine forgoing their company, which would happen if she and Grayson became lovers and he brought his wife to meet them.

Just as she would never ask Grayson to forgo his friendships with Randford and Sykeston on her behalf.

But if they became lovers, one of them would give up those precious friendships once he married.

It was odd to hear Grayson talk about marriage. Frankly, the idea he would marry one day didn't sit well with her. And she didn't know why. She'd given up on him a long time ago.

"Miss?" The little boy tugged on her skirt. "As I was saying, my ma wants to tell your fortune."

She came out of her revery and smiled. "No, thank you."

By then, both she and Grayson were surrounded by small children. Some were selling ribbons and others held small posies of flowers. Grayson retrieved a coin and purchased a small bouquet of flowers from a little girl who couldn't keep from smiling.

Beth felt the same when his undivided attention was on her.

"What's the harm?" Grayson asked jovially. "Let the boy's mother tell your fortune."

The children cheered at his words. He leaned close to Beth. "It's harmless fun. I'll go with you." He pulled away, his gray eyes twinkling with laughter.

She stood still and studied his face. What would their life have been like if they had married? Simple events such as these would have been memories that they shared together.

"Fine." It would put some much-needed distance between them.

"Come, miss." The small boy took her hand and led her to a tent without any signs.

As soon as she entered, a young woman wearing a black cloak stood from her table. She pushed the hood off her head. "You're here," she said with awe in her voice, and waved at an empty chair, indicating it was for Beth. With a slight smile, she turned her attention to Grayson. "I'm sorry, sir, but you'll have to wait outside."

"My ma won't tell the fortune otherwise," the little boy said with his arms across his small chest.

Grayson's gaze met Beth's.

Beth nodded. "It's harmless fun, right? This will only take a moment." She planned on giving the young woman a coin, then leaving without her fortune being told.

He took a moment to gaze around the tent, obviously seeing if it was safe. "Are you sure?"

"Positive," Beth answered.

"I promise she'll be in the best hands," the woman said with a soft smile.

He met Beth's gaze again, and she nodded. The boy took Grayson's hand and led him outside.

Beth took the seat facing the woman. "There are no cards or crystal balls on the table. You must read palms."

"My name is Prudence Stewart." She sat across from Beth. "I don't read palms. You must think this strange, but I dreamed about you last night."

Beth dug a coin from her reticule and placed it on the table. "There's no need to tell my fortune."

"But there is," she answered, pushing the coin back to Beth. "When I dream of people, it's rare that I can meet them and share a bit of their future with them. I don't want your coin."

Beth wanted to roll her eyes. Instead, she smiled. "What do you want?"

"A chance to tell you about my dream."

Beth placed her hands neatly in her lap.

"You're looking for a fortune, aren't you?" Prudence asked.

Beth lifted her brows. "Pardon?"

"You lost something very dear to you, and now you're trying to find it."

"How did you know that?" The vibrancy in the woman's voice caught Beth off guard.

Prudence shrugged. "I told you. I dreamed it."

"And you're going to tell me where to find it?" Beth tilted her chin, challenging the woman.

Prudence chuckled. "If I were sitting in that chair, I'd be skeptical too. When I was carrying my Sam, whom you met, I dreamed that I would have a son and a month later I would lose my husband. Both came true." She lifted an eyebrow. "It's a gift or a curse depending upon how you see it."

Beth swallowed. "I figured you would tell me how many children I will have or that I will meet my true love in an unexpected place."

"I don't make up tales," Prudence said a little defensively. "I only know what I dream. You'll find everything you're looking for." Prudence lifted her hand to her heart. "In here. If you open your heart, you'll find a fortune in love."

Beth stood abruptly, almost knocking the chair over in the process. "Thank you, Mrs. Stewart. But I'm not looking for love or marriage or any of the rattletraps or trifles that accompany it." She pushed the coin back toward the woman. "That's for your time." She turned toward the door.

"Your given name is Blythe, but your loved ones call you Beth," the woman called out.

Beth turned slowly. "How in the world did you know that?"

Prudence shrugged. "I dreamed it. Also, you're worried about your reputation. Don't be. It means nothing."

Then everything clicked into place. The woman must follow the London gossip rags that gleefully proclaimed Beth's ruination. Of course, the woman probably recognized her from the prints that had been drawn of her likeness and posted next to the lies and rumors regarding her marriage to Meriwether. By telling Beth not to worry about her reputation, she was trying to earn another coin.

"You know who I am because of the gossip that's been spewed about me. That's how you knew my name." She shook her head in disbelief.

"I don't know your last name. I'm telling the truth," the woman proclaimed. Suddenly, her cheeks reddened, and she appeared to deflate before Beth's eyes. "I never learned my letters."

The woman's embarrassment plunged a knife in Beth's heart. She struggled with what to say. "Perhaps someone read you those stories."

Prudence shook her head. "I don't lie. I don't know who you are."

Without another word, Beth placed another coin on the table, then walked out of the tent. All she could think of was escaping from the fortune-teller and the fair. Thoughts swirled in her head. The farther she walked, the angrier she got. *How dare people make fun of her misfortune.*

"Beth, wait," Grayson called out as he rushed toward her. "Did she tell you your fortune?"

By then, they were some distance from the crowd.

"Are you all right? What happened?"

She came to a stop. "Everything and nothing," she growled.

"Tell me." The raspiness of his voice sent a shiver through her.

But remembering the woman's words doused any passion that threatened to rise. "She told me that I'd find my fortune." She practically spit the words because she was so angry. "In love. It was all a hoax."

"She was a charlatan?" He gently gripped Beth's arms.

"Of course she was. She knew I'd lost a fortune. She even knew my name." Beth fisted both hands. "But the cruelest thing she said was that I didn't have to worry about my reputation, as it meant nothing. Though she told me she couldn't read, it was obvious that she'd known what had been printed about me and the other wives in the London gossip rags."

"Perhaps she's right," he said softly as he brushed back a fallen lock of hair behind her ear.

She closed her eyes at the gentle touch. Yet it did nothing to tame her resentment.

"Oh for the love of heaven," she murmured. "You're agreeing with her?"

"Maybe," he said cautiously. "I do believe that if your heart is open, you'll find love."

"Now who's being delusional in their optimism? I don't care about love or my reputation." She was lying. She didn't want to admit that it hurt every time she was mentioned in the gossip rags or pointed at on the street. The only way she could protect her heart was if she pretended not to care.

But not tonight.

She turned to face him so quickly that her skirts snapped to attention. She'd not leave without saying her piece. To make her point, she spoke the words crisply and succinctly in a low voice. "You should be worried about your reputation. Since everyone in Kingsclere apparently knows who I am and how I was ruined."

"My reputation isn't the point of discussion," he said warily.

"Yet mine is?" She sighed in frustration. "You wear yours like an armor."

"Beth," he said softly. "Why are you angry at me?"

"I'm not. I'm just angry." She huffed out a breath. "I'm tired of receiving advice that is based in fantasy." She held her arms wide and tilted her head to look at the star-filled sky. "I'm so tired of it all." Indignant, she stopped for a moment, but all those old wounds split open. "My father promised me that I was the most marriageable young lady of the Season. He said I'd make a brilliant match one day. All I had to do was marry a man chosen by my family. He said my husband would be worthy of me, and I'd be worthy of him. Well, my brother chose Meriwether."

Grayson didn't move an inch at her bluntness. He kept staring at her.

"But do you know what really hurt?" She shook her head. "Society and all its machinations had promised that if I was good and played by their rules, all my hopes and dreams for a brilliant future would come to fruition."

God help her, she'd once believed in those fairy tales.

"It was all lies. When Meriwether died and the whole sordid tale came to light, I discovered the truth." By then, she was laughing. It was the only way she could hide the pain. "My world fell apart through no fault of my own, and society does what it does best. It turned its back on me as if Meriwether's fraudulent marriage to me was my fault."

"But your friends didn't desert you," he said softly, then closed the distance between them. "I'm one of your friends. I won't turn my back on you."

But he had before. She took a deep breath and forced her gaze to his. She had to move forward and not look backward.

"Sometimes, I think about taking out an advertisement in the daily papers to make certain everyone knows who I am. I'd proclaim that I'm an heiress without any money. I gave my virtue to a man I wasn't married to. Perhaps then I can live in peace. The headline would be 'Beth Howell Is Ruined, and She Accepts It.'"

His eyes narrowed at her sarcasm.

She wanted to shake her fist at the heavens for the betrayals she'd had to bear in her life. Shake her fist at Meri and St. John. Her throat burned and her eyes blurred. She would not cry. She was stronger than this . . . even if her life was in shambles.

"I protected my reputation," she blurted out. "I know how to prepare and pour a proper cup of tea. I know how not to be compromised. I know how to be a hostess at a dinner party or at a ball of three hundred. I can sit gracefully. Dance as if I floated on air. I know how to stay out of trouble." She clenched her fists together at the unfairness of it all. "Yet I'm still ruined." She heaved a breath and narrowed her eyes. "I'm not going to waste another minute of my life on the false expectations hoisted upon my shoulders. I'm going to take whatever days I have left on this earth and pursue what I want."

The silence around them grew deafening. All the insects and birds had grown quiet. Even the slight breeze had stilled.

With an expression of gravity that he seldom wore,

Grayson nodded once. With his familiar voice of reason, he said, "I don't think you're ruined. I never have."

His words stole whatever remaining emotion she felt from her long diatribe. "Then what do you think I am?"

He clasped his arms behind his back and stared at the ground for a moment. Slowly, he raised his gaze to hers. "I think you're opinionated, stubborn, and sometimes prickly." He blinked twice, but his countenance continued to be serious. "You remind me of a scorpion I once saw in a book of animals. You sting when you feel threatened. You have a hard time laughing at yourself. Sometimes, you're entirely too serious, and other times, I wonder if you have any feelings at all."

She scoffed slightly. "If you're trying to make me feel better, you're doing a miserable job."

"You're also blunt."

"Then why do you have anything to do with me?" She didn't hide the hurt or the challenge in her voice. He was another man who'd failed her.

"I'll tell you in a moment." He studied her as if he could see inside her all the way to her heart, which had been battered and bruised by the men in her life. His gaze fell to her lips before he slowly raised it to her eyes.

If she didn't care anymore, she'd prove it to him by doing something outrageous. She leaned closer. "Kiss me." The challenge in her voice clear.

"Kiss you?" His brow furrowed. "Would you like that?"

"What do you think?"

He chuckled softly. "All right. Where?"

"You know where," she said bravely, knowing she'd shocked him.

His gray eyes flashed with humor as he brushed his fingers across her cheek. "Here?"

"No."

"Here?" This time, his lips met her forehead.

"Lower," she urged.

"Ah, here." He kissed her nose.

The gentleness of his touch had her leaning into him where her softness met his hardness. Like a cat, she moved closer to rub against him. "A little lower."

He pressed his lips to hers, and she sighed in relief.

His mouth molded over hers as if he were a starving man and she was the only nourishment he needed. She moaned as he deepened the kiss. When his tongue stroked hers, she could almost feel her feet lift off the ground, carrying her to a place where they were the only two that mattered. Her body thrummed. For the first time in her life, she needed to be closer or she feared she'd disappear into a puff of smoke.

Her kiss turned desperate, begging him to not stop until she recognized real passion and desire. All she wanted was to forget about all her disappointments.

He broke away and a moan escaped her. His kisses could bring her to her knees. Finally, the sensual fog that had enveloped her seemed to dissipate. By then, he was panting as if she'd stolen his very breath.

"You asked why I have anything to do with you." He cupped her cheek with his hand. "Because to me, you're just about perfect."

She had no idea how many seconds, minutes, or hours she stood there with her mouth open.

He'd insulted her earlier, but then his words had turned into one of the loveliest compliments she'd ever received in her life.

The hot sting of tears threatened as a melancholy embraced her. She stepped away and wrapped her arms defensively around her middle, hoping to shield herself from him. She would not make the same mistake with him as she'd done before.

She stared at the dazzling display of stars but only saw Grayson's face. She'd have given anything to have had him as a husband.

Now it was impossible. She'd not allow herself to be vulnerable, even with someone as honorable as Grayson.

After all, he was a man.

Chapter Eight

The next morning, Beth sat in the forward-facing seat trying to sew, but her attention kept drifting to Grayson. Every time she glanced at him, his attention was directed out the window. However, she could feel the heat of his gaze straying to her. When she'd look in his direction, he'd be staring out the window again.

She took a deep breath and inhaled his bergamot-orange scent. Was it possible to become addicted to a fragrance?

"We should discuss last night." Like a cat's rough tongue, his words prickled her skin.

"There's no need." She crossed her ankles and tried to situate herself on the bench. Heat bludgeoned her cheeks at the scandalous words she said to him last night.

Well, that wasn't exactly the truth. She wasn't embarrassed for what she said, but of his response to her. No one had ever pointed out all her all negatives, then kissed her.

Nor had anyone said she was practically perfect.

"You've said exactly two words to me today." He moved to the middle of his seat across from hers all the while careful not to touch any part of her. But with his natural leonine grace, he situated himself so he faced her directly, with his muscular thighs framing her body.

"This trip will be miserable for both of us if we aren't comfortable with one another."

With little effort, she could lean forward and be pressed against him.

"By chance, are you flirting with me?" The question popped out of her mouth before she could think. But that was the problem. Ever since last night, her musings had tangled into knots when she thought of him.

"No." A crooked smile tugged at his lips. "You would know if I was flirting with you. Would you like for me to?"

"Yes . . . no." She shook her head. "I don't know . . ."

His lips should be outlawed. No, his entire mouth. They made her want things, things that should cause her to be embarrassed. Instead, they made her hungry and tongue-tied.

When he stared at her like that, she had little doubt that he could see every want and desire she possessed. If he looked hard enough, he'd see she was desperate for a life that would be of her own making and filled with love and family.

He lifted his hand to her cheek, then stopped. "A lock of hair has fallen. May I brush it back for you?" His gaze never left hers.

Riveted and barely able to form any coherent words, she nodded. With the lightest of touches, his fingers brushed against her cheek, then tucked her hair behind her ear. The sensation so erotic that she couldn't help but inhale sharply.

She closed her eyes. This was the touch that she'd always wanted from a man. One that made her feel cherished and valued for who she was and not what she was. It wouldn't make any difference that she wasn't an heiress. Unable to turn away, she only hoped he couldn't see how desperate she was for more.

He drew his hand back. "There. I think you are set to rights."

She'd only be set to rights if he brought her into his embrace and she lost all sense of time and place. She wanted to protest the loss of his fingers against her skin. It would take little effort to lean in and feast upon his lips until she was satisfied.

But what if she never was satisfied?

For the briefest of moments, she wondered where all her compunction had gone, then was thankful that it had disappeared. Always before she'd planned every action, then thought through the consequences. It was her way to protect her reputation as a proper lady.

It had been such a wasted effort. One thing she'd learned from Meri's death, time was precious, and she shouldn't squander it by worrying about her reputation. After her marriage to Meriwether and her brother's shenanigans, she'd never again be considered a proper lady. Hence the reason the aging but civil Marquess of Siddleton had garnered her brother's attention.

From now on, she'd do what she pleased.

"About last night," she said.

"What about it?" A playfulness came over him that softened his face. Yet his eyes seemed to smolder with a fire that could ignite her from within. "Did you want to discuss last night's dinner conversation?"

My God, he wasn't just handsome, but breathtaking when he looked at her like that.

Somehow, she managed to shake her head.

"The food served?" His whisky-dark voice possessed the power to make her drunk just on his words.

"Stop teasing me," she said.

"I don't think I can." He leaned closer. "I've become

quite fond of the way your mouth twists when you're try-ing to think of a retort."

The silkiness of his voice mesmerized her. "I want to discuss . . . your kiss."

"From last night?" he asked.

Her chest rose and fell with every breath, betraying how affected she was by his nearness. "Your kiss . . . reminded me of one of your steam experiments."

He chuckled. "How so?"

"It shows promise, but it's not quite hot enough."

"You want hot?" The heat blazing from his eyes made her squirm in her seat. "The next time I kiss you, I'll make you burn."

She sat there with her mouth gaping and her entire body quivering as he stared at her with an intensity that left little doubt he'd deliver what he promised. His eyes raked over her mouth as if ready to claim her, causing her pulse to beat faster and faster.

"What about not becoming intimate with one an-other?" What was the matter with her? She challenged him to kiss her last night, and now she sounded as if she was running away from it.

That wouldn't do. She was more resilient than the girl he'd first met.

"It was unusual circumstances last night." His gaze fell on her mouth, then lifted to her eyes. "And I don't regret it. Do you?"

"No." Her heart pounded with the speed of a runaway carriage. "I want to try again. We'll see if you can make me burn."

The carriage slowed with Cillian's command of *whoa*.

"Lord Grayson, we've arrived," his valet proclaimed.

"Deuced bad timing," Grayson muttered as he caressed her cheek before slowly pulling away.

"Horrendous timing." The breathlessness in her voice surprised her. She'd never sounded that way with Meri. She leaned back against the squab. She was playing with fire, and nothing good would come from it. But she didn't want to stop.

The valet opened the door, unfolded the carriage steps, then stood at attention.

Grayson jumped down with ease, then extended his hand. As she took it, he smiled reassuringly. "Miss Howell, I believe your destiny awaits. If I'm not mistaken, there's a pig farmer or two standing outside that quaint little cottage ahead of us."

"One of them is a dairy farmer," Cillian offered.

"How can you tell?" Beth eyed the two farmers. They looked the same to her, with practically identical clothing. Both were in their late forties, give or take a few years. Each wore brown pants, a light-colored linen shirt, a handkerchief tied around his neck with a cap over his head.

"By the looks of them," Cillian answered. "The man on the right is the pig farmer. I'd stay close to him. Contrary to popular belief, pigs are notoriously clean and picky about their pens. Cows aren't that discriminatory. Besides a little mud on his boots, the man on the right is neat and tidy." Cillian nodded in the farmer's direction. "The dairy farmer looks as if he's been rolling in the mud with his herd."

"Thank you for the agricultural lesson. Now if you'll go see which of these gentlemen is the one Miss Howell needs to meet?" Grayson asked, a hint of impatience in his voice.

After winking at Beth, Cillian immediately assumed his footman persona, then practically marched to where the two farmers stood evaluating the scene playing before them.

"Are you nervous?" Grayson asked, smiling slightly.

"No. This is my path. Even if my search ends here, I'll know I tried."

"That's one of the things I admire about you, Beth." He practically purred her name. "You're never afraid of a challenge or the outcome."

If only that were true. But even Beth would admit that she was masterful at feigning boldness.

Grayson held out his arm. "Let's go meet your farmer."

Quickly, she took it and they started forward. She suddenly realized how tense she was. She hadn't been this unsettled since she'd stepped foot into the solicitor's office and understood she was wife number three. "Truthfully? I am a tad anxious. I don't want Meriwether's trail to end here."

Unobtrusively, he patted her hand. "I am a bit unnerved myself. We should have kissed in the carriage. That would have kept our minds occupied with other things beside this." He looked in her direction and winked without his serious countenance changing one iota.

Instantly, her unease melted away at his affectionate teasing. It felt marvelous to be the center of someone's attention.

"Good morning, gentlemen. My name is Grayson."

Though her hand slightly trembled, his arm was as steady as rock.

"Good morning, my lord," the pig farmer announced. "I'm Monday. This here is my sister's husband, Robindale."

"How do you do." Grayson bowed slightly. "Miss Howell, may I introduce these gentlemen to you?"

"Of course," she answered, with her most optimistic smile.

After the introductions were made, Mr. Monday came right to the point. "What can we do for you?"

"Well . . . I . . . " She swallowed. How in the world was she supposed to introduce Meriwether? As if he knew her quandary, Grayson nodded in reassurance.

Now was not the time to turn into a blathering ninny. "My friend the Countess of Sykeston was married to Lord Meriwether Vareck. It seems Lord Meriwether purchased a prized Hampshire pig from around these parts."

Mr. Robindale chortled and peeked at his brother-in-law. "Aye."

"Oh good." The butterflies in Beth's stomach seemed to have settled and would roost for the time being. "I was hoping you would know, Mr. Robindale. Your name was on one of Lord Meriwether's receipts."

"I'm the farmer that fancy lord got a pig from," Mr. Monday explained.

Grayson looked at Beth. "Did anyone have a receipt from Mr. Monday in their pile?"

Beth shook her head. When Beth had studied them, Monday's name never appeared.

"That fancy lord didn't buy it from me," Mr. Monday offered. "We traded for it."

Mr. Robindale shook his head and looked to his brother-in-law. "It's a day no one from around here will forget in a long time."

Mr. Monday nodded his head.

"That fancy lord pulled up in a coach with four white horses. A footman opened the door, and the man emerged like an angel descending from heaven. At least, that's what my wife says," Mr. Robindale offered.

Mr. Monday chuckled and shook his head. "My sister always favored the blond ones. She came running out of the house as if he was visiting her."

Mr. Robindale took off his cap and rubbed his bald head. "It wasn't too long ago I looked like that fancy lord."

Mr. Monday started howling with laughter.

His brother-in-law chimed in.

Finally, the laughter died down, and Mr. Monday wiped a tear from his eye. "You never looked like him." He turned his attention to Beth and Grayson. "He stayed for an hour. By then, my missus had sent one of the laborers to the surrounding farms inviting the women to come. There were more people in our home than at the parish's Christmas Eve service."

"He was the prettiest man I've ever seen," Mr. Robindale crooned in a high voice, then slapped his hat back on his head. "If I heard that once, I've heard it a thousand times. My wife still brings him up."

"Lord Meriwether always made quite an entrance." These two men would howl once again if they knew the truth about her and the *fancy lord*. "Could we talk about the trade?"

"Of course," Mr. Robindale said. "Would you like to see my statute?"

"Statute?" Grayson lifted a brow.

Mr. Robindale nodded enthusiastically.

"He means *statue*." Mr. Monday laughed, then stuck out his chest, obviously quite proud. "I've got one too."

Beth looked his way and nodded. "We'd be delighted. But what does it have to do with Lord Meriwether?"

"His lordship traded two from his personal collection to me," Mr. Robindale said. "I traded one cow and one statue to Monday."

Mr. Monday lifted a brow. "So, for payment to the fancy lord on Robindale's part, I traded two of my prize Hampshire pigs to Lord Meriwether."

"How did this three-party trade come about?" Grayson

moved a little closer to her by angling his body. Then, with the lightest of touches, he rested his hand on the curve of her lower back, offering comfort.

Which she appreciated. This was the first step in finding her dowry, and unbelievably, she was glad Grayson was beside her.

Mr. Monday shrugged. "Lord Meriwether wanted my pig. I wanted Robindale's latest heifer, and he"—Mr. Monday pointed to his brother-in-law—"wanted one of Lord Meriwether's statues. When I saw the statue, I wanted one. That's why I threw in the second pig. That fancy lord traded two statues."

Mr. Robindale lifted a shaggy black brow. "Mine is quite a piece of artwork. People come from miles around to see it. Then I send them to Monday's for a peek at his. We charge admission."

She wanted to slap her hands over her eyes. If they were talking about what she thought they were, there was no way she wanted to see what Meriwether had traded for the pigs. Her former fake husband had an extensive collection of erotic statuary that he'd given to his half brother, the Duke of Randford.

"I've become a connoisseur of art, though my sister and my wife think it's anything but art," Mr. Monday said without a hint of embarrassment. "I'm looking for more pieces to add to my collection."

"Lord Grayson, is that you?" a voice called out.

They all turned in the direction of the voice and saw a bright yellow curricle come to a stop in front of the farmhouse. One man tied off the reins as another gentleman jumped down and assisted the two young ladies who'd accompanied them.

Mr. Monday moaned. "They're back."

Mr. Robindale cursed under his breath. "They've come

here every single day for the last week except Sunday to see our statues. That's why we started charging admission." The farmer shook his head. "They stay hours drawing them."

When Beth recognized the foursome who had arrived, her insides seemed to crumble. The men were members of the same set as her brother. It was just her luck that one of them was Monty Portland. Word would find its way to St. John before tomorrow evening. The women were Portland's sisters. By the look of their dress and mannerisms, they appeared to have carried their hunt for a husband from London to Portsmouth.

"Grayson," she murmured. "Why don't you go greet them, and I'll stay with Mr. Monday and Mr. Robindale."

"No." His deep voice held an unbendable hint of steel to it.

"I really don't want to be seen here. They've recognized you, but not me."

The farmers weren't paying any attention to her and Grayson, as their steady gazes were on the quartet approaching them.

"Please," she begged softly.

His eyes bored into hers, and at first, she thought he was going to refuse her.

With a silent exhale of resignation, he nodded once. Then like a Shakespearean actor, he turned on one of his brilliant smiles and lifted a hand in greeting. "Hello, Stanton. Imagine seeing you and Portland here in this small piece of God's country."

"Gentlemen, shall we?" Beth asked. "I've never seen a piece of Lord Meriwether's famous statuary, but all of London was atwitter about it not too long ago." Without waiting for their invitation, she strolled right toward the house.

Chapter Nine

Grayson gritted his teeth so hard that he thought he was in danger of breaking a tooth. The two men approaching him would blend into a place filled with a flock of peacocks. How appropriate that they were coming into the barnyard.

Howard Doxley, the young Earl of Stanton, strutted forward in a blazing scarlet and yellow morning coat. Not to be outdone, Mr. Monty Portland, the second son of an earl, approached in an emerald-green morning coat. Each was obscenely wealthy and happened to have a lady holding his arm, the Portland sisters. Many described the two women as the catch of the Season with their hefty dowries dangling as bait.

Grayson almost had to shade his eyes at the bright morning coats. To say they clashed was an understatement. Thankfully, the women on the men's arms wore white and ivory.

Before the four reached his side, two roosters barreled at full speed from the other side of the house like highwaymen. Immediately, they blocked the newcomers' paths. Both plumped up their feathers and released the loudest and most unearthly crows he'd ever heard.

Stanton and Portland came to a stop. In an uncustomary bravado of chivalry, they stepped in front of the ladies.

By then, the ladies were cackling at the danger as loudly as the roosters' growls.

Grayson took a step forward but was halted by Portland's raised hand. "Don't come any closer. We've handled these marauders before."

"Marauders? They're roosters." Grayson pointed out.

"Grayson, you're not aware of the danger these menaces provide. This heathen"—Stanton pointed at the black rooster, then at the white one—"and his best friend chase anyone who they see as a threat."

"Explains why they didn't chase me," Grayson said. These men were idiots, and he didn't have time for this. He should be inside with Beth.

"Lord Stanton, I knew we could depend upon your heroics," Lady Clementine, the younger of the Portland sisters, proclaimed as she held on to her sister's arm.

Portland took a step forward. As soon as he moved, the two roosters charged with guttural growls and their wings flapping. Portland backtracked to stand with Stanton and his sisters. Smoothing his waistcoat, he kept his gaze glued to the fowl, who had their eyes on him.

Portland and Stanton were favorites within the *ton* because they loved to share gossip—Portland especially. Their manners were impeccable, but they possessed no real integrity.

Without giving the fowl another glance, Grayson joined the four on the edge of the barnyard. "They're chickens."

Portland wiped his brow. "But they're vicious, with a peck as sharp as a knife."

Lady Henrietta nodded in agreement. "Their talons are

sharper than that. Poor Monty has been a victim of their violence before. Mr. Robindale says he shouldn't wear red or green. Apparently, they loathe the colors and turn ferocious." She turned to her brother. "But Monty looks so dashing in those. As do you, Lord Stanton." Her eyelashes fluttered.

Grayson turned away from the group and rolled his eyes. God save him from such nonsense. The two "marauders" stood beside him pecking the ground for food. With gentle clucks sounding from their direction, the two dandies went on about their business, ignoring the quartet.

If only he could do the same.

"Oh thank you, Lord Grayson. You've saved us," Lady Clementine Portland said dreamily.

Lord Stanton's mouth pursed into a straight line. "We were the ones who put our lives in danger."

"We?" Portland smirked, then turned his attention to the ladies. "I did it."

As the two men verbally battled for dominance, Grayson bowed in the ladies' direction. "Good morning, my ladies."

Lady Henrietta Portland and Lady Clementine curtsied.

"It was lovely seeing you at the Duchess of Langham's ball," Lady Clementine said, then flirtatiously blinked several times. All of London knew that Lady Clementine wanted the title of marchioness or duchess.

"I enjoyed our dance," Grayson said matter-of-factly.

"Whatever are you doing here?" Lady Henrietta batted her eyes. "Come to see the famous Pan statue?"

Lady Clementine giggled behind her glove. "It's quite sensational." She waved a hand at the curricle behind them. "Monty, Henrietta, and I are visiting our aunt. Lord

Stanton came with us. With you here, we'll make quite the party." She turned to her sister. "Right, Hen?"

"Indeed." Lady Henrietta slid to Grayson's side and looped her arm around his. "You must join us for dinner this evening."

"Unfortunately, I can't. I'll be heading back to London after this." At the sound of the ladies' disappointment, he smiled contritely. He could think of no worse torture than spending even an hour in their company. Yet weren't they exactly the type of heiresses he should look for if the consortium didn't invest with him? It felt like a spider crawled down his back at the thought. His chest tightened with a pressure much like a vise squeezing him.

On top of it all, he didn't want Beth worrying about Montague Portland. He was close friends with St. John Howell. Anything he discovered about Beth would be shared with St. John.

He had to convince them to leave before Beth returned. Where were those roosters when he needed them?

~

"The statue is in the other room, Miss Howell." Mr. Robindale swept his hand down the hallway. "I'll ask my wife to prepare ye a cup of tea."

"No, I don't want to impose," Beth said politely. "If I could just ask a few questions, Lord Grayson and I will be on our way."

"Don't you want to see the statue?" Mr. Monday scratched his head and glanced at his brother-in-law. "We won't charge you admittance. You're not like the rest who come to see it. They just want to gawk, but I can tell you're a lady of fine taste who'll appreciate it as the treasure we believe it to be."

"That's very kind." She smiled at their sincerity. Life was so much easier if people were nice to you.

Mr. Robindale preceded her down the hall. The farmhouse itself was quite large and well-kept. The front room sported several windows that were covered in fresh white linen curtains. It was certainly homey and there was a unique charm to the place.

"Here we are," Mr. Robindale exclaimed, the pride in his voice readily apparent.

"Isn't it something to behold?" The reverence in Mr. Monday's voice stopped her in her tracks.

She struggled to find the words. Before her was a giant marble statue of Pan, the half man half goat. With a man's face and torso, the statue looked like other classical pieces of artwork that might decorate a London home. It was rather out of place in a farmhouse. But even London homes lacked a statue of this type. It was a Greek god with donkey ears and horns. As her gaze swept over the marble, Beth inhaled sharply. His lower half resembled the legs of a goat with a very erect penis.

She struggled to say something at the expectant look of the two farmers. "It is something."

They let out a matching set of relieved sighs as if she'd said it passed muster as a magnificent piece of art.

"Pan was once considered the god of shepherds and flocks. Monday and I flipped a coin for him. I won," Mr. Robindale said proudly.

"Your luck certainly turned that day," she said with a smile. Surely, she'd spent enough time appreciating the blasted thing. "What did Lord Meriwether do with the pigs?"

"He kept one here for his wife." Monday scratched his

forehead in thought. "Said he'd come back for it later. Eventually, I sent it to the Duke of Randford's home after I learned of Lord Meriwether's death. That's what Lord Meriwether's solicitor told me to do."

Beth nodded. That explained how Katherine received her pig. "Do you know what Lord Meriwether did with the other pig?"

Mr. Monday nodded. "Took it with him to one of those fancy towns like Cheltenham."

"Bath or Amesbury," Mr. Robindale offered. "Said he was off to gamble. Thought the sow might bring him luck."

"Did Lord Meriwether ever mention the Jolly Rooster?" They nodded.

Beth practically bounced on the tip of her toes. She was in possession of lodging receipts from the inn in Amesbury. It was notorious for high-stakes games of chance. Many of the wealthy and jaded gentlemen who grew bored with London and its offerings of ribald entertainment received exclusive invitations to the inn. Outrageous games of chance were played while massive fortunes were won and lost at the small inn owned by the Duke of Pelham. It was famous among the *ton* for when they wanted to gamble outside London.

"Thank you for your time. I'll collect Lord Grayson, and we'll be on our way." Already, she was calculating how far they could travel before it grew dark. It would be close, but they might be able to make it to the inn late that afternoon.

"Would his lordship like to see our Pan?" Mr. Monday asked.

"I'll inquire." She waved a hand at Pan, hoping to never see anything of its ilk again. "However, I find some people just can't appreciate true art." She blinked innocently.

"Unfortunately, they're in abundance." By then, Beth was at the door. She couldn't wait to share with Grayson what she'd discovered. "Thank you for all your help."

They quickly exchanged farewells. As soon as the door closed, she came to an abrupt halt. She'd forgotten that the Portland sisters, Montague Portland, and Lord Stanton were with Grayson. Just as she was about to slide her way back into the house without drawing attention, she heard her name called.

"Blythe Howell, what are you doing here?"

A chill slid down her back at the sound of Portland's voice. Listening to gravel ground together on a millstone would be more pleasant than hearing his voice.

It was only natural she'd feel that way. Monty Portland would deem it his business to inform St. John of her whereabouts. Then she'd face the wrath of her brother's lecture on marrying again. He'd accuse her of ruining his reputation by being seen unescorted with Grayson. He might even demand she marry Portland to save face.

She squared her shoulders. *Let him try.*

"Good day," she answered politely. She forced herself to smile. All she had to do was mimic the behavior she performed every time she had a visitor call or when she stepped into the ballroom. She nodded at Lady Henrietta and Lady Clementine. "How amazing to see the four of you here."

A crooked smile twisted Portland's mouth. "What are you doing at this farm? I doubt if your brother would approve if he knew that you were accompanied by Lord Grayson unescorted."

Before she could defend herself, Grayson did the honor for her. "What are you about, Portland? I wasn't aware that you'd appointed yourself the overseer of Miss Howell's travels. Who are you to pass judgment on her business?" His voice could cut steel.

Lady Clementine bent her head toward her older sister. "Since she entered into a false marriage with Lord Meriwether."

No one overheard the snide remark except for Beth. Lady Henrietta looked down her nose, then sniffed as if smelling something rotten.

A river of red flashed before her eyes. Beth prayed for the strength not to knock the two women into a pile of manure. Grayson cocked his brow at her. He seemed to always sense when something had upset her.

Monty Portland swung his gaze to Grayson. "Good manners and gentle breeding dictate that an unmarried woman should not be traveling with a man not her husband."

She could tell by Grayson's face that he was getting angrier by the minute.

"Indeed, sir? I never thought you so small in your thoughts to judge someone before you even understood what their business might be." Grayson's nostrils flared. "Furthermore . . ."

Beth stayed him with a light touch of her hand on his arm. "It's all right." She turned to the foursome. "I am seeing about some business that is personal. But my brother knows I'm traveling." It wasn't a lie per se. She did leave St. John a note saying she had urgent business to attend to. "Lord Grayson was kind enough to have provided me with an escort today." She laughed, hoping it would defuse the bubbling anger between the two men. "We must be on our way."

"And where might that be?" Lord Stanton asked. He tipped the brim of his hat back so he could see them better.

Lady Clementine and Lady Henrietta leaned closer to hear Beth's answer.

"It's not your concern." Grayson smiled, but his eyes warned Stanton and Portland they'd gone too far.

"You seem to be enjoying playing the knight-errant." Monty Portland laughed, then turned to Lord Stanton, who joined in.

The Portland sisters had the good sense to understand that things were not as jovial as they appeared to be. Instantly, Clementine waved a hand in the air. "Be kind, Monty." She blinked, then tilted her head Grayson's way. "I would hate for Lord Grayson to form the wrong impression of us."

It took mammoth strength, but Beth kept her expression even. Everyone knew that these two debutantes and their brother thought they were God's gift to the *ton*. Lord Stanton was more of a puzzle. St. John had some connection to the young lord, but she couldn't recall. Perhaps he'd purchased a racehorse from her brother. She'd never heard any rumors or innuendo about Stanton, but if he was in the company of Monty Portland then the odds were favorable that he enjoyed the same entertainment—gambling and horseraces.

"Lady Clementine, I assure you that my opinion of you would never be tarnished by such a simple conversation." Grayson bowed to the foursome, then extended his arm for Beth to take. "You mustn't keep the Prince Regent waiting, Miss Howell."

The women's eyes widened, and the men grew quiet at the mention of the prince. These four were desperate to become a part of the Prince Regent's inner circle.

Quickly, they said their goodbyes. As Beth walked beside Grayson, the muscles of his forearm seemed to constrict with each step as they approached to their carriage.

"Grayson," she said softly so as not to be overheard. "There's no harm here. Why did you tell them I was off to see the Prince Regent? He's a customer, but I'm finished with the Royal Pavilion."

"Because they insulted you with their insinuations," he bit out. "Portland is a sniveling coward."

She'd never seen him that angry before. When they were within ten yards of the carriage, Cillian jumped from the coach box and opened the door. Grayson gave her his hand for assistance in getting into the carriage. This time, she sat in the backward-facing seat. Grayson followed behind her.

"We're not too far from Sykeston's house." Grayson made his way to lean out the window with instructions.

"Wait." Beth twisted in the seat to face him. "We must travel to the Jolly Rooster."

He leaned back against the squab. "The Duke of Pelham's inn?"

She nodded, then leaned out the window to inform Cillian of their new destination.

"And why, pray tell, are we traveling there?" Grayson asked with a lift of a brow. "For a game of chance? We can find one of those in Portsmouth."

The teasing in his voice made her smile, and for a moment she felt like a debutante all over again, flirting with the man of her dreams . . . at least for one night. She sighed at such a silly thought.

"No. We're off to find a pig."

"Another?" he asked. "What is it with you and barnyard animals?" He stared intently at her face. "I presume Meriwether used the pig as money in one of Pelham's games?"

"That's what I want to discover." She let out a soft sigh. "Even if he lost it, which probably occurred, then I know what happened. Maybe someone there can tell me if he had a large amount of money to gamble with. Perhaps that's where he spent my dowry." The thought made her stomach twist into a knot.

"You have a speck of mud on your cheek. May I?"

She nodded. He reached across the coach and leisurely brushed a finger against her cheek. The tenderness of his touch practically undid her.

"It's gone," he said.

The deep, smooth timbre of his voice reminded her of whispers and bedrooms.

Her face heated at the intense way he regarded her.

"Be careful, Grayson," she chided as if unaffected by him. "Before you know it, I'll have you under my spell."

"Who says that I'm not already?" He regarded her from his half-lidded eyes as his voice dropped even lower.

"I thought we'd agreed not to allow ourselves to become entangled with one another," she said nonchalantly.

He glanced out the carriage window. Slowly, he turned his gaze back to hers. "It killed me that you were hurting last night." He closed his eyes for a second as if grappling with what to say. "I wanted to make you forget in that moment everything you'd been through." He bent his head and stared at his hands. "Beth, I thought to comfort you and got carried away." He lifted his gaze to hers. "I apologize."

"Don't apologize," she said. She hadn't realized that she needed consoling, but he had. And he'd cared enough to help her. "I appreciate what you did." She grinned. "If you hadn't, who knows how long I would have berated the world and the men in it."

Without warning, the coach dipped. Since she was sitting on the edge of the seat, Beth's body vaulted through the air. She mentally prepared for the impact, but Grayson caught her midair and gently placed her on the seat.

"Sit beside me. I promise not to take up all the room."

Carefully, she took his hand, his grip secure. Even with the bumpy roads and the swaying carriage, she felt safe.

Simply because he held her hand and wouldn't let her fall.

"I never asked you about your latest invention," she said once she was settled.

He twisted in the seat and rested his arm behind her on the bench.

"My new steam engine is being considered by an investment consortium that wants to develop more efficient technology. I heard about them and invited them to see what I'm creating." He sat so near that the soft vibrations of his voice gently thrummed against her. "I had a visitor from the consortium. He was suitably impressed. He's sending one of his men to my London warehouse to evaluate what I've created. He'll be there within three weeks. If everything meets with his approval, and I have the necessary capital, he'll return to the investors with his findings. Hopefully, I'll be meeting with the entire group for a presentation."

She tilted her gaze to see him staring at her. His gray eyes sparkled with excitement. He was the only man she knew who created technology with his own hands. "Which one of your engines will you show them?"

"The compound one." He smiled, then picked up his ever-present journal. He flipped it open and pointed to a drawing. "The operation is the same for the two-chamber and three-chamber engines. Steam forces down one piston, then it escapes to a second chamber, where it forces movement of the second piston, and so on. It's working so well that I may try to make it a four-chamber engine. I'm a little concerned about the design, though. The fourth chamber is too large. There won't be enough steam to push the piston."

She examined the drawings. "When I cook and need to boil water quickly, I either use a smaller pot or make the fire hotter." She met his gaze. "Perhaps you can make the chamber smaller or add more heat to the last chamber?"

His eyes widened and a smile brighter than the sun creased his lips. "That's brilliant, Beth. With a few adjustments, I can make the chamber smaller." He leaned over and smacked his lips against her. He pulled a pencil out of his waistcoat pocket and started scribbling in the book.

She lifted her hand to her lips. He'd just kissed her and didn't even realize it. This was a habit she could become quite fond of, especially on this trip.

He slowly raised his hand to his forehead. "I was so enthralled with your idea, I got carried away. I apologize again."

"I enjoyed it." She took his hand with hers. "Perhaps we can have the type of friendship where kisses are allowed."

Slowly, he put down his journal and pencil. "What do you mean?"

She shrugged with a smile. "Friends kiss all the time under mistletoe. At weddings."

That wicked grin of his appeared. "So, kisses won't cause problems between us?"

"Not to me," she said in satisfaction. There were so many aspects to him that others didn't see. He reminded her of a rare jewel. When you examined it in your hand, each facet seemed to glow with an energy from within. She grinned at such a thought. "Once we return to London"—

she crossed her fingers—"everything will return to the status quo except we'll be sharing a fortune."

His blank expression didn't betray his thoughts. "If that's your wish."

She nodded. Why shouldn't she be able to enjoy his kisses? She was her own woman living her life.

"All right. I agree." He exhaled. "Speaking of London, I must get Raleah House ready for the members of the consortium. Cillian and I will play housekeeper and staff before their visit." He chuckled slightly. "We have one apron to share between the two of us." He winked and her heart fluttered in approval at the gesture.

"Can't you hire someone to help with the cleaning?"

He shook his head. "I don't want to waste the coin."

"Are things that dire?" she asked softly.

His cheeks reddened. "One of the reasons I decided to accompany you is that I need capital if the consortium wants to see another engine. I'll have to build it."

"I have a few coins saved that I could lend you," she offered.

"I would never take advantage of our friendship like that." He dipped his head until they could see eye to eye. "Friends are too important to risk over money." His voice had deepened as he said the words. "And yours mean a great deal to me."

"But friends help friends. At least let me pay for last night's lodging," she said.

"No." Adamantly, he shook his head. "It was my gift to you."

At the start of this trip, she never considered him a friend. Two days ago, it would have been a terrifying thought. But not now. It was comforting to have a friend you could rely on.

"Since we're friends, if you ever need anything, I will help." She scooted a little closer until they were touching shoulder to shoulder and thigh to thigh. "At least, let me help you clean."

He shook his head slightly. "Thank you, but you work too. I'll not see you exhausted after a day, then come to my home and clean with us. Lean against me." He placed his arm around her shoulders, and she rested her head against him.

He pressed his mouth against her head, then softly said, "We'll need rest to keep our wits about us when we arrive at the Jolly Rooster."

"Why is that?" she asked, reveling in the feel of his body close to hers.

"If the Duke of Pelham is at the inn, he'll insist we play cards."

"Oh, I don't gamble." Her voice muted as she turned her head toward his chest, where she could feel the steady beat of his heart.

"It doesn't make any difference whether you gamble or not. He'll demand we put skin in the game."

"What does that mean?" she mumbled.

"Have enough blunt to play. Do you know how to count cards?" This time, he pressed his lips against her forehead and pulled her a little tighter to him.

Like a contented kitten, she snuggled closer. "I'm a good counter. I count stitches all the time."

He chuckled slightly. "Oh, darling Beth, you must sharpen those skills. We'll need them."

Chapter Ten

When Cillian opened the carriage door in the Jolly Rooster courtyard, Julian stepped down and surveyed the area before extending his hand to aid Beth. Several coachmen and a groomsman or two were the only people present. There didn't seem to be the usual bustle at the inn that would signal the Duke of Pelham's presence. Located in the village that adjoined his ducal seat, it was the duke's favorite haunt, and he owned it.

"Not many carriages, my lord." Cillian gazed around the courtyard as well.

"Excellent. Less chance of discovery." He slapped his hat against his thigh. "Will you see about lodging?"

"Of course." Cillian nodded. "How many?"

Normally when he and Cillian traveled, they stayed in the public rooms to save money. But with Beth, they needed to secure her a room. "Just one."

Cillian nodded, then proceeded toward the inn's entrance.

Julian reached out a hand and slowly Beth's hand came to rest in his palm. She'd not rested for long on the way to Amesbury. Excitement thrummed through her like energy during an electric storm.

"I expected there would be more activity," she said in

wonder as she glanced around the inn's yard. "It looks just like an ordinary inn on a major thoroughfare. Nothing at all like its reputation."

"Looks can be deceiving," he answered. "Have you been here?"

She nodded. "St. John likes to stay here when we travel to his estate next to yours. When we go home to Cumberland, we completely bypass it. For years, my brother has spent more time there than Somerset."

"For both our sakes, stay close with me."

She bristled slightly. "Is it not safe?"

"I don't know." He turned toward her so that his back was to the courtyard. She couldn't see anything over his height and broad shoulders. "Promise me that you'll stay by my side." He lowered his voice much like a lover would with another.

"I promise," she said softly. Her honeysuckle fragrance wrapped around him. He closed his eyes briefly and inhaled again. No matter what, he'd not leave her side. He'd been to enough of these types of places when he traveled to know what could occur at such an inn. Pampered lords and other gentlemen became enamored with their cards and drink. When they lost, which was the likely outcome, they'd typically wash away their disappointment with more drink. Afterward, they might attempt to find solace in the arms of a woman, if they could find one. Without inhibitions, they forgot what manners even meant.

God forbid if anyone dared muss a single hair on her head.

If anyone dared touch her, he would pummel the bloody oaf into the ground.

If anyone hurt her, he would kill them.

He brushed a hand down his face. He was turning into a barbarian, and they hadn't even left the courtyard.

Because it was Beth.

"What's wrong?" Beth tilted her head to his with a quizzical look about her face. "You look as if you're in pain."

If she only knew how much misery he was feeling right now, she'd probably kick him in the shin for such thoughts.

"Only a bit weary. Shall we?" He continued to lead her to the inn.

Just as they made their way to the entrance, the devil himself appeared. Dane Ardeerton, the Duke of Pelham, stood on the front step. With his blond hair and tall stature, he looked like King Midas. A lesser man might have been intimidated by the duke. He was one of the rare millionaires in the kingdom. Everything he touched turned to gold. His lands were some of the most fertile and profitable in all of England. On one of his lesser estates, tin was discovered, resulting in two extremely profitable mines. And if that weren't enough, the rest of his wealth came from his superb luck at the gaming tables and horseraces.

As soon as the duke saw them, he smiled, which transformed him into a handsome man. Many a woman had swooned at the sight of one of his rare smiles. But underneath that easy smile was a man who found great pleasure in winning high-stakes games against his opponents.

The duke nodded Julian's way. "Grayson."

He acknowledged the duke the same. "Pelham."

"Are you finally here for a game?" There was still a hint of hopefulness in his voice.

"Unfortunately not, Your Grace."

"You haven't changed. You're still a stick in the mud." The duke sniffed before his gaze stole to Beth. "Is your brother here?"

"Your Grace." Beth dipped the briefest curtsy ever. "No, he isn't."

"Pity," the duke answered. His gaze swept over Beth as if evaluating whether she was worth his time or not.

"Are you hosting a game?" Grayson asked.

"Perhaps." He grunted slightly while still looking at Beth, then addressed Julian. "I thought I'd see who shows up this evening."

The duke turned toward the inn, then stopped to face them. "I couldn't help but overhear the conversation that your coachman had with my innkeeper." With a wry smile, Pelham chuckled, and his gaze landed on Julian. "He only asked for one room. That's why I thought you were here for a game."

"I've no interest," Julian answered. It was the truth. He'd much rather spend his time and coin on inventing something. At least with those endeavors, he had something to show for it.

The duke grimaced before turning his attention to Beth. "I've heard all those rumors about you and the other wives." He straightened his shoulders. "I have no idea what Lord Meriwether was thinking. One wife is too many in my opinion, but to collect three?" His mouth puckered as if he'd sucked on a sour lemon. "That is the definition of hell." He turned his gaze back to Julian. "I'm not one to dictate what can and can't happen underneath this roof, but I must advise caution if you've only secured one room."

"Is it any of your concern?" Julian let the disdain drip from his voice.

The duke chuckled, then turned to Beth. "Miss Howell, the rules are that whatever happens under this roof is not to become gossip or blackmail. That applies to you. If you're looking for a husband, common sense says your best chances are elsewhere. I recommend London." He looked to the road and sighed. "It appears it'll be another dull evening. Well, I don't have anyone to dine with this evening, so why don't you both join me."

It wasn't a request, but a royal edict as if he were the king of all he surveyed. Without waiting for their agreement, he strolled back into the inn.

"Well, that was the most unenthusiastic invitation I've ever received." Beth tipped her nose in the air. "As if I'd be looking for a husband. Especially here of all places," she muttered.

"Let's get you settled. May I?" He pointed to the small travel valise.

"Yes, you may." She laughed. "Thank you for asking."

She was much more at ease with him tonight than last night. He couldn't help but smile in return. He picked up the valise, then extended his other arm for her to take. "I had Cillian order you a hot bath."

"Grayson, how kind."

The musical lilt in her voice made his stomach clench into a tight knot. Instantly, he could imagine her calling out his name when they were in the wild throes of passion, when neither of them knew where one began and the other one ended.

"Why is there only one room?" she asked.

He swallowed, not wanting to explain that it was the way he traveled when it was just him and Cillian. He was saving money. If the consortium came through, his life would change, and he could . . . what? Pursue Beth? She still didn't want marriage. "Let's save that discussion for later."

"Gladly." She smiled at him as if he'd picked the brightest star from the sky and presented it to her on a gold platter.

As soon as she wrapped her arm around his, Julian breathed a tad easier. He didn't like the way Pelham had looked at Beth. He'd recognized the hunger in the duke's eyes.

It was exactly what he felt for her.

———

After her heavenly bath, Beth dressed in the single evening gown that she'd brought with her during this trip. It was designed so that she didn't need a lady's maid's assistance when dressing. Earlier, she'd washed her hair and dried it by the cozy fire. She was finally feeling relaxed.

The simple but elegant room had a table and two chairs that overlooked the courtyard so a guest could see the comings and goings of other guests. Tonight, it appeared that it was just her and Julian who were staying here. Cillian had already found a bed in the stables to watch over the horses.

Her gaze landed on the four-poster bed against the wall as she evaluated the linens. As a designer of such goods, she always looked for inspiration. The coverings were simple but were edged in a beautiful black lace that added a bit of drama. Perhaps she'd invite Julian upstairs for a glass of wine after dinner. Perhaps they'd kiss again.

Such a thought made every inch of her skin break out in goose bumps. She could just imagine his large hands stroking her skin and his body covering hers as they kissed each other into oblivion.

Or at least, she hoped it would feel like that. She wanted a grand passion. If it occurred only once, it would be enough.

She left her room and locked it with the key the innkeeper had given her. She descended the stairs, where Julian waited for her.

The tilt of his lips and the way he stared at her made her smile even more. It was as if they both shared a secret without either of them saying a word. She couldn't remember smiling so much.

"You look beautiful," he said. "But then you always do."

Her cheeks heated at his tender words. She dipped her head, then raised her gaze to his. "My lord."

He took her hand in his and slowly raised it. The press of his lips against her skin stole her breath. It was almost as if he was . . . courting her again.

"No matter what the duke serves this evening, I won't taste a thing. All my attention will be directed at you."

Her heart raced, yet she didn't want this moment to end. The warmth and affection in his eyes were devoted completely to her. There was even a hint of hunger in his gaze.

Whatever he was offering her, she would take it with open arms and not let go until they were both satisfied.

"Lord Grayson?" Her own voice softened as if beckoning him to come closer and kiss her as she stood on the bottom step. Thankfully, the inn was empty, and in that moment she felt bold and determined to take what she wanted. "I want to kiss you."

A wicked smile graced his lips. "Go right ahead."

She closed the distance between them and pressed her lips to his. The taste of coffee and cinnamon greeted her. She flicked her tongue against his lips.

"Beth," he growled. "What are you doing?"

"Having an appetizer before the main course," she teased, then pressed her mouth to his, inviting him to join her.

"What's the main course?"

At the deep rumble of the duke's voice, they broke apart.

"I'm starved myself." Pelham leaned against the wall next to the staircase with his arms indolently crossed over his chest. The gleam in his eyes wasn't mocking but questioning. Whatever it was, it certainly was uncomfortable.

Julian's gaze had hardened at the duke's appearance. "Nasty habit to sneak up on others."

"I can't help it if you're unaware of your surroundings." He pushed away from the wall and strolled to them. "Of course, if I was being seduced by someone as lovely as Miss Howell, I wouldn't waste my time on admiring the décor either."

"Pelham." The warning in Julian's voice sounded much like the growl an animal makes when it defends its territory.

Before Beth could say a word, the duke walked away from them. Abruptly, he stopped and turned their way. "Are you coming?" Without waiting for an answer, he continued down the hall.

"What an arrogant arse," Grayson muttered. He swiped his hand through his hair. "I apologize if I—"

She pressed her finger to his lips. "I owe you an apology. I should have never kissed you like that in the open." Her stomach suddenly somersaulted as if she'd just flown over a fence on one of her brother's jumpers. "But I couldn't resist."

She was flirting, and the man she was flirting with seemed completely spellbound by her.

"Come, my little siren, let's find some sustenance."

A man cleared his throat.

They broke away from their conversation to now find

one of the duke's footmen standing at attention in the hallway.

"My lord." He nodded at Julian, then turned his direction to Beth. "Miss Howell. The duke is anxious for you to join him."

"Thank you," Beth answered.

As the footman turned to escort them to the duke's dining room, Julian leaned close. "Pelham reminds me of a spoiled child who opens his Christmas presents two days before everyone else just because he can."

"Hush," she scolded with a laugh. "Do you know him well?"

"We were at Eton together. Everyone hated him, including the staff. He used his privilege whenever he felt like it."

"Did you hate him?" she asked.

"No. I was one of the few who tolerated him. For some unknown reason, he apparently cared for my company. I would dine with him once a week in a private dining hall. His father gave a large endowment and insisted a room be reserved for him and his son exclusively." Julian frowned. "The duke rarely visited. I think his son acted out to gain the old man's attention, but it never worked. I was more fortunate. My father visited me whenever he could."

The look in his eyes told so much more. He loved his father, and his father loved him.

"I think you both were lucky," she said softly.

"Indeed." Julian slowed and pressed his hand over hers and squeezed. "I cared deeply for him. It was hard when I lost him."

"It was the same for me," she murmured. God, she loved her father and missed him every day.

"I know." His eyes glowed with compassion.

She stood on tiptoes and kissed his cheek, willing him to understand how much that meant to her.

By then, the footman stopped and opened the door to a room at the end of the hallway. Beth was the first to step through and her breath caught in her throat. The room looked like it came straight from the duke's residence at Pelham Hall. There was no expense spared in its decorations. A burl-wood table surrounded by six chairs was placed in the center of the room. Footmen stood off to the side to serve them. A brilliant chandelier overhead glittered with candlelight.

The duke stood slowly. A footman approached to pull out Beth's chair, but the duke waved him off and did the honors for her. With a graceful assuredness, he helped Beth to her seat, then resumed his position at the head of the table.

"I hope you're both still hungry after your *appetizer*," the duke drawled as he waved a hand. The footmen quietly but efficiently started serving the first course, turtle soup.

At the sight, she groaned.

Immediately, the duke turned his heavy-lidded gaze in her direction. "Is there something wrong?"

"It all looks simply divine," she said in her most pleasant voice.

The duke nodded, completely appeased at her answer. He turned his attention to Julian. "Tell me about your work."

While the men were busy eating and catching up with each other, Beth fiddled with her wineglass. She hated turtle soup. It reminded her of her dinner with Lord Siddleton and St. John. Siddleton had lost his false teeth in the turtle soup that night. That's when she escaped to Grayson's house.

Without a word being spoken, the footman assigned to serve her took away the bowl. Beth relaxed and turned her attention to Julian.

"A group of investors is interested in my machines." Julian looked her way. His eyes questioned if she was well.

She nodded slightly, then smiled.

The duke huffed a breath and rolled his eyes. With the snap of his fingers, a footman approached. "Decker, will you bring Miss Howell something else?" He turned his attention to Grayson once again.

In seconds, a bowl of clear consommé was placed before her. She slid a glance at Grayson, who winked her way as he continued his discussion with the duke.

Perch in a hollandaise sauce, buttered spinach, and baked partridge in a truffle and wine sauce completed the meal. The food itself was exquisite and the company entertaining until the duke turned his attention to her.

"Tell me, Miss Howell, what brings you and Grayson in the direction of the Jolly Rooster? You're not one to gamble, are you?" He leaned back in his chair and regarded her.

She pressed her serviette to her mouth, then rested it in her lap. "I'm here to see if I can discover the whereabouts of a pig."

The duke blinked three times in rapid succession, then burst out laughing. "What, pray tell, does this porker look like?"

"It's a Hampshire pig that Lord Meriwether Vareck owned."

At the word *Meriwether*, the duke let out a frustrated breath. "I'll never forget that day. He rode in on that immaculate white horse of his. Could see the bloody bastard from a mile away."

"Pelham," Julian warned.

The duke had the sense of manners to look ashamed. "Pardon my language, Miss Howell." He lifted his chin an inch. "Soon thereafter, his carriage pulled into the courtyard, followed by a cart with a pig you could very well be looking for." Pelham shook his head slightly, then took a long drink of wine. When he put the glass down, there was an odd gleam in his eye. "Would you like to know what happened then?"

"Please continue." Beth leaned forward in her chair ever so slightly, anticipation coursing through her veins. This new information would lead her one step closer to finding her dowry.

The duke smiled and waggled his eyebrows. "You'll have to play me for it."

Chapter Eleven

Julian leaned back in his chair. He'd seen the exact same look on Pelham's face when he'd organized a whist tournament at Eton. Within nine hours, he'd managed to win the monthly allowance of five earls, two marquesses, and six viscounts, including Beth's brother. St. John Howell had been so enraged at the turn of the cards he'd insinuated that Pelham had somehow cheated all of them.

When Pelham had demanded satisfaction to protect his honor, the viscount had sputtered like a dunked cat. Nonplussed, St. John had sulked off after muttering that he'd been mistaken and apologized.

No one could best Pelham at a game of chance, which was really a misnomer, as there was probably little luck involved. People believed the duke had an uncanny memory that allowed him to remember what cards had been played or discarded.

"I don't have extra coin to fritter away in a card game." The color had leached from Beth's face. "You would keep such information from me?" The curtness in her words echoed around the room.

The duke fell back against his chair as if she'd slapped his face. "Of course not. What kind of a man do you think I am?"

"A scoundrel," she said.

Julian had seen the same forthrightness on her face when she had politely informed him that with or without him she would find her missing dowry.

The duke turned his gaze to Julian. "I suppose you don't have coin you could let her play with?"

Julian arched a brow in answer.

"Fine," Pelham huffed. "I'll give you enough coins so we can play." Without waiting for their acquiescence, the duke lifted a hand.

Immediately, the footmen who served them cleared away the dishes. The duke stood and waited for Beth and Julian to do the same. Without a word, he marched out of the room and crossed the hall to where another footman stood. At the appearance of the duke, the footman swung open the door.

As they followed the duke, Beth leaned close. "Do you think this is safe?"

Julian bent his head. Her hair smelled of roses. He inhaled the sweetness, like that of a perfect dessert, and smiled. "He's all bluster. He has two sisters who have him wrapped around their little fingers."

When they entered the room, Pelham already had a decanter of brandy in his hand. Quickly, he poured two glasses. He glanced behind his shoulder in their direction. "Miss Howell, may I pour a glass of sherry for you?"

"Port," she answered.

"Why am I not surprised," the duke muttered as he reached for another decanter.

Within moments, they were seated around a small, round gaming table.

"Since there are three of us, shall we play vingt-et-un?" The duke handed the deck of cards to Julian. "The person with the cards closest to twenty-one without going over wins the hand."

Julian shuffled quickly, then presented Beth the deck to cut. There was nothing unusual about the deck, which proved his earlier theory that the duke knew how to count cards. With a flick of his wrist, he dealt the first hand. They placed their bets.

Naturally, Pelham won.

The duke motioned for his footman to bring the decanter to the table. Everything appeared as if they were three friends enjoying one another's company after dinner. However, the tension emanating from Beth oozed around the room.

Julian won the next five hands.

Pelham threw his cards on the table. "Miss Howell, you're not even trying."

"I don't play games of chance."

Grayson tsked playfully. "Pelham, don't be glum. Since I'm winning, why don't you tell her what she wants to know?"

"Fine," Pelham huffed. "What do you want to know about his pig?"

"What did Meriwether do with it?" Amazingly, her poise never wavered even though the duke acted like a spoiled child.

If Julian hadn't been watching her so closely, he might have missed the slight trembling in her fingers.

"He took it with him." The duke shook his head. "Along with my racehorse, Poison Blossom. He won a ten-year lease on an iron ore mine from the Marquess of Montridge." The duke shook his head. "Montridge was furious. I thought his groomsmen were going to take Meriwether behind the stable . . ." He blinked as if remembering Beth was there.

"Did Meriwether say where he was going?"

The duke nodded once. "The Poppycock Shoppe."

"Pardon?" she said.

Pelham pointed out the window. "There's a haberdashery by that name in the village that has games, cards, puzzles, and other knickknacks." He chuckled slightly. "He didn't tarry there for long, as the gentlemen who'd lost to him were furious. I've never seen fate favor anyone as she did Meriwether that night."

Beth frowned. "I knew about the horse and the iron ore mine. But what would he want from the haberdashery shop?"

"I have no idea, but he didn't return that night. If I recall correctly, he didn't return for several months after that night." He chuckled again. "He must have thought all had been forgiven."

Julian stood and retrieved the bottle of port. As he replenished Beth's glass, he asked, "When did Lord Meriwether return?"

Pelham studied the leaded cut crystal glass he held in the palm of his hand. "Exactly one month before he died. Asked for my sister's hand in marriage." He straightened his shoulders, and a pure look of disgust crossed his face. "Under no circumstances would I allow that no-good wastrel anywhere near my sisters. It's one thing to come here and gamble. But my sisters? Never." His voice rumbled with outrage. "It was obvious he wasn't interested in either of them. He was only interested in their dowries. Offered to help me with my investments." A slight sneer crossed his face. "I sent him on his way."

Beth's face was frozen. She sat so still that it reminded Julian of an empty shell. A slight breeze could have shattered her into a million pieces.

"Beth," he said softly.

"How fortunate your sisters are to claim you as their brother, Your Grace." She attempted a smile, but it failed miserably. "If you'll excuse me? It's late, and suddenly, I've found that I'm quite weary."

When she stood, all her usual energy and fire had disappeared into thin air. She looked as if she'd didn't have a friend in the world.

"I'll see you to your room." Julian came to her side.

"One of my footmen will escort her," the duke offered. As soon as the words were out of his mouth, the door opened, and a footman bowed.

"No, I'll see to it." Julian offered his arm, but Beth shook her head.

"Why don't you stay here with His Grace?" She didn't even look at him as she followed the footman from the room.

Julian stared at the door long after she was out of sight. Beth had a way of doing what she wanted when she wanted. It wouldn't be the first time that she'd summarily dismissed him without another thought when she wanted to be alone. But this was the first time he'd ever seen her devastated.

"Give her a moment by herself, and then you can . . ." The duke raised his hand, the lace at his wrist falling neatly against his black evening coat. "Whatever it is that you two have planned for the evening."

"We have nothing planned," Grayson answered.

"Of course." The duke lifted one arrogant brow in a move he must have practiced for hours in front of a mirror. "I, myself, have experience with the fairer sex who are in a high dudgeon."

This time, Grayson arched a brow. "While I'm sure your exploits are legendary, I beg you not to share."

The duke continued, completely ignoring him, "Sisters. They're the devil to deal with."

"I see." Grayson sat for a moment, then looked at the door again before addressing Pelham. "How long do you think—"

"Another five minutes should do it," the duke said confidently.

Grayson collected his winnings and handed them to the duke. "Thank you."

The duke shook his head. "They're yours." He placed his glass on the table without a sound and gathered the cards into a neat stack. "If you didn't have the blunt for another room, now you do. You're more than welcome—"

Julian clenched his teeth so tightly that it was a wonder he didn't break every tooth in his mouth. He hated that people were aware of his dire financial circumstances. He drew a deep breath and silently released his anger. "No, thank you. I planned to stay in the common room."

"Pelham," a voice called out.

When the duke saw his visitors, his entire demeanor changed. "Look what the devil brought in." He stood and held out his hands wide in welcome. "My salvation. I thought I was going to have to face a dreary night without company."

Julian stood and turned to the newcomers. One was the Earl of Rigby, a notorious gambler and womanizer. He wasn't as familiar with the other gentleman, Mr. George Sutton. Two other men followed, and Grayson suppressed a curse. It was Portland and Stanton.

"Grayson," Portland called out. "Imagine meeting you here."

Stanton acknowledged Julian with a nod. "Weren't you going to Brighton?"

"Change of plans," he answered without acknowledging Portland. "Thank you for the invitation, but I'm calling it an evening."

After he quickly said his farewell to the others, the duke followed him into the hallway. "With Rigby at the inn, stay in the room next to hers. You'll be doing me a favor. If anything would happen to Miss Howell, it wouldn't be good for business."

Ice ran through Grayson's blood at the thought of someone hurting Beth. "Good evening, Your Grace." Grayson nodded slightly, then exited the room as if the hounds of hell were nipping at his feet.

Cillian could stay in the room offered by Pelham.

Grayson was staying with Beth.

After thanking the footman for his escort, Beth silently closed the bedroom door. She rested her forehead against the oak panel and closed her eyes, praying for composure. She would not weep.

She hadn't had a good cry since Meriwether had left her bed that night.

Pushing herself away from the door, Beth walked across the room to a cozy fire that blazed in the hearth. A maid or one of the duke's numerous footmen must have made it when Beth had dined with Grayson and the duke. She extended her palms toward the heat, but she felt no warmth. Her teeth chattered slightly as unease swept over her, leaving in its wake a chill that blanketed her.

It wasn't that the duke had said anything purposely to hurt her, but his affirmation that Meri still hunted for another wife nauseated her. As she sat and listened to Pelham retell Meri's movements, Beth shriveled inside. If she'd ever wanted more proof that she was only valued for her dowry or what her brother perceived as her worth, tonight proved it.

Pelham could see through Meri's charade. Why couldn't St. John?

A little voice inside her hummed, *Because he only thinks of himself.*

She broke away from the fire and walked to the oak dressing table, where a beveled mirror was attached. She didn't recognize herself, as her features were drawn and pale. Dark circles surrounded her eyes, a testament to her weariness of life.

She'd laugh if her situation wasn't so dire. She had no idea who she was without that dowry. Of course, she was a partner to Katherine, the Duchess of Randford, in their linen business. But Kat was the one who'd created it, not Beth. Any success was directly related to Katherine and all her efforts.

A brief knock on the door broke Beth's reverie.

"Beth, let me in." Grayson's raspy voice seeped through the door and enveloped her.

Without a sound, she crossed the room. She took a deep breath in resolution. Of course he'd see how she was faring. When she opened the door, he stood before her with one elbow resting against the frame. Without a word, he studied her.

His gaze exposed every weakness she owned. Instinctively, she crossed her arms over her middle.

"Let me inside," he said softly.

She wanted to rush into his arms, but instead she stepped aside.

In turn, he matched her step and gently closed the door behind him. Their eyes locked, and the resulting silence between them was blown asunder by the thundering of her heartbeat. Her body trembled as if recognizing he was near, a welcomed sanctuary where she could find solace.

He opened his arms. She didn't wait for him to step forward. Instead, like an enchanted fool, she rushed into his embrace. She burrowed her head against his chest, seeking a haven at least for a moment or two.

"Beth," he crooned gently.

In response, she burrowed deeper against him. She inhaled his fragrance, determined to memorize it so that in the future when she was alone she'd remember. Her fingers trailed against the satin embroidery of his waistcoat, learning each thread.

"Do you want to talk about it?"

She shook her head gently against his chest, then relinquished her hold on him. "There's nothing to discuss." She forced herself to smile. "As I said, I'm tired."

He narrowed his eyes in disbelief.

"I'm perfectly fine." She tilted her chin an inch higher, daring him to contradict her.

"You're always fine in my opinion." His voice dropped an octave on the word *fine* as if she were a rare wine. "Tell me."

The tenderness in his gaze practically undid her. She closed her eyes and shook her head briefly. "Pelham."

"Pelham," he repeated, coaxing her to continue.

"He shared a bit about Meri's travels." She shrugged a shoulder much in the manner of dissuading a tiresome bee from giving chase. "Meri was already looking for another wife shortly after leaving me." She turned away from Grayson and, as best she could, walked nonchalantly toward the fire. "He wanted another. That's all."

"*He* was a fool." He followed her, then leaned close enough that she could feel his breath against her neck. "If you were my wife, I'd have never . . ." He quieted for a second. "If you were my wife, I'd have damn sure made it a priority that I told you every day and night how much I valued you."

At the unmistakable growl in his voice, her throat cinched tight, and her eyes burned with unshed tears. That was the problem with Grayson. He knew exactly what to say to tear down her defenses. As if that weren't enough, with the stealth of an accomplished thief he reached inside her chest without her taking notice, then gently plucked out her heart.

The urge to turn around and face him grew fierce, but she forced herself to face forward. "You had a chance to marry me long ago. Why say such things now?"

"Because it's the truth," he murmured.

It could be her imagination, but she thought he stepped closer. From the reflection in the window, he was reaching one hand to touch her. Everything stood suspended in that moment as she willed him to take her in his arms and pull her close.

Instead, a knock sounded on the door. "My lord?" Cillian called from the other side.

A slight brush of air met her back as Grayson stepped away.

Without turning around, she listened to the door opening.

"My lord, I have hot water . . ."

"Thank you," Grayson murmured.

"Miss Howell," Cillian called out in greeting.

Beth pasted on a slight smile and turned around. "Good evening, Cillian."

The servant nodded. "I've brought fresh hot water. They don't have the staff to bring it up right now. If either of you would care . . . to freshen up."

"How thoughtful. Thank you." Awkwardly, she returned to her study of the darkened window. With the candlelight reflecting against the dark pane, she saw Grayson point behind a woven screen where a slipper tub was hidden. It was where she'd taken a bath earlier. Her eyes widened. Was Grayson staying in her room? He would want to bathe this evening. She twisted her fingers together. If he bathed, what would she do?

Be tortured by listening to the water sluicing down his body.

She pressed her hands down her dress to calm the runaway beat in her chest. She shouldn't be nervous with such a common, everyday occurrence as Grayson bathing in her room. But tell that to her thundering heart and sweaty palms.

Besides, she had a lot more on her mind than a naked Grayson bathing behind a screen.

"I'm sleeping in the next room," Cillian said.

"Excellent," Grayson answered. The door closed, signaling Cillian's departure. "I'm sleeping here."

"Is there trouble?" she asked quietly.

"A few gentlemen arrived for play. One of them wasn't to the duke's liking. So, out of an abundance of precaution, he's keeping the room next to ours occupied. I'm sure Pelham wouldn't like for your sleep to be disturbed." Grayson glanced toward the screen. "Shall I prepare you a bath?"

Without turning from her sentry position by the window, she shook her head. "You take one."

His reflection revealed a slight smile tugging at his lips as he dipped his head.

Her breath caught at the sight. He resembled the man from her past. Eight long years ago, he was her future.

"I would fancy washing this grime away, but only if you don't want it instead."

"Yes, I'd fancy that too." *What an idiotic thing to say.* He might think she wanted to wash instead of him. She clenched her thighs together at the image of him washing after her, sharing the same water. She had to hold her tongue or she'd likely suggest they take a bath together. "You need a bath."

"I hadn't realized that my body was so offensive." He glanced at his clothing. "I must reek from traveling."

"I don't think you're offensive. Not at all. Quite the opposite." She swallowed when she realized what she'd said.

Of course she found him attractive. Every marriageable woman within all of England thought him appealing on so many levels. Every young heiress looking for a title was after him, according to the gossip rags. Yet she was the one who would share a room with him.

"What I meant . . ." Heat licked her cheeks at her verbal blunders that multiplied like field rabbits by the minute. "I think it'd make you more comfortable."

That sounded sensible even if her voice wobbled slightly.

His gaze was artless but observant. "Are you certain?"

"Positive." She'd always prided herself on being a strong, level-headed woman. She repeated that mantra again. It allowed her to find her backbone, which seemed to have scurried under the bed in hiding. She straightened her shoulders. "I think the more important question is whether you're comfortable with me." She turned and forced her gaze to meet his. "Because I'm sleeping in the bed."

Chapter Twelve

Grayson held her gaze and smiled at the confidence in her words. "I'll sleep on the sofa." As he set about pouring water into the empty slipper tub, he called out over his shoulder, "We could share the water." When she didn't answer, he turned her way again.

She shook her head so brusquely, it was a wonder she didn't injure her neck. "No, you take it. My pleasure will come later."

"And what pleasure might that be?"

"Your company." Her alto voice trembled slightly.

He couldn't help but smile. All her earlier sadness was forgotten. He could feel her gaze on his back. She was slightly flustered with him being here. This was a side of Beth that he rarely saw. It was wicked on his part, but it was extremely satisfying that she couldn't seem to tear her eyes away from him.

With slow and deliberate movements, he stripped out of his wool coat, carefully folded it, then laid it across a small chair next to the slipper tub. She fidgeted behind him. Next, he carefully unbuttoned his waistcoat and let it fall open. He poured another bucket of warm water into the tub before slipping the unbuttoned garment off his body.

As he'd done previously, he folded the waistcoat and laid it carefully on top of the coat.

A murmur of impatience escaped Beth.

As he untied his cravat and pulled the neckcloth out from under his collar, he glanced her way. Her blue eyes seemed to darken before him as if she wanted him to tempt her. Her gaze slowly rose from his hands to meet his, and a slight smile tugged at one side of her mouth.

This woman could charm every land-loving snake into the North Sea with such a look.

"Are you purposely teasing me?" The playful challenge in her eyes gave him the slightest pause.

"Why would you think that?" He had to be careful for his own sake. It would take little to sweep her into his arms and make love to her. With her tart tongue, she would be the sweetest indulgence, filling him with everything he wanted. Passion, temptation, and emptying the yearning that seemed to occupy his lonely days.

Sadly, they'd agreed to only kissing.

"I believe a turtle could complete a mile-long race faster than you can undress." She laughed, the sound echoing like the finest crystal chandelier prisms striking together.

"I didn't know that you were waiting for me to disrobe," he said innocently.

"Grayson," she admonished. "I never thought you a person to torment another."

"Julian," he said softly. "The sound of my given name on your lips would give me great pleasure."

"Only when we're alone." She bit her lip.

Even in the dim light provided by the candles and the fireplace, he couldn't miss the deep pink staining her cheeks.

"Julian . . . take off your shirt." Beth took a step closer.

"Perhaps you'd help me?" He extended his arm while exposing his gold sleeve buttons.

She nodded, then stilled for a moment before moving forward. The energy they created when they were together practically vibrated between them. When she took her first step forward, it grew in strength.

Every part of him hummed in awareness.

Her fingers settled on his wrist. She raised her gaze to his as she flicked the button free, then set it on the side table before him. He extended the other arm, and she repeated the task never once taking her eyes from his.

"Now, *Julian*."

At her gentle demand and the sound of his name on her lips, he swallowed, trying to tame the pent-up desire thrumming through his veins. But his unruly cock was having none of it. He didn't need to glance at the placket of his breeches to know that it had swelled. The thickened outline against the falls of his breeches made it clear how she affected him.

Perhaps this game was more dangerous for him than it was for her. She took a step closer until only an inch separated their chests.

She reached out and tugged at his shirt. "Shall I help you?"

He lifted his arms in response. Slowly, as if unveiling a valuable painting, she tugged his shirt from the waist of his breeches. When the cool air hit his stomach, he sucked in a breath.

She studied him much like one of her elaborate embroidery designs. Either way, the current that hummed between them grew in volume.

He bent slightly so she could pull the linen over his head. When it was off, he straightened to his full height so she could look her fill. When her gaze slowly rose to his, he felt like a veritable peacock showing off for a delectable peahen.

"Do you need my help undressing?" he asked.

She shook her head, but a slight grin tugged at her mouth. "You should bathe now." With that, she picked up his coat and waistcoat, then scooted the screen into a position that ensured his privacy.

For some odd reason, he had hoped she'd make a comment about his physique. Perhaps it was fortuitous she was silent. Otherwise, they might be courting trouble. He filled a washbasin with water, then shaved quickly. He unbuttoned his falls, took off his boots, then shed his stockings.

Carefully so as not to cause the water to overflow, he lowered himself into the slipper tub. He allowed his mind to rest as he relaxed in the deliciously warm water. Taking a piece of rose-scented soap, he washed himself all the while wicked thoughts crowded into his brain as he considered their sleeping arrangements. As he washed his body, his cock twitched. He closed his eyes and thought about her nearby.

Everything seemed on edge, like a dam ready to burst. He released a deep breath.

No matter how much he wanted her, he couldn't have her. Yet he couldn't deny the truth. It was Beth and had always been Beth who had captured his interest.

"Julian?"

He cautiously sat up in the small copper tub. "Hmm?"

"I've brushed your coat and waistcoat," she called out from the other side of the screen. "I know Cillian's been busy with the horses and driving today. If there's anything else I can do for you or him, I hope you'll let me know."

A warmth spread in his chest at her thoughtful gesture. It was something a wife might do for her husband.

"I'm in your debt. I appreciate you gallivanting around the countryside with me."

"It's my pleasure," he called out.

The room grew quiet again until she broke the silence once more.

"Julian?"

"Hmm."

"I should have mentioned this earlier, but I couldn't organize my thoughts." The outline of her body halted in front of the screen. "I've always thought you handsome."

He sat up. The water lurched at the sides from his movement. He turned his full attention to her silhouette.

"Your chest," she declared, then laughed. "It's most impressive."

"How so?" He sounded starved for attention.

"I have never seen a man's naked chest before. A few of the farmhands at St. John's estate roll up their sleeves when the heat of the summer is upon them. I'd wager that not even one of them looks like you. Your chest is much broader, and you have muscles on your stomach. I've never seen that before." From the shadows that flittered against the screen, the outline of her stretching her arms overhead commanded his attention. "I'm going to bed."

"Wait." He stood so quickly that the water sluicing off his body sounded like a waterfall. He grabbed a linen toweling to dry his body, then wrapped it around his waist. Within seconds, he'd stepped around the screen. The sight that was before him stole his breath.

Nestled under the bedcovers, Beth relaxed against the headboard. Her brown waves cascaded like yards of chocolate silk behind her.

She watched him just as he watched her.

The playful minx raised a perfectly arched brow as she smoothed one hand across the satin covering.

"Did you like it?" he asked.

"What?" She locked her gaze with his.

"This." He waved a hand down his chest. God, it would be a sleepless night if he stayed in this room with her a mere twenty feet away.

She turned slightly toward him. "Didn't I tell you that you were handsome? That includes your chest."

She settled under the covers as if they'd finished the discussion, but then a slight smile appeared.

At the sight, he could have sworn that the sun had just risen in the night sky.

~

He was the most magnificent male specimen she'd ever seen. Of course, he was the only one she'd ever seen this close. Her supposed husband had come to their bed on their "wedding night" dressed in a nightshirt. She hadn't seen anything except for his head.

The Marquess of Grayson could only be described as a masterpiece, and he was in her room. With him, she might discover what really occurred between a man and a woman.

Based upon what Constance had shared about her own experiences, Beth had been shortchanged on all accounts.

A crooked smile crossed Julian's lips that promised he knew exactly what pleasure was and he'd use every weapon in his arsenal to show her.

She let out a shuddered breath.

He stepped behind the screen and soon emerged in his shirt and breeches.

She frowned at the sight. Meri had done the same thing

when he'd come into her room. He'd doused the candle, taken off his clothing, then slipped on the nightshirt.

The only conclusion she could draw was that it must be some common ritual for men when they were about to bed a woman. Perhaps they learned it in school or it was some unwritten rule that only men shared. Whatever it was, she wasn't too pleased with it. If the rest of Julian's body was as magnificent as his chest, then she was being robbed.

Grayson sat on the edge of the sofa and extinguished the candle. With an athletic ease, he swung his body around until he was lying on the sofa staring at her.

"Shall I stay here, or would you prefer that I sleep in a chair outside the door?"

"A chair?" She sat up abruptly. With his arms behind his head, Julian was spread out like a buffet of sweets.

"I don't want things between us to become uncomfortable."

That was like closing the barn door after the cows had escaped. Of course she was uncomfortable. Everything inside her felt heated and anxious. She wanted him to kiss her again.

"Where is your nightshirt?"

"Nightshirt?" His brow furrowed. "I don't sleep in one."

Unable to wrap her thoughts around such visions, she blinked and debated whether to ask him more. Trying to act casual, she waved a hand toward the space between them. Yet her hand fluttered like a nervous robin on the first day of spring. "I thought all men went to bed in nightshirts."

"I've not slept in a nightshirt since childhood." When he chuckled, his chest rose and fell. It was enough to hypnotize a woman.

"What do you wear to bed?" She wanted to cringe. Her voice sounded incredulous, not at all disinterested and composed like she'd hoped.

"Nothing."

The low baritone of his voice went straight to her center, which was already warm and achy—like an arrow to the target, his aim perfect.

"What else do you want to know?" he asked softly.

She'd wanted to ask Constance and Kat all sorts of things about their married life but never had the courage. Here in the dark, she felt comfortable asking him questions that haunted her. "I once saw Kat and Randford come out of Kat's office looking quite disheveled. I think they might have been intimate." Her voice dropped. "I'm curious. Do people make love outside the bedroom?"

"Yes." His voice deepened. "A barn. A carriage. A field filled with fresh summer grass, a pond, a pantry, a folly, a table, a chair."

"How can people make love in a chair?"

"For a man and a woman, she could be sitting on his lap facing him or . . . facing away."

"What?" she asked breathlessly, staring across the room. Shadows kissed his handsome face. For the world, she wanted to be one of those lucky shadows. Or a moonbeam. She didn't care as long as it were her lips against his skin. "I thought . . ." Her mind whirled with images of her and Grayson making love in all those places. Some were easier than others to imagine.

"Beth." Her name on his lips sounded like a claim, a declaration that she was his. "You could try all of that . . . with the right man."

Her heart jolted at his words. Then something between them shifted in those infinitesimal moments. Perhaps they were destined to be more than friends.

"Are you the right man?" she asked softly. She sat up and pulled her legs beneath her body. In the darkness, it was so much easier to share these secrets and longings.

"Perhaps." His bold stare never wavered. "If I was your husband, we could share more than kisses."

She stilled. All the stormy passion swirling around her evaporated instantly. "Did you just ask me to marry you?"

Even from this distance, his hooded gaze didn't hide the controlled fire that smoldered in his gray eyes. She'd have been mesmerized by such a look if it had not been accompanied by the talk of marriage.

"I don't have money now, but soon I'll come into enough to marry—"

Before he could finish the sentence, she slid out of bed. Grabbing a silk dressing gown, she donned it. "Don't." Instinctively, she walked in the direction of the door. "Thank you, but you're wasting your breath."

"Where are you going?" His bearing was stiff and proud, but it didn't hide the shock on his face.

"If you're referring to my life, I wish I knew." She turned and walked back in his direction. "But wherever it is, a husband won't be part of it."

He propped one arm on a bent knee, the pose like that of a pirate ready to rule the seas.

"Quit looking at me like I'm a creature you've pulled from the deep," she huffed.

"In that dressing gown, you look like a mermaid who's come to the surface to serenade me. Like all those poor souls who listened to such a creature's song, I've fallen—"

Beth skidded to a halt and raised her hand to stop his poetic nonsense. She forced herself to take a deep breath. "I promised myself I'd never marry."

"That's a pity," he said softly. "I thought if we married, then we could explore everything between us." He sat up. "I don't want to lose my friends, nor do I want to lose you."

"It's a good thing you haven't asked for my hand . . . again." She blew out a breath. "We'd be at an impasse. Because you see, I don't want to lose myself."

Chapter Thirteen

Julian counted Beth's steps as she paced. The number was exactly ten, then she'd pivot gracefully on the ball of her foot and proceed in the opposite direction. She made four complete turns before he spoke.

"Shall we continue our conversation, or shall I just watch you pace like a caged animal?" He leaned back against the sofa and patiently waited.

She stopped midstep and blasted him with a stare that no doubt was designed to roast him alive. She had perfected such a look, and it took real talent to keep it steady. If they were in a London ballroom and she'd leveled that same gaze over the crowd, there would be a mass exodus. A smile tugged at his lips at such a vision. If that happened, then they'd be the only souls left. He'd waltz her around the floor and hold her scandalously close.

Though they'd known each other for years, they'd only danced a few times. The first was at her brother's house, and it was a quadrille. He'll never forget that night. She was young and carefree, simply vivacious. He couldn't take his eyes off her.

Much like now.

"There's nothing to discuss." She threw the retort straight at him. "You're aware how adverse I am to marriage. The very fact that you brought it up"—she pointed a finger at him in accusation—"indicates that you don't take me or my position seriously."

"Beth, that's not the situation at all and to insinuate otherwise misrepresents my intentions." The urge to take her in his arms grew fierce, but he stayed seated. Otherwise, she'd flee the room. "You must understand my intentions. I am an honorable man. I can't"—he sliced a hand through the air—"and won't make love to you otherwise. It would change both of our lives. You know that."

"I understand the situation perfectly." She lifted her chin and stuck out her chest.

Such a gesture emphasized her breasts. He sighed, then swung his legs off the sofa. Slowly, he approached her like she was a cornered animal ready to attack.

"Let's not argue." He held out his hands to her, and reluctantly, she took them in hers. Gently, he pulled her close, into his embrace. She snuggled up to him, and in response he lightly rested his head on hers. "I didn't anticipate my saying the word *marriage* would be so unsettling for you. Is there something else that's bothering you?"

She pulled away. The fire in her eyes had dulled.

"Perhaps I can help." He cupped her face and rubbed his thumb against her cheekbone. Her skin was luminous in the candlelight. "Tell me."

"I'm not the marrying kind," she muttered. She took his hand and led him to the sitting area by the fire, which still burned bright. She threw a small log on the fire, then arranged it to her satisfaction. Finally, she came to his side and sat down. "You'd be the last person in the world I'd marry."

For a moment, he was speechless. "Are you saying

I'm good enough to take to bed, but not good enough to marry?"

But it made sense. He'd failed her once. Why would she give him another chance?

Beth scooted closer and smiled apologetically. "What I meant . . ." She studied her clasped hands. "You're too valuable to me."

"If you value me enough, then marriage would be the next logical step, wouldn't it?" He smiled and caught her gaze. "Of course, this presupposes I was asking."

She shook her head, then studied the fire for a moment. The wood crackled in the robust flames as if vehemently disagreeing with her. "You must understand. Every man in my life has in some fashion failed me." Her eyes widened, and he saw the earnestness come from deep within her. "Meri walked away from our marriage before he'd even arrived."

"What do you mean?"

"He was already married to Kat, then Constance, who was carrying his baby. I wasn't even second choice, but a distant third." She heaved an anguished sigh. "My brother is another story. First, he arranged my marriage to Meri. Now he wants me to marry a poor elderly man for his money." She shook her head. "That's what I mean by failure."

At the word *failure*, it conjured the time when he'd walked away from her, all for his sense of pride and honor. He'd soon learned that neither of them offered the joy and comfort that marriage to Beth would have entailed.

"What about your father? You told me once you adored him." He reached over and smoothed a fallen lock of hair, then tucked it behind her ear. The firelight played and glistened among the strands. He wanted to plunge his fingers into her tresses and feel that softness against his skin.

A sad smile crept across her full lips. "I did adore him. But he failed me too." She stood slowly.

"How so?" He stood as well beside her. Wherever she traveled, he'd be right beside her—if she allowed.

"He died." Her lips quivered for a moment before she turned away.

"Beth, look at me, please." Grayson took her hand and entwined their fingers. "Beth," he whispered.

Finally, she turned his way.

"I would never hurt you. I would always have your best interests at heart."

She nodded slightly. "Marriage curtails a woman's freedom. I've earned it, and I won't give it up. Ever."

His lungs ceased working and his heart tripped in its beat when he saw the single solitary tear streaming down her face. By itself, it appeared as lonely as Beth did in that moment. But the tear stood suspended on her cheek, refusing to budge. It reminded him of her stalwart determination to live life her own way.

She squeezed his fingers. "Let's not talk anymore. I'm tired. Shall we get some rest before we leave for London tomorrow?"

"Of course," he said, then waggled his eyebrows with a smile. "On one condition."

She wiped the forlorn tear away and mightily tried to smile. "What's that?"

"Let me hold you." He tugged her toward the bed. "I need to feel close to you tonight."

She nodded gently.

With great ceremony, he went to her side of the bed and straightened the bedding. Then, with a flick of his wrist, he turned the covers back and waved a hand as if she were the Queen herself. She slid past him and untied her gown. With her usual grace, Beth sat on the bed and tucked her feet under the covers.

At the reveal of her slim ankles, Grayson sucked in a breath. He had little doubt that the rest of her was as beautiful as the promise of her shapely and delicate legs. What an excruciating but satisfying night he had ahead of him. He'd get to hold the woman of his dreams in his arms.

He bent down and pressed his lips to her forehead. "Sleep well."

He tended the fire once more, then blew out the candle on the side of the bed. As soon as his weight hit the bed, she turned to face him.

"What did you mean about holding me?"

The uncertainty in her voice brought out the need to comfort and protect this priceless jewel of a woman. Whatever he had to do, he wanted her safe from worry.

"I want to hold you all night long." He turned on his side, then dipped his head. He pressed his lips to hers. While the always present sensuality simmered between them, he wouldn't let it turn into an inferno. His darling Beth ached because the men in her life weren't there for her and ultimately disappointed her. And he'd been one of them. But tonight, he'd be damned if he added any more heartache.

He pulled her close. She was his—at least for this trip—whether she realized it or not. It wouldn't make up for his own failure to her, but he'd do everything in his power to help her find that dowry or what remained of it.

She settled into the crook of his arm, using his shoulder as a pillow. He relaxed and brought her closer. Her hand splayed against his chest as if ensuring that he'd stay beside her all night. The restful movement of her breathing next to him should have been an inducement to sleep. But it was her hand on his chest that gave him pause.

He held his breath as her hand drifted lower on his abdomen. Half-aroused this entire trip, his unruly cock sprang to attention, but Beth was sound asleep. He nuzzled her head and drank in her scent. This was what made life important. These simple moments of sharing the same air, the same space, and the same specks of time together were what defined the best of life.

Beth woke first and, with a stealth that she'd learned from sneaking out of the house, had performed her morning ablutions and dressed in record time. Before she left the room, she studied Grayson, who was lying on his back. His wide chest, the one she'd clung to all night, rose and fell gently as he slept.

If she married him, this would be what she'd wake up to every morning. A husband who promised everything in his power to comfort and protect her.

She shook her head to clear such a thought from her mind. She didn't want a husband, and she didn't want Julian. Though he was perfect last night, he'd walked away from her before. Apparently, it was easy for him.

Just like Meri had walked away from their marriage.

Perhaps she was being unfair to Julian. But she couldn't believe otherwise. She needed to keep her heart in its cage and not let the thing flutter about in hopes of something extraordinary.

Extraordinary things didn't happen to her.

Only calamity.

She'd made it out the door and down the steps without a single piece of flooring squeaking in protest. She entered the public room and nodded at the innkeeper, who was eating his morning meal.

"Miss Howell," Cillian called out, and stood at a table in the back.

She wove around the empty tables and chairs to meet him. "Good morning, Cillian. I trust you slept well?"

"Like a newborn babe." He helped her sit, then took his own chair. Without batting an eye, he poured her a cup of tea.

"When my friend Lady Sykeston had her firstborn, she hardly slept. Neither did her daughter Aurelia. Is that what you meant?" she asked with a wink.

Before he could answer, a commotion erupted at the entrance of the pub. Cillian practically growled under his breath. "It's those fancy lords and ladies from Portsmouth. I almost swear they're following us."

"What?" Beth froze while sweeping her gaze across the back of the room looking for an escape. Of all the blasted luck. There was only one way in and out of the main pub room.

"Lord Stanton." Cillian wrinkled his nose. "They're holding court at the front of the room." Casually, he looked around her. "The Earl of Rigby is with them. Another man I don't recognize is with them."

She didn't dare turn around. Thankfully, she'd worn her serviceable navy dress. If they even took the time to gaze in her direction, they'd think she was part of the ducal staff.

"For the love of a marquess," Cillian hissed.

"What?" she asked.

"Lord Grayson, how wonderful to see you again," a feminine voice called out.

This time, it was Beth who wanted to growl. "That's Lady Clementine."

"With Lady Henrietta." Cillian nodded. "Mr. Portland, Lord Stanton, and the Earl of Rigby are with them." He caught her gaze. "They all came to play cards with the duke."

"Good morning, Lady Clementine," Grayson answered politely.

Cillian buried his head in one hand. "He doesn't have his neckcloth tied. He looks like a disaster."

"Julian?" she whispered.

The valet stilled with wide eyes at her calling the marquess by his first name. Slowly, he twisted his head to peek again. "Now she's dressing him."

"Who?" Beth didn't hide this time. An overwhelming urge to see who dared to touch a single hair on Julian. She swung around in her seat to an unbelievable sight. Lady Clementine had Grayson bending toward her as she tried to tie his cravat.

That was only the domain of a man's valet or his wife. Perhaps his mistress would qualify, but a title-hungry slip of a girl who had barely been introduced to society? Nay. It would not happen while Beth was present, even if meant discovery.

When Beth stood, Julian's gaze whipped to hers. His body stiffened in shock.

"Come, Cillian." Beth strolled in Julian's direction. When she reached Julian's side, she stopped. "Lady Clementine, perhaps something that intricate should be left to Lord Grayson's valet." Only then did she turn and greet the others.

When Lord Stanton narrowed his eyes, the tiniest hint of unease crept up her back. In response, she lifted her chin an inch. She'd not be intimidated by such a man. Her brother's title was at least a hundred years older than Stanton's.

When Portland smiled, it was a warning shot across the bow. "Why, thank you, Blythe, for instructing my sister. A lady of your impeccable manners and bearing should rightly remind us of all the hidden pitfalls that might ruin a young lady's reputation."

While the words sounded like a compliment, there was no mistaking the insult that resided there. She inhaled silently. Lady Clementine's and Lady Henrietta's faces paled.

"Portland, apologize immediately." Grayson took a step forward in the man's direction.

Portland took a step back.

"Now," Grayson growled.

"Grayson." When he didn't turn Beth's way, she cleared her throat. "Lord Grayson, there's no harm."

His hands were clenched into fists by his sides as if he was holding himself back from hitting Portland. "Oh, there's harm all right. No one will insult you like that when I'm present."

"I didn't insult her," Portland argued. "It's the truth. Miss Howell was once above reproach."

"Meet me outside," Grayson seethed.

"Not a duel," Lord Stanton muttered as he stared at the floor. "It's too early in the morning for such nonsense."

"No." Beth reached and put her hand on Julian's arm. "Don't do this. I beg of you."

Both Portland sisters' gazes followed Beth's hand. Their eyes widened in horror that she dared touch him.

Lady Clementine cocked her head in interest. "Why is it that you can touch the marquess in such a familiar manner and yet, when I'm only seeking to help him, you chastise me?"

"Because he's a friend," she said in her haughtiest voice. "We've known each other for years."

Lady Clementine huffed softly. "If my father has his way, Lord Grayson will be much more than a friend to our family. Be that as it may, let us all sweep aside the ugliness of the morning. There's no reason to ruin a perfectly marvelous day. Monty, I think you should offer an apology to Miss Howell."

Lady Henrietta nodded.

Portland narrowed his eyes as he offered the apology. "Forgive me, Miss Howell, for my choice of words."

The Earl of Rigby seemed to come out of his stupor. "As long as the lady accepts your act of contrition, then there's no harm." He turned to Julian. "Wouldn't you agree, Lord Grayson?"

Grayson took a deep breath as if trying to wrangle his anger into a semblance of control.

Before anyone said another word, Beth nodded. "I accept your apology."

Rigby smiled and Lord Stanton exhaled in relief.

"My lord, why don't you find some air?" Cillian's quiet voice was directed at Julian. "I'll see Miss Howell to her room."

Grayson stared for an eternity at Portland, his nostrils flaring with each breath. After a full minute, he stepped back and nodded once. He turned to Cillian. "Don't leave her side." Without waiting for a reply, he walked away briskly. His boot heels echoed through the public room.

She'd never seen Grayson so angry. She smoothed her hand down her stomach hoping to stop the riot of butterflies that still lingered. Since the drama was slowing, resolving itself, the others meandered toward a table—all except Montague Portland.

"My lady, I left my coat at the table," Cillian said. "I'll fetch it and escort you to your room."

She nodded, unsure where to escape. Humiliation

licked her cheek, leaving an unbearable heat in its path. How did something as simple as breakfast become a spectacle? Because she was jealous and couldn't keep quiet.

Her breath hitched at such a thought. Surely, that wasn't what she felt.

"Miss Howell, thank you for accepting my sincerest apology." The sarcasm rolled off Portland's tongue quite easily. "The disinterest you feign at the truth I speak is as transparent as your bravado toward my sister. What she says is correct. Your 'gentleman friend' will be receiving a summons from my father. He'd very much like to arrange a marriage between Lord Grayson and one of my sisters. Alas, my sisters wanted a duke, but since there are none available, they'll have to settle for less. The Grayson title is a well-revered one even if the marquessate lacks funds. It seems Clem has her heart set already. Like an indulgent sister, Hen didn't fight her. She just declared Stanton was hers." He chuckled.

"Marriage?" It was the only thing she could summon to say. The idea that Grayson would marry one of the Portland sisters tied her insides into knots. Not to mention that her heart had stopped midbeat.

"Indeed." Portland looked over at the table where the others sat and smiled.

Grayson would be miserable with either of the sisters, but especially Lady Clementine. She was a spoiled young woman who skated on the edge of impropriety. Her only interest was keeping herself entertained.

When Portland turned his attention back to Beth, there was no smile. There was simply nothing, but an undeniable anger rose from him like smoke from an extinguished fire. There were embers of fury still burning.

Cillian had gathered his coat from the back of the room and walked their way. Portland extended his arm to stop him. "My good man, if you'll allow me to finish my conversation with Miss Howell in private." Without waiting for the valet's reply, he continued with his voice almost a whisper, "May I suggest whatever your relationship is with Grayson, you finish it quickly and quietly. If you marry Siddleton, I don't care what you do. But if you marry me, I expect fidelity. If Grayson marries Clem, I won't tolerate him keeping you as a mistress."

"I'm not going to marry Siddleton or you, and I'm not Grayson's mistress," she hissed. "To suggest otherwise is another insult."

"I suppose you want another apology. I thought I'd heard that you were sharing a room last night." He leaned closer and lowered his voice. "Be that as it may, this so-called nonsense will be relayed to your brother as soon as I arrive in London. I heard that Siddleton might pursue another. Marry him and save us all any additional grief. Including me and your brother."

Without another word, he left to join his sisters and the others.

"My lady, is everything all right?" Cillian asked, as his eyes followed Portland.

"I don't know." Why did it seem the entire bottom of the world had fallen away and she was tumbling with no direction?

For the first time ever, she realized she was going to lose Julian. For years, he had been in her life whether it was in her dreams or in her memories. When she'd befriended Kat and Constance, Julian had appeared again. It had been easy to hold her anger against him, but now he offered comfort. She'd even admit to experiencing excitement when she was with him.

His warning that they couldn't be friends if he married another stole her breath.

"You look as if you've seen a ghost." Cillian swept his hand for her to precede him. "Let's find the marquess."

She blinked, then somehow found the energy to nod in agreement.

It was a ghost from her past that wouldn't leave her be.

Chapter Fourteen

⌒

For thirty minutes, Grayson had walked the grounds outside the Jolly Rooster, desperate to contain the ire that still simmered. Without a doubt, if he came face-to-face with Montague Portland he'd punch the bastard in the mouth.

Grayson was more than annoyed with the nuances and slight insults that Portland directed at Beth. No one would demean her for the circumstances of her life. He rubbed his arm where Beth had touched him. It felt as if she'd branded him. In that moment, all he could think about was her touch and her desire for him to stand down.

"Grayson," a voice called out.

Julian lifted his gaze to see the duke approaching.

"Morning," the duke announced. "Not good or bad, just stating the obvious."

"Indeed," Grayson agreed. The shadows under Pelham's eyes revealed that the duke had little sleep last night. "Did you enjoy your evening?"

The duke grunted. "It was acceptable. Those pups who came in last night aren't deep enough in the pockets for me." Looking down, the duke took his walking stick and slapped his boot. "One of my footmen informed me of that Portland incident."

Grayson took a steadying breath as his anger threatened to erupt again. "I'll not allow anyone to insult Miss Howell. What he said to her was despicable."

The duke held up his hand. "I agree. If it was one of my sisters, I'd have blown his head off. But Miss Howell isn't one of your sisters, is she?"

Grayson lifted an eyebrow at the quiet, but nevertheless didactic, tone. "We both know the answer to that."

"May I be blunt?" the duke asked, then proceeded without Grayson answering, "I don't care what you and Beth Howell are up to. But this is my playground. I don't want her brother storming in here and upsetting what I've created."

"What you've created is a rural gambling hell that's trying to mimic the ones that are in London."

He smiled gleefully. "I know, and it's mine." He suddenly turned serious. "I told Portland to stay clear of you. Now, what are your plans?"

"I suppose we go back to London." Grayson shrugged. "Miss Howell was hoping to discover more of Meriwether's travels after he left here."

"Hmm." The duke's gaze traveled down the small cobbled street in front of them. "I suggest you pack your carriage and, on the way out of town, stop at the haberdashery."

"Why?" Grayson didn't hide the hint of distrust in his voice. Though a reliable friend, Pelham had always been a little misguided.

"Remember the puzzle boxes I told you about?"

Grayson nodded.

"The reason Lord Meri left was that he was run out of the inn. That night, my guests didn't appreciate his long winning streak at the tables. They all thought he was cheating." The duke studied the ground as if debating whether to finish his thoughts, then lifted his gaze to Julian.

"Was he?"

The duke shrugged. "I have no idea, but I doubt it. My dealers come from London. They've seen it all and would have alerted me if something foul was occurring. I think the man was on a winning streak. Luck deserted him on his midnight steeplechase when he drowned in that mud puddle." The duke sighed gently. "Anyway, the old boy stopped at the shop on the way out of town. He bought a couple of puzzle boxes. Perhaps the proprietor knows where he was headed or what his plans were."

"Thank you. I'll inform Miss Howell."

"Good," the duke said. He pulled something out of his coat. "I've had this in the pocket of my waistcoat since I broke my fast. It came from London this morning via special delivery."

Grayson took the sealed missive. His title was written on the front. From the seal, he could tell it was from Sir Jeffrey. He tore open the letter, then cursed softly when he read the contents.

"Trouble?" Pelham asked.

Grayson sighed. It was the worst type of trouble. The consortium wanted to move up their date for evaluating his engine. They wanted to meet with him a week earlier. "I have a business appointment that the parties want to move."

"The consortium?" Pelham asked.

"How do you know?"

"There's not much in London that escapes my notice." The duke chuckled. "I put a little money into their projects."

Grayson could see in his eyes that Pelham was telling the truth. He might seem like an arrogant, privileged fop, but his eyes held a gleam that betrayed his intelligence and his rare ability to ferret out what was taking place around him.

"Are you investing in my project?"

The duke shrugged. "I can't tell you. They sell shares of investments, and I always throw money into it every month. I even invest a bit for my sisters. That's one of the reasons why their dowries are so large." His eyes widened. "Might you be interested in one of them? For marriage, I mean."

Grayson took a step back. This came from out of the clear blue. Never had he and Pelham discussed such an undertaking. "I'm sure they're amiable." He struggled with what to say next.

The duke smirked. "No, they are not. Never have you met such opinionated, boisterous, and clever women in your life. However, they're an acquired taste." He patted Grayson on the back. "Just think about it. You might need an heiress one day. You'd be an excellent match."

"I appreciate your good opinion of me," Grayson answered.

"It takes a special man to take on one of my siblings. One who has patience and fortitude," the duke confided. "What occurred in there with Portland and Miss Howell required the patience of Job."

"I try not to act in haste," Grayson agreed.

"Except with Miss Howell?" The duke shook his head. "It's not my business."

Grayson nodded toward the inn. "I need to write a response. May I ask if one of your footmen could deliver it?"

Pelham nodded. "I have one leaving within the hour to secure some new fashion plates my sisters want. He could deliver your note while he's there."

The sentimental look on the duke's face revealed more than he probably wanted Grayson to know. "There's not much you wouldn't do for your sisters."

A sheepish smile graced the duke's face. "I'd do anything for my sisters except let them step foot in London without me."

Before Grayson could ask more, the duke turned on his heel, then strolled away.

Grayson watched him retreat, then reread the letter.

It was a good thing that they would be returning to London soon. The consortium's request didn't give him much time to prepare for the demonstration, but he'd make it work somehow. There was no mention of capital. He'd needed to tell Beth his plans. By his calculations, he could afford another week of travel before he had to return to London.

Perhaps his fortune was finally changing.

~

Beth stood outside the courtyard in front of the carriage with her travel bag beside her. She couldn't shake the melancholy that hung around her. Of course it was Portland and the fact that he'd said that Lady Clementine wanted Grayson as her husband. Such a thought nibbled away at her optimism like a mouse stealing food.

She couldn't think of Grayson as hers. Not now. Not after she told him she wouldn't marry him. Yet the idea of him being with anyone else was inconceivable.

It didn't help matters that the leads to where Meriwether had traveled next were nonexistent. Outside of Kingsclere and his visit to the Jolly Rooster, it was as if he'd disappeared into thin air until he landed in Perth, one of the last places he visited.

The door to the inn opened, and Grayson strolled into the sunlight. Its rays kissed the top of his dark hair as if favoring him out of all the men in the courtyard.

She'd always seen him as someone special too.

He came to stand beside her. "You must forgive my outburst in there. I would never make you feel uncomfortable or fearful of my presence. But I cannot tolerate anyone insulting you or your good virtue."

"It's all right." She placed her hand on his arm much like she did when he was confronting Portland. Only this time it wasn't to dissuade him from his actions, but to give comfort. The lines around his eyes betrayed his lingering anger. "I'm not offended by what you said in there. It's the first time that anyone has ever bothered to uphold my so-called honor. I quite liked it."

His eyes narrowed as if he wasn't pleased with her answer. "That's a shame, Beth."

"Well, you can't blame people for wanting little to do with me or thinking that I'm ruined."

"I can blame them for being small-minded and without a conscience." He lowered his voice even though the entire courtyard was abustle with carriages, horses, and groomsmen.

It made this moment intimate in a way she'd never experienced before. He stood so close that all she could see was him. Slowly, she lifted her gaze to his.

"I've never seen a person more honorable and noble than you. You proved it by keeping your head high even though the circumstances you were dealt would have felled a lesser person."

She rolled her eyes to keep from exposing how his words wrapped around her heart and squeezed, stealing her breath for a moment. "Besides my dear Kat and Constance, no one understands what my marriage to Meri and his subsequent leaving did to me." She studied her half boots peeking out from underneath her gown. "I'm rebuilding myself or at least trying to. I don't know if I'll recognize who I am when I'm finished."

"I'll recognize you," he said softly. "No matter how you change, I'll know your heart."

She blinked, unable to form a response. It was the most romantic thing anyone had ever said to her.

"Tell me about this rebuilding yourself?" he asked.

A heat swept across her cheeks. "It's nothing really."

"Tell me," he coaxed.

"It's just a dream." She grinned. "But if I find my dowry, perhaps I'll create a school or an institute for women like me."

"What do you mean, like you?" His brow furrowed.

"Women who lost their place in the world but still have a desire to be respectable. I want them to learn a trade so that they can make a decent living and not have to worry about being ignored for the rest of their life and dependent on their extended families. Perhaps they can open a school or a business." She shrugged. "Start a newspaper."

Why was she telling him all of this? She hadn't even told Kat or Constance about her whimsy for fear they'd insist on funding it for her. If she did find her money, she'd do it herself and prove that others' opinions didn't define a person.

"Beth, I admire you."

The tenderness in his voice and gaze stole her breath. She blinked to wrestle her unruly emotions under control.

"Shall we depart?" she said before she made a fool out of herself and tried to kiss him.

Grayson picked up her bag and stowed it inside the carriage.

"By the way, where are we going?" she asked. "London?"

"To the haberdashery. I'm in the mood to see some puzzle boxes." He held out her hand and helped her into the carriage. It dipped when he entered behind her. Cillian clucked at the team driving them, and the carriage lurched into motion. "Pelham suggested we stop since Meriwether frequented the shop when he was staying at the inn." Grayson glanced out the window, then turned his gaze to hers. "Portland was staring at us the entire time. Has he always had a fascination with you?"

She shook her head. "It's St. John he believes is fascinating. My brother possesses a cadre of friends who would do anything for him. Such loyalty comes from my brother's knowledge of horses and horseraces. Portland considers my brother one of his closest friends. I'm sure they've discussed my situation numerous times. If Lord Siddleton doesn't marry me, Portland told St. John he would." She lifted a brow. "In exchange for half of his stables, Portland will give him a nice settlement."

"Portland?" His lips thinned, and she felt the same irritability. "He asked for your hand in marriage, then treated you . . ."

"Disrespectfully?" She shrugged. "He hasn't asked, and he means nothing to me."

She didn't belabor the point that Monty Portland shared that a possible marriage proposal was coming Julian's way if Clementine Portland's father had his way. The Portland family was rich and could offer Julian money in rebuilding his marquessate. It was too ghastly to even contemplate he would marry someday. Not that Clementine couldn't be a good wife. She seemed pleasant enough when she wasn't insulting Beth, but this was Julian.

Her Julian.

By then, Cillian pulled the team to a stop in front of the last shops in the village. He opened the door. Grayson stepped down with an elegance that few men had, then lifted his hand, offering her assistance.

They walked to the front door of the shop. When Grayson opened it, a merry bell tinkled in excitement announcing their arrival.

A middle-aged man looked up from the books on his counter. "Welcome. How can I help you today, sir?" He nodded Beth's way. "Madame."

"Good morning. I'm a friend of the Duke of Pelham's, and he suggested we stop here."

"I'm Ian Bingley. And you are?" Mr. Bingley came around the table to stand beside them.

"The Marquess of Grayson." He nodded in Beth's direction. "Miss Howell."

Bingley narrowed his eyes as he looked at Beth. She knew the exact second when he'd recognized her name.

She swallowed, then forced herself to respond. "It's a pleasure to meet you, Mr. Bingley."

"Miss Howell." The man kindly smiled. "I'm so sorry for your loss."

"Thank you," she said softly. It wouldn't be considered good *ton* to ask if he referred to the loss of her "husband" or her reputation. "We're looking for information regarding Lord Meriwether."

Grayson nodded. "According to the duke, he shopped here the last time he was at the Jolly Rooster."

Mr. Bingley turned his attention to Grayson. "My lord, I remember the day Lord Meriwether shopped here as if it were yesterday." The man chuckled slightly as he turned to Beth. "It looked like a traveling menagerie. He'd won that famous racehorse . . ."

"Poison Blossom?" Beth offered.

"Yes, that's the one." Mr. Bingley shook his head. "And he had that pig with him." He turned to Julian. "Such a unique man. When Lord Meriwether first walked into my shop, he became fascinated with the puzzle boxes. They're exquisite, but expensive because of all the carving and inlaid craftsmanship." He took them to a table where ten boxes of various shapes and sizes were displayed. Mr. Bingley picked one up and handed it to Julian. "Open it."

Grayson took it, then turned it over in his large hands examining it like he would one of his steam engines. He looked to Mr. Bingley and smiled. "It's this lever here." He showed a side of the box where a small indention was. It was hidden by the exquisite mother-of-pearl overlay and carving that covered the entire box.

"Press it." Mr. Bingley waved a finger at the lever.

Grayson caught Beth's gaze, and with his eyebrows lifted he pressed the button. Instantly, a drawer in the bottom of the box slid open.

"That's one of the easier ones. I always recommend those for the children." Mr. Bingley picked up another one, then gave it to Beth. "You try, Miss Howell."

Beth carefully examined the box. "My father gave me one of these for my birthday."

She turned the box in her hand over, then examined each side. With a smile, she found what she was looking for. She showed the hidden lever to Julian. Instead of pushing a button like Grayson did with his box, Beth pulled the lever. A drawer popped open on hers.

"Clever." Grayson leaned over to study the box. "But what's in the rest of the box?"

"Yes, please show us." Beth smiled at Mr. Bingley. "I've only been able to open one compartment in the box my father gave me."

Funny how when she was with Julian she smiled more with strangers.

Mr. Bingley took the box from her, then turned it upside down. On the outer lip, which had been hidden by the closed drawer, was another button. He pressed it, and a lid popped open, revealing a large space inside. "This is one of the simpler ones. Some of them are like moving pieces that you have to twist and put in the right place, or they won't open." He handed the box back to Beth. "Is this like yours?"

Beth nodded.

"Well, open yours and see if yours has a button release on the bottom. If you're ever in this direction again, bring yours to me, and we'll see if we can figure it out." He rocked back on his heels. "I've seen just about all of the varieties."

"Thank you, sir." Beth looked at the box once more, then handed it to him. "Did Lord Meriwether share anything else with you besides his love of puzzle boxes? Or about the pig?"

"Oh, the pig. I forgot." He chuckled. "The night before Lord Meriwether came to the shop, there was a loud argument outside the duke's inn. It was Meriwether and another man who thought he'd cheated to win Poison Blossom. The man thought he'd have won the horse if Lord Meri hadn't played. Then the man proclaimed he wanted satisfaction."

Beth's hand flew to her chest. "A duel?"

"Lord Meriwether called his bluff and shouted he'd be more than happy to give the man satisfaction. Immediately, the other man backed down."

"Who was it?" Grayson asked.

"I don't know."

"What happened to the pig?" Beth asked.

The man chuckled. "I have the pig. Lord Meriwether gave it to me the last time he was here for safekeeping. He couldn't travel with it and the horse. Poison Blossom was rather a moody mare. She didn't like sharing the road with others. That's what makes her a great racehorse."

Beth wanted to sigh. Seems every human male was an expert on the requirements for a successful racehorse. "She *was* a great racehorse. She foaled not too long ago. The Duke of Randford has retired her."

The man looked crestfallen, but then his face brightened. "Will the duke race her offspring?"

"I don't know, sir," Beth answered. "But can you tell us more about the pig? Did Meriwether say who it was for?"

He shook his head. "No, he didn't. Do you want it?"

Beth shook her head. "I think you should write the Duchess of Randford. Lord Meriwether bequeathed her a pig. Perhaps she'd want it."

"Pelham said that Meri won a mineral lease from the Marquess of Montridge. Do you know if he won anything else that night?"

"I believe he won something from Mr. Portland, or was it Lord Stanton?" Mr. Bingley tapped his chin. He shrugged, then picked up a journal, not seeing the glance the two of them shared. "This is where I keep all the invoices from previous purchases." He thumbed through the journal until he found the page he was looking for. "The second to last time that Lord Meriwether shopped here, he bought three puzzle boxes that day, a new morning coat, two shirts, and a velvet brocade waistcoat. It was one of my most successful days ever."

"Did he purchase anything the last time?" Grayson asked.

"Clothing and two satchels. Said he needed to keep his affairs in order." Mr. Bingley crossed his arms over his chest.

Strange to hear of Meri's last travels and what he'd purchased. Perhaps he had another home or, God forbid, another wife. All the information Mr. Bingley shared had to do with Kat and Constance. There was nothing here for her, it appeared.

Why was she not surprised?

"Did he say where he was going?" Beth asked. She placed one hand behind her back and crossed her fingers. *Please give me another destination. Please.*

"Bath."

"Bath?" Beth couldn't keep the incredulity out of her voice. Meriwether would never be caught in such a place. Only the infirmed patrons and matrons of society visited Bath anymore. Since the Prince Regent quit visiting regularly, Bath's popularity had waned.

"Bath." Mr. Bingley nodded. "He'd received an invitation to gamble with some merchant types and a marquess with new money." He chuckled slightly. "Plus, they wanted Meriwether there to give them an air of society." He scratched his head. "Some people are never satisfied with who they are."

"Do you have any names?" Grayson asked.

"There was a Farnsworth and Tidwell." Mr. Bingley nodded, then shrugged his shoulders. "I'm sure anyone in Bath would know who they are. Made their fortunes from coal and iron ore mines."

Beth's heart beat a little faster at the news. Her trail wasn't cold yet. She could travel to Bath in less than a day.

"We're continuing to Bath." Julian caught her gaze and that wicked half smile of his appeared.

Her stomach fluttered in answer, but the rest of her

sighed in relief. Perhaps he was a man who kept his promises.

Julian turned to Mr. Bingley. "Can you remember anything else?"

"No, sir," Mr. Bingley stated.

They exchanged goodbyes, and just as Julian held open the door for Beth the shopkeeper called out, "Sir?"

Beth and Julian turned around.

"The Marquess of Montridge. Lord Meri said he'd call on him."

"Thank you," Beth answered.

"Let's be on our way." Julian donned his hat as soon as they were outside. "For some reason, a Roman bath sounds quite refreshing."

Chapter Fifteen

~⌒~

Julian tried to work on sketching a new drawing of a larger compound engine but kept stealing glances Beth's way. She was busy embroidering a piece of odd-shaped fabric. Trying to be considerate of her comfort, he sat on the rear-facing seat this time.

"What are you working on?" he asked.

"A gift for a friend."

"You have a lucky friend. Whatever it is, it's beautiful."

"Thank you." She blushed prettily. "It's a secret, or I'd tell you who it's for."

"Of course. All ladies must have their secrets." He turned his attention back to his work.

"Julian?"

He looked up from the journal where he'd been scribbling notes. "Hmm?"

"What are you working on?" She leaned close and peered at the book.

"A new engine." He turned the journal around so she could see his drawings.

She scooted across the bench and peered at his drawings. "You're talented. I've always admired that about you.

You come up with such ingenious designs and ideas. Tell me more." With such an expectant look on her face, she appeared to be waiting for him to respond.

He closed the book gently. "Do you really want to discuss steam engines?"

"I want to talk about what interests you." She looked out the window and frowned slightly. "Reading in the carriage has never been an agreeable pastime for me. I'm tired of sewing." She smiled sheepishly. "You must think of me as a spoiled child."

He rested his elbows on his thighs and regarded her. "On the contrary. You never throw tantrums, beg for candy, or insist upon sitting on my lap. Though the latter I would enjoy very much."

She burst out laughing. "Thank you for making me laugh. Sometimes, I'm too serious."

He winked. "We all are at times. I think you and I are similar. We can become lost in our work. Now, what's troubling you?"

She set aside her embroidery. "How did you know?"

"You're chewing on your lower lip." Driving him to distraction at the same time. He wanted to groan aloud when her tongue swept across the tender skin. With little effort, he could lean across the coach and kiss her until they both forgot what day it was.

Completely oblivious to his turmoil, she nodded. "I can't help but think about what happened at the inn. My outburst at Lady Clementine." She shook her head. "I'm angry at her brother and not her."

"There's no harm done. Lady Clementine didn't seem upset." He lowered his voice. "However, Portland is another matter."

She studied her gloves. "After you went outside, Portland

approached me. He warned me away from you as Lady Clementine has . . . Oh, this is ridiculous," she muttered.

Not to add any further worry to Beth's shoulders, he chose his words carefully. "Firstly, did he say anything to you that caused you concern?"

"Yes and no," she said softly.

"Tell me."

She stared at her embroidery for a moment, then turned her stalwart gaze his way. "He told me that whatever this was between us had to end this trip. As soon as you arrive back in London, their father is going to summon you."

"For what purpose?" Julian's mind went through all the possible scenarios. The earl couldn't be in the consortium, as his investments were mostly in financial instruments from everything that Julian had seen and heard. But perhaps the earl was looking for different investments. After all, Pelham had shocked him with the news that he invested with the group.

"Marriage." Beth straightened her back. "She has a significant dowry." She lifted her chin in defiance. "You're in possession of a noble title, and your estate is the most beautiful in Somerset. She looks at you much like the way a cook evaluates a piece of meat."

For a moment, all he could manage was a blink. Frankly, he was taken aback at how vehement she sounded. "Beth, I'm practically insolvent. Her father, the Earl of Foxthorp, has no interest in matching me with his daughter."

"Nonsense. Heiresses don't care," she sniffed. "They want titles. Since there are no dukes available, a marquess will do quite nicely for such purposes."

He bit his lip to keep from laughing. He'd never seen

her so riled. Her cheeks had colored into an extraordinary deep-pink flush.

"Don't laugh," she huffed. "A beautiful estate and your eligibility make you an outstanding marriage candidate. You must be careful."

Was that jealousy in her tone? It couldn't be. She'd made her position on marrying him plainly clear. She was simply looking out for his welfare. That's what friends did for one another.

Bloody hell. He didn't want to be friends anymore.

She appeared to be finished with the conversation, as she scooted to the far side of the bench to better see out the window.

He studied her profile. She was such a strong, confident woman and always had been. When they'd first been introduced, she'd asked about his interests and what he'd found enjoyable in London. When he'd answered, her gaze never left his. Her brother had interrupted their conversation and insisted that Beth leave with him. His judgmental glare was a sight Julian would never forget.

But she didn't leave. She politely told her brother she'd find him when she'd finished their conversation. Clearly dismissing him, she turned her attention back to Julian.

That was the moment he'd first fallen for her.

"I have a proposal for you."

She turned his way with a nonchalant look on her face. "What kind of a proposal?"

"I suppose it's more a favor." He presented his most earnest look. "Since I'm helping you find your fortune, you could give me lessons on how to woo a lady."

By the shocked look on her face, he'd completely taken her by surprise. That didn't happen often.

Suddenly, they hit a rut, and she bounced up in the air.

His arms shot out to grab her to keep her from falling.
When she landed, she grimaced.

"Beth." He searched her face. "Are you all right?"

She nodded.

"A thousand pardons," Cillian called from the coach
box. "It couldn't be helped. The rut took up half the
road."

"Understood," Julian answered as he studied her face.

"It's nothing," she said softly. Slowly, a grin appeared.

The entire mood between them shifted. He was on
alert ready to parry an attack, while she was ready to go
toe-to-toe with him. He could tell by the look on her face
that Beth Howell was dangerous when she was in this
mood.

"So now you want payment for accompanying me on
this trip. Tit for tat. Half my fortune isn't enough?"

She had a point. That sounded rather scandalous on
his part. What kind of an honorable man would demand
payment to help a friend? "Forget I said anything."

"Oh no." Her laughter followed, and the sound was
pure mischief. "I would very much like to pay you. I never
want to be in anyone's debt." The words were soft and
seductive. She lowered her eyes modestly, then lifted her
not-so-shy gaze to meet his. The slight smile on her lips
was sweeter than the first honey of spring. "Where would
you like to start? Perhaps the first thing in your wooing
lessons is to show a lady how grand your kisses can be
when you put your mind to it."

"Are you saying I need practice?" He lifted a finger to
brush it across the softness of her cheek when a sudden
dip threw them both up into the air, followed by an ex-
plosive crack. Instinctively, Julian grabbed her around
the waist as they succumbed to gravity and his body
slammed into the carriage seat.

He grappled with his breath after the air was knocked out of him.

"Julian?" Beth asked as she clung to him. "What was that?"

Until his lungs finally filled with air, he couldn't speak.

"Bloody hell," Cillian called out as the carriage wobbled to a slow halt.

The carriage lurched to the right side, tilting at an odd angle. Julian gulped in air. "Are you hurt?" he asked, his voice raspy.

"I'm fine," she answered. She scooted off his lap, and the carriage protested with a creak that sounded like a moan.

By then, Cillian opened the carriage door, and by the stark look on his face Julian knew the damage to the carriage was severe.

"Are either of you hurt?" The normal Irish lilt in his voice had become more pronounced.

"I'm not, but Lord Grayson took the brunt of the force of the accident," Beth volunteered.

Questioning, Cillian's gaze locked with his.

"No harm but a bruise or two."

"Julian? You didn't tell me that." She reached out to touch him. When she saw Cillian watching them, she drew her hand back swiftly. A deep flush colored her cheeks.

A thrill erupted in Julian's chest at the alarm in her voice, though his backside hurt like the devil.

"I'll get out first, then I'll help you," he said.

"Begging your pardon, I think Miss Howell should leave first." Cillian's gaze darted to the wheel, then back to Grayson. "If you're first out, it might tip over."

"That bad?" Quickly, he placed his hand over Beth's. Immediately, she covered his hand with her other one, then squeezed.

"You'll see for yourself shortly." Cillian lifted his arms. "Miss Howell, let his lordship lift you gently to me."

Julian put his hands around her waist, and she froze. "Don't squirm when I lift you. Otherwise, the entire carriage might fall on its side."

She nodded. When he went to lift her an inch off the seat, she hissed softly.

"Ticklish?" he asked.

She shook her head, then regarded him with a slight smile. "Something else."

He felt it too. That earth-shattering energy that seemed to swarm them when they were touching. Carefully, he lifted her to Cillian while balancing his body so there was minimal movement of the coach.

Within seconds, Beth was on the ground. Her eyes grew as big as dinner plates when the carriage tilted slightly toward her and Cillian.

"Beth, stand clear," Julian said.

"But—"

He shook his head. "No buts."

Cillian regarded her and nodded. "What Lord Grayson says is the safest for all of us."

With Julian's strength and speed along with Cillian's hand, Julian jumped to the ground with minimal movement of the carriage. He could hardly believe the sight before him. The wheel looked like it had been broken in two.

"Let's get the horses unhitched before a strong wind knocks it to the ground." He and Cillian freed the horses, attached leads, then led them to a copse of trees. In seconds, they were tied and munching on the sweet grass beneath their feet.

Beth joined the men. "Isn't there a coaching inn about ten miles down the road?"

"Yes," Julian answered, then turned to Cillian. "Why don't we ride the horses into town, and let the stablemaster come and get the coach?"

"There's no stablemaster," Cillian answered, wiping his brow with the arm of his jacket. "It's a small inn, but the innkeeper should know of some farmers who would help us for a coin or two. I'm going to take a closer look at the wheel."

As Cillian walked back to the carriage, Beth announced, "I'm not riding one of those."

Julian slowly turned his attention to her. All the color had drained from her face. "Why is that?"

"I hate horses . . . unless they're tied to the coach."

He leaned closer. "You hate horses?"

She nodded brusquely. "I'm not riding one. Certainly not without a saddle."

"But your brother owns an impressive stable of racehorses. You used to help him with the finances of his hobby."

One of her perfectly arched brows lifted. "I didn't do the bookkeeping riding a horse."

"I thought you were comfortable with the animals."

She continued to stare at him as if he'd turned into a full-fledged ass in front of her.

"I've an excellent seat. You can ride in front of me on one of the horses."

"I'll stay with the carriage," she announced as if it were a foregone conclusion. "Someone needs to guard it."

"Deuced bad timing for this revelation, Beth." He swept a hand down his face. "Perhaps we should have taken a different road." He delivered a sly grin. "If you'd have stayed in that tent with the fortune-teller, perhaps she could have warned us about this."

"You think she could have planned our itinerary

better than I did?" Beth rolled her eyes. "For a man of science, you have some undeniable quirks."

"And you are one of them," he parried.

By then, Cillian motioned him to follow.

"If you'll excuse me for a moment." Grayson left her there and met his valet at the carriage.

"Examine the wheel." Cillian stood to the side.

Julian rested on his haunches and ran a hand over the back of the wheel. It had been cracked in two pieces down the middle as if some giant had taken it in their hands, then broken it apart like a biscuit ready to dunk in a cup of tea. Julian tilted his gaze to his servant.

"Are you thinking what I'm thinking?" Cillian said in a low voice so Beth couldn't hear.

"Someone sabotaged our carriage." Grayson returned to study the wheel once again.

"That's what I reckon as well." Cillian took off his hat and wiped his brow on his sleeve.

Grayson lay on his back and scooted under the carriage body to examine it closer. It'd been chopped with an ax or weapon of some type, making the wood too weak to tolerate a rut-ravaged road. He turned his gaze to Cillian. "Did you see anyone near the carriage?"

He shook his head, then put on his hat. "I didn't even think to check the wheels before we left. We were at the Duke of Pelham's inn."

Though Pelham was a trifle irritating and obnoxious about his guests, he'd never tolerate such dangerous behavior.

"We could have been injured or worse." Grayson looked at Beth. The thought that she could have been seriously hurt made his chest ache. "Why don't you take a horse and ride to the inn and see if you can find us some help."

Careful not to tip the carriage, he reached inside and opened the compartment where he kept his pistol. Quietly, he stuck it behind his back. He didn't want Beth to see it and worry. But Julian would do his best to protect her.

"I'll try and convince her to ride with me, but for some reason she's adamant about not getting on a horse."

"I'll inquire if they have another carriage to let, then come back for you." Cillian walked to one of the horses, untied it, then swung onto its back with little effort. With a wave of his hat, he was off.

Beth stood far enough from the horses that Julian could tell she was wary of them. Even the slightest flick of their tails or a shifting of their weight, she'd look their way, then back up a couple of steps.

As Grayson walked toward her, he purposely patted the three remaining horses on their shanks. Perhaps if he showed her that they were gentle beasts she'd relent and ride to the inn.

"They're very docile. I don't think we'd have much trouble riding them." He stopped next to her and pointed to the carriage. "Cillian can return for our things."

Before the last words quieted, she was shaking her head. "You go ahead. I'll stay here. If you leave now, you should be back in three hours, give or take."

"Beth, I'm not leaving you alone." He looked around the sloping hills and the small glen about a quarter of a mile away. There were perfect hiding places for highwaymen, robbers, or other more dangerous sorts to hide. "What if someone came upon you?"

"I have a pistol." Beth opened her reticule and pulled out a small firearm that fit in the palm of her hand. "Once when I was visiting Constance and Jonathan, he gave it to me." She tilted her chin in a manner meant to exhibit her bravery, confidence, and independence. "I'll be perfectly fine."

It still didn't sway him. There was a hint of fear lurking in her blue eyes.

"Well, you can protect me then. I'm not leaving you."

Chapter Sixteen

❧

After two hours of sitting in the hot sun, Beth was willing to give one of the horses a go. The two black geldings that kept slipping her the evil eye were definitely out of the race. However, the calm bay mare might be worth the trouble and anxiety.

Julian wiped the sheen of sweat from his brow. "Why is it that you hate horses?"

"It's not that I hate horses. I just don't trust them." She shielded her eyes and looked in his direction. The marquess looked as tired and parched as she felt. "Not after St. John's favorite racehorse, Saltpeter, bit the skin underneath my arm."

Julian winced as she showed him where the scar was. Of course, the long sleeve of her dress covered the hideous sight. "I have that scar to this day because of that fiend."

"I assume you're speaking of your brother?" Julian asked innocently.

For a flash of a second, she was about to defend St. John. Her gaze wandered before it landed on the carriage. Then the absurdity of their situation hit her full force. In the middle of nowhere, she was stranded on the side of the road with a man who happened to be her friend. The truth? She considered him a best friend.

And it was all St. John's and Meriwether's fault. If her brother had been looking out for her welfare and sent Meriwether on his way, she'd still have her dowry. But the truth was if she still had her dowry then she wouldn't have met Constance and Kat, her other best friends in the world.

Nor would she be on this trip.

Nor would she be having this exact moment in time with Julian.

A grin tugged at her mouth, then turned into a snicker. Who on God's green earth would have thought she'd be thankful for marrying that lout of a trigamist, Meriwether? Or thankful her brother had convinced her to marry Meriwether? Before she knew it, she was laughing so hard, she couldn't catch her breath and her stomach muscles protested.

When Julian's deep baritone laugh joined hers, it made the moment sweeter.

It could have been seconds, minutes, or even hours, but they shared their laughter with each other. Finally, their merriment died, and she wiped the tears from her eyes. "I believe that's the first time I've ever cried because of laughter." A lone giggle escaped, not wanting to miss the silliness of the moment.

"What caused all that?" Julian asked.

With the smile on his face, and the lazy way he leaned against the tree with one leg bent, he reminded her of the man who'd once asked her to marry him all those years ago. She'd always thought him attractive then, but in this moment, he was more. He was her confidant. As she drank in the sight of him, she realized something: If one was lucky in their life, they experienced moments with another person that would never be forgotten. Such events were rare.

Just like now.

Just like when he asked her to share his life with him all those years ago.

She released a deep sigh. "St. John didn't warn me that the finicky horse disliked having his ears touched. So, all of this"—she waved one arm out in front of her—"being stranded on the side of the road is because of Saltpeter." She turned toward Julian. "And I'm having the time of my life. I've never felt so alive as I have since we started on this adventure together." Suddenly unable to look at him for fear he'd see everything she truly desired, she looked at her lap as she twisted her fingers together.

What she wanted was for this never to end. She wasn't Blythe Elizabeth Howell, the ruined heiress who'd lost her fortune. She was simply Beth enjoying a perfect moment with him. *Best friend* wasn't an adequate description of Julian. He was so much more than that.

"Beth, what are you thinking?"

"About our rabbit family and the stories you'd tell me when you called on me."

He narrowed his eyes. "The rabbit family?"

She leaned forward and peeked at him. "When we first went for a walk in Hyde Park and we found a nest of bunnies there."

Smiling, he tilted his head back and closed his eyes. "You always enjoyed hearing about Mr. and Mrs. Hare and their brood, didn't you?"

"I couldn't wait for you to come see me. You were always so animated. I'll never forget their proposal. You came into the sitting room with the biggest grin on your face. 'Beth, you'll never guess what Bonnie did today. She has a beau and he kissed her in broad daylight. I think a proposal is coming.'" She sighed in pleasure. "You told such grand stories about them exploring Hyde Park.

You named them, remember?" She didn't wait for him to answer. The memories rushed through her thoughts. "Joshua and Edna were the parents. Beatrice, Bonnie, and Bertram." She shook her head. "Did Bonnie's beau ever propose, you suppose?"

There was laughter sparkling in his eyes, until it transformed right before her. His gaze grew incredibly tender, signaling that something momentous was about to happen. "Yes. They lived happily ever after. The wedding made all the hare society papers."

"I would have liked to have seen that," she said wistfully. "It was everything she always wanted with him."

Her heart pounded against her ribs in a rhythm, moving faster and faster to reach him. Always before, she'd tell herself to remain calm and not show how much he could affect her. But it was a losing battle.

"Thank you. This day, this trip, all of it is . . . something I'll never forget. Just like that rabbit family. Nor will I forget what you did for me at the Jolly Rooster. Thank you for thinking I'm worth defending."

"I know your worth. I consider you priceless," he said softly. The velvet-edged strength in his voice sent prickles of awareness through her. His words forever etched across her heart.

Suddenly, the air around them changed. They seemed locked in place. She couldn't move and neither did he. Somehow, he broke through the invisible barrier that kept them apart, then leaned close. She found the sudden strength to do the same. He studied her face until he reached her lips. His parted ever so slightly.

She parted hers in answer, then stared at him. His eyes slowly closed as he leaned forward and brushed his lips against hers. Her unruly body trembled as she closed her eyes.

Another moment to remember. They'd kissed before, but there was a newness about this one that was unrecognizable. *A tentativeness* might be a better description. The one they'd shared before had an ending. For some reason, this felt like a beginning where they unfurled all their deeply held feelings and wants that tied them together but were never exposed to the light of day.

He cupped her cheek with such tenderness that she felt treasured. She'd best be careful, as his lips worshiping hers was totally addictive. When his tongue licked her lips, she moaned at the overwhelming sense of perfection between them.

This was another moment to remember. Whatever he wanted she was prepared to give—but only to him. Frankly, if she ever trusted a man with her body, it would be Julian.

She might even trust him with more.

"Beth." The whisper of her name on his lips was a plea, a sweet one at that. Or perhaps it was a call to surrender.

Either was fine with her.

Before she could answer, a hauntingly eerie sound reached them. Before Beth could turn and discover where it came from, a moan reached a crescendo before turning into an earthshaking crash.

Her hand flew to her chest as the carriage fell on its side.

But it was the sight on the other side of the overturned carriage that caused her heartbeat to explode in her chest.

A man stood on the other side with a smile. She would have thought it an ordinarily friendly smile.

Except he held a pistol in his hand pointed straight at them.

"Don't say a word, and stay behind me." Grayson stood slowly and she did the same.

Of course she wouldn't stay behind him. He'd not

become a sacrificial lamb—or ram, as the case may be—on her behalf. She stayed next to his side so she could see.

The man strolled toward them. From a distance, he looked young and well-dressed. He wore a fitted blue morning coat, a matching waistcoat, and buckskin breeches.

Yet as he closed the distance between them, the façade faded. He had to be in his forties, as his long black hair was peppered with gray. His clothing wasn't as fine as she'd once thought. His appearance could only be described as disheveled and dusty, as if he'd ridden on horseback for days. His boots were covered with dried mud.

When he reached them, he continued to point the pistol, but he dipped a bow as if possessing the manners of the gentleman. "Cameron Cochran at your service."

"There's no need for a pistol." Grayson's voice had deepened until it reminded her of a growl.

"Probably not. But I've always prided myself on my sense of preparedness." He turned his attention to Beth but kept his pistol trained on Grayson. "Ma'am."

Beth stood still.

Mr. Cochran motioned to the carriage. "You must not have heard me approach since you were occupied." He chuckled softly. "Ah, there's nothing like lovebirds to while away a summer's day."

She slid a sideways glance at Julian. Though his face was expressionless, she could see the wariness in his narrowed eyes.

"Beth, behind me," he said without looking at her.

Beth did as Julian instructed. With any luck, he would keep the highwayman busy as she opened her reticule and pulled out her pistol.

"Do you always heed his commands?" Mr. Cochran asked as his gaze never left Julian's. "My missus would have my head if I talked to her like that."

"And what way would that be, Mr. Cochran?" She peeked around Julian's left side. If she could keep the man engaged, it was highly unlikely he would notice her rifling through her reticule.

"Ordering you about as if you're a child or a dog?" He turned his gaze to hers and smiled. "Now, ma'am, if you're thinking you can hide whatever is in that bag of yours, I can assure you that I'll find out for myself what's in there."

"Are you a thief, Mr. Cochran?" she asked.

Mr. Cochran laughed. "I like to consider myself a man of honor who borrows things. At least, that's what I tell my wife." He shook his head, the affection clear in his eyes. "I'd do anything for her."

"Even steal?" she asked.

"Yes," he said curtly. "Anything and everything to keep her safe and happy. Keep her belly full so she'll laugh." His voice grew faint. He shook his head as if trying to brush off the emotion. "It's my job to care for her, and I'll do it any way possible."

The anguish was clear in his voice. This man had experienced hardship in his life. Hunger and more, she'd wager. "I'm sorry," she said softly.

That snapped him out of his sorrow. "I don't need your sympathy." He threw a thumb toward the road. "My men will be here soon. Five strong lads who'll be coming up the road any minute now." He looked Beth up and down. "It's a shame you're married to him." He flicked the pistol in Julian's direction. "One of my men is looking for a biddable wife."

"I don't believe the law looks favorably on a woman having two husbands." By then, she had her pistol in her hand. "Wouldn't you agree?"

"Indeed," Mr. Cochran said, holding out his hand that didn't hold the pistol. "Give me your bag."

Was this the moment she should shoot him? Or wait until he opened the reticule to see what was inside? When Sykeston had taught her how to load and shoot a pistol, they never discussed how best to surprise someone. For the love of heaven, she was considering shooting the man. She'd never shot anything besides a target in her life.

"Ma'am, my patience isn't long for this world," Mr. Cochran said.

Her fingers tightened on the strings of her reticle. All her money was in that bag except for the five guineas she had tied around her waist in a pouch. It was her emergency fund. Her governess had instructed her to always keep some money hidden. She'd always said that a woman didn't know when some mild disaster would strike.

This qualified as a disaster of epic proportions.

"Beth, perhaps you should give it to him," Grayson murmured.

She sighed her reluctance.

"Yes, *Beth*, give it to me," Mr. Cochran mimicked.

What happened in the next second was something straight out of a gothic novel. She threw the reticule at Mr. Cochran's feet and pointed her pistol as he bent down to pick it up. Julian reached behind his black morning coat and pulled out his pistol.

Both pointed the weapons at Mr. Cochran's head.

In that moment, all sound hushed. The birds calling for their mates quieted. The wind stilled.

None of them moved.

"Well, this is awkward," Mr. Cochran said charmingly with a smile. Slowly, he rose, leaving her reticule on the ground but keeping his gun pointed on Julian. "Ma'am, perhaps it would be best if you'd drop your weapon before I shoot your husband."

"Why would she do that?" Julian asked, pulling the striker back on his gun. "You're the one at a disadvantage."

She did the same, slowly easing the striker back with her thumb as Sykeston had taught her.

Mr. Cochran shrugged, then slowly turned the pistol on Beth.

Her breath hitched loud enough that everyone heard it.

This time, the robber's good humor had completely disappeared. "If you don't drop your weapon, I'll shoot her. I swear I will. I've done it before."

"Leave her be." Julian inched ever closer to her side. "I'll put mine on the ground. Promise me that you won't hurt her."

"You're really not in a position to ask for such." Cochran's gaze flitted back and forth between the two of them.

"What do you want? We have no jewels and not much money," Julian asked. He still pointed the gun at the robber.

"Your carriage is mighty fancy to claim that you don't have any money or jewels." He eyed Beth's person. "She doesn't have any jewels, but that pin in your neckcloth might bring enough for a meal." He sighed. "I don't have all day to dally with the two of you. Put the pistols down."

At the change in the thief's demeanor, Julian nodded, then slowly knelt to the ground, where he laid his pistol. "Beth, I think it best to do as he says."

Julian stood so near that she could sense the shift of his body, the tension increasing all around them.

Slowly, she stepped out of his reach. Whether it was instinct or to draw Mr. Cochran's attention to her, she couldn't rightly say. Perhaps it was simply that she wanted to make her own decisions.

"Beth," they both said at the same time.

"I know what I'm doing, Julian," she said with an awakening bravado that surprised even herself. "I'm going to shoot that pistol out of his hand, then we can all get on with our day." When the thief started to laugh, her back stiffened, but she didn't take her gaze from his. "This is your last chance, Mr. Cochran."

"You'll miss, then what will happen?" Cochran warned.

"I will not," Beth argued.

"You will. Those small pistols are notoriously unreliable." Cochran shrugged slightly. "I hate to be uncivil. But if I even see you twitch a finger, I'll shoot you."

"Not if I shoot you first," she said. Never in her entire life could she have imagined being in this position. The rush of energy and excitement through her entire body heightened every sense. She could hear the wind humming through the trees. The air was sweeter and the feel of the sun on her skin seemed hotter.

She faced death's door, and she'd never felt so alive.

"Beth, it's not worth it." Julian's voice sounded raw. "Let him have whatever he wants and be done with it."

"Listen to your husband." Sweat dotted Cochran's brow. He was nervous.

Or perhaps it was the heat. Either way, she'd see this through.

"I beg of you, do as I ask," Julian implored with a hint of exasperation in his tone.

"Don't worry. I'm an excellent shot. Sykeston said so."

"The Earl of Sykeston?" Cochran asked.

She nodded slightly. "He's the one who taught me to shoot. I assume you know that he's a marksman." The pride in her voice was unmistakable.

"Well, that sheds a different light on our situation." Cochran narrowed his eyes as if seeing her for the first time.

"It looks like the same light to me," Julian countered.

Completely ignoring Julian, Cochran chuckled, but his steely gaze was solely locked on Beth. "I wager you're not a marksman."

"You have no knowledge whether I'm a marksman or not," she said curtly. "Let me correct you. I am."

"With targets?" Cochran arched an eyebrow.

Beth answered with her own arched brow. "I can hit apples lined on a fence twenty yards away."

Remarkably, Cochran's stance relaxed somewhat. "That's impressive. Why don't you show us then?"

She wanted to roll her eyes but kept them trained on the thief in front of them. "And if I did that, then I couldn't shoot you. When you underestimate my ability to shoot, you underestimate me. That is a huge mistake."

"Pfft," Cochran huffed. "I've not underestimated you. But I know I have the advantage." Slowly, he swung his pistol to point at Julian. "I'll shoot him first, then you can shoot me. But I warn you that the hole in his gut will be worse than what you do to me."

Every ounce of Beth's bravado and exhilaration fled only to be replaced with primal fear. "Don't," she said, hating the tremble in her voice.

What had been the best day of her life suddenly turned into one of the worst. She couldn't lose Julian again. Yet the idea that another man would best her didn't sit right either. She was finished with men telling her what to do.

That only left her one way to proceed. "I'm so sorry, Julian. I never wanted you hurt."

"Beth," he said gently. "We were both caught unaware. You tried your best."

She stole a glance his way and smiled. "I know what to do. Thank you for believing in me."

"I'll always believe in you."

With a new resolve bolstered by Julian's confidence in her, she didn't hesitate.

She pulled the trigger.

In that split second it took for the powder to ignite, Cochran jerked his arm out of the way. The shot cracked through the air as her hand jerked from the recoil.

"You." Cochran shook his head in disbelief, then grinned. "You might be a markswoman, but you don't know the first thing about shooting a moving target."

The shot still echoed in her ears as she stared at the smoking gun. Slowly, she lifted her gaze. Whatever advantage they'd had was lost.

"I can't believe you did that." Julian's widened eyes latched onto hers. He shook his head as if clearing his thoughts.

With his free hand, Cochran pushed his tricorne up to his hairline, then scratched his forehead. "You've got spunk." He waved his gun at her. "Now, you throw your gun to me."

"This is my gun." She would not allow herself to be bested by the highwayman again.

"He does this for a living. You can get another gun," Julian said quietly.

"But I've trained with this one," she argued, but she knew it was a losing battle.

Still pointing his pistol at Julian, Cochran reached out and pried the gun from her fingers, then grinned. "You sound like me and my missus. How long have you been married?" His eyes widened in understanding. "You're not. If you were, then your husband would have known you could shoot and were an *excellent shot.*" He chuckled as he shook his head. "I can't waste any more of my valuable time listening to the two of you."

"No, we're not married," Beth answered. "And we never will be."

"Is that relevant to the conversation?" Julian gritted his teeth.

"Enough," Cochran shouted. "While you two bicker, I've had a chance to go through the lady's reticule. There's nothing in there except for about ten quid. I need at least twenty quid from the two of you to make this afternoon worthwhile." He examined her pistol. "This is worth about three. Now, let's see if you can find another seven between you." He picked up Julian's pistol, examined it, then shook his head. "There's no ball? Not even powder?" he asked incredulously.

"What?" Beth placed her hands on her hips. "Your pistol wasn't even loaded?"

"I'm not foolish enough to keep a loaded pistol stuck down my breeches. If you're such an expert with weapons, you'd know the danger."

His sarcasm infuriated her. "If we're stuck out here—"

"Quiet," Cochran roared.

Everything stilled around them at his outburst.

"Now, that I have your attention," the thief said with a smile. "Take off your clothes."

Chapter Seventeen

Julian quit arguing with Beth for a moment to look at Cochran. "What did you say?"

Beth bristled beside him. "That is preposterous and unacceptable," she scolded. "I will not undress."

Cochran raised a single black eyebrow. "My wife is a lot like you. She wouldn't be taking too kindly to my demands either. But this is business."

Julian ran a hand through his hair. Bad enough that he quarreled with Beth, but things were progressing from a poor situation to a dire one. "Why do you want our clothes?"

Cochran waved the pistol around them and pointed at Beth's reticule. "I need to make a profit today. To make it worth my while, I'm taking your clothes and selling them." He waved the pistol at their feet. "Boots and shoes too, if you please."

"Why don't you take the horses?" she asked.

Cochran tsked. "*Beth*, you know that would make it too easy to find me after I leave."

"This is barbaric." She took a step back.

Julian bit the inside of his cheek. Why did she have to be so argumentative? Her spirit was one of the most attractive things about her, but not at this moment.

"We would not be in this predicament if you'd gotten on that damn horse."

Her eyes narrowed.

He'd seen that look before. It's the one she always had when she was about to dress someone down.

"It's my fault that we're here?" The incredulity in her voice would have been comical if Cochran's gun hadn't been pointed at them. "After you gave up your pistol?" she added.

"It wasn't loaded," Cochran pointed out.

She shot the thief a look. "You didn't know that. Nor is this your argument."

"I'm just trying to be helpful," he said sheepishly. "We men have to stick together."

She didn't answer but turned her attention to Julian once again. "Perhaps if *you'd* had your fortune told, she would have advised you to keep your pistol loaded," she bit out.

"She didn't dream about me." Immediately, Julian's blood started to pound, and his head ached in similar rhythm. He should just tackle the miscreant to the ground and take his chances with the pistol. If Beth weren't there and in danger, he'd have done it already.

Mr. Cochran ran his gaze over her body.

Immediately, Julian sneered and made a move to shield her from the scoundrel's perusal.

The thief had the good sense to hold up one hand. "Hold there, sirrah. It's not what you think. My missus is about the same size as your wife . . . lady. I'll be taking her garments to give to the missus. That ought to keep me out of the dungeon for a least a week—"

"I . . . I embroidered this ensemble myself," Beth protested.

"There, there, ma'am. I'll leave your chemise." He

frowned. "What kind of a gentleman do you think I am?"

She blinked, incredulous at the thief's question.

"Hurry. I don't have all day. Dinner will be ready soon." He smiled. "Tomorrow, I can take these to the market—" He shook his head. "It almost slipped." He waggled the pistol toward them. "You'll not catch me."

"But we already have your name," Beth said.

"You don't know if that's my real name or not." Cochran sniffed in defiance.

Julian tugged her close with an arm around her waist. "Darling, let's not dawdle. The man needs to get home to his wife." He motioned to her feet. "Take off your shoes."

When she exhaled loudly, Cochran looked sheepishly at Beth. "Sorry. Those look brand new."

"Custom-made." She lifted a brow. "Your wife will enjoy them."

Cochran chortled a full belly laugh that echoed around them. When the sound died, he waved them over to a large tree. "You should marry her. She's entertaining. Now, undress."

"Come, we need to do this." Julian placed his hand on the small of her back.

"Preposterous," Beth murmured as she turned away from him, breaking all physical contact between them.

As soon as she had her dress removed, Cochran motioned with his gun. "Take off the stays. My missus will quite enjoy them. And so will I." He nodded to Julian. "What a lucky bastard you are."

"I made these myself. I embroid—"

"Yes, I know. I'll tell my missus. She'll appreciate it." He motioned to Julian. "You do it."

"I'll do it," Beth growled. In seconds, she was bare

except for her chemise. She wrapped her hands around her chest in a protective manner.

Cochran motioned to Julian. "Everything except your breeches. I can use your shirt. Your boots should bring a good coin or two."

"I've only had them a month," he protested as he stood on one foot, then the other as he twisted off his boots.

"And they're already scuffed." Cochran evaluated the fine leather. "I'd have gotten twice the half quid if you'd taken care of them. Don't you have a valet?"

"Sometimes," Julian said.

"Fire him," Cochran demanded. "The man should be taking better care of your possessions."

"Why does he keep his breeches?" Beth piped up.

"I'm not going to leave the man without any dignity."

"I'm in my chemise."

Cochran pursed his lips. "You're fully covered. Quit being so missish." He turned to Julian. "Is she always like this?"

Julian shook his head. "She keeps me on my toes."

Cochran nodded. "So does my wife. Never a dull moment." He turned to Beth, keeping Julian in his sight. "You have a lot in common with her. Face the tree"—he pointed the gun at Julian—"face the opposite direction. Now, stand next to each other and don't try anything heroic." He glanced at Beth and raised an eyebrow. "Particularly you."

Soon, Cochran had them both tied together around the tree.

"There now." He stood back and put his pistol in a pocket inside his coat. "I'll be on my way." With that, he hurried toward the overturned carriage. He reached inside and withdrew their two small bags but left Julian's journal and Beth's embroidery. "I'll be taking these with me." Then, he launched himself onto his horse, tipped his hat, and galloped away.

"Well, at least he has manners." She rested her head against the tree. "You had all our money in your bag, didn't you?"

He could still hear the anger vibrating in her voice. "Yes, and all my clothes."

"Mine are gone as well. This is all your fault." She turned slightly toward him, giving him an excellent view of her cleavage. Though it was damn difficult, he kept his gaze on her face. He'd always known she was a beautiful woman, but he'd never been this close to seeing the perfection that was Beth.

Her gaze drifted to his chest. He almost smiled when she sucked in a breath, then slammed her eyes shut.

"Is something the matter?" he asked innocently.

"Of course there is, you vain man." Her gaze met his. "I'm tied to a tree practically naked."

When she swallowed, his eyes locked onto the pulse at the base of her neck that fluttered in agitation. He inhaled, desperate for a hint of her scent.

"My face is a little higher than where you're currently staring," she said, not hiding the sarcasm in her voice.

When he slowly lifted his gaze to hers, a beautiful blush had crowned her cheeks in a glorious pink color. "I wasn't looking at your chest. I promise."

"What were you looking at?" she snapped.

"The pulse at the base of your neck. I wish I could put my lips there and feel it." Fear, relief, and a sense of failure bounced through his thoughts like a hard billiard break. "It's the beating of your heart. It reminds me how alive you are right now." He grappled with the emotions stuck in his throat as tears threatened.

What a catastrophe. He hadn't cried since his father died.

Julian tilted his head to the blistering sun and closed his eyes. He despised that she had to bear this indignity. He also despised that he'd failed her again. If he'd loaded the gun, they wouldn't be here.

"Are you all right?"

"No." He'd never be all right after today. "I don't care about the consortium, my engines, or even that albatross around my neck called the marquessate." He finally had enough control over his emotions that he could look her in the eyes. "You are the only thing that matters. If I'd have lost you . . ."

"I felt the same way." Her voice trembled. "I wasn't going to let him hurt you." She looked to the ground. "I wish I had that shot to do over. I would have aimed for his chest. You could have tackled him to the ground, then *he* would have been tied to this tree."

Their declarations hung in the air between them. Everything in that moment seemed hard and ungiving. Beth, the tree, his body, and his cock.

To make matters worse, she slid up against him and somehow managed to twist herself until they were chest to chest. Her gaze dipped to his chest, then shot straight to his face. She swallowed and the slight movement of her throat made him want to kiss that spot even more.

She moved just an inch, but he could see the outline of her soft breasts and hard nipples through her chemise.

In response, his cock jerked against her stomach. Bad timing on its part, but even it knew he wanted to kiss her and ensure for himself that she was alive and well.

"Ouch." When she leaned her head away, the movement pressed her lower body harder against his. The pain that lashed from a steam burn was child's play compared with the torture of being pressed against her lush body and unable to do anything about it.

"Is that a branch poking me?" As soon as she asked, her eyes widened.

He lifted a brow in challenge.

"Oh God," she groaned.

"A little early, but I would expect no other response from you when I give you pleasure."

This time, he could practically see the steam rising from her body. "Another reason you're an arrogant ass."

"Quit wiggling." When she started to protest, he shook his head and dropped his voice until it was almost a whisper between lovers. "I wouldn't have been able to live with myself if you'd been killed."

There. He said it.

"But I'm an excellent shot." This time, her protest grew weaker. "You were worried about me?"

He locked his gaze with hers. "I'll always worry about you." He blew out a breath. "Don't you know that?"

She shook her head slowly, not turning away from him.

He drew a deep breath, then released it. "I'd have gladly taken the bullet for you. I wouldn't want to be here without you."

He tried to stretch the rope to no avail. Though Cochran hadn't tied it tightly, the rope wouldn't give much of a stretch or twist. Only because of Beth's lithe form could she slide her body over his. He blew out a breath and forced himself to relax. Cillian would reach them shortly.

Her brow wrinkled adorably. "When you say you wouldn't want to be here without me, what do you mean?"

Leave it to her not to leave any stone unturned.

Her question reminded him of a trail leading to the

top of a mountain, one riddled with dangerous curves and sheer drops that could leave a man decimated. How to answer without scaring her and making her retreat from him once again?

He blew out a breath.

The truth? Since they'd been together, she'd become as vital to him as the air he breathed, the water that quenched his thirst, and the food he ate for sustenance.

She was everything.

"All I meant was that your health and happiness mean the world to me." His vague answer sounded feeble to his own ears.

Her eyes glistened with unshed tears. Perhaps his answer proved to be stronger than he first believed.

"Then why didn't you come back to me and tell me what happened to the rabbits?"

"What?"

"Beatrice, Bonnie, and Bertram." Her voice cracked. "When you never returned to *me*, I went to Hyde Park to see for myself how they were faring. There were all gone . . . just like you." She pursed her lips and closed her eyes as if in pain. "Why did you not stand and fight for me? For us?" Her breath hitched in a half sob.

"Are you talking about Cochran?"

She swallowed, the movement again drawing his gaze to her neck, where her pulse pounded. "When you asked for my hand, then walked away. St. John said you didn't even try to convince him otherwise. He said it proved you didn't care for me." She blinked as a ragged breath escaped. "If what you say is true, then why, for the love of God, didn't you fight for us?" Betrayal shone bright in her eyes. Its power was ten times greater than that of the sun beating down upon them.

"Oh, Beth," he whispered. He longed to take her in his

arms only to be thwarted by the burn of the rope that refused to yield.

"You promised me you'd return. You promised me we'd have a happy life together." She sobbed once but didn't turn away, her pain raw and exposed.

If Cochran had shot him, it would have hurt less than seeing her like this. Instantly, he tried to move closer again. The tree bark bit into the skin of his back, the pain welcome.

"I thought your brother shared . . ." He let the words die when he saw the wretched disappointment in her eyes. It reminded him of how his father had reacted when he'd told him that St. John had refused his suit.

As he watched her expression change to shutter her agony, it explained so much that had transpired between the two of them over the years. He'd never realized how much she'd wanted that marriage. For a moment, he wanted to ask her the same. Why she hadn't come to him? When he never heard from her again, he concluded she felt the same as Howell. This explained why she was always so distant when they'd seen each other at Randford's and Sykeston's houses.

He'd always known she was fond of him, but he'd never thought she had her heart set on the two of them marrying.

His chest heaved as if he'd run ten miles. The intense shame threatened to swallow him alive. He struggled to find a response. The truth was he couldn't pursue her until he'd proven himself.

His damnable pride and honor wouldn't allow him to be labeled a fortune hunter.

At the jangle of a harness, they both turned their attention to the road.

Cillian brought a two-horse cart to a halt in front of

their broken-down carriage. When he looked in their direction, his eyes widened as he jumped down.

"For the love of Saint Christopher, what happened?" He broke into a sprint. Once he reached them, he pulled out a knife and cut the rope away.

With an awkward step, Beth stumbled, but Julian steadied her by grabbing her arms. He searched her eyes and saw the humiliation that dulled their accustomed brilliant blue.

"Thank you." She turned away from both him and Cillian with her arms crossed over her chest. "I'm indecent." Without looking their way, she darted around the tree in an attempt at modesty.

With his freckled complexion and green eyes, Cillian's cheeks burned brighter than the sun.

"Is there a blanket?" Julian asked.

"No, my lord."

Julian motioned with his hand, and immediately Cillian stripped out of his jacket and handed it to him.

He walked behind the tree and found her resting her forehead against the rough bark of the tall oak towering above them.

"We're not finished with this conversation," he murmured into her ear. He rested the jacket over her shoulders. "'I'm . . . sorry' isn't enough," he whispered hoarsely. "However, make no mistake, Beth." Unable to resist, he pressed his lips to the tender skin below her ear. "I've always wanted you. Every single day. Every single hour." He gently squeezed her arms. "Shall I help you put this on?"

Without a word, she shook her head no, so he stepped away, giving her some privacy.

When he turned to face Cillian, the mischievous man gave him a thumbs-up in approval and silently said, *Bravo*.

Julian rolled his eyes and was rewarded with a waist-coat hitting him in the chest.

"You can't go into the inn without something covering you. What happened?"

"We were set upon by a highwayman. He took advantage by pointing a loaded pistol at us. He took everything he could except the horses. Our clothes, pistols, bags."

"Pistols?" Cillian asked with raised eyebrows.

"Beth had one."

"Your talent never ceases to amaze us, Miss Howell," Cillian called out. When she didn't answer, he frowned.

"It's been a dreadful afternoon," Julian said softly.

Cillian pursed his lips. "That's unfortunate."

"In more ways than one," Julian said glumly.

Just then, Beth joined them. She shuffled her bare feet as if trying to hide them. "The thief called himself Mr. Cochran. I still have five guineas."

"Five guineas," Julian exclaimed. "Where did you find that?"

"It's tied to the inside of my chemise." She sighed gently. "But he took all the rest."

"Our situation is unfortunate, but it's not impossible." Julian kept his gaze focused on her face. "That's five guineas more than I thought we had. More importantly, you're not hurt."

Cillian pulled out a small coin pouch tucked inside his breeches. "I took upon myself to take his lordship's coins when I went to the village. I figured I'd need more. And I was right. I had to buy the cart and nags driving it. I've only got about two quid left. The good news is that we can sell the nags back to their owner when we return to the inn and use our horses. That'll make seven guineas, not including Miss Howell's money." Cillian bent his head to look at Julian's feet. "But even with that amount, those are going to be a problem."

"How so?"

"There is little chance of finding anything to fit those monstrosities." Cillian chortled at his own joke.

"Enough." Julian slid the waistcoat over his chest and buttoned it. "What did you discover?"

Cillian tipped his hat back and regarded Julian. "This was not the best place to have suffered a carriage mishap. The only person who has the tools to repair the carriage is visiting his sister in Northumberland." With his thumb, he pointed behind him. "That cart is our conveyance to Bath, my lord."

"The sun will set long before we arrive. Too dangerous to travel in the dark. We're a good twenty-five miles from there."

Beth's stomach rumbled with the volume of a small volcano. Instantly, she slapped a hand over her middle. "I haven't eaten since last night."

"Let's not tarry then." Julian held out his hand to her. She stared at it.

"I'll have you in Bath by tomorrow afternoon. I promise."

Cillian turned and walked to the cart.

She hesitated for a moment, then took his offered hand. Immediately, he entwined their fingers together.

In response, she squeezed.

His heart skipped a beat. He still had plenty of time to escort her to Bath, then arrive in London for his meeting with the consortium. That meeting now was more important than ever.

For the rest of this trip, he planned to use every spare moment minute wooing her.

First, he had some explaining to do.

Chapter Eighteen

While Julian sat with Cillian on the cart bench, Beth had huddled in the back, hoping beyond hope that no one would see her practically half-naked and dirty. Never in her life had she been brought so low. She'd always prided herself on her ability to manage her own affairs, but today proved the opposite.

To make matters worse, she'd forgotten her vow never to tell or even hint to Julian how devastated she'd been when he'd walked away from her. She'd seen the look of shock in his eyes when she'd asked him why he hadn't fought for them. Perhaps she'd discover why when they finally had a chance to discuss it in private. She stared at the embroidery in her lap and continued to sew. The slow hum of conversation in front of the cart drifted in and out of her consciousness. With all other men, she could ignore them.

But not Julian.

When she'd felt his hard body next to her soft one, the contrast had almost made her melt on the spot. The perfect fit of their bodies and the evidence of his arousal against her awoke a need to press closer to him.

And the need to press for answers.

But did she heed her own warning to not reveal her thoughts? *Oh no.*

She should have just let it lie in their pasts. Yet he said the loveliest words she'd ever heard. He was the rare man in her life who had once put her above all others.

Why couldn't he have done that when St. John had said no to their courtship?

The cart slowed, then finally came to stop at a small inn with a faded sign proclaiming its name as The Merry Maiden.

Cillian jumped from the cart, and Julian placed his arm over the bench and turned in her direction. "He'll tell the proprietors our circumstances." He twirled a loose lock of her hair around one finger, then lowered his voice. "It's such a shame about that fortune-teller. We could have skipped this whole day and headed straight to Bath."

Beth opened her mouth ready to defend herself.

"Darling, I'm joking. I wish she would have dreamed about me years ago and told me everything."

The affection in his voice caused an immediate rush of goose bumps to sprint across her arms.

"I would have done things so differently, Beth." He continued to play with her hair. "Soon, you'll have some other clothing and a refreshing bath."

The promise in his deep voice made her want to lean close and kiss him.

Moving with the speed of honey on a brisk January day, an elderly couple tottered out of the inn with a middle-aged woman following.

"Oh, you poor lass," the woman cried. "To be set upon by highwaymen and robbed of everything." She tsked. "I'm Mrs. Drummond, and this is my husband, Mr. Drummond. This is our inn, and we'll take good care of you."

"Now, Lily, don't suffocate the poor woman until she and her husband are inside." Mr. Drummond smiled. He turned to Julian. "What did you say your name is?"

"Julian Raleah, and this is my wife, Beth," he answered. He waved a hand down his chest. "I apologize for our appearance."

"Horrible nonsense." Mrs. Drummond's voice trembled. "I ask you, Mr. Drummond, is this not the most horrible news you've ever heard?"

The elderly man took his wife's hand. "Indeed, Lily. But with your care and good food, they'll recover quickly." He beamed at his wife, then at Julian. "Best cook this way of Somerset, sir."

Julian delivered his notorious, charming smile, the one designed to make every female within fifty miles quake inside like a fresh pudding. "We look forward to it." He turned to Beth. "Right, dear?"

Beth nodded and held his gaze. "I couldn't have said it better."

Mr. Drummond turned to the middle-aged woman. "This is our daughter, Sarah."

"Good afternoon, Miss Drummond." Julian dipped his head.

"It's Mrs. Drummond." Sarah blushed. "I married a second cousin on my da's side of the family. So, I kept the name I was born with. My husband runs the public room at the inn. He'll fetch the water for a bath. When your coachman arrived the first time, we prepared our very best room for you."

When Beth's gaze landed on Mr. Drummond, he smiled again. He had a kind face, as did his wife and daughter. When Beth returned the smile, tears welled in her eyes. Whether it was the joy of being here or what she and Julian had been through earlier, it wasn't something she wanted to examine too closely.

Julian jumped from the cart, then came to her side. "Ready?"

She nodded. For some unfathomable reason, she was suddenly shy. It wasn't because she was half-naked. It had to be the tenderness she heard in his voice. A tremulous breath escaped, and a single tear slipped free. She shouldn't have shared so much with him.

With the gentlest of touches, he wiped it away. "Here now. None of that. The Drummonds and their daughter will be wondering what could possibly have made you tear up when I'm near you."

"Nothing and everything," she answered. When he lifted her from the cart, she set her hands on his shoulders. When he released her, she didn't let go. "Thank you for being so wonderful today."

"Well, Mrs. Raleah, don't you know that I'm wonderful most days?" Julian winked. "But not all." Then he did the unexpected.

He swept her into his arms.

"What are you doing?" Startled, she wrapped her arms around his neck.

"Since you don't have shoes, I'm carrying you." He winked. "After what you went through today, it's the least I can do. I'm not going to let you step on a rock or a piece of glass in the street."

"Oh." It was a lame answer, but it was all she could think of in that moment.

When they entered the main room, several locals who sat swilling a pint jerked their gazes toward the sight. Julian nodded in their direction. Beth hid her face against his shoulder. It felt divine and familiar being in his strong embrace. Almost like home.

"Mr. Raleah, if you'll take your lovely missus up that flight of stairs and enter the first door on your right you'll find your room," the elder Mrs. Drummond called out.

"Thank you, ma'am," Julian said. At the rumble of his

words in his chest, Beth burrowed deeper against him. In mere seconds, he had her in the room and shut the door behind them. Without warning, he sat on the bed with her on his lap and kissed her. The move was so surprising she didn't have a chance to protest.

This was not like any kiss they'd shared before. It felt like a hunger that had gone too long without a satiation. His tongue begged entrance, and on a moan, she parted her lips. When his tongue met hers, he groaned in response. It was like finding your haven from a storm, and she never wanted to leave.

He broke the kiss, then stared at her lips. She licked her lower lip only to discover how swollen and wet it was. His was the same.

"What was that for?" She brought her hand to his chest and let it rest against the pounding of his heartbeat.

He pressed his forehead next to hers and closed his eyes. "I had to make certain you were unharmed."

She laughed at the ridiculousness of the statement.

Before she could offer a response, he swept his mouth against hers, then pulled away. "Everything appears satisfactory." His expression turned serious, but then the rogue winked. "However, I won't be content until I do a more thorough examination."

A knock pounded on the door.

Julian gently placed her on the bed. Had she ever realized how strong he was? A devilish thrill swept through her. Perhaps she'd need to do her own investigation of how he'd fared from their ordeal.

As soon as Julian answered, the younger Mrs. Drummond swept into the room with a business-like efficiency that left no doubt who ran the inn.

"I've brought a few pieces of clothing that will suffice until you've had a chance to purchase something new." In her arms was a pile of clothing. She walked to the small dining table in the room and pulled out two chairs. Swiftly, she placed a dress, chemise, stays, stockings, and a well-worn pair of half boots on one. On the other chair, she placed a serviceable brown coat, black trousers, stockings, and a linen shirt that probably had been white and pristine before but now appeared almost threadbare. She'd also brought a worn pair of men's shoes. She eyed Julian's feet, then shook her head.

"Mr. Raleah, I doubt that these will fit, but try them."

"Thank you, Mrs. Drummond," Beth said as she wrapped her arms around herself again, hoping to reclaim some of her dignity. "How can we ever repay you?"

"There's no need, ma'am. These are various pieces of clothing other travelers have left. Me and my mum have cleaned them and kept them for situations just like this." She nodded as if satisfied with what she'd brought up to them. "This isn't the first time that Mr. Cochran has left his mark on travelers who've been left stranded by the road."

A man entered the room followed by two young, strapping boys carrying buckets of water. With a finger pointing, the man directed the boys to empty the water into a serviceable copper hip bath that sat next to the unlit fireplace.

As the boys went about their task, the man regarded Mrs. Drummond. "Don't say anything out of turn, Sarah." He turned to Julian and nodded. "I'm Sarah's husband, Tom."

Julian extended his hand, and the two men shook. "Thank you for your generous hospitality."

Tom Drummond nodded. He instructed the boys to retrieve more water. As soon as the lads left, he shut the door slightly. "I'm not defending Cochran, but I'll say that he and his missus have come upon hard times. They've lived around here since they've been born. Unfortunately, the landlord tripled their rent. They've not been able to farm for the last three years." He shook his head. "I'm sorry you've suffered at his hands. It's just . . ." Tom bent his head and stared at the floor for a moment. "He's had to do things that no man should have to do to keep his family fed."

"Stealing and threatening people?" Sarah shook her head. "No matter how hard times are around here, there's no excuse for thieving."

As if Julian suspected Beth was about to speak, he glanced her way. "My Beth and I have not been strangers to hard times ourselves. But I don't take kindly to a man who points a loaded gun at my wife." A simmering fury raged within the sharpness of his gaze.

When he turned and stared at Tom Drummond, the man had the good sense to look sheepish. "I'd feel the same as you, Mr. Raleah. I expect they'll be leaving the area soon."

"He told us he had men who would join him," Beth added.

Tom shook his head and stared at the floor. "It's only him and his wife."

"Is there a magistrate in town?" The rigidity of Julian's body told everyone in the room that the matter wouldn't be resolved until he saw justice done.

"Aye," Mrs. Drummond answered.

"Sarah," Tom warned.

"One of these days he's going to choose someone to rob who doesn't care what he's been through. When he goes around brandishing a loaded pistol, someone is going to be hurt." Sarah stood by her husband's side, then placed her hand on his arm. "Perhaps it's best if Mr. Raleah speaks with the magistrate."

"Julian," Beth said. When his attention came to rest on her, she smiled. "Perhaps we should settle a bit, then consider our options."

After a moment, he nodded. "You're right. We've been through enough for one day."

The boys returned with more jugs of water. Mr. and Mrs. Drummond took their leave after promising to send up food and wine.

"You go ahead and bathe. I'm going to see after Cillian." Julian walked to the door, then executed a perfect turn. With his arms crossed over his chest, he took a gander at her. "I'd have never taken you as one to dismiss something this egregious."

She shrugged. "With my experience, especially with my brother and Meri, I've learned that actions don't always tell you everything about a person."

"Beth, no matter a person's circumstances, there's never a justification for breaking the law or acting immorally. We all must abide by the rules."

"If that were the case, then the rules would forbid us from sharing a room together since we're not married or even lovers for that matter." It was a bold thing to say, but not everything was so black-and-white. She'd had enough experience in her twenty-six years to learn that. "You're a man of science," she said. "Surely, you've expected things to work one way, but then you're surprised because something happens that you didn't take into account."

"It's a poor comparison. Scientific principles and theorems always behave in a like manner."

"Even if the circumstances and conditions differ each time they're tested?" she asked. "Perhaps your steam engines wouldn't work the same if they were subjected to stress that was suddenly forced upon them. Maybe that's what happened to Mr. Cochran."

His jaw twitched twice as he pursed his lips. She'd made her point, and he couldn't refute it. People under the stress of poverty and hunger act differently than they would if they didn't have to live with those challenges and constraints.

"My own family and tenants have suffered much like Mr. Cochran and his family. Yet they never lost their dignity or resorted to thievery." His voice was quiet, but there was a hint of reproof in his words.

He walked to one of the chairs with the clothes tossed on them. With his back to her, he stripped Cillian's waistcoat off. Then picked up the linen shirt and tossed it over his head in a quick movement. The linen stretched across his back as if two sizes too small. He donned the stockings and slipped his feet into the shoes. His heels extended three inches over the ends of the shoes. Yet he didn't complain. Finally, he slipped on the only piece of clothing that fit appropriately, the sturdy but worn coat.

He turned to her. "I'll consider what you've said. We'll have that talk when I return."

"Thank you," she answered.

Julian nodded, then swept from the room.

When he closed the door, she released a sigh. Perhaps it was a poor comparison. But even she could see breaking the rules and the law if her own family was frightened or hungry.

She'd do the same for Julian if he was suffering.

And that was the scariest thought she'd ever contemplated.

~

Julian ignored the shock of horror that appeared on his valet's face. When the man shuddered as if he'd eaten a sour lemon, he ignored that too. But when his valet and coachman cackled at his foot apparel, Julian drew the line.

"Enough," he growled as he slid into an empty chair across the table from where Cillian sat drinking a pint.

"Can I pour one for you, Mr. Raleah?" Tom Drummond asked. But it was rather a moot point, since the good man was already pouring a draft for him.

"Thank you," Julian answered. When the pint was set before him, he took a long drink. The ale quenched at least one of his desires, but the thirst for more of Beth's sweet kisses sang through his blood with each pump of his heart. But the heavy weight of regret rested on his shoulders. How to explain why he'd left Beth all those years ago without opening old wounds?

"Hits the spot, doesn't it, sir?" Tom stood beside their table and waited for Julian to pass judgment.

"It's extraordinary." He wasn't just saying that. The ale in his cup could rival any he'd ever had before. "Did you brew it yourself?"

Tom nodded. "Best in the county."

Cillian nodded in agreement. "Why don't you bring us another round."

"My pleasure," the innkeeper said, then left the table.

"How is your wife faring?" Cillian kept his voice low. When Tom approached with the other two mugs, Cillian grew quiet and nodded his thanks.

Thankfully, Tom's wife called for him and he left the room.

Julian took another long swallow of ale, then set the empty mug on the table and picked up the other and set it before him.

"She's fine, but I'm not." He slid back in the chair, then leaned forward over the table. "Out of nowhere, she pulled a gun from her reticule. Told us both that Sykeston had taught her how to shoot. She aimed the thing straight at his hand where he held his gun, then pulled the trigger. She missed and it all went downhill from there." He shook his head, then took another drink. "We'd just had a special moment between us where she was finally opening up to me, then with his pistol drawn that bloody bastard interrupts us."

"I'm glad you're both safe." Cillian's serious expression turned impish. "You haven't done anything foolish, have you?" Cillian asked.

"What are you referring to?"

"You haven't taken her to bed, have you?" When Julian's expression didn't change, Cillian rested his head in one hand. "Oh for the love of heaven, don't tell me you did. My mother always said, if you give the milk away for free, then you'll never find a buyer no matter how sweet the taste. Now she'll never agree to be your wife."

Julian delivered a look meant to skewer his valet to the table. "It's none of your business."

"Good," Cillian said confidently. "I can tell by the defensiveness in your tone that you've listened to my advice."

Cillian finished his mug, then took a sip of the second. He wiped his mouth and continued, "She's a feisty one, our Miss Howell."

"She's not yours." Julian surprised Cillian and himself with the warning growl in his voice.

"Of course she's not mine." Cillian frowned. "My lord, you forget that I work for you. My job is to see you happy, and that means securing Miss Howell's hand in marriage."

"Quiet." Julian glanced about the room, but no one was there to overhear. "I don't want anyone to know our true identities." He rested both elbows on the table and held his head between his hands. "She wants me to forgive Cochran and not go to the magistrate."

"And?"

"I don't know if I can do that. All I can remember is him pointing that weapon directly at her heart while she was aiming for his hand. If anything had happened to her this afternoon, I . . ."

"It's over, Grayson." Cillian smiled, offering comfort. "She's upstairs, safe and sound. No doubt she's waiting and wondering where you are."

"She's taking a bath."

"There you are, Mr. Raleah." Sarah walked into the room with a tray. "I'm just about to take this tray upstairs to your room." The delicious smells of roasted chicken, carrots, buttered potatoes, and fresh bread filled the room. Sarah leaned over the barkeep's area and pulled out a bottle of wine and two glasses, then set them on the tray.

Julian's stomach rumbled loud enough that Sarah turned in his direction and smiled.

"No need, Mrs. Drummond. I'll take it," Julian called out as he winked at Cillian, then lowered his voice to just above a whisper. "I imagine you can keep yourself entertained this evening. My wife and I are due for a long chat." As Cillian started to object, Julian stood with a wolfish smile. "You have a way to woo women, and so do I."

Chapter Nineteen

〜〜

At the sound of the door opening, Beth slid down into her bath, which was rather large. She could immerse her whole body.

"Beth, I brought food."

At the sound of Julian's voice, she relaxed and straightened. The movement sent the water slushing against the sides of the tub. "I'm bathing."

"I know." His deep chuckle vibrated in the air. "Shall I make you a plate and pour a glass of wine?"

"Please. I'll be just a moment." Hidden behind a beautiful four-panel screen painted gold and green with pastoral scenes, she glanced around the bathing area for her linen toweling and clothing. "Smells delicious."

"No need to hurry. Enjoy yourself."

"Thank you," she called out. He was such a tranquil person to be around. There was never a sense of impatience or annoyance about him . . . except when she held a gun in her hands. She smiled to herself and took the lavender-scented soap and ran it over her body again. Her nipples pebbled in the cool air, but the warmth from the water brought forth a languid feeling of contentment. She leaned back and closed her eyes. She should be nervous with him so near, but instead, it felt natural and perfect. She should invite him to join her.

That would shock him.

Around the screen, he was completing various tasks, but from the subtle sounds she couldn't determine what he was up to until she heard him pouring something. She leaned her head against the tub and opened her eyes. "What are you doing?"

The single candle flame flickered when the air changed. In an instant, he stood before her with a tray in hand and a roguish smile on his lips.

"Serving you."

She stilled in the water.

He set the tray on a small side table before sitting on the floor beside her. He lifted a glass of wine and held it out to her.

She seemed incapable of moving. The entire lower half of her body was submerged, thankfully. One quick glance proved what she was afraid might happen. Her breasts bobbed on the water as if gleeful that he'd arrived. The turgid nipples pointed as if trying to garner his attention. She could either order him away or submerge her whole body, including her head, underwater much like a turtle when trying to hide.

Like nothing was amiss, he rested one arm on his bent knee and regarded her. Unaware of her turmoil, he smiled slightly while still holding her wine.

Oh, she hated to be vulnerable. And she was the one putting herself into that position. With a deep breath and a wish that her pounding heart would quiet, she stretched her arm and took the glass.

"Thank you." She took a sip for fortification, then handed it back.

He gently wrapped his fingers around her wrist and took the glass she was holding with his other hand. Frowning, he tilted his head. "Is that where the horse bit you?"

Oh for the love of equines everywhere. Water was dripping down her arm, and she'd forgotten completely about the hellish scar.

"My God, that had to hurt like hell." He gently lifted her arm higher, which in turn lifted her breasts out of the water.

A hot flush bludgeoned her cheeks. She'd never been one to be mawkish about her body, but this was Julian.

And the first thing he noticed about her body was that horrid scar.

With his attention devoted completely to the scar, he trailed a finger up her arm until he reached the puckered flesh. Gently, with the roughened tip of his finger, he outlined it.

The deep concern in his eyes tore another piece of her heart. By the end of the evening, she doubted she'd have any part of it left. The traitorous thing was jumping ship and swimming straight for him. "It's fortunate for St. John that Sykeston hadn't taught me how to shoot yet."

A true smile of affection graced his lips before he pressed his mouth to her scar. Slowly, he pulled away. Never taking his eyes from hers, he kissed her hand.

"We should finish our conversation." When she started to shake her head, his hand tightened slightly on hers. "Please."

After a moment, she nodded.

"I thought . . . it for the best . . . that I walk away." He cleared his throat.

"What do you mean?" She started to sit up, then remembered she was naked. She slid back in the water.

"I was the first man to offer for you. Your brother vowed he'd not allow you to marry me as destitute as I was. He called me a fortune hunter. It was offensive to me as my affection for you was true and pure." He blew out a breath. "He said if I continued to see you he'd buy every one of my father's debts and demand payment. Thus, ruining my father. I didn't try to convince you to go against your brother or elope, because that's what a fortune hunter would do. I couldn't stand to be seen as someone less than honorable. I thought my foolish, prideful honor was the only thing of value I had to give to you." He released a painful sigh. When he ran his hand down his face, the movement scraped the whiskers of his beard. "But it cost me something valuable because I could have had a happy marriage with you. We both would have had the money we needed."

She blinked away the sudden tears. "I see."

She studied their clasped hands, then tugged them closer. "I despise my brother for doing that to you." She pressed her lips to his fingers. "Every event, I looked for you. I was desperate to find out why you chose to walk away from me," she confided. "I should have defied convention and written a note asking you to come see me."

"I never went to any other events because I couldn't bear to see you in the arms of another man. I went to Raleah House and worked on the estate and on my engine designs." He tilted his head to look at the ceiling and gripped her hand tighter. Finally, he looked at her.

His eyes bore his pain, and she inhaled swiftly.

"I knew that industry was undergoing a rapid change. Now, with the consortium, my fortune is changing." He leaned close enough to kiss her.

She held her breath as her heart squeezed in her chest. Most men wanted to marry her for her money. But the one sitting across from her wasn't most men. Fate had been cruel to keep them apart.

She slid closer and pressed her lips gently against his. She pulled away and cupped his cheeks. "I'd be lying if I didn't say that I've wondered for years what had happened. I'm sorry I didn't think about it from your perspective."

"There's no need to apologize." He smiled faintly. "I've experienced failure on so many levels, but none have ever brought me so low. I'm sorry I failed you, and for that I'll never forgive myself."

She put her hand to his lips. "As you said, no apologies. Let's start anew."

He pressed a kiss to her outstretched fingers. "I'm relieved that I told you. I don't want you unhappy because of my actions."

The air between them sparked with a new energy. It was as if they'd reached a new understanding and acceptance between them.

Finally, he glanced at her body. Without looking away from his eyes, she could feel his gaze slowly sweeping over her, almost as if he were touching her.

With a tremulous breath, she waited for him. She didn't know if she'd survive if he didn't say something soon. His silence would be ten times worse than what she'd experienced when she'd spent her wedding night with Meri.

"Julian?" She bit her lower lip, dredging forth every ounce of courage she could scrape together. The candle cast shadows that flickered around his face, making it even more difficult to see his expression.

His nostrils flared as his gaze slowly swept across her breasts before meeting hers.

"I need to ask you something," she said.

When he swallowed, his Adam's apple bobbed in his throat as if he were dying of thirst. "Go ahead."

"Have you been with many women?" It was a bold question, but it would open a conversation that she longed to have with him.

"If you're asking if I have a mistress, the answer is no."

"That's not what I'm asking." She smiled. "We both know they're expensive."

He grunted, and she laughed.

When he joined in, she knew she'd said the right thing. "Tell me, please."

When their laughter faded, he turned serious. "I don't recall. Less than ten."

"You want me to believe you don't remember how many women you've made love to?"

"Five, then." He smiled, but it didn't hide his discomfort.

"What were they like?" She leaned closer, and the water lapped at the edges of the tub. "What were you like with them?"

"Beth," he admonished.

"Julian," she said in the same tone. "I'm not asking if you were in love with them, or if they were in love with you. I want to know if . . . if they enjoyed it."

His eyebrows shot up. "This entire conversation is spiraling into something I don't understand."

She grabbed his hand again. "This is hard for me. You see . . . I didn't enjoy it . . . the consummation. There"—she released a breath struggling to explain—"wasn't any affection. Neither of our hearts were in it." She blew out a breath. "That didn't come out right either. You see, Constance and Kat enjoy being with their husbands." She glanced at the water, then returned her gaze to his. "I just don't see what all the fuss is about."

The heat in his eyes warmed every inch of her. "Let me show you." She made a move to stand up, but he shook his head. "No, stay there. It'll be easier here."

"Here?"

"Trust me?"

After a moment, she nodded.

He cupped her cheek and brought his mouth to hers. His slow kiss promised more. Before she could deepen the kiss, he pulled away. He gave her wine. "I trust you also. Take a sip."

When the wine hit her tongue, her entire mouth awoke. The tart flavors of grapes and blackberries meddled together into a perfect taste. He handed her a plate of roasted chicken, grapes, and fresh bread and butter. He picked up a piece of chicken and held it to her mouth. "Eat."

Her lips parted and he fed her. After she took it, he rubbed his thumb gently over her lips, the touch simple but filled with tenderness. The food tasted like something her brother's finicky cook might have created. Each succulent bite satisfied her but didn't fill the hunger that resulted from him being this close to her. His eyes never left her mouth as he watched her eat, then fed himself. It was decadent and his attention made her feel like a queen who had an attractive man satisfying all her cravings.

Except for one.

Once she had her fill, she shook her head when he offered her more.

"Now we have that hunger satisfied, shall we try another?" he asked with a cocky grin.

She wanted to beg him to hurry, but she didn't say a peep. Yet her rapid breath had to tell him that she was impatient.

Slowly, he stood, watching her, then, in the slowest motion imaginable, rolled up his right sleeve. Inch by tantalizing inch revealed a muscular forearm. Her breath caught at such a sight, and instantly she moved her lower body toward him.

But why?

She'd seen men's forearms before. They were ordinary. Tonight, she couldn't tear herself away from such a sight. The unveiling of his arm was the most erotic sight she'd ever witnessed. Her entire body seemed to quiver in anticipation. Surely, the unveiling of the rest of his lean body would be as riveting as the unveiling of his forearm. Even though he was clothed, she could tell that he possessed a flat stomach, muscular thighs, and broad shoulders. It was a feast for her eyes. She'd always thought him handsome, but tonight he seemed to be promising her all sorts of wicked pleasures.

And he wasn't doing it fast enough.

His gaze never left hers as she examined him.

When he finished one arm, he repeated it with the other. As each minute floated by, her body, particularly her lower half, ached.

He moved behind her with ease, then dipped his hand in the water and hummed lightly. His breath tickled the back of her neck since she'd pinned her hair to the top of her head.

"Lean back," he directed.

When she did as he instructed, his hard, solid chest was directly behind her.

His arms came around her and he rested his hands on the edge of the tub. His lips touched the tender spot below her right ear. "Have you ever touched yourself in the bath?"

She made a motion to turn around. "Of course. How do you think I wash myself?"

He laughed softly, the sound relaxing. "You're being too literal. I'm asking if you touch yourself for pleasure."

"No." She shrank a little inside. If she was going to be honest with him, she had to tell him the truth. "I'm not really good at it."

"By the way you kiss me, I'd wager you are exceptional." His words turned her body into a tuning fork as everything within her seemed to vibrate. He pressed a light kiss to her skin. "Do you ever desire a man's touch?"

She closed her eyes and let the sensation wash over her. "Sometimes."

"Now?" he asked gruffly.

"Yes." Just answering him took Herculean strength.

He leaned back and she wanted to protest the loss of his heat. A soft rustle sounded behind her before he wrapped one arm around her waist right below her breasts.

"Your shirt?"

"I decided to take it off." He rested his chin lightly on her shoulder. "Look at my hand."

She watched as his large hand cupped her left breast. She hissed softly at the sensation of the rough skin of his palm caressing her tender breast. When he flicked his thumb on her nipple, she gasped.

"Do you like that?"

"Very much," she answered softly.

"Good." He trailed his lips from the base of her neck to her ear, where he nibbled gently. He trailed his other hand over her stomach until he reached the nest of curls at the juncture of her legs. He raked her fingers around her curls, then whispered, "Open for me."

She leaned one leg against the side of the tub. She ached *there*, and prayed he'd touch her. She moaned and leaned her head against his chest. "Please," she pleaded.

"Kiss me," he demanded softly.

She angled her mouth toward his. As their lips met, his fingers descended into the water. She lifted her hips and whimpered against his mouth as if giving directions.

He chuckled slightly, then filled her mouth, his tongue examining every inch of her, learning what she liked. His fingers went on an excavation of their own, finding the tender nub and circling it as if in a dance.

She groaned into his mouth as her tongue met every thrust and parry of his as they ravished each other.

But it was his wicked fingers that were her undoing. He was masterful at stroking her with the lightest touch. Each press of his fingers against the most sensitive part of her made her senses race, careening out of control.

He moaned against her mouth as if he found pleasure in her response. He squeezed her nipple between his thumb and forefinger. The perfect play of pleasure and pain made her see stars. Unable to help herself, she lifted her hips higher. His fingers moved faster, pushing her to find her release.

She closed her eyes as the sensation became everything. She gasped as it ripped through her, igniting a peak of pleasure that she'd never experienced before. She cried out his name, a heartfelt benediction for him to never stop.

As her body slowly floated back to earth, his kiss turned gentler and achingly sweet.

She took his hand, the one that had touched her so intimately, and brought it to rest against the runaway beat of her heart.

After a moment, she could speak again. "That was it?"

"You tell me." He pressed another kiss to her lips as if he couldn't stop touching her. "What did it feel like?"

"Like a thousand glowworms were lit up inside me and proclaiming to the world they were alive and looking for their mates." She giggled and shook her head. "I think I understand now why my friends get such faraway looks in their eyes when they're discussing it. So addictive. I want to experience it again."

"I think it has everything to do with the people you experience it with." He arched an eyebrow, then smiled like a child who'd found the hidden location of the biscuit jar. "You liked it, then?"

"Are you looking for praise?" Beth splashed him lightly with water and laughed.

As he grabbed her hand to keep her from splashing him again, Julian stole another kiss. When they broke apart, his entire face softened into an emotion she didn't want to study too closely. An examination best left for another time, when she was alone. When she stood, the water sloshed down her naked body.

Julian's gaze raked over her, devouring her. Never had a man studied her with such a hunger in his eyes, as if he'd take her right there and never let her out of his sight.

She grabbed a linen toweling and started drying herself as she stepped out of the tub. "The water is still warm, if you'd fancy a bath."

Amazing how casual she sounded as her body still tingled from her release.

As she stood there naked, he started to strip. He flicked the buttons on the falls of his breeches. With ease, he inched them over his hips.

Her breath hitched. From the black nest of curls at Julian's groin, his swollen member proudly jutted upward.

Her curiosity almost bested her. She lifted her hand to touch it as her mouth watered. There was *no* conceivable circumstance in which that engorged appendage would fit inside her.

Chapter Twenty

Was there anything more desirable than the woman of your dreams salivating at your naked body? He'd immediately recognized her insatiable curiosity. She'd licked her lips, then bit her lower lip as if contemplating him and his cock.

When she reached toward him, then withdrew her hand as if afraid he'd burn her, he'd wanted to shout.

For the love of humanity everywhere, touch me.

It was wicked on his part, but he'd tightened his abdomen and silently willed Beth to look at him.

Finally, she lifted her head until their eyes met. She stood before him like a goddess. With her plump breasts, pink nipples, and never-ending curves that would make any man fall to his knees, she was more beautiful than Aphrodite emerging from that damnable giant shell. God, he ached to have her.

"You can." The deep growl of his voice surprised him.

"I can what?" Her voice had a dream-like sound to it.

"Touch me." Without a second thought, he grabbed himself and tugged hard. "I'm not breakable."

She didn't move, and for a moment he didn't know if he'd just dreamed that he'd said the words. Then she blinked.

"I don't know." She hesitated. "I've never touched"—
she pointed at his member—"one before. Would you like
for me to?"

Underneath her uncertainty, something wasn't right.
And no doubt it had to do with Meriwether.

"I'd very much like for you to put your hands on me,
not just there but everywhere." He turned and regarded
the tub. The fragrance of the lavender-scented soap she'd
used wafted in the air. He turned back to her. It was best
not to push too fast if she wasn't ready. "But I'm going to
bathe before the water gets any colder."

Her eyes brightened. "I could bathe you?" A flush
pinkened her cheeks. "If you need help."

A grin tugged at his mouth, and he nodded.

As he made his way into the water, she approached.
With a deep but silent inhalation, she knelt by the water
and took the soap. Completely naked, she rubbed the soap
between her hands. It was absolute torture to watch as all
he could think of was her touching him. She took a clean
piece of linen toweling and dunked it in the water.

Gently, he grabbed her wrist. "There's no need for that.
I want your bare hands."

"For a husband, you're pretty demanding," she teased
as she put her soapy hands on his chest. "By the by, how
long have we been married?"

"Not long enough," he groaned. When he lifted his
hips, the water sluiced over his body.

"Why isn't it long enough?" she asked as her talented
hands skated down his torso. He dug the soap out of the
water and washed his arms and shoulders.

"Because I'm still mesmerized by everything you do.
If we were an old married couple, I wouldn't be praying
to the heavens for your hand to continue stroking my skin
in the direction you're heading."

She caught his gaze as her hand slowed to a stop on his stomach. "Do you like this?"

"Yes." Her hand was literally an inch away from his cock, which was pointed straight at her.

Boldly, she encircled her palm around his engorged member. They both hissed at the same time.

"Am I hurting you?" she asked.

"You're killing me," he managed to spit out. "Harder."

"Harder?"

"For the love of heaven, Beth," he pleaded. He placed his hand around hers, then squeezed. "Like this."

Then, the clever minx never took her eyes from his as she squeezed, coaxing him, giving him the pleasure that he'd craved from her. He'd wanted this for years, and it was as sweet and beautiful as he always knew it would be. "You're a natural."

She leaned close and pressed her lips against his. "Silly man, but I thank you."

He cupped her head with his hands, then deepened the kiss. For this woman, he'd do anything.

And everything.

"Faster," he whispered against her lips. He kissed her again and his tongue danced with hers as if they'd done this a thousand times. As she stroked him harder, he could feel his climax building. His bollocks tightened and his spine tingled. He clenched his eyes tighter as everything within him exploded into a riot of pleasure.

He tugged Beth closer, desperate for her touch, her body, and her kiss. His heart pounded and his blood raced. Never had he had a climax like this—one that took the very essence of him and molded him into someone new.

He was a man who would give everything he was and would ever be for the honor to call Beth Howell his forever.

As his breath started to calm, he opened his eyes and kissed her again. "You," he whispered affectionately.

"You," she repeated with a laugh, then turned serious. "You appeared as if you were in pain. Did I hurt you?"

"I've never felt such rapture." He swept his lips against hers, then washed away his seed from his belly. Quickly, he rose and extended his hand to assist her to stand. Once she stood, he dried himself, then stepped from the tub. "I should have asked for a dressing gown for you, but I'm glad I didn't."

"Why?" Her brow crinkled into perfect lines much like an architect's next masterpiece.

He waggled his eyebrows. "I can gaze upon your body without having to imagine the perfection underneath. I'll try to get my fill, but I know it's an effort that will never be satisfied."

She dipped her head as she shook it. However, her telltale flush gave away the impact of his words.

He was a gentleman, and it didn't sit well that she felt uncomfortable in front of him. He bent and picked up the worn linen shirt the Drummonds had provided.

"Let me put this over you."

She held up her arms, and her breasts lifted at the movement. He'd never tire of her body. Just as he'd never tire of her even when they were in their eighties. He felt like he had the energy of a hundred-man army at that moment.

He slipped the shirt over her head, and it fell in gentle waves about her body. The sight rendered him speechless for a moment, but then that hum of excitement came to the forefront of his thoughts, and he couldn't keep silent.

He brushed the backs of his fingers against her cheek as she gazed up at him. "You're beautiful."

"Julian, I . . . I . . ." She turned from him and walked

to the table where the remaining food lay. "Are you hungry?"

He narrowed his eyes at the change of subject. "Can we talk about what happened?"

She shook her head and laughed. But the sound wasn't reflective of her normal confident self. There was a hint of nervousness about her that hadn't been present when they pleasured each other.

Seeing her enveloped in his shirt did strange things to his insides. It was as if his stomach, heart, and brain had been tossed together, then rearranged. Yet his senses were still heightened. Her fragrance, slight though it was, made him take notice. In response, his nostrils flared as he filled his lungs with her scent. Her hair seemed to be curling in front of his eyes as it dried. He could still taste her kiss, the one flavored with the sweet wine.

He blew out a breath. His future had always been defined by his work. But now he wanted more. He wanted Beth by his side.

She turned and faced him. The open V of his shirt trailed down from her décolletage to her stomach, but her breasts were hidden, as if teasing him to come and find them.

He forced such thoughts aside. There were more important things to discuss. "Beth, there's a tax bill waiting for me. If I couldn't find a way to earn the funds, I was afraid I'd have to marry an heiress, or lose everything. But the consortium offers me a different path. A path that leads me to you. A path that leads us to a chance at starting over."

"I need time." She returned her attention to the food.

"Why is that?" he asked gently.

"You know my promise to myself. Also, I don't want to jeopardize our friendship."

"I've never done *that* with friends before."

"No." She whipped around and faced him. "But you've done it with others, though."

Now the irascible woman was throwing his words back in his face, and he wouldn't let it stand. "You were the one that asked about my experience."

She shrugged one shoulder, not answering. Her indifference didn't fool him for a second, particularly as she'd piled every piece of food from the tray onto her own plate.

"Marriages have been started with far less than friendships, and they've been successful. My own parents had an arranged marriage." He tipped his chin in the air, daring her to deny his words. "It didn't take much effort on either of their parts to fall in love."

"Do you love me?" The challenge in her voice shot across the room, and the glare in her eyes could have cut him in two if he didn't know why she asked. It didn't take a genius to understand she was frightened of being hurt again.

He stood motionless while his heart raced. If he said what was in his heart, he was afraid he'd scare her.

"Don't answer that."

"I will answer," he said gently. "It's my prerogative." He casually walked to her side and leaned close. Then he lowered his voice until it was barely above a whisper. "I know the moment you walk into a room. Automatically, my eyes find you. Honestly, I can't help but walk to your side even when we're with a group of people. It's like a phenomenon that I can't control."

She tilted her gaze to meet his. A glimmer of wariness marred the brilliant blue.

He released a silent exhale. She'd been hurt too many times by the very men who had promised to love and protect her. Her brother. Her husband.

He'd also hurt her. But never again. *His Beth* should never doubt whether the men in her life would nurture, protect, and care for her.

"Let me share something else." He ran a hand through his wet hair, desperate to gather his thoughts into something that wouldn't send her running from the room. "Whenever I make a new discovery or build a new engine, my first thought is to share it with you." A grin tugged at the corner of his mouth. "Immediately. Especially if it's the middle of the night."

"I do that too," she said with an answering smile.

"I've never told this to anyone." His gaze held hers. "When Randford told me that you'd married, my heart stood suspended in my chest before it broke into a million pieces. Then I—" He picked up his wine and drank the rest of the glass for courage. "I'll go to hell for this confession. But my heart started beating once again after Randford told me that you were the third wife. I realized I still had a chance."

"A chance?"

The look of bafflement on her face surprised him. Did she really have no clue?

"We could still find our way back to each other." He took her hand and squeezed, willing her to see how committed he was to her.

"Too much time has passed." She huffed a breath in protest. "We have different lives. What about our friends?"

"We could solve any problems that would arise, don't you think? I know this, Beth, no matter where life takes us." He pressed his lips to hers. A vow, a solemn promise she could believe him. "I want that journey with you."

Her lips trembled beneath his. "You never answered my question . . . whether you loved me."

"You weren't listening then." He took a step back and

narrowed his eyes, assessing what thoughts could possibly be tumbling in her head. One thing about her, she had a sharp mind. But when it came to trusting men, she wore blinders. If he said he loved her aloud, she'd leave before the last syllable was out of his mouth.

How could she not see what was before her eyes?

"You're being fanciful," she declared. She turned away from him and pulled the coverlet off the bed and wrapped it around her.

"The consortium will change our fortunes. We'll have enough to live on." He raised his hand to stop her from arguing with him before he finished.

"I work. I don't want to lose that independence." She shrugged. "Your marchioness would be in trade."

"Well, your marquess would be in trade. It's like the kettle calling the pot black, don't you reckon? I'm not giving that up."

"We're too different. You're a scientist. You work with metal and steel and steam. I . . . I work with soft linens and embroider beautiful—"

"Pieces of art," he finished for her. "You create," he said softly. "You create positions and livelihoods for others. You create masterpieces that grace people's homes. I create too, only with different materials."

"Please don't." Her back straightened like a ramrod. "I can't discuss this now." She studied the window as if trying to gather all her courage.

He slowly clenched his fist, praying she wouldn't turn him down flat.

"I need some time alone to consider everything you've shared," she pleaded softly.

Somehow, he managed to nod an answer.

"I'm exhausted." She walked to the bed, then regarded him. "Where shall you sleep tonight?"

"I presumed here."

She sat on the bed with the coverlet wrapped around her. She wriggled a bit, then suddenly threw his shirt at his chest.

Which meant she was naked under the covers.

Just the thought of it sent his blood boiling. He slipped his shirt over his head. He donned his breeches, stockings, and shoes. "I'm not quite tired yet. If you need me, I'll be downstairs with Cillian." He waited for her to answer, but she simply stared at him. With his remaining dignity, he stepped from the room.

Tonight proved why he would never be a successful gambler.

He always laid his cards on the table too early.

Chapter Twenty-One

As soon as Julian stepped out the door, Beth flopped on her back and put her hand over her heart to stop the ache from everything shared tonight and all the lost opportunity between them. They both were at fault for not pursuing the other.

While her heart encouraged her to move forward, her mind was a different matter. The problem with Julian? When she'd kissed him, she'd felt as if she were in a different world, one where she was welcomed and appreciated. Just as she felt the same for him.

She drew a shallow breath. When she'd asked if he loved her, his words nearly knocked her to the floor. She'd asked the question thinking it an effective but harsh way to end the conversation. Yet he'd completely turned the tables on her by saying such lovely things that made her feel cherished. She had no idea he felt that way for her.

Or had she?

Did she have the courage to trust him again?

Julian was like a chameleon. He could change to fit in anywhere. Wasn't that what he was doing at this inn? He was a marquess masquerading as a . . . gentleman.

Because that's who he was. A gentleman no matter his station in life. Most men in his circumstances would be gambling trying to change their fortunes. But not him. He was trying to turn his fortunes around by creating. The same as her.

She got out of bed and started to dress. She needed to walk outside and breathe the fresh air. Perhaps that would clear her muddled thinking.

As she put on the worn dress and half boots that Sarah Drummond had generously provided, memories rippled through her thoughts. In years previous, she'd have turned her nose up at wearing such items. When she was younger, she never wore a dress twice. Slippers and half boots in a rainbow of colors lined her dressing room cabinets. They were replaced every year. Though her circumstances had changed, one thing became a constant. She had to rely on herself.

But tonight made that personal vow teeter like an unbalanced top.

As she stood to leave her room, her heart skipped a beat. The fickle and totally unreliable organ's rhythm was a reminder that she could marry him. Yet love, marriage, tenderness, and affection were not her forte nor her destiny. Her previous attempts at marriage were proof.

The soft lilts of a fiddle came from downstairs, accompanied by the sound of people clapping. It would be the perfect cover as she slipped out of the small inn for an evening stroll. Perhaps that would help her wrangle her recalcitrant heart under control.

When she opened the door, the muffled sounds of a country tune became louder. For a moment, she stood there letting the music wrap around her. The tune reminded her of a simpler time when she attended assemblies at the country village next to her father's estate in Somerset. Her mother and governess attended with her. But it was her father who had made those nights special.

"Miss Howell, may I have the next dance?"

She had her back turned but already recognized the voice. Smoothing her dress, she turned and found her handsome father before her with his hand outstretched. "Oh, Papa. If you dance with me, then none of the young men will ask me for at least an hour. They're too scared of you."

That's my intention," he growled, but the laughter in his eyes conflicted with his serious countenance. "Come, I want to dance with the prettiest girl here." He leaned close and whispered as if sharing a state secret, "Except for my viscountess."

She slid a side-eyed glance his way and caught him winking at her. Though her father appeared gruff to most people, she and the rest of the family knew him to be the kindest and gentlest man in all of England. Her gaze met that of her mother, who was beaming at the two of them.

"Indeed, Mother is breathtaking." Dressed in a brilliant red and blue silk gown, she was stunning. The love her parents shared made the world a brighter place. Beth was never lonely, even when St. John was away at Eton.

"And you, my favorite daughter, will be received just like your mother when you have your introduction in society." Her father grinned. "A rare, brilliant diamond of the first water."

"I'm your only daughter," she pointed out with a laugh.

"It doesn't make any difference that you're the only one." His gaze turned serious. "You will always be my favorite."

She didn't think he was simply discussing just daughters, but also wayward sons.

He grinned as he led her out to the dance floor. "I want you to have what your mother and I share. A love that makes even the dreariest days exciting simply because *your love is right beside you. I promise I'll help you find a worthy man who will cherish you the way I cherish your mother.*"

God, how she'd wanted that too, but it was another broken promise.

Just as having her parents still alive wasn't meant to be. How many times had she wondered what her life would be like if her parents were with her today?

Too many to count, and it was wasted effort anyway. But her stubborn heart had always kept that wish nearby along with all those tender feelings for Julian.

It was all a bother. Beth didn't want what her heart wanted. She doubted if either of them could mend if Julian's offer turned into another broken promise. Because love didn't guarantee neither of them would be hurt.

Maybe if she kept repeating that she'd believe it.

⁓

Julian slid into the chair next to Cillian. At this time of night, the inn was bustling with activity. A fiddler was tuning his instrument and the people in the public room fairly shimmered with excitement.

"What'll it be, love?" A barmaid sidled up to the table and smiled at Julian.

"Whisky."

"Another ale?" She waggled her eyebrows at Cillian. When he nodded in answer, she continued, "Save me a dance, then."

Julian leaned back in his chair and regarded Cillian. "Dancing?"

"Apparently, whenever the fiddler comes in for a pint there's dancing. Sally said it happens practically every night."

"Sally, is it? How long have you sat here swilling ale?"

Cillian lifted an eyebrow in challenge. "I can't help that all the ladies find me enchanting. That is, all except Miss Howell." His face turned serious. "I don't try and charm her. That's why she's immune. You have a better chance with her."

Julian released a sigh as the barmaid returned with their drinks. By then, the place was crowded. "Perhaps you could lend me some of your charm. She's immune to me also. I'm at my wit's end."

"What happened?"

Julian took a sip of whisky. Best to tell the truth and not soften it. He'd mucked everything up with Beth.

"I told her I loved her in so many words."

Cillian blinked as his brow furrowed in disbelief.

"After she was in danger, my gut ached. Plus, all those hours that I was with her upstairs made me even more confident."

"You did what?" Cillian's voice pitched higher than the strings on the violin that the fiddler tuned.

Julian winched at the shrill sound. "Not so loud. I didn't say those exact words, but I told her what happens when she walks into the room."

Cillian nodded once in agreement with a slight smile. "That's promising."

Julian finished his drink, and before he could order another, Sally was there with another glass.

"I thought it was promising too, until she told me to leave."

"Ack, man. Am I going to have to write you instructions? Bring her down here." His valet shook his head. "While she's wondering what your declaration means, you don't leave her. You woo her." He waved an arm around the public room. "The inn this evening is the perfect place.

You dance with her a couple of times, then you take her outside for a breath of fresh air. For the finale, you kiss her." He leaned back in his chair quite satisfied.

"Hmm," Julian grunted, not acknowledging the advice. If he had Beth outside, he didn't know if he could leave it at just a kiss. At that moment, his blood thrummed with heat for her. There was nothing he wanted more than to take her in his arms and give her a kiss that told her everything she meant to him. She was the only woman who'd ever had this effect on him. It was as if a part of her had seeped into him.

Beth Howell was his life, and she was scared to death to take what he offered her.

A marriage based on love and a lifetime of commitment. What he couldn't offer her before, security and a happy life, he could offer now. A part of him wanted to go to their room and argue with her until he could change her mind. Another part of him thought it best to leave her be until she had enough time to come to grips with what happened between them.

How could he blame her for not trusting him?

He regarded Cillian once again. "How do I prove to her that I won't fail her now or in the future? That's what she's afraid will happen." He traced the rough edges of the table, desperate to find some mooring to keep himself grounded. "What would I do if I failed her again?"

His valet rubbed his hand down his chin. "That's a conundrum. But I think you're looking at it the wrong way. Success is not the absence of failure. It's the ability to learn from our mistakes and try again. And, if necessary, try again and again until we get it right. You do that with your designs. You can do that with Miss Howell. I have faith in you."

"More Irish wisdom?" Julian scowled.

Cillian shrugged.

Julian lifted a brow. "How convenient that you lock your lips when I need your counsel now more than ever."

"You don't need me. You know what to do."

Julian nodded, then stood as the fiddler started playing a lively tune. Immediately, several couples moved enough tables and chairs to form a makeshift dance floor. They took their positions for the lively country dance.

"Wish me luck. I'm off to find Beth and see if she'll dance with me."

As Julian turned to leave, Cillian stood and put his hand on his shoulder. "Don't give up. You've always carried a torch for her."

"What if it's impossible?" The words slipped free, and he wished he'd never uttered them. He had always believed that his future and happiness lay with Beth. "What if I can never convince her?"

Cillian squinted his eyes with a pained look on his face. His sympathy laid bare for Julian to see. "If that's your fate, you'll know when to walk away. But I have every confidence in you and Miss Howell." Suddenly, he broke into a grin. "This is too somber a conversation for the entertainment that's promised this evening. Go, find her." Cillian smiled at Sally. "I'm off to find a pretty girl and dance with her."

Julian glanced about the room not really seeing anything as he contemplated what he'd say to Beth. *I can't stay away from you. You're as much a part of me as my own heart. My life, my future, are defined by you.*

He had it bad. Blythe Elizabeth Howell was under his skin.

It would be best to let her have time by herself. She always enjoyed her own company. Perhaps she was rethinking what they did in the bedroom. He certainly was. Just touching her awoke a hunger that had existed for years, one that he'd kept harnessed for as long as he could. Now it threatened to consume him.

He glanced up to the ceiling hoping to calm his musings.

"Mr. Raleah?"

At the sound of Sarah Drummond's voice, he bowed slightly. "Mrs. Drummond, how are you this evening?"

"It looks to be a busy night." She gazed at her husband and smiled. "The entire village seems to have come to dance away the summer evening. Where's Mrs. Raleah?"

"Upstairs. I'm on my way to join her." As sure as the sun would rise tomorrow, he'd not be sleeping with Beth this evening. Even he needed a little distance. But he had no idea where. With the crowd gathering in the pub and common areas, it wouldn't be here with all the noise.

"Have a good evening, Mr. Raleah." Sarah nodded at the next table, where several men held up their tankards asking for another ale.

"You do the same, Mrs. Drummond." Julian headed out of the public room. As soon as he reached the stairs, he discovered Beth standing on the landing.

He moved to go to her, and immediately she practically flew up the steps. Then and there, Julian decided he'd be sleeping outside her door.

It was as close as he dared get to her this evening, for both their sakes.

Chapter Twenty-Two

It was the quietest cart ride Beth could ever recall. Of course, she'd never really traveled in a cart this far a distance. This morning when they'd left the inn, Mr. and Mrs. Drummond had promised they'd see Julian's coach repaired and returned to London.

Beth sat in the back of the cart finishing the waistcoat she was making for Julian. Sitting in the driver's box, he had worked on his steam engines since his journal had been retrieved from the wreckage of the carriage. It was silly, but she just wanted him to glance her way once and smile, letting her know that the world was right between them.

Last night when she saw him standing at the bottom of the stairs, Beth had been struck by how strong and capable he looked. Even today, dressed in the borrowed clothing from the inn, he still possessed the proud bearing of an aristocrat.

Yet his eyes shone bright when he found pleasure in something. He'd looked at her like that last night. Such an expression made her heart pound a little harder just as it had when they'd been intimate with each other last night. Funny, but the slight touch of his hand against hers melted every part of her into a sentimental puddle of emotions.

She forced herself to exhale and took in her surroundings.

From the rolling hills in the distance, she could tell they were nearing Bath. It wasn't too long before they were on the outskirts of town.

Cillian pulled the cart to a stop in front of a little shop. "I'll see what I can find."

Julian nodded.

When Cillian was out of earshot, it gave Beth the opportunity she'd been looking for all morning. "Did you have a pleasant evening last night?"

Finally, he raised his head from his journal and regarded her. "Pleasant enough."

"Did you dance?"

"I really wasn't in the mood for dancing." He studied her with an intense gaze.

"Why are we here?" she asked.

"Mr. Drummond told me to stop here on the way to Bath. It seems Mr. Cochran likes to frequent this shop and sell many of the items he 'finds' on his routes to the shop owners. I'm hoping that's the case. Cillian is seeing if our items are in there. If they are, then he'll purchase them."

"Oh, I see. Do you need money? I still have my five guineas."

He shook his head. "Cillian has the remainder of my money. Plus, I still have good credit."

"Julian, I wasn't avoiding you when I saw you at the bottom of the stairs. I wouldn't have been very good company. I wasn't even good company for myself." She leaned toward him and rested her hand on the back of the bench seat. "Can't we pretend that our discussion didn't happen?"

"That's like letting the canary out of its cage, then ignoring it while it flies around the room." He turned slightly in her direction.

She smiled, and wonder upon wonders, he did the same. "I was hoping . . ."

Several songbirds were singing their hearts out. It was almost as if they were serenading them.

A wistfulness in his deep gray eyes betrayed the winsome smile he presented.

"I don't want to lose . . . our friendship." She'd said the wrong thing, as his grin vanished and a seriousness that she'd never seen before clouded his visage. But she had to try and make amends. "I think you're my best friend."

"Oh, Beth. What am I going to do with you?" He reached out and brushed his hand against her cheek. "As you are mine. Our friendship hasn't changed." He blew out a breath and leaned away from her. "But other things have."

She wanted to protest the distance. Why was this so difficult?

"After what we did and what I said, there's a logical solution to all of this."

Before his words were out of his mouth, she was shaking her head. "I've thought about last night. You don't have to give me a proposal."

"I know you believe you're not the type of woman who needs a proposal, but I beg to differ. I want to marry." When she started to protest, he held up his hand. "And I'm the type of man who wants to offer a proposal, especially after what we shared."

"But you said you'd had other lovers. Did you offer them proposals?" It was a rather sound argument, if she did say so herself.

"I didn't offer them marriage as we had an understanding between us. Both of us were fully aware that our time together was something that brought pleasure to each of us with no future." He stared straight into her eyes, holding her in place. "You and I are different. What I shared with you yesterday . . . was everything. Didn't you feel it?"

That was the problem. She did feel it. She couldn't imagine sharing her body and all those new experiences with anyone but Julian. "I felt it more than you know." She reached out her hand as an act of mending this rift between them.

The bell over the shop door jangled, and Cillian strode to the cart with an armful of clothing and boots. "It's just as Drummond said. All your clothing was there except for your shirt. I managed to bargain for a used one that should fit you." He held up Julian's boots and a pair of evening slippers, then laughed. "These I practically stole. The shopkeeper said that he'd never seen any this big before. You, sir, do not have to wear your boots to a formal affair this evening."

"Excellent." Julian laughed as he took the boots and a pair of stockings from Cillian's hands. "And Miss Howell's clothes?"

Cillian's lip pressed into a grimace. "I'm sorry, Miss Howell, I didn't have luck recovering any of your valuables."

And neither did she if her conversation with Julian was any indication. The most valuable thing in her life, and she was frightened she'd lost it.

"But I did manage to pick up this gown and the other . . . items you'll need to dress. The clothing is clean, and I think it'll fit. If it needs any altering, I can do it."

"Thank you." She took the pink gown from his hands

along with stockings, chemise, stays, and a pair of slippers. The gown was several seasons out of date and a little faded. But it did appear that it would fit and there was no odor.

"Thoughts?" Julian said softly.

Oh yes, she had thoughts.

She thought she was going to cry.

Not because her circumstances had fallen once again. At one time, she would have scoffed at wearing second-hand clothes, but now she welcomed it. No, her sadness came from her confusion. She didn't know what she had to do to recapture the easiness she once shared with Julian.

Now that she lost it, she finally understood how extraordinary it was.

Julian stood outside Beth's door at the Royal Hotel. He'd splurged on connecting rooms for them. It gave them both a little distance, which was needed at this point. But it kept him close to her. For him, last night had been torture. He'd slept in the chair outside her room, ensuring that no one disturbed her. But that was like the fox watching the henhouse. He wanted to walk through that door and take her downstairs to dance while he wooed her, as Cillian would say. It was easy to tell from her expression when she enjoyed him. If she'd keep her preconceived notions at bay for a while, he could convince her that they'd have a happy life with each other.

Though he'd promised his father he'd marry well and bring the marquessate back to its original grandeur, he could accomplish what he needed with Beth by his side. His work with the consortium would provide enough of a living to at least put the estate back in order and live modestly. They didn't need the social Season, servants, or extravagances that would normally be expected of them. They both liked to work hard.

He blinked. Perhaps that's where he made a tactical error. It would be better if he laid all of this out on paper and went over it with her. Then she'd see what he was trying to accomplish and how they could marry.

"My lord," Cillian called out as he walked down the carpeted hallway.

Julian turned his attention away from the door to his valet. The man had spent the entire afternoon trying to put Julian's clothing in order for tonight's event.

"What did you discover?" Julian asked.

Cillian nodded in respect, then looked in both directions in the hallway. "The Marquess of Montridge is in residence here with his sister. They're attending the assembly tonight. He wasn't receiving callers today, as he had a bad night at the gaming tables."

"Where at?"

Cillian shook his head. "I couldn't determine, but it was at some gentry's house. Whoever the man is, his games run deep. Apparently, Montridge has quite the temper and let it out last night."

"How did you find all this out?" Julian leaned a little closer.

"His mistress."

Julian's eyes widened. "What the devil were you doing with his mistress?"

"Nothing. I was checking on our horses when she marched into the stables in a high dudgeon. She stood and waited as her groomsman and driver readied her carriage. She was anxious to return to London. She told the whole story to her staff and didn't care who overheard it."

"What was she upset about?" Julian didn't know much about Montridge. He was a man in his early forties who not only possessed a prestigious title but also appeared to be as rich as Croesus by the way he gambled. His games were legendary with Pelham at the Jolly Rooster.

"Apparently, when he returned to his residence this morning he informed her that her clothing allowance was reduced by half, then promptly rolled over and fell asleep. She told a groomsman that the marquess's sister could deal with him." Cillian shook his head, his disgust clear. "His sister, the poor lass, is only seventeen." He motioned to Beth's door. "Are you on your way to see Miss Howell?"

"Yes." He reached into his jacket and pulled out a small pouch. "There is a modiste shop down the street. I've written a note to be included with the dress and another instructing that I wish to purchase her a new gown. It's the one in the window. Have them send me the bill in London."

Cillian nodded as he took the money. "What color is it? Not black, I hope."

"It's dark blue and exquisite." For one night, he wanted her to feel like a queen of all she surveyed. "Do you know the lake at Randford's hunting lodge?"

His valet nodded. "Bluest water I've ever seen."

"It reminds me of her eyes. The blue of a perfect midnight summer's sky."

A snort of laughter escaped Cillian. "By heavens, I'm going to make a poet of you yet." Then he turned suddenly serious. "Remember that and say it to her. She'll melt like ice that same *midnight summer night*."

"*Sky*, not *night*," Julian growled. "Remind me, why do I keep you employed?"

"Because you're loyal." He pointed at Beth's door. "Just like Miss Howell. Remember that."

"Begone before I lose my good temper." Julian waved his valet away.

"I think you lost that a long time ago, my lord." Cillian chuckled, then bowed briefly. With purely theatrical precision, he turned on his heel.

Once Julian was alone in the hall, he slowly lifted his hand and knocked briskly.

When the door opened, his gut clenched in a knot. She'd bathed and donned her secondhand dress. Though it was worn, the dark-pink gown highlighted her complexion, and her blue eyes twinkled. Her earlier wariness had disappeared.

"Come in," she said softly.

"I shouldn't. What if someone—"

By then, she grabbed his arm and pulled him into the room, then closed the door. "What we have to say to each other shouldn't be overheard by anyone else." She smiled briefly, then waved at a sitting area next to the fireplace at the far end of the room. "The room is lovely."

He glanced around the room. The walls were painted white, which made the gilded bed the centerpiece of the room. Lush bed linens covered the bed and pillows embroidered in gold thread were tossed haphazardly across the mattress.

Just like he wanted to do with her. Toss her on the mattress and satisfy the urge to take her into his arms and never let go. Sup at her lips and fill himself with her sweetness. In his dreams, she'd do the same with him. An image of them together on the bed—naked and entwined within each other's arms—branded his thoughts. Everything within him tightened, as did his cock.

"I'll pay for my portion of the room."

The image of them faded. "What?"

"I'll reimburse you." She smiled sweetly. "Where are your things? Cillian hasn't brought them yet."

He cleared his throat. "We're not staying in the same room together. Not here. There's too much of a chance someone might see us together. But our rooms are joined together through there." He pointed to a locked door at the end of the room.

Her face fell.

He ran a hand through his hair. "Beth, I'm trying to give you some distance. I don't want you thinking I'm pressuring you."

She clasped her hands demurely in front of her, then walked to the fireplace without seeing if he followed.

She didn't have to. They both knew he would.

He always did. Every breathing moment he wanted to share with her.

When they were both seated, she turned that rapier-sharp gaze to his, slicing through him, seeing everything inside.

"I appreciate your thoughtfulness. Just so you know, I care about you and me." She glanced out the window momentarily.

"I'm aware of that," he said gently.

With a deep breath, she turned his way again and picked up a bundle that had been tied in a red ribbon. "This is for you to wear tonight. I made it myself. Cillian helped me with the measurements."

Carefully, he untied the ribbon and held up an ivory silk and satin waistcoat. The needlework was exquisite. Decorated with an embroidered black Greek key design, it was the most elegant and luxurious piece of clothing he'd ever owned. "This is what you were sewing. It's beautiful." The awe he felt crashed through him, leaving him stunned. For a moment, he was speechless. "No one has ever given me anything this grand."

Her eyes flashed like diamonds. "Do you really like it?"

"Very much." He wanted to add he adored her too but thought the better of it.

She sat on the edge of her seat, her excitement practically making her quiver. She leaned near and pointed to the inside of the garment. "On the silk lining I've embroidered one of the Raleah lions that's on your family crest." She dipped her gaze. "It's close to your heart as I know how much your ancestral seat means to you."

His breath clenched in his chest. No one understood his devotion and loyalty to his marquessate. He never discussed with anyone how the entire estate was being sold off piece by piece. The two marble lions that guarded the entrance to Raleah House might be the next items he had to sell. His throat thickened at the thought.

"I will treasure this always." He smiled, then studied the lion again. "It's magnificent," he said reverently as his forefinger traced the design. The lion was surrounded by a flower of some sort. "What's the flower? It's not on the crest."

The defiant upward tilt of her chin undid him. It was a gesture she used to guard her heart. "It's not. It's a pink dianthus. The first time you called on me after we danced together at my first ball, you brought me a bouquet."

The memories slammed into his thoughts. How could he forget that day? The entire entry of her house had been literally covered in exquisite bouquets from the finest floral shops in all of London. He had arrived with a meager bouquet of flowers that he'd bought from a flower seller on the street. They'd reminded him of Somerset and Raleah House, where they grew wild. That winsome, carefree day she'd marveled at them as if he'd brought her the Crown Jewels as a token of his affection.

He couldn't not touch her anymore.

Slowly, he stood, then took her hand and gently pulled her to her feet. He took her into his arms and pulled her tight against his body. Her supple curves melted into the hard planes of his chest. He trailed his hand down her back.

"It's perfect, Beth. Thank you."

They stared at each other, both breathing heavily from the pent-up passion that had been ignored for too long. Unattended it threatened to explode.

"Are you going to kiss me?"

He narrowed his eyes. "What was it that you said to me? Oh, I remember," he rasped softly. "You said that my kiss was like one of my failed steam experiments. It wasn't hot enough. I'm about to prove you wrong. So, yes, I'm going to kiss you and prove that I don't need any lessons on how to make it hotter or learn how to make you beg for more. By the time we're finished, your entire body is going to be smoldering and aching for more."

He searched her eyes and saw the desire ignite within them. Her perfectly kissable lips formed an O.

"Get ready to burn." He bent his head and claimed her lips with his. He pulled her tighter and his cock throbbed against her belly. He bit her lips gently, then teased his tongue over the plump flesh of her perfect mouth. When she opened, he didn't hesitate. His tongue left no inch of her tender lips or mouth unexplored. When she whimpered, he didn't relent but kept on tasting, feasting, and driving her wild.

Just as it drove him wild.

"Bloody hell," he murmured before he lifted her in his

arms and stormed across the room. His entire body was about to combust if he couldn't taste all of her. When he reached the bed, he gently lowered Beth to the soft linens covering the mattress. With an efficiency that didn't betray his nerves, he managed to take off his boots. Once that was finished, he kissed her again. Easily, he could become addicted to her kisses . . . become addicted to her. With her, he'd never get his fill. Not even when they turned eighty and had to help each other climb the steps to their bedroom. He chuckled at the thought of them stopping on each step for a sweet but unchaste kiss. They'd shock their servants with their amorous behavior.

"What are you laughing at?" There was a certain shyness in her voice.

It would not do for her to turn bashful or think he was laughing at her.

"Myself and how much I'm looking forward to kissing you again." He swept his lips lightly over her lips. When she parted hers, he deepened the kiss, then crawled onto the bed, never breaking contact.

His knees framed her hips as he continued to feast upon her luscious mouth. But his Beth was a fast learner. She turned the tables on him without him even knowing it. She wrapped her arms around him and pulled him until his body rested against hers. She canted her hips to his and ground against him.

"Please," she said as she bit his lips.

"Please, what?" he groaned.

"I need more." He lifted his head until he could look at her entire face. Her lips were red and swollen from their kisses. Her face was flushed, and she was panting as hard as he was.

"I can never say no to you. You're temptation, ruination, and salvation all combined into a frenzy I can't resist."

He slid his body to the side so he could touch every inch of her. As he kissed and licked the tender skin of her neck, his hands cupped one of her breasts. With a pleasurable sigh, she arched her back, giving him better access. He stilled as he traced the hard nipple through the soft muslin of her gown. "Where are your stays?"

She turned to him and smiled like a mermaid intent on seducing the poor sailor to crash upon her rocks and stay forever. "They didn't fit." Her gaze slid down his body until she openly stared at his erection begging to be released from his breeches. "It looks like your pants don't quite fit either. Whatever shall we do?"

"Minx," he growled playfully, then took possession of her mouth again. "This is what we'll do. This trip is a treasure hunt, and we're about to go exploring." He slid down her body, nestling his face against her breasts as he lifted the hem of her gown. He lightly nipped her nipples through the cloth.

"What are we looking for?" she asked breathlessly while running her fingers through his hair.

"Pearls." With a devilish smile, he caught her gaze. "One in particular."

Her eyes widened. "Pearls?"

"A precious pink one," he replied. By then, he had her dress to her thighs. "I think we should start here." He scooted down and positioned her bent leg to his liking. He pressed a kiss to the silky skin that would lead to the jewel he was seeking. "Hmm," he murmured next to her skin. "Not quite what I'm looking for, but it's a masterpiece in and of itself."

She rested on her elbows and peered down at him with a quizzical look. "You're not . . . hunting there, are you?"

"My darling Beth, I don't think we should"—reverently, he placed another kiss on the inside of her opposite thigh, then trailed his lips upward—"leave anything to chance, do you?"

"Julian," she moaned softly. Her smile sent a rivulet of sensation through him.

"Put your legs around my shoulders." He'd uncovered what he was seeking. The very heart of her was unveiled and he couldn't wait to taste her and bring them both pleasure. He parted her nether lips and found the precious jewel he'd been seeking. To think he'd be the first and, if he had his way, the only man to bring her pleasure this way. She was his beloved, cherished and treasured for the wonder she brought to him. What a fool that others didn't see the rare gift she was.

He worshiped her by placing a light kiss on that hidden pearl. But with the first taste of her arousal, he couldn't resist and feasted upon her like a starving man.

He worshiped her like she was his heaven.

Chapter Twenty-Three

〰️

Beth's heart threatened to break through her chest. Julian was kissing her *there*. With each stroke of his tongue, he sent flashes of pleasure exploding through her. With each breath, lick, and suck, he was leaving no stone unturned as he gave her pleasure.

She flopped back on the bed with a groan that came from the exquisite fervor he brought forth with his lips and tongue. Her fingers bunched in his hair of their own accord, locking him in place.

"That's it," he said softly as he raised his head. "Show me what you want."

At the tenderness in his words, her eyes grew misty. No man had ever treated her as if she were precious and vital to him.

"Julian," she crooned. She canted her hips and pressed his head closer as the sensations started to rise and fall like waves undulating during a tempest. As he pleasured her, she moved one of her legs and slipped her stocking foot underneath his body. When she found his cock, she rubbed the top of her foot under him. The slight hiss that erupted from him ensured that she found her efforts pleasurable.

Suddenly, he pulled her leg out from underneath him,

then smiled down at her. "Allow me to treasure hunt first, then you can have your turn."

"A woman sometimes becomes impatient when there's a promise of a golden shaft in her future," she said huskily.

"A golden shaft?" He waggled his eyebrows.

She rolled her eyes with a smile tugging at her lips. "I'm referring to Cupid's arrow. 'How she will love when the rich golden shaft / Hath killed the flock of all affections else / That live in her.'"

"Amazing the things I discover about you," he teased. "A devotee of *Twelfth Night* and Duke Orsino."

At the sound of the deep rumble of his laughter, she smiled.

In response, his eyes blazed. "If I ever saw you dressed in breeches, I'd throw you over my shoulder and take you into my bedroom and we'd not come out for a week."

She bit her lip and slowly closed her eyes. To hear such words from him made her heart somersault in her chest. "I need to find a pair. I'd like that."

"As would I." He blew air lightly against her nub and she shivered in response.

The intensity started to build once again. Her blood felt heated, and her breath grew shallow. Each one of her senses responded to every lick and kiss he administered. Then, he attended her with a frenzy that made her body bow like an arrow ready to shoot across the sky. He drew from her a heady mix of emotions that she couldn't control. She wanted to laugh and sigh, then weep as the world delightfully careened out of control. Every nerve ending fired in concert, taking her body higher and higher. He took possession of her with his tongue, and the warmth of his breath undid her, making her feel attractive and alive in a way that only happened with him.

As she gasped for breath, he slowed his kisses, but he didn't stop caring for her as her orgasm rolled through her, then slowly gentled. Her skin felt on fire and dew covered her brow.

As if he cherished every part of her, he kissed her center, then her inner thighs before slowly moving up her body. His hands cupped her face as his gray eyes peered into hers. A look of smug satisfaction spread across his lips. "I found my treasure. A priceless pearl that can only be called incomparable."

At the tender words, she blushed and tried to hide the effect he had on her. With little encouragement, she'd give him her heart and soul.

Gently, he lifted her chin until she was staring into his eyes. Then like the gentle lover he was, he pressed his lips to hers. She closed her eyes and deepened the kiss, tasting her arousal on his lips. When her tongue swept to meet his, she tasted herself again. It was sensually wicked, and there and then she decided she never wanted to leave this room . . . certainly, not while he was in her bed.

He pulled back, then as if he couldn't bear to be parted from her, he growled softly before returning to kiss her. Finally, he pulled away and stared at her once again. The seriousness of his gaze took her aback but only for a moment.

"Is something wrong?" she asked.

"Indeed," he said, pressing a kiss to her nose. "I never knew a perfect moment until now." He pressed a kiss to her forehead. "However will I be able to walk out that door and return to my ordinary life, the one I had before I came in here?"

"I feel the same. I liked what we did," she whispered.

"I as well," he murmured.

His eyes burned with an emotion so intense she almost had to look away for fear he'd see inside her and discover all the riot of thoughts and ideas that were running amok in her head.

Oh, this was the problem with lovemaking. A person could easily confuse it with love.

Particularly with someone so caring and giving. Julian was a threat to her sanity, her world, and, most importantly, her heart. Even she couldn't deny that there was something uniquely extraordinary that she shared with him. She'd seen in his eyes a look that she recognized. A man who cared deeply. She'd seen that look in her father's gaze as he shared a laugh or a secret with her mother. Randford had it for Kat, and even the reclusive Earl of Sykeston had it for Constance.

Beth strummed her fingers through his hair. "When do I get to go on a treasure hunt of my own?" She ran her hands down his back, the firm muscles tightening and bunching under the linen shirt he wore. When she got to his buttocks, she pushed him into her lower belly, which still seemed to be humming in pleasure. His hard cock rocked into her where she was still sensitive. She sucked in a breath.

"Anytime," he said in that gravelly voice of his that seemed to make the inside of her vibrate in pleasure.

"Now," she whispered. "This instant, I want to make love."

He pushed up on his elbows and stared down at her, narrowing his eyes.

Before she could say another word, a knock sounded on the door. "My lord?"

"Cillian," he groaned, and collapsed on his back beside her, covering his eyes with one bent arm. "The man normally has such impeccable timing."

"My lord?" The man's Irish lilt rang through the oak panel.

"I'm going to kill him," Julian muttered.

"I won't allow you." She playfully swatted his arm. "The man has great fashion sense." She scooted to the edge of the bed to stand and answer the door.

Playfully, he pulled her back against his body and nipped the tender spot below her ear, then pressed a kiss to it. "Where do you think you're going? Stay here. I'll see what he wants, then send him on his way."

With a natural ease, Julian stood in his stocking feet, then within five steps he had his hand on the handle. He turned her way and smiled as if they shared a secret, then opened the door.

~

Cillian stood on the other side with a box in hand, which he handed to Julian. "My lord, the things you requested." He tilted back on his heels quite animated. "I think it will be to your and your lady's liking."

"Thank you, Cillian." He smiled at his valet and clasped the man's shoulder with one hand.

"Lord Grayson." Sir Jeffrey stood a few feet away from Cillian. He turned to the lady holding on to his arm. "Allow me to introduce my wife . . ." His gaze drifted down to Julian's stocking feet.

Instantly, Julian closed the door behind him.

"Sir Jeffrey." Julian nodded at the man, then executed a perfect bow to the woman. "Grayson at your service, madam."

Sir Jeffrey chuckled slightly and pointed at the box. "That's quite a box. I've purchased items from that modiste for my wife. I wasn't aware that you were married."

Julian's face turned crimson. "I'm . . . I'm not." He glanced at the closed door. "It's for my . . . friend." The words sounded like an insult to Beth.

Sir Jeffrey's eyebrows lifted to his hairline. "I see. We don't mean to interrupt you." The man cleared his throat. "Have a nice evening." He tucked his wife behind him as if trying to shield her from the spectacle.

"The assembly later this evening. Are you going to attend?" Julian asked, desperate to salvage their chance meeting. He couldn't afford for Sir Jeffrey to come to the wrong conclusion.

Sir Jeffrey blinked several times at the question. "Perhaps." He tugged his wife's arm. "Come along, my dear."

As they turned away, Julian overheard the wife's loud murmurs.

"How indecent. He didn't have on shoes. He looked to be in a state of dishabille. Who is he? Surely, you're not doing business with him."

"Hush," he scolded. Their voices faded to nothing as they continued their way down the hall.

"Ignore them," Cillian said. "Do you hear, my lord? Ignore them," he repeated.

"Thank you." Julian took the box, then returned to the room and closed the door.

Beth stood and straightened her dress. "Look how dreadfully unkept and slovenly I appear."

"You look beautiful," he said softly. "Like a woman who . . ."

What had he done by being so careless? Not only had he jeopardized his reputation but his Beth's as well. As soon as he had the chance, he'd set the matters to rights about Beth with Sir Jeffrey.

"Like a woman who is well-pleasured." She laughed and the sound, which normally made him laugh, also did nothing but ring hollow in his ears. She glided to the mirror, then groaned at her reflection. "My hair looks like a beehive with all the bees buzzing about." She released her hair from the pins, combed it with her fingers, then twisted the chestnut-colored locks in a knot and tucked it under.

Julian was by her side after placing the box on the bed. He took both of her hands in his. "I'm proud to be with you." He waggled his eyebrows. "I like bees even if they sting."

"Not everyone does." She laughed.

Her elegance captivated him. He could watch her for hours and never get bored.

He would not let thoughts of Sir Jeffrey ruin this moment for them.

With a couple of hairpins, she secured the knot. "Who was at the door?"

"Cillian." He smiled, then held out his hand. "Come. I want to give you something."

When she crossed the room, he picked up the box and gave it to her. "I feel like a boy at Christmas. I can't wait for you to open this."

"No man has given me a gift in ages."

"They're all fools." He smiled. "Except me."

She laughed, then tapped her chin with a finger as she thought. "The last man was my father. It was my sixteenth birthday, the last I celebrated with him. He gave me a sapphire ring in a puzzle box very similar to the ones sold at the Poppycock. I still have the box, but the ring is safely locked away at E. Cavensham Commerce." She frowned slightly. "It was the only way to ensure that St. John wouldn't sell it."

His chest tightened that she had to worry about

personal mementos such as gifts being sold. In so many ways, they shared the same experiences.

She sat on the bed with the box, and he sat next to her. The look of pure delight on her face was gift enough. Slowly, she pulled the lid away and pushed aside the gauze wrapped around the items beneath.

She drew in a sharp breath as she pulled out the exquisite ball gown, a taffeta creation in the deepest blue he'd ever seen. It was the exact same shade as when the flame of a candle illuminated her eyes. The netting that covered the gown was covered in clear crystals that reminded him of the constellations that decorated the sky at his ancestral home on clear summer nights.

With her hand, she traced the designs. "Only you would think of something so beautiful and romantic to give me. It's gorgeous." She raised his gaze to his. "I can't remember receiving anything so beautiful."

The tenderness in her face undid him, and he knew he'd done the right thing. "I saw it in the window of a shop when we rode into town. I wanted you to have it." He cupped her cheek.

A lone tear cascaded down her cheek.

Gently, he wiped it away with his thumb. "Darling, you're supposed to be delighted."

"I can't help it." She cupped her hand over his, holding it in place as she searched his face. "I can't accept it. It cost a fortune, and neither of us have the money."

He leaned close and pressed a soft kiss to her lips. In that moment, all he could think of was how much she meant to him. For the world, he didn't want her to suffer because of mistakes not of her own doing. Without any hesitation, she returned the kiss. They took from each other the tenderness offered. But as it always did with them, the underlying desire that seemed to shimmer between the two of them threatened to erupt.

With a slight groan, Julian pulled away. "For all my adult life, I've wanted to give you something that would be a reminder of how special you are. I wish it was more than a dress." He blinked several times. Perhaps he was as affected as she was by the moment. "Wear this for me this evening. It'll be another gift you give me. Just remember that no matter what we discover tonight, know that I'll always cherish you." He took her hand in his and lowered himself to one knee.

"Julian," she warned gently.

"I'm not proposing." He took her hand and raised it to his lips. "Consider it an act of fealty on my part. Know that I'll always put you first in my life."

"Oh, Julian," she said quietly. "That's beautiful."

"It's the truth, but I want to discuss our future." He looked toward the door, then returned his attention to her. "Soon, I'll be able to support us. You'll want for nothing. That's my life's goal, to take care of you."

Gently, she placed her hand on his mouth to stop him. Instantly, he pressed a kiss to her fingers.

"I won't be quiet until you hear everything I have to say. It won't be overnight. But I'm a hard worker, and I promise I'll give you everything you need and desire in life." He took her hand and squeezed it. "I finally have opportunities that will change our fortunes."

"I don't know what to say." She shook her head.

"There's no need to say anything now," he answered. He gently placed his hand under her chin and tilted it until her gaze met his. "But try and keep an open mind. I won't hurt you, nor will I fail you again. I'll disappoint you at times, but it won't be intentional."

"I promise to think about it." She bit her lip. "I should

have stayed with that fortune-teller. Perhaps she could have given us a little advice here." She slid her gaze to his.

He couldn't help but laugh at her playfulness. "I heartily agree."

"I'm lucky to have you as my . . . I can't say 'friend' as that term doesn't really define us anymore, does it?" She tilted her head as she regarded him as if trying to solve a puzzle.

He chuckled and shook his head. "Let's say we're each other's most intimate and ardent admirer." He waggled his eyebrows slightly. "Sounds wicked, doesn't it. Plus, I think it's perfect for us."

He stood and pointed at the box. "There are several more items you'll need for the evening." He looked to the gilded clock that sat above the fireplace. "I'll let you dress for the assembly. Afterward, we'll dine and discuss what we discover. I don't want to miss Montridge."

She stood as well, then walked him to the connecting door. Before he took his leave, she stood on her tiptoes, then kissed him once. "Thank you for everything. I don't know how I'll repay you."

"Same way I'll reimburse you for this exquisite waistcoat." With his best grin, he winked. "We're creative. We'll think of inventive ways to compensate each other, don't you think?"

~

Beth leaned back against the door and let her mind wander to places that she'd never let it go before. She had no doubt that his experiments would be commercially viable and he'd be a success and a celebrated scientist. No one was better at coming up with these steam machines than Julian.

She pushed away from the door and went to properly lay out the dress. As she held it up to admire it once more, she was again struck by the beauty of it. Since her first Season, she'd never possessed such an exquisite gown.

She picked up the box and pulled out the other items. There were new clocked stockings, a set of stays with exquisite embroidery of little blue flowers. The workmanship was so extraordinary that Beth had half a mind to visit the shop and see if she could convince the woman who created the masterpiece to come and work for her and Kat in London. Perhaps the designer could create custom pieces for them. She chuckled at such a thought. She thought of business as much as Julian thought of steam engines. Lastly, she pulled out a chemise made of the finest silk that matched the stays. She ran her fingers over the exquisite but delicate silk. She drew a steadying breath at the image of Julian taking it off her.

When she pulled out the dance slippers, she grinned. They were made of the same midnight color. The slippers sparkled with each turn in her hand because of the tiny inlaid crystals embedded throughout the shoes. Inside was a folded piece of parchment.

For the most beautiful woman, who only deserves the best. I can't wait to see you wear it. You must promise me the first and last dance of the night.

Would it be remiss of me to ask for all the ones in between also?

J.

Her heart stuttered in its beat. Julian was a born romantic. She'd be a fool not to marry him.

While it might be scandalous to accept such a gift from him, she would wear it proudly. The way he described how he saw her as stars in the night convinced her that for the first time in her life she had the possibility of a future with him.

Because she believed him. He'd not hurt her, nor would he fail her. But as with all the people we love . . .

Her heart stopped at the words. She loved him. She picked up the dress and hugged it to her. She loved him with every fiber of her being. How could she have been so determined not to acknowledge and accept it? She'd always tried to keep such emotions under lock and key, but what was the point?

She'd fallen in love with him the very first time he'd asked her to marry him. It's funny how so many years had passed, but no matter what life threw their way, he was the one true constant in her life.

Just then, a knock sounded on the door. Beth smoothed her dress and answered. A slightly older woman stood before her. "Miss Howell? My name is Beatrice Cooke. I'm employed by the Royal Hotel to help fine ladies such as yourself dress for our assemblies when they haven't brought their own lady's maid."

"How do you do," Beth answered. "However, there must be some mistake. I didn't ask for your services."

"No mistake, Miss Howell." She smiled demurely. "Lord Grayson made the request. He said you have a new gown for tonight and thought there might be the need for alterations."

Beth's cheeks heated. "You must think the worst of me. I'm not his . . ."

The woman's eyes were kind as her brow furrowed in concern. "I think nothing of the sort. You're a beautiful woman who needs help dressing. That's all I see."

Beth smiled at her kindness and wondered if Beatrice could also see before her a woman in love.

Chapter Twenty-Four

Julian knocked softly on Beth's door. He smiled as he ran a hand down the waistcoat she'd made for him to wear this evening. It fit perfectly, and it was the first time in ages that he'd worn anything except for his typical black formal wear. But what set his blood pounding was the anticipation of seeing her in the dress. Whatever sacrifices he'd make in the coming months to pay for her new dress, it would be worth it. She deserved fine things and so much more.

He could hear the rustling of footsteps behind the oaken panel. When it opened, a prim and proper maid stood before him. He smiled not so much in greeting, but with the thought *This is how Beth should always be pampered. With servants galore to wait on her and a multitude of beautiful gowns and the accompaniments.*

"Good evening," Julian said with a nod to the maid. "I'm wondering if Miss Howell is ready for tonight."

The maid nodded in reply. "Yes, sir."

He could tell by the sly smile the woman wore that Beth would be stunning, but when she stepped into view he hadn't been prepared for the magnificent sight. His heart slammed against his ribs. She looked like she'd stepped from a world that few mere mortals could ever claim to see.

He swallowed, trying to keep his wits about him. One look at Beth and all men would become tottering fools.

Just like him.

"My lord," she said softly. "I'm ready."

"I'm not," he muttered. All he wanted was to stay in this exact spot and bask at the sight of her. He inhaled through his nose, desperate to calm his racing pulse.

"Is something the matter?" She tilted her head and stared at him. "Do you need more time?"

Forever. But even that might not be long enough. Like a gift that begged to be unwrapped, and he was the man who would get to unwrap her if all the stars aligned correctly.

"Everything is perfect," he answered. His voice had deepened of its own accord. "You are a vision."

The lady's maid chuckled softly. She turned to Beth and dipped a curtsy. "Thank you, Miss Howell, for allowing me to dress you this evening." The maid's voice grew softer, but Julian could still hear every word. "If you need assistance undressing, please just ring. I'll make myself available."

Not if he had anything to do with it. No one would deny him the pleasure of performing the role of Beth's lady's maid this evening.

"Thank you, Beatrice," Beth replied. "I'm sure I'll be able to manage."

"I'll leave you to your evening then, ma'am." The lady's maid made another brief curtsy, then left. Finally they were alone.

Her gaze lifted briefly to his. Though she didn't smile, he could see the invitation that resided in the brightness of her eyes.

He stepped closer and took Beth's gloved hands into his own. "I've always thought you beautiful, but tonight, you're radiant." He gently squeezed her fingers. "I wish there was an artist present to capture this moment forever."

She blushed prettily, but he was rewarded with her saucy smile. "I'm glad there isn't one here. I rather fancy a dance or two with the handsome gentleman in front of me. An artist would take weeks, and by then I'm afraid the orchestra would be tired of playing."

"Good point." He chuckled, then bent slowly to her. With a soft press of his lips to hers, he groaned against her mouth. "I fear I'll not be able to resist touching you this evening."

"You're going to fill my head with such utterances," she chided playfully.

"That is my intention. I plan to give you so many compliments this evening that every other man fades from sight as you'll only have eyes for me." He brought one of her gloved hands to his mouth for a kiss.

"They already have," she replied as her gaze locked on his waistcoat. "How does your waistcoat fit?"

"Perfect, like you," he teased. "Thank you."

With a wink, she continued, "Shall we? I'm anxious to see what the evening brings."

He held out his arm. When she wrapped hers around his, he was instantly aware of that undercurrent of desire that always encircled them. He closed the door behind them, then leaned toward her ear, "For the first time in ages, I want to curse my lack of wealth for my own reasons."

"What do you mean?" She bent her head slightly, giving him greater access to her neck, and he took full advantage by pressing another kiss to that tender spot he'd discovered she possessed when they'd shared the bed earlier.

"I want to bedeck you in every jewel I can find that would be fitting your station in life."

"And what station would that be?" The laughter rang clear in her voice.

"The queen of my heart," he whispered.

"The things you say would make a woman in her nine-tieth decade blush."

"I'm not interested in her. Only you." When he looked up, Sir Jeffrey and his wife stood at the end of the hall-way staring at them. Of course, he and Beth hadn't made it ten feet from the door, as they'd been in their own world. He knew the minute Beth saw the couple. Imme-diately, she retreated into herself, losing all her earlier playfulness.

"Good evening," Julian called out, then looked to the man's wife and bowed slightly. "Madame." Just by say-ing the words, he made the couple acknowledge him, since his rank was well above Sir Jeffrey's knighthood.

Sir Jeffrey silently acknowledged him with a nod.

Julian turned to Beth and smiled in reassurance. "May I introduce my dearest friend, Miss Howell."

When he returned his attention to the couple, they had turned around and were walking away.

"*Bloody bastard*," Julian growled. Tonight, he'd make the time to find Sir Jeffery and drag him to Beth's side, where he'd apologize for his abhorrent behavior.

With a gentle touch, Beth placed her hand on his sleeve. "Perhaps they didn't hear you and didn't want to intrude."

He fisted his other hand. That was the tragedy of it all. Naturally, Beth would try to find an explanation for such abhorrent behavior. She stared at the empty hallway, then turned her gaze to him. "You don't think they recognized me, do you?" She stared once again down the hall as if seeking answers. "If so, then I apologize," she said softly.

He clasped her lightly around the arms. Instantly, she lifted her gaze to his. "Never apologize for us. You're everything to me."

Beth's stomach roiled at the thought the couple snubbed them because they recognized her. Not for her own discomfort but for Julian's. She didn't want his reputation to suffer because of her. God, would this overwhelming feeling of nothingness ever leave her be? She let out a silent breath. Would this happen for the rest of their lives when they met someone too highbrow?

She smoothed a hand down her stomach. Lightly, her fingers trailed the exquisite paste jewels that adorned her gown. She was stronger than that. All she had to do was concentrate on tonight's business. If the Marquess of Montridge was at the assembly, she'd find him and discover what exactly happened between him and Meri. She closed her eyes and inhaled a steadying breath. She'd not quit until there were no stones to upend.

She smiled though her heart felt heavy. "Julian, I must warn you to take heed. There's no advantage in being angry at that couple."

"You're right." He smiled down at her, but there was something in his eyes that betrayed his unease. He leaned close. "Your night awaits."

Every sense of hers was on high alert at the conviction in his voice. He'd never been more desirable in her eyes than he was right then. "Let's not waste any more time.

The quicker we find out what we can about Meri, the quicker . . . we can go back to my room."

She entwined her fingers with his and tugged him down the hall. Before they entered the public areas, she had her arm wrapped around his.

In minutes, they were outside the hotel. The scent of wisteria sweetened the air. People and carriages bustled about the street.

People residing at the Circus were descending Gay Street. Their excitement fairly made the air crackle, and Beth did everything in her power to tease and flirt with Julian. And he did the same with her. By the time they entered the Assembly Room, he was smiling and laughing again. The music and light from the inside of the building spilled into the street. The gaiety was infectious, and she found herself anxious to dance.

Once inside, she glanced around the room. The chandeliers' candles overhead winked as if greeting them on their arrival. The musicians were in fine form, and elegant couples danced in perfect formation.

"Shall we?" he asked with a gleam in his eyes that she was becoming quite familiar with. It was the one that promised all sorts of naughtiness in their future. "First, I think we should stroll about the room and see if we can find Montridge."

With Julian's superior height, he stood with an intrinsic authority that made every person in the room take notice. Women bent their heads together and whispered. Beth didn't need to hear their conversation to know what they were discussing. They all were lamenting the fact that she was the one standing beside the handsome marquess and not they. At such a thought, she smiled and didn't shy away from the direct glances she received.

Yes, ladies, you may look, but you can't touch. He's mine.

He leaned close. "Do you see that young woman who's with an older woman, her mother most probably? Is she wearing your gown?"

Her gaze latched upon a woman whose back was turned to hers. "The one in the green?"

Julian nodded. "Isn't that the dress you wore at our dinner with Pelham? The one stolen from you?"

"It is." She recognized the full drape of the gown's back. She'd had it custom-made. "You don't think she is Cochran's wife, do you?"

He narrowed his eyes, never looking away from the girl. "I don't have a clue. Let's go meet her. I'll engage the older woman, and you can ask her."

"Excellent idea." She tilted her gaze to his. "You're very astute to notice that it looked like my gown."

"I notice everything about you." He lowered his voice, ensuring no one could overhear him. "Including that chemise you were wearing when we were robbed. You embroidered pink dianthus flowers on it, didn't you? They match the one you sewed on my waistcoat."

She blinked in amazement as her cheeks flushed. What man would notice things like that?

"I love it when you blush, especially when it's because of me." He winked as he held out his arm, then led her to the women.

Good heavens. How was she to survive the night with such observations? She tugged his arm a little closer. "You are the devil, sir."

"Madam, thank you for the compliment," he answered with a smile. "Lucky for you, I've always found him in the details. That's how I recognized your dress."

Soon, they stood beside the woman in Beth's gown and the older lady.

"Good evening," Beth said sweetly. "My name is Miss Beth Howell, and this is Lord Grayson."

A pretty, young lady no more than eighteen or nineteen turned her attention to them and smiled. "Good evening. I'm Miss Amanda Winter and this is my mother, Mrs. Winter." Her eyes were bright with excitement.

After they exchanged a few comments about the assembly and the crowd that had already gathered, Julian veered Mrs. Winter away with his own conversation.

"Miss Winter, I couldn't help but notice what an exquisite gown you're wearing. It's beautiful. Did you purchase it here?"

"Yes."

"You're stunning in it. Such detail." Beth smiled. "If you don't mind me asking, what shop?" When the poor girl's face fell, Beth quickly tried to soothe her. "I apologize if I've made you feel uncomfortable."

"You didn't. I can tell by your manner you're being nice. I was afraid that someone might recognize the dress as their own tonight," Miss Winter said with a shy smile. "I purchased this at a shop that caters to . . . well, that caters to people like me." She bowed her head, but not before Beth had seen her humiliation. "I can't afford new clothing. This gown had just come into the store."

Beth put her hand over the young woman's and shook her head. "There's no need to tell me any more. I know exactly what shop you're referring to." Beth squeezed her hand. "I've had occasion myself to shop there."

"You have?" Clearly shocked, Miss Winter's gaze swept the length of Beth's gown. "Did you get that gown there? It's stunning."

Beth shook her head. "No, it was a gift."

"You're very lucky." The girl bit her bottom lip. "I had to pay for this one myself. I've been saving for over a year to buy such a gown."

Beth nodded. "I have no doubt you'll have the attention of every young man here tonight. I'm sure the previous owner would be delighted to know that someone as beautiful as you was wearing it."

"You're too kind." Miss Winter grinned as she smoothed a hand down the green silk. "I feel like a princess in it."

"You look like one," Beth said affectionately, and meant every word.

Just then, a young man approached them and asked for Miss Winter's hand for the next set of country dances. As the couple moved to the dance floor, the young girl smiled at Beth.

She'd seen that smile before on young women during their first Season, when they'd hoped to catch the fancy of some young man who might be the one to ask for their hand in marriage. She matched the girl's smile, hoping her dress would bring the needed magic for Miss Winter tonight.

As the music started, Beth turned to find Julian only to discover he'd gone, leaving Mrs. Winter standing beside the older ladies who were all supervising their charges.

Such a shame, as Beth was feeling quite like the princess herself.

The one who had found her prince charming.

Chapter Twenty-Five

After he'd escorted Mrs. Winter to the matrons' corner, Julian took a step to return to Beth's side. From across the room, he caught a glimpse of the Marquess of Montridge. Julian had never really cared for the man's company, and fittingly, the man looked to be glowering at the crowd before him. A young slip of a girl stood beside him in an ivory gown with an overabundance of lace. It had to be his sister.

Julian sighed slightly. The one good thing about finding the marquess early was that his and Beth's evening wouldn't require attending the assembly for much longer. Everything about this evening felt right. He could sense it in his bones that he should ask Beth to become his marchioness.

As he took a step in Beth's direction, a man blocked his path.

"Sir Jeffrey," Julian said. His dying irritation at the man's caviling, judgmental rudeness to Beth roared to life once again. "I'd like a word."

"We are of the same mind." Sir Jeffrey nodded, but a sneer tugged at his lip. "Allow me to go first." Without pausing to take a breath, the man continued, "I can't in good conscience go forward with the consideration of investing in your engines because of the iniquitous behavior you have flaunted tonight."

Julian clenched his hand in a fist and held it by his side. It took every ounce of self-control not to punch the man in the nose. "What are you referring to?"

"Your behavior with your paramour," Sir Jeffrey stuck his nose in the air as if he'd been proclaimed the gatekeeper for the high moral ground. "I've personally seen how reckless a man is when he forgets his principles. I won't invest with you. Too much is at stake."

His entire future or lack thereof flashed before his eyes at Sir Jeffrey's pronouncement. But Julian would not allow such a misconception to continue without correcting it or the man before him. For once in his life, he'd damn the consequences. This was Beth they were discussing.

"I've seen you answer her door while displaying a shocking state of dishabille." Sir Jeffrey sniffed, then lowered his voice. "My poor wife had to call for the smelling salts because of the shock to her sensitive system."

"Careful, sir," Julian warned curtly. "Miss Howell is a family friend, a dear one at that."

Sir Jeffrey narrowed his eyes. "No matter how you describe it, I know what I saw. I will not ignore such behavior." He tilted his nose in the air as if smelling something foul. "Miss Howell is not someone—"

"Have a care how you continue," Julian softly growled. "Otherwise, I'll invite you outside."

"You'd actually *fight* over her?" Sir Jeffrey asked incredulously.

"I'd die for her," he countered. "If you value your face, or your life for that matter, I suggest you stay out of my sight."

"You're a fool to have ruined your chances with us. As soon as you saw me here, you should have cut ties with her." He shook his head. "A pity, really. The consortium could have restored your fortune in a year, two at most."

"But at what price? To turn my back upon a friend. You don't deserve the title of *sir*, as there's nothing noble about you." By then, he'd raised his voice. People were starting to stare, but he didn't care. He'd not allow anyone to disparage Beth. Not the woman he would make his wife.

"Well, I would wish you luck in your endeavors, but you're holding fast to a course that will see you insolvent. One word from me and your name will be synonymous with debauchery. A rake may be welcome in aristocratic circles, but not in the consortium. We want people dedicated to their work, not their pleasure and dissipated living." He practically spit out the words.

"Better that than someone whose every action is amoral and judgmental," Julian bit out.

Sir Jeffrey stared for a moment longer, then turned on his heel. As the crowd watched, the man collected his wife and left the building without saying another word.

The relief that flooded the room was almost palpable. Then the music started up once again, and the dancers lined up for the next set. Beth entered the Assembly Room and gazed about until she saw him. A brilliant smile lit her face as she came his way.

Once she reached his side, her brow furrowed. "What happened?"

He ran a gloved hand through his hair. "Nothing. And I couldn't be any better now that you're here by my side."

"I can tell by your stance that you're angry."

To discuss it further would do nothing except hurt her. She'd already suffered enough blame for her marriage to Meriwether to last a lifetime. And now he'd made it worse by being seen going in and out of her room. Why hadn't he used the connecting door between their rooms? Uncharacteristically anxious, he'd taken the quickest route to find her. Which seemed to be a weakness he suffered when around her. But was it weakness to want to spend every moment with her, his love? He released a breath and straightened to his full height, then noticed Montridge staring at them.

"The Marquess of Montridge is glancing our way. I don't want him to leave before we've had an opportunity to chat with him." He smiled down at her. The worry in her eyes still clear as day. "That is why we're here tonight."

Thankfully, before she could answer, the marquess stood before them. "Grayson." He nodded slightly in greeting, then turned Beth's way and studied her.

"Montridge," Julian presented his most charming voice. "You remember Miss Howell?"

His eyes flashed in recognition, yet the man had enough manners to bow to her. "Miss Howell. I've been so long out of society that you'll have to forgive me for not recognizing you. How is your brother?"

"In fine health, sir," she answered. "How fortuitous you're here. I wondered if I could have a moment of your time."

"Whatever would you want to discuss with me?" The marquess's attention was glued to the dance floor, where he appeared to be watching a young lady dancing with another man.

Beth followed his gaze. "How is Lady Susan?"

The marquess grunted slightly, then smiled. "She's well. Next year is her come-out Season. She convinced me to stay in Bath for the summer so she could practice." He arched a brow. "I think she wanted to come just to bedevil me. Practically every young man in attendance has asked her to dance. The scourge of every brother's existence. Sisters."

"I've been spared such fortune," Julian said. "I have no siblings."

The marquess regarded him. "Consider yourself . . ." His gaze drifted slowly to Beth.

"Careful, sir," Beth warned with a genuine smile. "I'm one of those scourges."

"Point taken." The marquess laughed. His deep voice caused several matrons to turn their way. He clasped his hands behind his back. "However, I was referring to the young men sniffing at my sister's heels." He smiled, then regarded Grayson with a gleam in his eye. "These are not your usual haunts, Grayson. What's caught your interest in Bath?"

"You," he answered. "Tell us about Lord Meriwether."

At the mention of the name, Montridge pursed his lips. "I know it's a sin to speak ill of the dead, so I decline."

"I was the one allegedly married to him," Beth answered. "However, I share your regard of my late *supposed* husband. Let's you and I have an honest exchange about him."

Heat marched a path straight through Beth's body. With a snap of her wrist, she unfolded her fan and briskly tried to create some air between the three of them. For the love of God, how had Meri angered practically every person she'd encountered during this trip?

"Please, Lord Montridge?" Beth asked in the calmest voice she could muster, though it was becoming harder and harder to stay composed. "I'm trying to find out what he did with my dowry."

Both Julian's and the marquess's eyes widened at her
tone. Even she'd shocked herself, but the rogue deserved
it. She'd had enough of the games he'd played from the
grave.

"No one can definitively confirm nor deny if or how
he lost my fortune. Before I can lay the unfortunate circumstances of my so-called marriage to rest, I need to
discover what happened to my dowry. If you could tell me
where he went or what he did after he won the mineral
lease from you at the Jolly Rooster, I'd be most grateful."

In a tell that she was unsettled, Beth started to twist
her fingers together. Julian immediately moved closer
to her.

Montridge nodded brusquely, then sighed. "Of course.
If I were you, I'd want to know what happened." His gaze
darted to his sister, then back to them. "He won a ten-
year lease on an iron ore mine I owned." He shook his
head and stared off into space. "It was the damnedest
thing I'd ever seen. Meri couldn't lose a hand. Every card
favored him." He shook his head once. "I've never seen
such luck for a night, but the bloody . . ." He cleared his
throat. "Forgive me, Miss Howell, for such language."

"Believe me, I've called him worse." Her gaze sought
Julian, who smiled affectionately at her. The sight bolstered her resolve to see this through. Before, she'd always had Kat and Constance, but it was different having
Julian beside her. They were fighting together.

"Within the month, he'd drowned in a mud puddle,"
Lord Montridge continued, unaware of the distress she
was experiencing. "It's as if luck had enough of his behavior, then completely deserted him. Much like his so-
called friends. Really, that's all I know."

A frustrated sigh escaped from Beth. She understood

her husband seemed to turn every friend he acquired into an enemy. "Are you sure that's all you can remember?"

The marquess glanced at his sister again and narrowed his eyes as if retrieving a memory. "There were several others at the table that night. Some of the local gentry and a few men from London who made fortunes in banking and commercial endeavors. I don't recall their names. The stakes were too high for me. I called it an early night. The next morning Meri was gone."

"Do you recall the exact date of that game?"

The marquess shook his head. "I'm sorry. I don't recall anything except it was warm that evening. The windows were open."

A scream rent the air. "Someone, help. My daughter has been kidnapped. *Help!*"

Beth's breath caught in her throat at the cry of sorrow. Instantly, she turned to Julian. "That's Mrs. Winter."

Julian nodded at Montridge, then grabbed Beth's hand. "Let's see what this is about."

By then, the music had stopped, and a crowd was forming around the distraught woman. The soulful sound of her weeping filled the air.

They wove themselves through the mass of bodies until they were standing beside her.

"Mrs. Winter, when was the last time you saw your daughter?" Julian's manner was calm but direct.

Beth had little doubt he'd be on a horse within a quarter hour, looking for the girl.

"Oh, Lord Grayson and Miss Howell," Mrs. Winter's voice broke with fear. The blood had drained from her face. "I don't know what to do."

"I'll help, and so will Miss Howell," Julian said. "When did she leave?"

Still trying to tame her shock, Mrs. Winter shook her head. Beth took the woman's hand in hers, offering comfort.

"Mere minutes ago." With tears flowing down her cheeks, Mrs. Winter stared at Julian. "She was standing right beside me. We went outside for some fresh air when a man approached. He threw a cape over her head, then tossed her across his shoulder. I tried to pull his arm, but he shook me off. I fell to the ground, then . . . they were gone."

The crowd's murmurings grew at the horrific tale. With his sister trailing, Montridge butted his way to stand beside them.

"I'll take my sister home, then I'll join the search," he said to Mrs. Winter, then nodded at Grayson.

"I found her," a young man announced at the entrance to the Assembly Room. Beside him stood a disheveled but smiling Miss Winter.

As soon as she saw her mother, she rushed into her arms. The young man followed.

"My darling," her mother cried. After a tight hug, she pulled away and studied her daughter from head to toe. "Are you all right?"

Miss Winter nodded. "The man tossed me into the carriage. Then he took the cloak from my face. As soon as he saw me, he exclaimed, 'You're not her.'" She glanced at Grayson and Beth. "He stopped the carriage and practically threw me to the ground."

"My precious girl," her mother cried softly.

"If it hadn't been for Mr. Jenkins, I don't know what I would have done. That man was frightening." Miss Winter visibly shivered.

Immediately, the young man, Mr. Jenkins, took her hand. "You're safe now."

"All because of you," Miss Winter said with gratitude. Her normal color was returning as if she realized the ordeal was over.

"What did your abductor look like?" Julian asked.

Miss Winter shook her head. "His face was masked."

"What do you recall about the carriage?"

"The seats felt like velvet." Miss Winter looked to Mr. Jenkins. "Do you remember anything, sir?"

Mr. Jenkins still held her hand and smiled in reassurance. He turned his gaze to Julian and Montridge. "It was dark. The only thing I can tell you is that the four horses were black, the same as the carriage."

"That describes half the carriages in England," Montridge grumbled.

Julian's gaze settled on Beth. As the crowd's attention was devoted to the Winter family, he leaned close and whispered, "Ready to leave?"

"So early?" By the tic of the muscle in his chiseled jaw she could tell that he was worried. "What is it?"

"Not here." They took their leave of the marquess and his sister, then the Winters. As soon as they were outdoors, he pulled her close. "I'm going to escort you to your room, then see about transportation. Leave everything as is. Cillian can bring it tomorrow." He held her arm as they walked down the street. But his gaze was constantly sweeping the streets and alleys as if looking for someone.

"Where are we going?" Her voice was breathless, as she was having a hard time keeping up with him.

"To my ancestral seat." Realizing she was having trouble, he slowed his pace. By then, they were close to the hotel.

"Why would we do that?" She stopped, and he immediately did the same. People were strolling along the street enjoying the evening. Which was in direct contrast to what they were doing.

The intensity of his gaze nailed her in place. "Who exactly do you think the kidnapper was looking for?"

She shook her head, then suddenly her stomach swooped like a barn swallow being chased by a sparrowhawk. "The dress." The words were a faint whisper in the night air.

"Exactly. They were after you. Do you think it's your brother?"

"Impossible. He lacks the mental fortitude to come up with such a plot." She shook her head. "He's more likely to harangue me until I capitulate to his wishes."

"Portland?" he asked.

She shivered at the name. "I don't know."

Julian took her hand and squeezed it. "We can't stay here." He studied the street again. "Do you trust me?"

"Of course."

"No one will expect us to leave this evening. The kidnapper is long gone. We can cut through the fields and stay off the main road. The moon is full, so we'll have plenty of light." His gaze finally landed on hers. "We're riding on a horse. Together. We don't have time to argue."

Chapter Twenty-Six

Luck was with them that evening. With Cillian guarding her door, Beth had changed while Julian had acquired a fast horse. They'd left Bath with little fuss, and no one had been aware of them departing. Most importantly, Beth hadn't argued as much as he'd expected on their way there. She'd been tense the entire time. When she'd refused to relax in his arms, he'd slowed their mount down and wrapped his arm around her waist.

That had been the magic needed to get her to finally rest in his arms. It had been pure torture for him as her fragrance had wrapped around him. Whenever he'd had the chance, he'd pressed his lips against some part of her. But when the ugly thought arose that someone had been determined to hurt her this evening, he'd squeezed her tight, thankful she was safe in his arms.

"Look." She turned her head and smiled. "There's Green Hills."

Down in the dark valley below was a massive mansion. "I see it."

"My grandfather built it for his viscountess. My grandmother preferred it to London, so they resided here. My father and mother did the same. I have some clothes there. May we stop? I won't be but a moment."

"Would your brother be there?"

Beth shook her head. "No. He's in London for a horse auction at Tattersall's. Besides, he prefers the ancestral seat in Cumberland."

As they came to a stop, a footman hurried to help them. "Good evening, Miss Howell. We weren't expecting you. But it's always a pleasure when you're here." The footman's genuine smile lit up his face. He turned and bowed to Julian.

"Good evening, Harold," Beth said.

The footman's brow furrowed. "No carriage."

"Unavailable, I'm afraid," Beth answered. "Lord Grayson was kind enough to escort me."

Without waiting, Julian slid off the horse. He reached for Beth's waist, and slowly he eased her to the ground. He stood so close that her luscious body brushed his. At her sudden intake of breath, he smiled.

He couldn't wait any longer. As soon as they reached his ancestral estate, he'd propose. Tomorrow morning, he'd send a note to Randford and Sykeston telling them what had occurred. Then he'd get several of his tenant farmers and see if they'd help guard Beth as they traveled to London.

As they walked up the steps of her home, Beth took his hand and entwined their fingers.

He squeezed her hand gently. "You're safe."

She nodded with a smile. "All because of you."

The front door swung open, and he wanted to curse at the sight before him.

"I've been looking for you for over a week." St. John extended both arms in welcome. "The prodigal sister has finally arrived home." His gaze landed on their joined hands, and a frown appeared. With a huff of disgust, he turned his attention back to Beth. "Why is *he* with you? How many times have we discussed this, Blythe?"

Beth heaved a heavy sigh, then leaned close to Julian. "If the fortune-teller had made mention that my brother would be here, we wouldn't have stopped." She turned to St. John with an imitation of a smile. "Hello."

Before Julian could address the viscount, Beth straightened her shoulders and took a step in her brother's direction.

By her expression, it was a sound bet that she was about to give a dressing-down to her brother. Silently, Julian cheered her on.

"Lord Grayson kindly accompanied me. He's helping me with my business. Frankly, you owe him a debt of gratitude. Apparently, someone tried to kidnap me, and the marquess has escorted me to safety."

"That someone was me." Howell moved so they could walk through the door. "It wasn't a per se kidnapping but a call to come home. Do come in so we can discuss this like rational adults."

"You?" Beth's eyes widened.

Grayson fisted both hands. He'd just delivered her to her kidnapper.

"It's not as sordid as it sounds. Come in. You must be famished." He waved them in and then called out, "Richards, have a tray prepared. My sister and the . . . Marquess of Grayson have arrived." The butler nodded, but Howell stopped him with a raised hand. "Bring a bottle of champagne. We've much to celebrate."

When Beth walked toward the door, Julian stopped her. "We should leave," he murmured as Howell turned and walked into the house as if they were following him. "This isn't safe."

Beth took his hand and pulled him through the door. "It's St. John. He's harmless."

They followed St. John into a small informal dining room. He waved for them to sit as he poured a glass of champagne for all three of them. After a maid brought in the tray, she curtsied, then left the three of them alone. Beth served Julian a plate of roasted chicken, cheese, bread, and strawberries. She made the same for herself.

"Blythe is right. Pardon my abruptness. Thank you, Grayson, for escorting her all over the hills and dells of England." He leaned back in his chair.

"It was an honor." He studied the viscount. The man practically trembled in excitement. "Why would you kidnap your own sister? Wouldn't a note asking for her to come home be as efficient?"

Howell regarded him, then laughed.

At the sound, Beth put down her fork. Her displeasure plain to all. "What's so amusing?"

"It's just that the marquess doesn't know you well, does he? If he did, he'd know you never do anything I want. Hence, the need for tonight's events." He finished his glass of champagne, then poured another. "But I shan't keep you in suspense." He leaned close to Beth. "The arrangements have been made. You're to marry the Marquess of Siddleton in three weeks. The bans will be called on Sunday unless he decides to pay for a special license, which I expect he will." He took another sip of champagne. "It will be the wedding of the Season."

Julian had been holding the stem of his champagne glass so tightly that it broke in two.

"You did what?" Beth instantly stood and glared at her brother.

"You'll marry Siddleton. I've signed the settlement." He sniffed, then regarded her. "That's an ugly dress. But your fortunes are changing. You'll be relieved to hear that the marquess wants to gift you a new trousseau. Imagine the clothes you'll have as a marchioness."

"No," she said softly.

"He'll be more than generous with you."

"Stop it," she said curtly. "I told you . . ." Her eyes drifted to the entrance of the room and didn't move.

Julian turned to see what caught her attention. He stood when he saw another man approaching the door. "What are you doing here, Stanton?"

That's when everything clicked into place. For the love of God, why didn't he see it before now?

"You're the one who tried to kidnap her. It makes sense that we were seeing you everywhere, including in the company of the Portlands. You bastard," Julian hissed.

"Thought you were headed to Portsmouth." Lord Stanton shook his head. "I met up with Monty in Kingsclere, and there you were."

Stanton looked the worse for wear. Scratches trailed down one side of his face. He rubbed his face, then took the glass that St. John handed him.

"It was bloody inconvenient too. Whoever I took was a vicious little thing." Stanton tipped the glass and drank the entire amount. With a thud, he set the glass down, demanding another round. "Then I had to deal with that swain who was chasing us."

Beth narrowed her eyes. "You scared that poor woman half to death. And her mother. If the swain you're referring to is Mr. Jenkins, he's a gentleman."

"She had on your dress." Stanton looked her over. "I recognized it and thought it was you. I should have just taken you at the Jolly Rooster."

"Why didn't you?" Beth demanded.

"I didn't want any of my friends to know my situation."

Julian's attention turned to Stanton. "You must have been the one responsible for the carriage accident. You could have killed Beth."

"It was just to slow you down. But I couldn't find you." He looked Beth in the eye. "I apologize."

"Why are you helping him?" Julian pointed to St. John.

Stanton hesitated for a moment. "I need the money. The Jolly Rooster hasn't been the most hospitable with its luck at the gaming tables. I owe Pelham quite a sum." He shrugged. "Besides, Lord Siddleton is my great-uncle on my mother's side. I thought I'd help him with a good deed and make a little coin while helping Howell here." He had the decency to look sheepish. "I've been chasing you all over the countryside, and you end up here on your own accord."

"You are despicable." Beth turned to her brother.

Howell urged her to sit down by patting her chair. "Don't make such a fuss, Blythe. I heard all about the carriage accident, but you're fine. Safe and sound at home."

"It's Beth, you dreadful man," she seethed.

Julian smiled. "Bully for you, Beth."

"This is not your concern," Howell cried, before returning his attention to Beth. "Listen to reason. We need the money. You must marry him."

She shook her head. "Do you know what happens when you put yourself and responsibility in the same sentence?"

Howell pursed his lips, and Stanton's brow furrowed.

"Nothing." Like an arrow, Beth's sharp voice sailed across the room.

Howell had the good manners to wince but quickly recovered his bravado. "Now see here," Howell sniffed. "I promised Father that I'd look after you if he or Mother wasn't here. I'm giving you a marriage. A life that far exceeds what you could expect on your own. Our parents expected perfection in their children. I'm trying my best."

"They wanted perfection?" Julian felt his lip twist into a sneer. "That explains why they had Beth after you."

Beth's gaze never strayed from her brother's as she narrowed her eyes. "I'm of age. You can't order me around like a piece of chattel or a broodmare." She tapped her finger against the middle of her chest. "I make my own decisions and have ever since Meri left me." She pursed her lips, then shook her head. "What you believe is seeing after my welfare is nothing more than you trying to amend your failings."

She turned to Julian as if seeking comfort. He nodded in support. She smiled, then took a deep breath before returning her gaze to her brother.

"I'm going to gather some clothes and I'm leaving. When I return to London, I'll stay with the Duke and Duchess of Randford."

"Blythe, don't," St. John cried.

"And another thing." Her blue eyes darkened, then flashed like a thunderstorm rolling in. "I'll never forgive you for threatening Grayson when he asked for my hand. How could you threaten to ruin his family? My happiness was never a consideration." Her voice never wavered, but her anger was readily apparent to everyone in the room. "What would you do if someone threatened to call in your debts?" Her mouth tilted in a sneer. "I never want to see you again."

"You're my sister." Howell shook his head in disbelief.

"Semantics." She dismissed him with a wave of her hand. "If you seek me out, I'll either shoot you or, if I'm feeling magnanimous, I'll ask my friends' husbands to intervene." Calmly, she clasped her hands together. "Understood?"

"What about the settlement?" Howell croaked out a hiss.

Beth tilted her chin in the air. "Not my concern, as you so aptly said earlier. I'm sure if you dig deep enough you might find some of that perfection and honor our parents expected of you. It's time to practice putting it to use." Beth's voice was crisp and direct. It was clear she expected St. John to fix this on his own. "No matter the consequences." She turned to Julian. "Please excuse me for a moment. I'll return quickly."

They all watched her leave. Stanton's eyes were as round as saucers while Howell's face had turned beet red.

Julian walked to Howell's chair, then picked the man up by the scruff of the neck. It wasn't a difficult task. The man had to weigh at least five stone less than Julian and was at least seven inches shorter. When Stanton started forward to help the viscount, Julian turned his stare toward the man. "Do not move. Do not blink."

Stanton swallowed, then nodded.

Julian shifted his attention back to Howell. "I think she made her position clear. If she does ask Randford and Sykeston to help, I'll join them."

"She's my family," Howell managed to croak out.

"She dismissed that argument." Julian lifted Howell until his feet were dangling off the floor. "If and when she wants to see you, she'll make the decision. Not you."

Finally, the man managed to swallow and nod briefly.

"For once, you're thinking of Beth," Julian said, then threw Howell back into his chair. The momentum was so great, the chair fell over and Howell found himself on the floor staring at the ceiling.

Julian turned to Stanton. The silent conversation clear,

Stanton finally nodded. Without a look back, Julian went to the entry just as Beth flew down the stairs with a small satchel clutched in her hands. He held out his hand and she placed hers in his.

When he looked down at her, that's when he saw the devastation Howell had wrought. She looked vacant and empty. He'd seen that look before.

The first time they'd met after Meriwether had died.

When the butler told her good evening, Beth didn't look at the man. She appeared so brittle that one brisk wind would break her into a million pieces.

As soon as they started down the steps, Harold, the same footman who had greeted them on their arrival, held the reins of Julian's horse. "My lord, he's been fed and watered. He should be ready for the short ride to Raleah House."

"Thank you." Julian handed Beth's bag to the man. As the footman secured it to the saddle, Julian lifted her onto the horse. She turned away and stared into the night's sky.

"It was an honor to see you again, Miss Howell." When she didn't answer, Harold's gaze shifted to Julian's. "My lord, I . . . I wish you both safe travels."

"Thank you." With ease, he mounted the horse and settled Beth between his arms.

She sat stiffly as if desperately trying to rein in her tumultuous emotions.

"Beth," he said softly.

In response, she just stiffened. "I don't want to discuss it."

He pressed his lips to the top of her head. He'd give her all the time she needed.

She lasted until they reached the haven of his ancestral home, Raleah House. They were about to enter the drive when she shifted her body and buried her head into her chest.

And cried. Her shoulders shook, and her soft gasps ripped his heart apart. The relentless fall of tears dampened his linen shirt.

He'd never seen this emotion from her before and the pain he felt on her behalf crushed him.

Her bloody selfish brother caused this.

"Let me hold you," he said softly, then dismounted. Two huge granite lions flanked the estate's entrance. He'd always thought they stood watch over the home and the people who resided there. Tonight, they, along with him, would watch over his precious Beth.

He swept her off the horse and into his arms. In two strides, he sat on one of the statue's platforms with his proud and self-reliant Beth on his lap as her tears continued to fall. Carefully, he tugged her close and tried to soothe her. She snuggled closer as if seeking sanctuary.

She was grieving. Whether it was for Meriwether or her brother or both, it made little difference to him.

Just as long as he was the one holding her.

And he'd willingly stay here forever if she'd let him.

Chapter Twenty-Seven

B eth clung to Julian as he lifted her off the horse and carried her to the lions. She couldn't even recall the path they took, as all she could think about was St. John's betrayal. He'd not only planned to kidnap her, but even more egregious was the fact that he'd planned to have the first banns announced this upcoming Sunday with Lord Siddleton.

Her consent, her own free will, meant nothing to him. Just as *she* meant nothing to him.

"When St. John wanted me to marry Meriwether, I allowed him to convince me it would be a good match. He said my father would have approved. I believed him. But not this time." She breathed in Julian's comforting fragrance. "I think my brother would have drugged me to make me marry the marquess," she murmured. Her head tucked into Julian's chest, she acknowledged the betrayal for the first time. "My brother. My only family." Another sob broke free. Everything inside her crumbled into nothing. By now, she was crying so hard, she couldn't catch her breath.

"Breathe, darling," he soothed as his strong arms surrounded her and one large hand skated down her back in a calming rhythm. "He won't hurt you."

She wanted to laugh at such words. Instead, another soft sob escaped. It was too late. "I never want to see him again. He's gone too far this time."

"I would feel the same." He pressed his lips to hers, where they lingered. "You were so brave. I'm in awe of your confidence. Just like you were with Cochran."

"Thank you." She bit her bottom lip in reassurance that this moment was real. "Sometimes it's hard to be reliant on only yourself."

The soft touch of his mouth against hers made her shiver. How could such a man, one good and kind and noble, exist? At that moment, all her senses awoke as if coming out of a year-long slumber. Her hearing was more acute, her taste was more heightened, and her fingers longed to trace every inch of him.

"Beth?"

She tilted her gaze to his. The moon's light caressed his face. Even the heavenly bodies wanted to touch and be near him.

He cupped her face with his hands and rubbed her cheekbones with his thumb. His tenderness was endearing. "Come. Let's get you to bed. If you're wondering, I was thinking of putting you in my bed." A roguish smile creased his lips. "Will that do?"

Everything melted within her when he looked at her like that. A shuddering sigh escaped. "As long as you join me. I need to be near you."

"Agreed." He picked her up again and put her on the horse, where he joined her. As they traveled up the stately drive surrounded by trees on both sides, he lightly rested his chin on her shoulder. "No one will greet us. The house is . . . rather empty. I have an elderly butler and housekeeper, but they're abed and won't hear us. Cillian will join us on the morrow. The rooms are . . . sparse."

She turned and pressed a kiss to his cheek. She knew how hard that was for him to share that with her. He didn't entertain here or in London. He'd told her that he cut practically all his staff to save money.

His kindness was a gift. No one had ever treated her in such a loving manner. Certainly not since her parents had died. But Julian was special in a way that was hard to describe. It was ironic that they'd only shared days with each other. But that didn't change the truth. If she didn't have him in her life, it would be a rather bleak existence. Like living her life in the darkness without any light.

After he settled the horse, he escorted her inside the Palladian mansion. A candle buried in the entry. Shadows played against the walls, and it was difficult to see much. She'd been there once as a girl when her parents had visited the marquess and the marchioness, Julian's parents. Julian had been attending Eton at the time with St. John and others they knew.

The Grayson home had been magnificent back then. But she'd known that Julian had to sell practically everything that wasn't entailed. The Greek statutes that had lined the entry were gone. They looked like naked footmen when she'd seen them as a little girl. When she mentioned that to her parents, her mother had blushed while her father and the Marquess of Grayson had laughed.

With one hand, Julian held the candle to light their way. With the other, he held hers and led her upstairs. Portraits of his ancestors used to line the staircase to the family's living quarters. They'd been sold years ago. When she glanced at him, he stared straight ahead, not acknowledging what she was looking at.

"Julian, I'm sorry," she said softly.

He stopped. Pain flashed in his eyes.

"About your home. It's how I feel about mine."

"Come," he commanded softly. "Let's put all of it behind us and make something better than what we had before." His face was like a stone wall, impenetrable. At the top of the stairs, he opened a door and motioned for her to enter.

Anticipation and perhaps a little shyness overcame her as she stepped across the threshold.

He set the candle on the table, then opened the windows to let the breeze stir the air. But the room didn't smell musty, nor did it look to have been ravished by the estate's misfortunes. The biggest bed she'd ever seen commanded the middle of the room. A lovely sitting area was arranged in front of the fireplace. At the end of the room was a door that probably led to the marchioness suites. She swallowed the discomfort that had lodged in her throat.

After everything that had transpired tonight, she hadn't had time to consider that her dowry hunt had come to a dead end. If he asked for her hand again, she'd have nothing to offer him.

When she glanced his way, he was staring at her as if he were a starving man and she was the main course of the buffet. She took one step toward him, then it was as if a dam had broken.

She really wasn't certain who moved faster, but it made little difference. In seconds they were in each other's arms. He lowered his lips to hers, and at first touch she melted against him. This was home. This was always home. During the past few days, she had discovered that whenever she was lost or angry or sad it was Julian's arms she sought. It was his comfort that made her feel whole again.

She'd do everything in her power to offer him the same. She knew how hard it had been for him to bring her to his ancestral home after he'd had to discard so many of the treasures that made the house unique.

His lips gentled over hers as his tongue lightly touched the seam of her mouth. She moaned as he deepened the kiss. His tongue slid over hers, exploring and tantalizing with each stroke and each caress. Beth tried to move closer to him, if that was possible. Her breasts hurt. The only relief would be rubbing them against the hardness of his chest. She wanted his mouth on her again.

He groaned as if in agony, and she smiled. Only with him did she feel like an enchantress. Tonight, she'd wield that power without hesitation or apology. Both of them were out of breath. When they broke apart, he was panting and the hunger in his eyes made them gleam in the moonlight.

"Let's take off that gown," he said as he wheeled her around to unbutton the back. Instead of unbuttoning it swiftly, he did the exact opposite. With each slip of a button, he brushed his knuckles or finger or lips against her bare skin. If her chemise or stays were in the way, it didn't matter. He continued in the same manner. In many ways, the tender touch of his hand through the fabric sent the very best type of chills through her body.

"Are you cold?" he asked, pressing a kiss to the nape of her neck.

"No. I'm just happy." She swung her head around and kissed him on the cheek. "But I'd be happier if you hurried."

"Whatever you wish." With that, he made short order of her dress.

She turned around, then started to undress him.

"But I'm not finished," he protested as she slipped her

arms under his formal evening coat and pushed it off his shoulders.

With his height, she had to stand on her tiptoes. "You may have a turn . . . next." She unbuttoned his waistcoat, and he slipped it over himself.

Without his eyes leaving hers, he managed to toe off his evening slippers. "My turn." He reached to the blue ribbon at the top of her stays and slid the knot free. Without his gaze leaving hers, he loosened the ribbon that was woven so intricately through the eyelets.

Every second that went by felt like an hour. "Hurry."

He chuckled lightly. "All good things come to those who wait."

"I never liked that saying," she said playfully, then took a step back. If he wanted to tease her, then she'd do likewise. Inch by inch, she loosened the ribbon. When her stays were loose enough, she took a deep breath, then let it out. Her poor breasts were still tender, and her nipples were unusually hard. Even brushing up against the silk chemise felt like torture.

"Beth, if I didn't know you better, I'd think you were punishing me." His voice deepened. "Go ahead and do your best." His gaze lowered from her face to her breasts. "I think I rather enjoy this."

She smiled, then loosened the stays enough that they fell to the floor. His gaze met hers again, and she pulled the string from inside her chemise and untied the knot. She pulled the neckline until the material slackened, then let it fall to the floor.

A sudden rush of air left his chest, and his eyes brightened. Slowly, his gaze swept down her body, then back up to her face. He stepped closer, then gently cupped one breast. "So soft." He rubbed his thumb over her hardened nipple. "Except perhaps here." He looked into her eyes. "When I take you to bed, I promise you one thing. You'll never think of lovemaking as something you're not accomplished at. Because I know you want me as much as I want you."

His deep voice rasped, sending shivers through her.

"I'm sure if I touched you right now you'd be wet for me."

Her eyes widened and she felt herself flush at such a statement. "I feel as if I've waited my whole life for this night."

"As have I." He lowered his mouth to hers and pressed the sweetest kiss to her lips. With infinite care, he pulled the pins from her hair.

When it tumbled down her back, she closed her eyes and let the sensations rush over her skin. The feel of his soft, full lips against her contrasted with the roughened skin of his hand cradling her breast. With his other hand, he reverently combed her tresses. She groaned slightly, wanting more, but first he had to disrobe.

"You're still dressed," she whispered between kisses.

"Hmm, let's rectify that immediately."

When he scooped her into his arms, she laughed. All her earlier worry and hurt had been swept away just by being in his presence. Gently, he laid her on the bed. Towering above her, he drew his shirt over his head. The sight never ceased to amaze her. She sucked in a breath when his hand stilled on the fall of his breeches. Slowly, he flicked the buttons open, revealing the taut muscles that bracketed his narrow hips. As her eyes followed the unveiling of his body, they landed on his erection, which seemed to be standing at attention.

She swallowed at the sight.

When he finished discarding the rest of his clothes, she whispered his name on a sigh, then held out her arms. He came over her and she wrapped her arms around him, holding him tight. If heaven was a place on this earth, she'd found it in that moment.

He rested his weight on his elbows, then stared down at her. Gently, he brushed away several stray locks that lay across her brow.

"After tonight, things will be settled between us," he whispered.

"Agreed."

"Then, let's not tarry." He bent down and kissed her with a passion that made her body hum and her toes curl. She'd never had a kiss like this, one that made her heart accelerate its beat. As their tongues chased and caressed each other, she was filled with the absolute rightness of the moment. This was what her friends had experienced with their husbands. Every touch and stroke of his mouth and hands threatened to whip her into a frenzy.

Her fingers traced the muscles of his strong back as they flexed when he moved. By now, he was nibbling on her neck, then soothing it with his tongue. With a torturously slow movement, he kissed her shoulders before taking one of her nipples in his mouth. She arched her back at the feel of his hot mouth against the sensitive skin. Never in her life had she experienced something this intense.

Julian seemed to sense when it was too much, as he turned his attention to the other nipple. Yet he didn't leave either of them alone. He cupped her breast and squeezed gently as he sucked the other nipple. A moan that seemed to come from the very essence of her broke free.

The sound seemed to excite him, as his attentions became bolder. He nipped her sensitive nipples, then soothed them with his tongue. With his free hand, he thumbed her areola and nipple to the point of pain. Yet she found it pleasurable.

"Too much?" he asked breathlessly.

"I've never known any of this," she answered. Her own voice breathless. "But it feels divine."

He gazed at her through half-hooded lids. "I promise it'll get better."

She continued to run her hands down his back, marveling at its size and strength. He was beautiful, and he was in her arms tonight.

He started to kiss the sensitive skin under her breasts, then trailed openmouthed kisses across each rib. She gently pushed one hand into his soft hair, just relishing the moment and the exquisite feelings. Only he could make her feel that there was no place else she belonged except in his arms.

His hard cock rested against her thigh, and she lifted her leg slightly, desperate for more of the feel of him. He growled softly in response, then pressed harder against her. He rolled his body toward her as if enjoying it.

By then, he was licking her navel, kissing her hips, and, finally, trailing his mouth to her curls. "Did Meri kiss you here?"

She shook her head.

"Good. Because what I have planned for you should only be shared between the two of us. Look at me," he softly commanded. Only when she forced her gaze to his did he continue, "You are the most beautiful woman I've ever seen. And that beauty is not only on the outside, but more importantly, it's on the inside as well." He placed one hand between her breasts, where her heart pounded. "In this special place where it counts."

She huffed out a breath. "I feel the same about you."

He strummed a finger through her folds. When he touched the sensitive nub, she gasped at the sensation.

He closed his eyes as if in pain. "You're so wet . . . for me." Before she could answer, he lowered his mouth and started kissing her there. "I love the way you taste."

Pleasure radiated from where his mouth touched her. With his tongue, he circled her nub, teasing her and pleasuring her at the same time. Then he licked her as if feasting upon her flesh, before inserting his tongue inside her.

She grabbed ahold of the bedcovers, desperate for purchase. The sensations were building one upon the other, lifting her higher to a pinnacle that she'd experienced only once before and that was with him.

He returned to stroking her nub and she was close to coming. Unable to fight the sensations any longer, she called out his name. Indescribable pleasure unfurled at the speed of light. Tiny stars exploded behind her closed eyes. Everything in that moment disappeared except for Julian and her.

He continued kissing her and fondling her until her body once more came under control.

She ran her fingers through his hair while murmuring his name over and over. To be loved by a man who cared for her and not her fortune was everything she wanted.

He kissed her stomach, her breasts, then the side of her neck below her ear. Slowly, he moved up her body, kissing her, worshiping her. With his knees, he straddled her body, and rested his weight on his elbows as he stared down at her. With only the candlelight, she could see her reflection in the beautiful gray of his eyes.

"How did you like that?"

"I'm not certain," she said coyly. "You might have to do it again before I can answer that question."

He chuckled. "Gladly. Anytime you'd like."

He bent and his mouth met hers. She could taste herself on his tongue. She sucked it and he groaned. Another riot of emotions marched through her, determined to conquer her. She'd gladly surrender as long as she had Julian with her in her bed.

He dipped his body, and his cock slipped through her wetness. This time, she was the one to moan. He did it again, and she closed her eyes as all the nerve endings in her body awoke, desperate for the feel of him.

"Don't tease me." She reached for him, and he hissed.

"We can't rush this, my love. I want to make this an experience you'll never forget."

The tenderness in his eyes almost undid her. Never had she felt more cherished or, indeed, loved. "I need you. Now," she commanded softly.

He nodded once. "Wrap your legs around my waist."

She did as he asked. He kissed her again with a groan that vibrated through her. In answer, she deepened the kiss.

With his hand, he placed his cock at her entrance and gently pushed it in. She sucked in a breath as he pushed more of himself in. With his girth, the pressure increased, and she felt stretched.

He leaned back slightly, then lifted her hips. The slight movement alleviated the pressure.

"Are you all right?" He cupped the sides of her head while never taking his gaze from hers.

She nodded. "This means everything to me."

"And to me." He pushed his hips against hers, then slowly pulled out. He did the same movement again, but this time he rubbed against her clitoris. Pleasure shot through her body. She could feel it all the way to her fingertips.

"Good?" he asked.

"Perfect," she answered.

His mouth met hers again as he plunged inside her over and over, gradually picking up his pace. With each thrust, he managed to tease her nub, resulting in her gasp. She raised her hips to meet his as the sensations started to build again. It was as if she were already on fire as she was close to coming again.

As he moved faster within her, she held on to him, desperate to reach that pinnacle again. He repeated her name over and over as if it were a benediction. Pleasure filled her body and the moment her orgasm flooded her with the most exquisite sensation she cried out his name. He did the same, then withdrew, and his hot seed shot across her stomach.

He'd marked her as his, just as she felt she had done with him. He pulled her close as if he'd never let her go. Sweat dripped from his brow onto hers. It was the most sensual but intimate moment she'd ever felt in her life.

He rested his head in the crook of her neck and whispered, "Christ, Beth."

She ran her fingers lightly through his dampened hair. "Is it always like this?"

He lifted his body so he could look her in the face. Gently, he pressed his mouth to hers. The gesture was filled with tenderness. "Only with you."

At the words, tears filled her eyes. "I love you."

"I love you and always will." He took her in his arms and rolled them both until she rested on him. "I didn't want to come inside you. Not yet."

She'd seen and heard enough at her brother's stables to know that could result in pregnancy. The idea of carrying his child should have terrified her, but frankly, a warmness spread through her as she realized she'd cherish such an outcome.

"Perhaps . . . another time." She would not hide from him. Ever. "I wouldn't mind if there was a child."

He grinned. "You and I think alike."

"It seems like a lifetime ago that we were at the assembly." She pressed a kiss to his chin.

"Indeed." He pressed a kiss to her nose.

"Now that the trail is cold for finding my dowry, we should return to London. You'll have plenty of time to be ready for the meeting with the consortium." Immediately, his body stiffened underneath her. She drew back so she could better see his face. "What is it?"

He looked out the window but stayed silent.

"Be honest with me," she pressed.

Slowly, he turned his gaze to hers. His mood had darkened. "Sir Jeffrey and I decided that we would not work together in the future."

She cupped his chin to keep him from turning away from her. "But the consortium is still interested in your designs?"

"No," he answered. He pressed a kiss to her forehead, then gently lifted her off him. He stood and walked to a pitcher and basin on a nearside table.

As he poured water into the basin, she sat up. "Why?"

Julian had a piece of linen that he'd dunked in the water and was wringing out. "Difference of opinion."

The air around her stilled. "About what? When did you see him?"

"I don't recall." He returned to her side. "Let me clean you." He pressed a sweet kiss to her lips and lingered as if not wanting to be separated from her.

Flames licked her cheeks. "I can do that."

He dipped his gaze to hers. "Allow me?"

She nodded. With a tender touch, he washed away all traces of his seed on her body. Once he was finished, he cleaned himself. He tossed the used linen onto the table, then climbed into bed beside her.

She nestled into his embrace, resting her head on his shoulder.

He pressed a kiss to the top of her head.

"Could you approach other members of the consortium with your disagreement? Perhaps get another opinion? I'm sure you can work it out." She leaned away to see his face when he responded.

He wouldn't look at her and didn't respond. After a moment, she sat up and whipped her gaze full at him. She was unable to move as numbness spread throughout every inch of her.

"Sir Jeffrey was the man in the Assembly Room you were arguing with. He was the man in the hallway earlier." Grappling with the conclusion she didn't want to hear, she held her head between her hands. "What were you arguing about?"

"Work, ethics," he murmured. "Let's leave it."

"No." Like one of the puzzle boxes, everything clicked into place, and she could see what had transpired. "You were arguing about me. He doesn't want to do business with you because he saw you coming out of my room and kissing me in the hallway tonight. He knows who I am." She shook her head in disbelief. "Oh my God. My reputation is ruining yours."

Chapter Twenty-Eight

Julian threw his arm over his eyes. *Damn*. Beth always possessed a keen sense for when something wasn't right.

"Tell me." The quiver in her voice betrayed her disquiet. "After what we just shared, you can't keep it from me."

Her warm hand rested on his stomach. If she had punched him, it would have hurt less. He slowly sat up and faced her. He rubbed the back of his neck as he struggled with the appropriate words to say. All he wanted was to hold her in his arms, then make love to her again and again. They could sleep in the carriage on the way back to London tomorrow.

She sat with the sheet pulled against her chest as if it were a shield. "Sir Jeffrey doesn't have a high opinion of me."

"It makes no difference what he or any of the consortium members think." He turned, then took her hands in his. "We can marry," he assured her. "I have some ideas on how to sell my engines. Both Sykeston and Randford have offered me loans. I told you that I'd never borrow from them, but I'm going to accept their offers. Things are different now." He gently squeezed her hands. "I can't lose you again." He leaned nearer. "Hear me out. I can build a few more prototypes and rent more warehouse space to show them. I'll find other investors."

Her shoulders hunched as she dipped her head, staring at their hands.

"I'm confident this can be turned around." He tugged her chin slightly up so he could see her face. What he saw in her eyes terrified him. Her eyes flashed with the sheen of tears. "Don't cry. We can do this. The first years will be hard, but I'll succeed. My mechanics and engineering are solid . . ."

By now, she was shaking her head with her familiar mulishness that he'd always adored. "I agree you need to go to Sykeston and Randford."

He let out a silent sigh of relief.

"And have them go with you to the consortium and tell them it was all a mistake. Apologize to Sir Jeffrey and tell him I seduced you."

"I would never do that," he exclaimed.

"Well, I would," she said in her most haughty manner. "You are on the verge of financial security, and you threw it away because of what Sir Jeffrey said about me? That I was a whore?"

He narrowed his eyes. "If he even whispered the word about you, I would have called him out then and there."

"The problem is you still think of me as that young woman from so long ago." She lowered her voice and smiled slightly. "I haven't seen her in years." She scooted away from him. "Not since Meriwether."

"Don't say such things." When she continued to move farther away, he reached across the bed and halted her progress. "Where are you going?"

"To think," she answered. "We can't resolve this sitting here with you naked before me."

"Is it a problem that I'm naked?" Things were quickly

spiraling out of control. "You've been trying to get me out of my breeches this entire week. When I finally capitulate, you're ready to run."

She tilted her head with a smirk. "Julian, stop it. I'm not running from anything. But I'm ready to face reality. If I stay here then things will happen, and you'll weaken my resolve."

"Is that such a bad thing?" he asked with a brow lifted. "I enjoyed our lovemaking, and I think you did too. I think we need to make our plans for marriage."

She smiled serenely, but he was aware of the hidden danger there. Like the scorpion he'd compared her to once before, she was about to sting him. The only question was how badly it would hurt.

"We can make love as many times as you want. I did enjoy it. Thank you for showing me how wonderful it is."

"Then come into my arms, and I'll show you again."

"I would like that." She traced a pattern on the walnut-colored coverlets, then raised her gaze to his. "A woman would never tire of you."

"That's promising for our future." He waggled his eyebrows. Perhaps he was wrong and she wasn't going to sting him. "When shall we get married? I say as soon as possible."

"Julian, I can't marry you," she said softly. "Not now."

"But you promised," he argued.

"No, I didn't. And it's a good thing." Her voice trembled with emotion. "Don't you see what you'll face every time you're with me?" When he tried to close the distance between them, she stayed him with her hand. "Can you fathom the teasing and bullying that would come our children's way when it was discovered their mother was the third wife of the most famous trigamist in the history of England? Our children will be haunted by such truths.

I love you too much to impose that type of cruelty on you and your family. I won't put you through that."

"I can handle whatever others think, because I know you and your heart."

"You might be able to weather all the cruelty. But I can't. Not anymore." She sniffed, trying to hold back her tears, but it didn't work. "It's exhausting."

The sight tore another piece of his heart.

"Beth, please." He sank to his knees before her and took her hands in his. "I'm begging you."

"Oh, Julian," she exclaimed softly, shaking her head. Her eyes narrowed in pain. "I know the agony of having promises broken. I know that it made me doubt my worth." She cupped his face with her hands and stared into his eyes. "Never, ever doubt *yours*. Over the last week, you've taught me so much. How to love. How to live. Though others have a different opinion of me, I know who I am because of you. I'm someone who deserves to have promises kept." She pressed her palms against his cheeks and closed her eyes. "Oh God, why does this have to be so difficult." She took a deep breath, then opened her eyes. "I made a promise to myself that I'd never marry, and I intend to keep it."

They stared at each other as her words echoed around the room. This time, she was the one to blink first. He rose from the bed. It was unfathomable, what she was saying.

"What do you mean?" He waved a hand between them. "What exactly do you think happened here?" He kept his voice even, but the anger was building like the steam from one of his engines. "We made love."

"You gave me comfort when I needed it," she countered.

He heard the hitch in her voice, and like a hunter he

homed in on the sound. "You said earlier that you wanted to continue making love with me. If we don't marry, how can we continue?"

"We can be lovers." Her voice weakened. "It's over when you find your wife."

And there it was. The sting he'd been dreading. The poison that oozed through his veins caught fire. His nostrils flared. He'd never felt such exasperation and vexation in his entire life. Not even when her worthless brother had declined Julian's offer of marriage for her. In the most dramatic fashion he could muster, he held his arms wide. At his stance, her eyes grew wide.

"You want this body in your bed," he growled. "Then my suggestion is that you put my ring on your finger. Otherwise"—he waved a hand down his body—"you can't have it. Not tonight. Not tomorrow. Not in the foreseeable future."

"I understand." With the bearing of a queen dismissing her disloyal subjects, she regarded him. With a sure and inherent grace, she stood. She found her chemise and quickly donned it. Next, she gathered her clothing and gave him a final look. Without another word, she left the room with her head held high.

Bloody hell. Without hesitation, he followed her naked as the day he was born. Thankfully, no one would be about, as the housekeeper and butler slept in the other wing of the house. Without breaking stride, he reached her and gently grabbed her hand to stop her movement.

"Beth," he said softly.

She twisted herself free and stared at him.

"You can't storm off like that when we're having an argument."

She crossed her arms over her chest, using her clothing as a barrier between them. "It's not an argument." She

arched one perfect brow. "It's a difference of opinion."
She turned around and started down the stairs.

"Where are you going?" he asked. "Allow me to dress,
then I'll join you."

She turned on the step and faced him. "Don't bother. I
don't want your company." Then she threw his words right
back in his face. "Not tonight. Not tomorrow. Not in the
foreseeable future." She stopped for a moment almost as
if lost in thought. "Forgive me. Sometimes, I'm too opinionated, stubborn, and prickly. Your words, not mine."

"Beth," he cajoled.

"Think of your future." Her small smile was bittersweet.
"I am, and I'm thinking of mine."

Cillian's words that Julian would know when it was
time to walk away drifted into his memory like a ghost
haunting him.

Never.

His gut tightened. He wasn't ready to let her go.

Beth spent the rest of the night in Julian's study. It was
the only room in the house where the furniture wasn't
covered in Holland cloth.

She hadn't slept a wink. She'd either paced the room or
cradled her head in her hands as she tried to make sense
of their conversation. After what she discovered last night,
there was no way that she could marry Julian even after
she'd entered his bedroom with a different decision. After
what she'd been able to pry from him about his conversation with Sir Jeffrey, she couldn't and wouldn't do that
to Julian. He'd never be able to sell a single design or
engine in all of England if he married her. His entire estate would become insolvent. No, she couldn't marry him.

Last night was a revelation. Everyone knew her reputation and therefore considered her ruined. She'd always pretended not to care. But it hurt. When it started hurting Julian, it became unbearable.

He had to face reason.

She couldn't live through it again.

She let out a soulful sigh. She'd been so close to having her dreams come true—a husband who loved her, a family, children—but it was all gone. How could she be so selfish to inflict her taint on Julian?

When the sun had crested the horizon, signaling it was morning, Beth stood and looked in a mirror. It was worse than she'd imagined. She'd managed to dress, but several of the ties in the back of her gown were loose. She twisted her hair into a semblance of order, but her dress was wrinkled practically beyond recognition.

At the sound of a knock, she turned, expecting to find Julian, but it was Cillian.

He came to an abrupt stop and stared at her. He blinked, then glanced around the room, obviously trying to find the marquess. "Good morning, Miss Howell. Where is Lord Grayson?"

"I believe he's still asleep."

"I'm here." His deep voice entered the room before he did. When he crossed the threshold, his gaze locked with hers. "Good morning, Cillian. Miss Howell."

The tension between them thickened, making it almost impossible to breathe, but she'd not reveal her discomfort.

Cillian glanced between the two of them. He shifted his feet as if uneasy. "Yes, well . . . I'll prepare tea."

"There's no need," Beth said, not taking her gaze from Julian. "I'm ready to depart for London."

"So am I," Julian curtly agreed.

"What's happened?" Cillian asked.

"Nothing," they both answered at the same time.

Beth was the first to look away. She had to keep her wits about her if she wanted to avoid getting into another argument with Julian.

"On second thought, fetch a tea tray. Take your time," Julian said softly to Cillian. "Miss Howell will need a chaperon to London. Will you see if the vicar's daughter and her husband would be willing to travel to London with us? I'll ride my horse."

"Yes, my lord," Cillian answered with a bow, then scrambled from the room as if the hounds of hell were nipping at his feet.

Julian closed the door, then strolled to his desk. Beth's attention was fixated on his movements. They reminded her of last night, when he'd so tenderly made love to her. She brought her hand to her heart. Yet there was something different about his demeanor.

Oh, but this was ridiculous that they did not speak with each other. "How did you sleep?"

"Not well." He leaned back in his chair in a relaxed pose, but the muscle in his jaw tensed. "And you?"

"I didn't either." She clasped her hands. "I stayed here all night."

"I know." Before she could ask how he discovered that, he continued, "I came to check on you. I was worried."

"There was no need," she said softly.

"There was every need. When you love someone, their well-being comes to the forefront of your mind no matter if you argue or have a difference of opinion." He placed his hands on the desk and bent his head. After a moment, he patted the desk lightly as if he'd come to a resolution of some sort. Finally, he regarded her. He motioned for her to sit in one of the club chairs in front of his desk. "Please sit."

Once she sat down in the chair, he rose from the desk and knelt beside her. He took her hand and squeezed. "Have you changed your mind about last night?"

She shook her head.

"Will you at least reconsider if not for you, then for me?"

"I can't, Julian." She held his gaze, willing him to understand.

"I see." The dullness in his voice set her on edge. He stood and then returned to his desk. "This is the last thing in the world I want to do. The hardest thing I've ever done." He stared at the floor, then turned to her. He continued to stare as if waiting for her to say something.

"No, Julian."

He swallowed, then closed his eyes as if grappling with his emotions. "I've come to a decision. And I'm just going to say it. If you don't marry me"—he ran a hand down his face, but the pain from last night still lingered in his eyes—"then we can no longer associate with one another."

She drew her head back, then turned away. For a moment, she couldn't think of a reply. The words hurt worse than a slap across the face. Tears welled in her eyes, but thankfully, he couldn't see them. She refused to let them fall.

Why should she be surprised that this would be their outcome? She'd do the same if she were him. She bent her head so he couldn't see her pain. The heaviness in her chest made it difficult to inhale.

She sat silent for a moment, then lifted her gaze to his. "I understand."

"No, I'm afraid you don't." He studied her, then grimaced. "I can't love you and not have you. It isn't fair to either of us." His Adam's apple bobbed several times as he swallowed. "You're a beautiful, giving, and strong woman. I hope you find someone you want to share your life with. But I can't stand by while that happens." The despair in his eyes twisted her heart. He gripped one hand into a fist as if fighting his own pain. "I can't be your friend. Everything within me would wither to ashes if I saw you with another." The softness in his voice belied his resolve. "But if you ever find yourself in trouble and need me, I will be there for you."

A tear threaded its way down her cheek, and she angrily swept it away. He had needs. Every man did in his position. He needed to marry and produce an heir. He needed an heiress to help him rebuild his estate and create a family together.

She wanted that for him. And she'd wanted that for herself. But it was impossible for her to be that person.

"I failed you when I didn't fight for you the first time. I've lived with that regret ever since I asked your brother for your hand in marriage. But this failure is different." The roughness in his voice betrayed his pain. "I accept your decision that we not marry. You see, I let you go the first time without trying. But this time? I've given my best to win you over and failed. But I've discovered something important about myself. There's no shame or regret in this failure." He released a heavy breath. "You don't have to worry about your friendships with Kat and Constance and their husbands. I want you to have them in your life." He wiped his hand across his face. "I'll see Randford and Sykeston when we return. I'll tell them that I can't socialize with them anymore."

Her heart ceased to function. At least, it felt that way. He was giving up his friends for her.

In those few seconds, everything became clear. It wasn't St. John or Meri who had disappointed her. It was herself. She allowed her brother to manage her life for so long that she had no one to blame except herself for not taking control of her own destiny.

Because of that she was losing the most important person in her life.

Somehow, she'd been unaware that he'd moved from his desk and now stood before her. Gently, he cupped her cheek and tilted her face to his. "Tell me I'm wrong or tell me you've changed your mind. I'll drop to my knees this instant and beg you to marry me. If you tell me you want more time, I'll give it to you."

She loved him too much to have her name associated with him. Nor would she see him fail with the consortium or other investors because of her.

She cleared her throat. "You're not wrong." She prayed he didn't hear the tremble in her voice that betrayed her anguish. Unable to stay in the room any longer, she stood slowly. "I'll find Cillian and tell him we're finished here."

She might be a social pariah, but she knew honor. He was an honorable man, and he deserved so much more than what she could offer. With her head held high, she left him standing there, staring out the window.

She would not allow another tear to fall. There was no need. She sucked in her stomach.

Once she reached London, she had the rest of her lifetime to cry for all she had lost.

Chapter Twenty-Nine

Three weeks had passed since Beth had arrived back in London. The world continued spinning on its merry axis without a care whether she was involved in life or not.

Which was fine with her.

Constance and Kat had visited her every day trying to cheer her up, but it helped little. There was really nothing to look forward to anymore.

Her work at the linen workshop had always given her pleasure and a sense of purpose, but lately it had become dull. Thankfully, the woman she'd put in charge of the workshop, Mary Anne Lucas, had managed the shop and business with finesse while Beth had been gone and was still willing to take on that responsibility.

It gave Beth more time to sit in the salon of the small town house where she had lived with Kat and Constance after they'd discovered that Meri had married all three of them. Kat's husband had purchased it after they all had parted ways and was allowing her to live there until she decided what to do with her life.

She looked around the room decorated in black and white with touches of turquoise and pink spread throughout. Kat had decorated it, and it was lovely.

But it didn't feel like home.

Because Julian wasn't there.

A knock sounded on the door, and her housekeeper, Mrs. Manners, peeked into the room. "Ma'am, shall I say you're accepting visitors?"

The worried look on her face gave Beth pause. Her poor housekeeper thought she was moping over her brother's latest scandal. He'd been banned from White's as he couldn't cover the dues. He'd come knocking on her door no doubt to ask for the small pittance of savings she owned, but she'd refused to see him. He'd had to resort to selling his racehorses. An outcome she'd encouraged weeks ago.

The truth was she hadn't felt like receiving anyone since she'd left Julian's house except for Kat and Constance. The ride back to London still haunted her. Mrs. Millicent Williams had been her chaperon on the ride back and had never left her side. Julian had never once tried to talk with her.

But Beth couldn't help but notice that every time they'd stop to change horses Julian had found a way to converse with Mrs. Williams. She'd even asked the woman what they discussed, and she'd replied, *His lordship always asks how you're faring.*

"Ma'am?" Mrs. Manners reminded her about her visitors.

"Pardon me, my mind was elsewhere. I'm still not receiving."

"Unless it's the duchess or the countess?"

Beth nodded.

In seconds, both Kat and Constance glided into the room. Constance looked in fine health carrying her second child. Kat was radiant in a crimson gown that perfectly matched the rose she had pinned to her lapel.

"Darling, how are you?" Kat pressed a kiss to Beth's cheek and handed her a bouquet of fresh-cut roses. "These are from Randford. He wanted you to know that he was thinking of you."

"Tell him thank you." Beth took the red roses and inhaled deeply. If only someone else was thinking of her. Like a particular marquess. She chided herself for such thoughts. Breaking all ties was best for them. She realized that now. Only, she'd had no idea how overwhelming the pain would be.

Constance took her in her arms and hugged her the best she could with her big belly. Beth closed her eyes as those hateful tears threatened. The cause had to be that her dearest friends were visiting.

Mrs. Manners returned with a tea tray, then shut the door behind her when she left.

Kat and Constance settled on the black-and-white-striped sofa that faced Beth. She went through the motions of pouring the tea and serving her guests but didn't make a plate for herself.

"Are you eating?" Constance nibbled an iced biscuit. "You've lost more weight."

"She's right." Kat leaned near and covered Beth's hand with her own. "We're worried about you."

"I'm fine." Beth pulled her hand away and created a little distance between them. "I'm just not hungry." She took a sip of tea, then placed the cup and saucer on the side table next to her. "Did you hear the news? Grayson is supposedly going to propose to Lady Clementine Portland this week or next."

Just saying the words made her want to double over and cry out in pain. Miraculously, she kept her face blank. But her insides were a different story. This was what it felt like to die of a broken heart.

"It's rumors," Constance said softly. "I asked Jonathan about it last night. He said Grayson hasn't mentioned a word to him."

Her eyes widened. "I thought Grayson told Sykeston that he wouldn't socialize anymore."

Constance squeezed Beth's hand. "He did. Grayson doesn't call on him anymore. Jonathan visits him."

"I see. But it doesn't mean Julian's not marrying her." God, she hated sounding this weak.

Constance leaned forward and caught Beth's gaze. "Jonathan would know. They confide in each other."

"He hasn't mentioned anything to Christian either," Kat said in agreement with a sad smile. "Christian visits him also."

"There was a time when Julian would confide in me." She stared at them. "So, pardon me if I don't hold much weight in your husbands' claims that they're confidants of the marquess." She was dying inside. Still, it didn't excuse her behavior. "Please, forgive me." Her voice broke, but she straightened her spine. "I'm not myself today."

Her two friends gave her a sympathetic look.

"Truthfully, I haven't been myself since I returned from my trip." She picked up the inlaid walnut puzzle box that her father had given her and started to play with it. "I still find it hard to believe that Meri spent my entire fortune. After Bath, there's nothing except a game that he supposedly lost that was the start of his bad luck run."

"You know I'll always help you," Kat murmured softly.

Constance nodded in agreement. "Me also. We all are independent with our own means of making money." She narrowed her eyes and looked at the box in Beth's hand. "Is that a puzzle box?"

Beth nodded. "My father gave it to me on my sixteenth

birthday. It held my birthday present. He told me that I had to figure it out if I wanted my present." For the first time that day, she smiled. "It was almost my seventeenth birthday before I figured out how to open it. When Julian and I were at the Jolly Rooster, we stopped at a shop that sold these boxes. The proprietor showed me new ways of opening it."

"But you already know how to open it, don't you?" Kat asked.

Beth nodded. "I think there are more hidden compartments." She leaned forward and showed the box to her friends. "See these inlaid mother-of-pearl flowers? If you press the petals in a particular pattern, I'll wager that a new section of the box will open. But I haven't figured out the combination yet."

Kat sat on the edge of the couch. "I should get one of those for Arthur."

Constance laughed. "He's still a baby."

Kat waggled her eyebrows. "But Christian would want to figure it out before he gave it to his son. He'd enjoy it as much as, if not more than, Arthur would. What about your Aurelia? Your daughter is a genius according to your husband."

Constance smiled, then dipped her head. "He's so wonderful with her. Meri gave us a gift."

Beth's smile faded. It was another reminder of Meri's lack of regard for her. She forced herself to concentrate on the box and not Meri. She pressed one petal on a flower, then pressed another petal, then another on the other side. Anything to keep her mind off Julian too. Just thinking his name hurt.

Suddenly, something shifted in the box. Her eyes widened as she pulled the bottom out.

"You opened it," Kat exclaimed.

Constance clapped. "Brava."

"I simply pressed a combination I'd never tried before." She pulled the box apart, then froze.

"What is it?" Constance asked. "What's wrong?"

"There's a letter." Her voice grew weaker. "From Meri." She forced herself to open her eyes, then looked at both of her friends. "It's addressed to me."

They both stole a glance at each other, then turned to Beth.

"Would you like to be alone when you open it?" Kat asked softly.

Beth shook her head. "No, it's fortuitous that you're here. You were married to him also." She tried to smile. "If it's a horrible letter, then I'll need you both for strength."

Constance's eyes filled with tears and she placed her hand protectively over her stomach. "We'll always be with you. We love you, Beth."

"Whatever he's written, it's not a reflection of you." A tear streaked down Kat's cheek, and she brushed it away. "Out of all of us, you're the one who's suffered the most. If there's anyone who deserves happiness, it's you."

"Don't say that." Beth pulled the letter out and placed the box on the table beside her. Whatever it said, she'd not pity herself. "My life has turned out this way because of the choices I made. It wasn't Meri or St. John who caused my pain." She looked up at her friends. "I did it of my own free will."

The look of support and love that shone in her friends' eyes practically undid her. She took a deep breath for fortitude, then broke the seal on the letter and carefully unfolded it.

My dearest Beth,

*I have a confession. I won't ask your forgive-
ness, as what I've done is inexcusable. If you're
not aware, I've married two other women besides
you. Miss Constance Lysander and Miss Katherine Greer are their names. Like you, they're kind
and beautiful.*

*However, they're much different from you, my
sweet Beth. Neither are part of our society. I'm
afraid that once society hears that I've married
three different women, you'll be the one to bear
the brunt of the scandal. The* ton *has its own set of
rules and breaks them regularly without apology.
But I digress.*

*You have my deepest apologies. I would like to
make amends. I know you may not care at this point,
but I hope you'll allow me to explain.*

*When I lived with you, I came to realize what a
fool your brother was. He literally had the sense
of the blancmange we ate on our wedding day.
The fool gave me all your dowry to invest and
asked that I do the same for his fortune. Utterly
ridiculous and a poor excuse for a human being.
He knew nothing about me except for my knowledge of horses.*

*I know that my actions have ruined you for any
future marriage within the peerage. But you deserve so much better, my darling.*

You deserve a duke.

No, a duke isn't good enough.

You deserve a royal duke.

*Anyway, I've taken your dowry and wagered
with it.*

"He gambled with my dowry." She flinched at the sudden intake of breath from her friends but continued to read.

> *I played with a gentleman by the name of Sir Jeffrey Baker. Fate was kind that evening. I won everything that man owns or did own. It's the majority stake in an investment consortium.*
>
> *Now you do. I've signed the shares over to you. Congratulations, dearest. You should receive a nice annual income of seven thousand and five hundred pounds. Whatever you do, please do not share it with your brother. He's a wastrel.*
>
> *I hope that we all can meet to discuss where to go from here. I truly believe that if you met the other wives you'd become fast friends. You're all such unique, lovely ladies. There's another present in this box, but it's for all three of you to share equally.*
>
> *I only hope when we next see each other you won't hate me for ruining you.*
>
> *I've always found that there's a silver lining in every black cloud. I hope we all can find it together.*
>
> *My best for you always,*
> *Meri*

A key accompanied the folded piece of parchment. He'd spoken true. When Beth unfolded it, she discovered a legal document declaring that she owned sixty percent of the shares in the consortium. Like the sun popping out from behind the menacing storm clouds, everything brightened before her. For the first time in weeks, she had hope for her future.

Beth held the letter in her hand and slowly raised her gaze to her friends.

"Well?" Kat asked. "What did he say?"

"He gambled with my dowry, but he won . . ." She stopped for a moment to let the truth sink in. "He won a *bloody* fortune." She gave the letter to the women to read, then started to pace as her giddiness took flight. If what Meri said was true, then she'd never have to worry about money again. "There's something for all three of us to share." She held up the key.

Her friends quickly scanned the letter.

Kat was the first to stand and hug her. "Oh, darling, this is wonderful news. You're rich."

But then the truth hit her square between the eyes. "I own Sir Jeffrey's shares. This changes everything."

Constance's smile turned delightfully wicked. "Considering what he said to Julian privately, I agree."

Kat put on her gloves and pulled them tight. "Why don't you put on your best gown for calling. I think you should visit Sir Jeffrey. Constance and I will accompany you. We want to witness him kissing your slippers."

"Brilliant, my dear Kat." Constance laughed.

In fifteen minutes, Beth was downstairs in her favorite spring-green gown. It was striking and it gave her confidence. Her friends had arrived in Kat's carriage with the Duke of Randford crest boldly painted on the door. A footman assisted Constance in first, then Kat and Beth followed.

As the carriage lumbered down the street, Constance leaned back against the squab and sighed.

"Is anything wrong?" Beth asked. Her friend had a terrible time carrying her daughter, Aurelia, the last time.

Constance smiled. "I'm right as rain. I was sighing because this will be so fun." Her friend tilted her head and regarded her. "But I must ask, how did Meri come to have that puzzle box in the first place? I thought he'd never visited your Somerset home."

Kat nodded once. "I was wondering the same thing."

"After Meri left the Cumberland ancestral seat, I had some of my most precious possessions moved to Somerset, including the puzzle box."

"And to think this was in your possession the entire time." Kat studied the box. "What if that key is for the lockbox in Christian's possession?"

"Sounds plausible." Beth leaned forward. "I'm sure with the three of us working together we'll discover what he left us. Hopefully, it's not another pile of receipts."

"Well, even if he left us receipts, I'm grateful." Constance reached over and put her hand on Beth's. "He made amends."

"I'm grateful also." Kat joined in by putting her hand on top of theirs. "You weren't forgotten. As if anyone could forget you."

Beth swallowed at the thought. Had Julian forgotten her?

The carriage slowed to a stop in front of an exquisite town house on the outskirts of Mayfair. Carefully, they climbed from the carriage and made their way up the walkway to the front door.

"He seems to have done well for himself," she muttered.

"I wonder what's happened to the money that you've earned since Meri won the shares from him?" Constance asked.

"I think we're about to find out." Beth nodded, then pounded with the door knocker.

A young man opened the door and regarded the three. "May I help you, ladies?"

"We're here to see Sir Jeffrey." Kat whipped out her calling card. "You may tell him that the Duchess of Randford wishes to see him."

Constance gave him her card. "The Countess of Sykeston."

The poor man became so flustered that he didn't even ask for Beth's name and turned abruptly on his heel. He practically ran down the hallway without even inviting them inside.

But that had never stopped the three of them from going where they wanted. After they entered the house, Kat and Constance wrapped their arms around Beth in a show of solidarity.

"I'm so grateful you're here with me," Beth said softly.

"There's no place we'd rather be," Constance answered.

"Indeed," said Kat.

It was then that Beth's heart seemed to lighten. For the first time since she'd last seen Julian, she felt happy. Knowing what she was about to do was an act of love.

For all her days on this earth, Beth would love Julian and only him. She'd realized that when she'd left his study the last time. He was her lodestar. She'd not be centered unless she was with him.

But with the fortune that Meri left her, perhaps she could create that dream of funding a school or charity of some sort that would help others with tarnished reputations. It would be a worthwhile endeavor. Of course, she'd still work at the linen workshop. She'd enjoyed it in the past and, she hoped, would find her way back there.

"Your Grace and my ladies, if you'll follow me." The young man bowed, then motioned them forward.

Beth didn't correct him. If Sir Jeffrey knew she was there, he might refuse to see them.

The butler stepped out of their way after he announced

them. Kat entered first, then Constance, and finally Beth. Sir Jeffrey was already out from behind his desk and bowing profusely.

"Welcome, Your Grace." He nodded at Kat, then turned to Constance. "My lady."

Finally, he turned to Beth. "My la—" His eyes widened. "You all three were married to Lord Meriwether." He took a step back and the confusion on his face was laid bare. "What is the meaning of this?" He turned his attention to Beth. "You were in Bath with Lord Grayson. You're not a lady."

"I never claimed to be," Beth answered calmly. "But I do claim to be the majority owner of the consortium. Lord Meriwether signed his shares over to me."

Just then, Sir Jeffrey's wife swept into the room. "Welcome, Your Grace—"

Silence reigned as she saw Beth. It would have been quite comical if Sir Jeffrey didn't look as if he were about to faint.

"My dear, these ladies are here to see me on a matter of business."

"Of course," she said hurriedly, then scampered from the room, shutting the door behind her.

Kat and Constance both eyed Beth with an arched brow. They were all thinking the same thing. None of her friends would tolerate their husbands dismissing them from a conversation about business. They were all independent-minded and their husbands appreciated their business acumen.

"Please sit." Sir Jeffrey waved to a sitting area that overlooked a formal garden in the courtyard.

As they each took their seats, Beth regarded Sir Jeffrey. The look of utter defeat had turned his complexion an ash color.

She had felt the same when she'd discovered the trail for her dowry had turned cold. But it was nothing compared with the emptiness that had guttered her when she left Julian.

She closed her eyes and took a deep breath. He was the reason why she was here.

"Sir Jeffrey, let me begin. Since I'm the majority shareholder with the consortium, I have a few matters that should be addressed as soon as possible."

He nodded warily.

"What exactly happened to the monies earned that were due to Lord Meriwether after his death?" Beth asked with determination in her voice.

He cleared his throat and glanced at Constance. "They've been held in an account on his behalf. We were waiting to see if the Duke of Randford or Lord Meriwether's widow would come forward claiming the funds."

Constance shook her head in disgust.

Kat rolled her eyes. "Of course you were."

"It wasn't like that at all, Your Grace. The consortium had decided that if no one came forward, then we'd contact the solicitor and let him know about the money."

"How much is it?" Beth asked.

His brow furrowed as if she'd said something unseemly. "Money is rather gauche to discuss between us."

"I asked how much," Beth pressed.

"Forty thousand pounds," he murmured. "The shares are worth another one hundred and eighty-five thousand pounds."

Beth's stomach somersaulted at the staggering amounts. "I see. Have the earnings sent in my name to the attention of Lady Somerton at E. Cavensham Commerce. I will let her know to expect them."

He nodded once. "Is there anything else? I'm a busy man."

"How wonderful that you'll have more time on your hands," Constance said soothingly, then waved a hand in Beth's direction. "Now that Miss Howell is making the decisions for the consortium."

"Lady Sykeston, our arrangement with Lord Meriwether was that he allowed us to make the decisions for him." He wiggled his nose in irritation.

It reminded Beth of a mouse who'd lost his cheese. "Well, I won't be that type of investor, sir." She smiled sweetly. "I want to invest in Lord Grayson's engines."

His eyes widened in shock. "But he's your . . . you're his . . ."

"My friendship really isn't the topic here. The marquess is a talented and learned man of science. His engines will create an entire new way of weaving textiles." She tilted her head. "Unless there's some issue with his engineering skills?"

"No. They're the best designs I've seen of such an engine. However, the consortium tries not to . . ." He cleared his throat. "Miss Howell, we have very high standards that we uphold."

"As do I," she said with a hint of steel in her voice. "But I know genius when I see it, and Lord Grayson has it. And he's taken that gift and made an invention that will make us money."

He nodded slowly. "Yes, ma'am. I'll send word of your decision to the consortium. Most of the members were quite excited about Lord Grayson's endeavors."

"As am I," Beth said, then stood. "Are you still an investor?"

He nodded sheepishly. "After Lord Meriwether won

my shares, I was allowed to purchase a few from other members."

"From now on, I will be attending any meetings that the consortium holds." Beth nodded. "Good day."

Kat stood, then helped Constance to stand.

Before they reached the door, Sir Jeffrey called out, "Would you like to inform the marquess of your decision?"

"No," she said with a bittersweet smile. "You should, since you were the one who made the rash judgment and severed ties with him." She glanced at her friends, who nodded encouragement. "It will give you the opportunity to apologize for your behavior. The Marquess of Grayson is an honorable man, and you insulted him. I suggest you find a way to mend your differences."

"I'll inform him and let him know of your new status as majority shareholder."

Beth shook her head. A deep sadness enveloped her. She'd not have Julian change his course in finding an heiress because of her decision to invest in his machines. "There's no need to mention my name."

"I see." Sir Jeffrey regarded her with a sympathetic smile as if he could sense her sorrow. "I owe you an apology also, Miss Howell. I can see you're a woman of intelligence and integrity. I'm deeply sorry I caused you any pain."

The sincerity on his face gave Beth pause. Perhaps she'd been a little rash about her judgment of all men being undependable. It seemed that Sir Jeffrey had the ability to see the errors of his way and change his mind.

Meriwether may have made a shambles of her life when he married her, but now he was fixing it from beyond the grave.

Too bad she couldn't fix what was wrong between her and Julian.

The women took their leave and were soon in the carriage. As soon as they were in motion, Constance took her hand. "This changes things mightily, don't you think?"

"How so?" Beth asked.

Kat took Beth's other hand. "With Julian."

Beth squeezed both of their hands, then lowered her head. "Not a bit."

She forced herself to look at her friends, her sisters, and the two women she was closest to in her life. Though they didn't share a drop of blood between them, they were family and supportive of one another. Wasn't a supportive family the ones who had the hardest trouble seeing your faults?

"Meriwether's return of my dowry won't repair what's wrong between me and Julian," she said with a sad smile, though her heart was crumbling in her chest. God, she was so tired of the pain. Tired of the tears. Through her blurred vision, she tried to smile again but failed miserably.

Constance frowned. "You're not making sense. Your wealth is greater than ten times your original dowry amount. You would have married him with twenty thousand pounds years ago. Why isn't two hundred thousand pounds enough now?"

Kat slipped off the bench and sat next to Beth with her arm around her. "Dearest, I don't understand either. Why can't you be with Julian? You love him, don't you?"

She squeezed their hands until she was certain she was hurting them, but she couldn't let go. It was as if they were the only ones who keep her steady in the storm that raged in her heart.

"I love him so much, it hurts." She inhaled a stuttered breath, desperate to keep her emotions tamped down. "I've always loved him."

The empathy in Constance's gaze practically undid Beth, but of all of them, she was a realist. What her life had become couldn't be undone. "No amount of money would ever be enough to repair my destroyed reputation. I would never subject Julian to such pain, nor any children we'd be fortunate to have. I don't think either of you should have anything to do with me."

"Don't say such things," Constance chided.

Kat nodded in agreement. "Have you spoken with Grayson?"

Beth wiped the tears from her eyes. "I told him to find an heiress."

"Beth," Constance said softly. "Neither Kat nor I were born into the peerage, but they accepted us. Even with our history with Meri. You're one of the wealthiest women in all of England. With your wealth and birthright, everyone will accept you. They'll be clamoring to welcome you into society once again."

"He loves you," Kat said softly. "Besides, you're wealthy once again. Make the *ton* bow to you."

Constance caught her gaze. "The only reason he goes to any events is that he says he's trying to find a wife."

"And not very successfully," Kat added. "Do you know why?"

At the mention of someone else marrying Julian, her heart was shredded a little more. She shook her head.

"He can't, darling." Kat's gentle voice hitched as if she were about to cry. "He only loves you. He doesn't want anyone else. He told Christian that."

"Can't you see a way to put the past behind you and

build a future with a man who loves you with every part of his heart and soul?" Constance placed her hand on her rounded middle and leaned forward just a tad. "Both Kat and I found a way to be with our husbands. Our reputations were as tattered as yours." She looked at Kat and smiled, then turned her attention back to Beth. "It wasn't easy or pretty or smooth for either of us. But fighting for our love was the most worthwhile endeavor I've ever accomplished. It was my destiny to be with Jonathan."

"Same with Christian," Kat said softly. "Don't lose Julian, Beth. You'll regret it to your dying day otherwise."

All that tightly coiled control started to slip. With a wretched, woeful sound, a sob escaped, and her tears started again. Kat drew her into her arms and kept her steady.

"I don't know," she cried.

"Yes, you do, dearest," Constance said. "Don't let others define you. Define yourself."

After her heart had been split into thirty pieces, Beth somehow managed to mend it together. Her nose was running, and her face had to look a fright, but that didn't stop the newfound sense of hope that began to unfurl in her chest.

"You're right. I shouldn't allow anyone to dictate who I am or what Julian and I feel about each other. I hurt him by being so stubborn. You think he'll give me another chance?"

Kat and Constance laughed through their own tears.

"Without a doubt," Constance said with a huge grin.

"That's our girl," Kat cried as she pulled Beth tighter against her.

"I'm going to the modiste Madame Mignon and purchasing a new gown. I read that Julian is attending the

Duke of Pelham's ball. I'm sure the duke will welcome me if I attend." She laughed as she wiped away her tears. "He loves to be outrageous. Frankly, I'll fit right in."

Her dearest friends nodded in agreement.

"That's perfect," Constance declared. "What color dress are you going to wear?"

"Black and white," she said with a nod. "Those are Julian's colors."

Chapter Thirty

With little fanfare, Randford's butler announced Julian.

Julian had hesitated before answering Randford's summons and agreeing to this visit. He needed to keep his distance.

Yet the truth? Everything hurt inside. He needed his friends now more than ever.

When he stepped into the study, Randford and Sykeston stood.

"We were just discussing you," Randford called out.

As Julian greeted his friends, he realized that the duke's charity for the veterans who'd come home from war with nothing had become a celebrated success. And his duchess had helped him create it. Sykeston had found a way to accept his limitations and have a full life with his countess and their daughter.

If only Julian had Beth by his side, he could accomplish great things also. Her advice was priceless. And her kisses were his ultimate weakness. He closed his eyes briefly. He could not think of holding her or making love to her anymore. Since he'd returned to London his sleep was practically nonexistent. Besides, she'd made her position clear. They didn't have a future.

He tried to banish the gloom that surrounded him. "I assume you were discussing my stunning intellect and stellar conversation skills."

Sykeston looked at him as if he'd grown two heads. "Hardly. It was how dense you are."

"I'm offended," Julian declared, then smiled. "Tell me how you've reached those erroneous conclusions."

"Let's have a coffee first." Randford waved to a sitting area where a steaming pot of fresh coffee awaited them. After they all sat, Randford poured. He took a sip as he regarded Julian.

He set his cup down and stared at the duke. "What?"

"We were discussing how your hunt for a wife is progressing." Randford rested his elbows on his thighs and leaned forward. "Any promising candidates?"

"No." Julian let out a sigh. "I hate it."

Sykeston regarded him. "I find it hard to believe that no one is interested, particularly since Sir Jeffrey came to you with an apology and the offer to invest. Your fortunes have changed. You should have young marriage-minded women falling all over you."

"That's the problem. I don't care for any of them." He studied the floor as he decided how much to disclose. These were his closest friends. "They're not her."

Both Sykeston and Randford grew solemn.

"I find that no matter what social event I attend, I'm always comparing the other women to Beth. I look for her even though I know she's not going to be there." He ran a hand through his hair. "How ridiculous."

Randford gazed at Julian with his penetrating brown eyes. "On the contrary. I wouldn't expect you to feel any other way."

Sykeston leaned back in his chair. "Rumor has it that

you're about to offer for the Portland girl. What's her name?"

"Clementine," he answered. "It's nothing but rumors. Her father invited me to dinner to discuss marrying her, but I declined. That was after Sir Jeffrey had told me of the reversal of the consortium's decision."

"Speaking of which"—Sykeston finished his coffee and set the cup on the table—"my countess told me a rather interesting story."

"Do tell," Randford said with a chuckle.

"Do you know why the consortium changed its mind?" Sykeston's question pinned Julian in place.

Julian sensed the change in mood. "Sir Jeffrey said they'd not let such an opportunity pass and apologized for his earlier behavior."

Sykeston looked to Randford. "You should tell him. It's your brother."

"Half brother," the duke corrected, then regarded Julian. "It seems that Meri had quite the luck in a game of cards against Sir Jeffrey. He won the man's consortium shares. Sir Jeffrey had to purchase shares from other members to stay in the investment group."

"Go on." Julian sat on the edge of his seat at the news. Sir Jeffrey wasn't bluffing when he said he had personal experiences with reckless behavior. It almost made Julian laugh, but he'd lost Beth because of the man.

"Sir Jeffrey used to be the majority owner," Sykeston offered. "Then Randford's brother . . ." At the duke's dark glower, Sykeston laughed. "I meant half brother."

Randford smiled, turning his attention to Julian. "I'll give you one guess who he left those shares to?"

"Based upon Sykeston's mood, I'll say his countess." Such news would no doubt devastate Beth. The need surged to offer her comfort, but he knew it was impossible.

"Beth," Randford said.

"Beth?" he asked incredulously as his mind reeled.

"*Your* Beth," Sykeston said with a grin.

"She found it in a puzzle box that her father had given her. Apparently, Meri had hidden it there to ensure that St. John couldn't get his hands on it. When she discovered it, Kat and Constance accompanied her to see Sir Jeffrey. She told him to invest in you. It was her right as majority stockholder."

"Why didn't she come and tell me herself?" He wanted to withdraw the words. By the look in his friends' eyes, they knew he was wounded. He tried to smile. "It's fitting that she has it. I'll write a note and thank her." He fisted his hands together. Just thinking her name brought forth sweet memories that now sliced him into shreds.

Sykeston narrowed his eyes. "A note? You should see her."

"She wants nothing to do with me." He tried not to sound curt but failed. It still hurt like the devil that she wouldn't marry him.

Randford thrummed his fingers on his leg, a typical sign of impatience for the duke. "By the by, are you going to Pelham's ball?"

He shrugged.

"Constance wanted to go, but we're going back to Portsmouth and stay until the baby comes." Sykeston stood slowly and extended his hand. "Come and see us."

Julian stood and shook hands. "We shall see."

After they said their goodbyes, Randford clapped him on the shoulder. "You never answered my question. Are you going?"

"I hadn't really thought about it." He ran a hand down his face. The idea of going to another ball made him want to run to his ancestral estate and never return to London until the Season was over. But if he went to Raleah House, all he'd think about was Beth. After Sir Jeffrey's visit, Julian hadn't been able to concentrate on his engines or his estate. Beth was at the forefront of his mind always. "Are you and Kat attending?"

Randford lifted a ducal brow. "We're still deciding, but I think you should. I've heard that Pelham has arranged for a ball that is not to be missed."

A week later, Julian stood among a crowd of his peers at the Duke of Pelham's ball. Everyone around him was dressed gaily in colors of the rainbow. Wearing practically all black except for the handsome ivory waistcoat that Beth had made for him, he stood out like a mourner at a carnival.

Which was appropriate. His mood was as dark as his clothing. It didn't help matters that he'd kept his own company this week. Instead of working, he'd drafted letter after letter to Beth thanking her for her support of his engines. But it all turned to drivel each time. At first, he'd railed at the situation. He'd asked how she could leave him if she claimed to love him. The next set of letters had been questions about why she'd decided they couldn't be together. That had been disastrous. He'd sounded like a love-starved suitor because that's what he'd become.

He was out of options now. He had to accept her wishes and let her go. Just the thought of it made him want to howl.

"Lord Grayson, how lovely to see you again." Lady

Clementine had sidled beside him with her sister, Henrietta, and Portland next to her.

He greeted each politely but added little to the conversation.

"I beg your pardon." Randford's deep voice broke into the conversation. "A matter of extreme urgency requires the marquess's attention. If you'll excuse Lord Grayson and me?"

Julian nodded to the ladies, then turned on his heel and walked side by side with Randford. "I thought you weren't coming, as you hadn't mentioned it."

"My duchess wanted to attend. Said she wouldn't miss this for the world. When the woman who rules your heart decides a course of action, you'd best go along with her plans." Randford arched a brow. "Or get out of the way."

"I wouldn't know," he said glumly. "What's this about? Another Pelham spectacle?"

"You'll see." A smile tugged at his lips.

When they reached the bottom of the steps where guests entered, Kat, Constance, and Sykeston were waiting for them.

"I thought you and your lady wife were traveling to Portsmouth?" Julian asked, clearly bewildered.

Sykeston grinned. At the rare sight, the entire ballroom quieted.

"She said she wouldn't miss this ball and wanted to stay here." He nodded in her direction. "Frankly, I didn't want to miss it either."

The fact that Sykeston wanted to attend a ball was odd. The man normally hated functions such as these. "What 'it' are you referring to?"

Before anyone could answer, Pelham made an appearance at the top of the steps. With his navy velvet evening coat and matching breeches, the duke cut a fine figure. Several of the ladies giggled at the sight.

"My honored guests, may I have your attention?" Pelham's voice boomed from the top of the steps. "I'd like to introduce my guest of honor."

The crowd's titters grew to murmurs.

Julian glanced at his friends, but they didn't notice. All their attention was riveted to Pelham, who had his hand outstretched.

With a sure confidence and poise that Julian knew intimately, Beth came into view and took Pelham's hand. Dressed in a silk black and ivory gown, she looked like a goddess. Not any goddess, but Melinoë, the goddess of ghosts. Which was appropriate, as she haunted his dreams and every waking hour.

Pelham beamed like a besotted fool. "It's my pleasure to introduce you to my dearest—" The duke's gaze bounced between Grayson and Beth.

Julian took a step back to escape. He had no earthly idea where, but he couldn't stay in this room for another minute.

Sykeston shot out a hand and clasped him by the arm.

"Don't leave. It will only draw attention to you," the earl whispered for Julian's ears only. "After the pompous arse makes his announcement, then you'll be able to exit as the crowd will rush forward."

Julian tried to concentrate on the black marble baluster before him, but his traitorous eyes kept drifting to Beth, who wasn't even looking at him. Her gaze was on the duke.

"As I was saying, I'd like to introduce you to someone very special to me." Pelham's voice boomed like a death knell.

Julian didn't listen until he heard three words that sent chills down his spine.

"She said yes."

Julian sucked in a breath as a nightmare unfolded around him. There was only one conclusion to be made from such a spectacle.

Pelham was going to introduce Beth as his fiancée.

Chapter Thirty-One

Hidden behind a column at the entrance of the ball-room, Beth had stared at Julian as he and Randford made their way to the bottom of the steps that led to the magnificent room where the Duke of Pelham's guests had gathered. As the two imposing men walked across the dance floor, the crowd parted much like a magical river. She rested her hand on her stomach, hoping to calm the butterflies that were flitting inside. She prayed she wouldn't faint. She'd never done anything this outrageous before.

Pelham had his hand extended, signaling that now was the time for her to take her position beside him and address Julian. With as much grace as she could muster, she walked to his side. She could hear the crowd whispers grow like a gaggle of geese complaining, but she ignored them the best she could. This moment, this night, and her next words all belonged to the man she loved with her whole heart. She'd rehearsed her speech a thousand times during the last week, but her mind was a sieve right now. She would have to rely on her heart to guide her.

Without even realizing it, she'd grabbed ahold of Pelham's hand and held on for dear life.

"I'd like to introduce you to my dearest . . . friend. She

said yes to attending tonight," Pelham announced with a slight laugh.

She didn't hear the rest of the introduction as she directed all her attention to Julian. Her heart stumbled at the sight. He looked as if he wanted to be anywhere but here.

"Breathe," Pelham said in a voice that only she could hear.

"Thank you." She squeezed his hand and let go.

"My pleasure. We have everyone's attention, including Grayson's. Don't make him wait."

The duke took a step back and she was alone on the top of the steps with a restless crowd below.

"What is she doing?" one matron asked loudly, with condemnation in her tone.

"Creating another scandal," answered another woman across the ballroom.

Beth shook her head slightly, and her gaze met Sykeston's. The earl nodded slightly in approval. When she glanced at the Duke of Randford, he did the same in encouragement.

But when she looked to Meri's other two wives, Kat and Constance, her sisters of the heart, tears welled in her eyes. Their unconditional love and support surrounded her. And their own tears gave her the strength to see this through.

"If you'll indulge me for a moment, I have something I must say before the evening begins in earnest." With each word, her voice grew stronger. She would survive this, and she'd flourish no matter the outcome.

All because she accepted herself for who she was—a woman who controlled her own destiny and loved a man with her entire being.

"Lord Grayson, I must offer you my most humble

apologies." At the sound of his name, his eyes met hers. She didn't shy away. "Over the last several weeks, I've made some discoveries about myself."

His eyes narrowed slightly, but he didn't turn away.

"For years, I've been under the mistaken belief that the men in my life had failed me. But during those days when you graciously escorted me through the countryside, I came to realize something. The person who had failed me was myself. My heart had been telling me whom I could trust and love. No matter how much I tried to dismiss such wisdom, I couldn't. Because it was you. Only and always you."

A muscle in Julian's cheek jerked.

"My dearest Grayson, I beg your forgiveness," she said with a raw emotion that made her throat tighten.

He stared at her without any expression passing over his face. In that moment, she didn't know what he was going to do. It was quite possible that she had pushed him so far away that he was done with her.

She couldn't say that she blamed him.

"I've been obstinate and opinionated, and have proven myself pigheaded about many things . . . including a pig." At that, Kat and Christian laughed. Constance joined in, and even Sykeston smiled. It also earned a slight grin from Grayson, giving her hope. "But I never, ever stopped loving you. It just took me a little while longer than most to understand it."

He closed his eyes and shook his head slowly as if disbelieving her.

Despair nipped at her heels. Yet she continued, "Though I'm a tad mulish, I'm tenacious when I want something." She didn't take her eyes away from him. "I want you. I want you as my husband."

His gaze met hers and she was never so unsure of an

answer to a question in all her life, but she'd ask even if it resulted in humiliation.

Because that's what she'd learned about herself. Pride and honor meant nothing if it kept you hidden from the world and afraid to accept the rare gift of love.

At that final thought, she straightened her stance as the rest of the crowd melted away. "It seems I did listen to the fortune-teller. She was right and told me everything I needed to hear."

Another round of aghast murmurs flooded the ballroom again.

"I found my fortune here." She placed her hand on the center of her chest. "I'm giving you my heart again." She smiled. "Which in a way is silly. You've had it the entire time."

Everything came down to the next few minutes. If he said no, she'd have no choice but to walk away. She'd come this far, and she wouldn't back down now.

"Make me the happiest woman in all the world and agree to become my husband." At the sounds of shock that echoed through the room, she raised her voice above the din. "Will you marry me, my dear Grayson? I promise for all my days upon this earth, I will ensure that you're happy and know that you're loved every day."

Grayson continued to stare at her as the crowd quieted, waiting for his answer. This was the moment of reckoning. No matter his answer, she'd been true to her heart and to him with her proposal.

Pelham came to her side. "Allow me to escort you down the steps to his side."

"What if he wants nothing to do with me?" She hated the desperation in her voice.

"You won't find the answer if you stay up here all night." The duke held out his arm.

With a deep breath, she wrapped her arm around his and slowly descended the steps.

Once she reached her friends' sides, she gave a little smile to Kat and Constance, letting them know how much she appreciated them. She turned to her first and only love.

"Julian," she said softly. "I hope you can forgive me."

"Don't," he said.

Her brittle heart was on the verge of shattering, but she refused to turn away.

"Don't ask me to forgive you. Not in front of all these people." His eyes searched hers. "Especially when you have nothing to apologize for." Then, the most exquisite smile graced his lips. "The answer to your question is . . . yes. I would be honored to marry you."

Cheers rang out among their friends. At the sound, the crowd gathered closer.

She gasped and tears brimmed her eyes. "Thank you."

He cupped her cheeks and drew close. "It is I who must thank you for having the courage to take a chance on us," he said tenderly.

Somehow, Pelham stood by their sides. "If you don't ask her to dance this minute, then I will," he said with a true smile. "Congratulations. You're a lucky man, Grayson."

"The luckiest in all the world," Julian answered without tearing his gaze from Beth's.

As he led her to the dance floor, the crowd parted. When the waltz started, he swept her into his arms.

Unable to look anywhere except to gaze upon his handsome face, Beth danced with little thought to anyone else. She was completely captivated by the raw emotion in Julian's eyes. Magically, it healed every wound in her broken heart. With him by her side, all was finally right with the world.

Other couples joined them. They didn't look askance when Julian then led her to the terrace overlooking the exquisite Pelham gardens. The din of the music faded as he took her arms and kissed her with such heartfelt tenderness that she melted in his embrace.

He brushed away a stray tear, then rested his forehead against hers. "That was the bravest thing I've ever seen."

"I couldn't let you go unless you knew what was in my heart. I want to build a future with you. I love you." She nestled closer. "With you, I can be brave."

"Oh, darling, you were always brave. You simply needed to find it within yourself. And I had to learn patience." His eyes searched hers. "Only by letting you go could I have you. Because you had to decide you wanted me." He chuckled slightly. "This is the start of a wonderful life."

She smiled while another joyful tear fell. "You did promise me that."

With the back of his hand, he caressed her cheek. "I love you with everything I am." He pressed his lips to her.

When she moaned, his tongue teased her mouth to open for him. As their passion for each other ignited like a fire out of control, she said a silent prayer thanking Meri for ruining her.

For without that, she'd have never seen the best within Julian, her forever love. A man who kept his promises.

And without Julian, she'd have never found the best within herself.

Epilogue

One year later
The London home of the Duke and Duchess of Randford

The air shimmered with an undeniable excitement as Julian pulled his beloved wife, Beth, tight against him. She held their two-month-old son, Maxwell Aston Raleah, the Earl of Weyhill, in her arms. She tipped her head and flashed a grin.

Smiles came easier now for Beth than they ever had. It was a rich sight, one he would never tire of seeing.

And for good reason.

Their lives had been transformed since they married. They both successfully straddled the divide between the aristocracy and the rising middle class of industrial masterminds. They were the undisputed "it" couple in all of London. Everyone vied for their attention and advice.

Julian's steam engines were a rousing success. The factory he'd built was in full production. With Beth's guidance and support he'd rebuilt the Grayson fortunes and had managed to collect many of the Raleah House portraits and art pieces that had been sold. They were now safely ensconced within his ancestral seat. The ones that couldn't be recovered were replaced with new pieces that he and Beth had picked out together. Raleah House felt like home again along with their London manse. He'd helped Beth found a social club for men and women whose reputations were less than glowing. She spent much of her free time there giving advice and comfort to the young women and men who'd made mistakes. She helped them find a different course in life after the *ton* had shunned them. When his own business allowed, Julian was by her side and marveling at the confidence and change that she helped those people find within themselves.

Such efforts together were the epitome of their marriage, a true partnership. Even at night, when Max needed his feeding, Julian was the one to retrieve their son and place him in Beth's loving arms. He'd never tire of the sight. It was those tender moments when he fell even more in love with his Beth, if that was possible.

"We're ready to start," Beth said. With a sure hand, she gave Max to his nursemaid, Mrs. Cochran, who'd come to live with them after her husband, the highwayman turned land steward, had come to apologize with his hat in hand, begging forgiveness.

It was Beth's idea to bring the down-on-their-luck couple into their employment. One of the best decisions Julian had ever made. Under Cochran's supervision, the tenant farms surrounding his ancestral home were on the verge of turning a profit. His father would be proud of what Julian had accomplished over the last year, and he would have fallen in love with Beth. Julian was certain of it.

He stepped forward and joined Sykeston and Randford, who were as mystified as he at the purpose of this gathering.

Sykeston held his sleeping one-year-old heir, North Alfred Jonathan Eaton, Viscount Lyndale. "What the devil are they up to?" Sykeston growled softly so as not to disturb his son.

"Papa?" Aurelia, Constance and Lord Meriwether's child, peered up at the earl who had claimed her as his own. "It's a secret. You always said secrets are to be kept if they're not yours." She smiled adoringly at her father.

"How right you are, darling girl." Sykeston smiled down at her, then winked at Julian. "You need a daughter," he confided. "They remember everything you say and do. Keeps you honest." He laughed. "I'm teaching Aurelia chess. By the time she's five, she'll be winning every game against me. Utter genius."

Before Julian could offer his opinion, Kat, the Duchess of Randford, announced, "May I have your attention? We're all gathered to unveil a special portrait that Constance, Beth, and I commissioned. But first, we'd like to remember Meriwether. Today would have been his birthday, and in remembrance, we'd like to share what Meriwether has given to all three of us."

Randford picked up his son, Arthur, and beamed at his wife, who was carrying their second child. The duke was clearly besotted with his wife. It seemed to be the same malady that Sykeston suffered.

Julian did as well.

They were all fortunate men to be so afflicted.

Holding hands and looking very much in love, Jacob and Willa Morgan had joined them.

"Lass, don't keep the men in suspense. You know how they are with surprises. They tend to run in the opposite direction except for him." Willa threw her glance to Julian. "Lord Grayson, I admire the way you won Beth's heart. You may not be a Scot, but you've a Highlander's heart. Much like my Jacob." She leaned over and kissed her husband.

"Thank you, Willa," Julian said as he captured Beth's gaze. When his wife mouthed the words *I love you*, he fell in love with her all over again. Amazingly, it happened every single day.

"If it's an erotic statue, our butler Wheatley knows what to do with it," Randford chortled.

"Behave," Kat scolded playfully before turning to Beth. "Tell them, dearest."

Beth picked up the rusty lockbox that had been stored in Randford's London mews for over two years. "We didn't want to be premature with our news until Mr. Hanes verified the document was legal." She smiled at Constance and Kat, then continued, "You are looking at the three co-owners of the Belton Arcade."

Silence reigned around the room.

The thought was inconceivable. The Belton Arcade housed the most exclusive shopping area in all of London, including Greer, James, and Howell, the linen company owned by Kat and Beth.

"It's worth a bloody fortune," Sykeston exclaimed.

"Language," Constance reminded him, and pointed to Aurelia.

"Sorry, darling," the earl said to Aurelia. "Don't repeat that."

"It's worth a bloody fortune, Mama," Aurelia gleefully called out.

Randford placed his hand on Aurelia's head and pulled her gently to his side. "Are you telling me my brother won this in a game of chance and gave it to the three of you?"

Kat waggled her brow. "How fortuitous that you married me."

Constance nodded and set her gaze on her husband. "And you are quite lucky to have married me. Mr. Hanes says the building is worth over seventy thousand pounds."

Sykeston blinked. "That means the three of you must be the wealthiest women in London."

"Indeed," Constance crooned. "But not for the reasons you think."

"Mr. Wheatley, will you ensure everyone has a glass?" the duchess asked.

Quickly, the butler handed out crystal glasses of the bubbling wine and gave the children each a glass of apple cider.

Kat nodded, and Willa and Morgan lifted the Holland cloth off the portrait.

Randford, Sykeston, and Julian gasped at the sight. It was Meriwether in all his glory, dressed in white and sitting on his white horse with a smile.

"Please raise your glass," Kat said with a smile. "To Meri. Without him I'd have never found my true love."

Constance raised her glass. "To Meri. Without him, I'd have never convinced my husband to see the beauty of our life and love together."

"To Meri. Without him, I'd have never been able to find my way." Beth's tender gaze found Julian. "I'd have never been able to see that my heart was always safe with my best friend, my husband, and the love of my life."

His throat tightened at his wife's sweet words. When he glanced at his two friends, it was easy to see they were as affected as he at the toasts their wives had given to Meriwether.

"I'd like to make a toast." Ranford cleared his throat. "To my wife and my soul mate."

Sykeston grew silent, then slowly lifted his glass to the portrait. "To my wife, who's given me my family and rules my heart."

Finally, it was Julian's turn. For a moment, he struggled with what to say, but then he looked to his darling Beth, and everything became crystal clear.

He raised his glass to the portrait. "To my wife, the engineer of my happiness, my love, and all the bountiful gifts that make my life worthwhile."

Beth rushed into his arms. Without caring a whit who saw, Julian pulled her close and kissed her with all the love and passion he felt for her. His longing for and commitment to her and their family would never waver.

But what happened next was a story for the ages.

Julian kept his observations to himself until later that night when he held his darling Beth in his arms and privately confided what had occurred.

As a scientist, he knew it defied logic, but he saw it with his own eyes. It was the most unusual, magical, not to mention incredible sight he had ever witnessed. There was no explanation.

After Julian had given his toast and held Beth in his arms, an excited Aurelia rushed to his side and pulled on his breeches. Julian knelt beside the little girl, where she whispered that Meriwether's portrait had winked at her. He explained that couldn't have happened and pointed to the portrait. When he glanced up, his heart skidded to a stop. Meri's blazing smile seemed to have doubled in size since the portrait unveiling.

As Julian studied the painting, Meriwether's gaze moved over every couple. But what happened next had left Julian speechless.

As the cheers rang in celebration, Meriwether settled his gaze on Julian. With a smile that practically lit the room with a thousand candles, he mouthed the words *Well done*.

After Julian finished his story, Beth turned in his arms and kissed him soundly, then whispered, "I couldn't agree with Meri more. Well done indeed, my love."

Author's Note

The concept of using steam as an energy source for work has been around for centuries. As a matter of fact, the aeolipile was introduced by Heron of Alexandra around the first century A.D. It was a simple design using steam to turn a wheel. Fast forward to Georgian times and the industrial revolution, and the steam engine figures prominently in the rapid rise of technology during those years.

My inspiration for Julian Raleah, the Marquess of Grayson, were two brilliant engineers and men of science. The Scotsman James Watt was a leader in the creation of steam engines. He created the Watt steam engine, which was the workhorse of the industrial revolution. He was also known for suing anyone whom he thought infringed upon his patent. Arthur Woolf played a huge role as well. Born in Camborne, Cornwall, Mr. Woolf is credited for the compound engine, for which he was awarded a patent in 1804.

Julian was a little ahead of his time in his creation of compound steam engines for textile mills. Successfully using compound engines in these mill applications didn't occur until around 1850 in Lancashire. However, Julian shares several traits with Mr. Watt and Mr. Woolf. Those are patience and perseverance.

Those virtues helped Julian woo the marriage-shy Beth Howell. And that's lucky for Beth. I'm sure she appreciates the concept of "burning steam" now.